JAI JAI VALERIAN—the most
desirable woman in the world,
greedy for pleasure, in love
with the only man
in the universe rich enough
to afford her.

ALEXANDER RAIMONT—the most
handsome, sexually magnetic
and lonely billionaire on earth.
Until he met Jai Jai...

TOGETHER they weave a
tangled web of perverted
lives and loves, of
incest, lust,
jealousy—and murder.

THE RICH
AND THE
BEAUTIFUL

BY RUTH HARRIS

Jai Jai is reckless—her men dangerous.
Jai Jai is uninhibited—and so is her life.
Jai Jai's beauty is spectacular—and with
the help of a handsome billionaire her wildest
fantasies are suddenly about to come true.

THE RICH AND THE BEAUTIFUL

A sensuous novel by RUTH HARRIS

THE RICH AND THE BEAUTIFUL

BY RUTH HARRIS

BANTAM BOOKS
TORONTO · NEW YORK · LONDON

THE RICH AND THE BEAUTIFUL

*A Bantam Book/published by arrangement with
Simon & Schuster*

PRINTING HISTORY
*Simon & Schuster edition published October 1978
Bantam edition/September 1979*

ISBN 0-553-12811-6

Published simultaneously in the United States and Canada

Bantam Books are published by Bantam Books, Inc. Its trademark, consisting of the words "Bantam Books" and the por-
trayal of a bantam, is Registered in U.S. Patent and Trademark
Office and in other countries. Marca Registrada. Bantam
Books, Inc., 666 Fifth Avenue, New York, New York 10019.

PRINTED IN THE UNITED STATES OF AMERICA

for
Michael Harris,
with love

∾ CONTENTS ∾

PART ONE

LOVE
AND
MONEY

February 1976—April 1976

∾ ONE ∾

Jai Jai Valerian was an artist, and her greatest creation was herself. If she had lived in the eighteenth century, she would have been a great courtesan—the king's favorite, a woman admired and envied, a woman of influence, beauty and power. In 1976 she did the twentieth-century equivalent—she had an affair with Alexander Raimont, one of the richest men in the world.

Bequia is an enchanted island in the Caribbean Sea: an island connoisseur's island; a yachtsman's paradise; a millionaire's secret. Located in the eastern Caribbean, in waters considered perhaps the finest yachting grounds on earth, Bequia, part of the chain of islands called the Grenadines, is the kind of tropical paradise Caribbean islands are supposed to be but usually aren't. Its picture-postcard harbor is a superlative natural anchorage, and boats of all kinds—classic Alden yawls, nine- and twelve-meter boats, the wind-driven Ferraris of ocean racing, comfortable Morgans, graceful Hinckleys, motorized floating palaces built to the specifications of Norwegian shipping magnates in Japanese shipyards and flying Panamanian flags—pause there for provisioning and pleasure. Bequia, pronounced Beck'-wee, was Jai Jai's favorite port on the cruise through indolent waters from St. Vincent to Grenada—away-from-it-all enough to be exclusive, yet a lively, gossipy social center.

The island itself is green and unspoiled. There is no jet strip; there is a sunny, breezy climate, deserted beaches, electricity that works now and then and a raffish, to-hell-and-gone-in-the-tropics, Somerset-Maugham-in-the-forties ambience. On the southern shore of Bequia is a two-mile-long white beach accessible only by boat. No roads lead to Grand Anse. Crystal sand dips into transparent water, palms and sea grape provide natural shade and the hills of Bequia rising behind form a living, constantly changing

3

landscape. Grand Anse is a superlatively beautiful beach, and because it is, Alexander Raimont owned it. He planned to build a resort there, adding luxury to beauty in the lavish, discreet style that was his trademark and the basis of his fortune.

"You can't leave anything alone, can you?" his son, Sergei, would say. "Especially anything beautiful."

The first time Alexander saw Jai Jai, he was in a powerboat, a sleek Riva he had had custom-made in France, returning from Grand Anse with Peter Cameron, the tropical architect in charge of the project. Jai Jai, wearing only the bottom of a black bikini, was sunning herself on the deck of the big yacht, a ninety-six-foot two-masted schooner, *Bel Air*, lying at anchor in Bequia's harbor. She was very slender and very strong, so strong that the long, fine muscles of her body were as articulated as an athlete's. Her breasts were flat and suntanned so that the nipples were barely visible. Her head, in the kind of imperfection that makes beauty memorable rather than merely decorative, was too big in proportion to the rest of her. Her hair, wet from a swim, showed the marks of a wide-toothed comb, and her eyes, which reminded Alexander of fine Colombian emeralds, dominated an unusually wide mouth. Almost naked, without makeup, she was dazzling. Jai Jai raised her head at the noise of the Riva and waved as the *Bel Air* rocked gently in its wake. Peter had been on Bequia all winter, and Jai Jai had seen him every time the *Bel Air* had anchored there and listened to his admiring stories of the perfectionistic, egomaniacal man who employed him, a man said to be one of the few genuine billionaires in the world. Jai Jai realized that the man with Peter must be Alexander Raimont. He was younger than Jai Jai had imagined. Much much younger.

Alexander and Peter inclined their heads toward each other as they spoke in order to make themselves heard over the noise of the powerful two-hundred-eighty-horsepower engines. They were talking about Jai Jai. Alexander wanted to know who she was.

Jai Jai was one of the young beauties who are drawn by the international rich as inexorably as the tides are drawn by the moon. They are the chic-est girls in the world, origins mostly unknown, and you see them going in and out of the revolving doors of the Hôtel de Paris across from the casino in Monte Carlo, at the Corviglia Club in St. Moritz, on Greek islands undiscovered by tourists, at backgammon tournaments in *salons privés* in the South of France, at Formula One races in Watkins Glen and Brands Hatch, at grand balls in Ferrières. They are the satellites of rich men, their companions, confidantes and mistresses and, sometimes, their wives and ex-wives. Of all the prizes money can buy, a beautiful woman is the most envied. Jai Jai, as beautiful as any woman on earth, valued herself as far more than a rich man's possession. She was, she knew, born to be an empress.

One of anything was never enough for Jai Jai. When she was a little girl, she had had two favorite dolls, two favorite uncles and two favorite flavors of ice cream, strawberry and chocolate. The uncles competed with each other to please and win her, and her parents, charmed by her inability to choose between strawberry and chocolate, always treated her to both. It was clear to Jai Jai from her earliest years that her greed and the extravagance of her needs made her special. That—and her extraordinary beauty, of course—set her immediately apart from other people, and it had never occurred to Jai Jai that she couldn't have all of everything she wanted. Meanwhile, she would settle for two of everything, and on the day Alexander Raimont first saw and wanted her, Jai Jai was traveling with two lovers, one a poet, one a pirate.

After a broken engagement followed by a broken love affair, Jai Jai, temporarily unattached, met Ian McKenzie early one morning at New Jimmy's in Monte Carlo. Jai Jai was with a group of young, beautiful people whose primary passion was the worship of youth and beauty. Ian was alone, incongruously sipping beer in a nightclub where champagne was ordinary. He asked Jai Jai, the most beautiful girl in sight, to dance and, over the loud disco, told her he was a poet, a published poet. He was living aboard a yacht he had just bought from a retired general in the United States Army who had just suffered a stroke and was no longer able to enjoy her. The *Bel Air*, a teak beauty, had been built in the twenties to the specifications of a Wall Street tycoon who threw himself out of a window of

the Plaza Hotel on the Saturday after Black Friday. The
Bel Air, rated +100A by *Lloyd's Register*, was a spectacular beauty. The brightwork and spruce masts were scraped
by hand and varnished monthly, the saloon was mahogany
and the bathrooms, incredibly, were Italian marble. The
Bel Air slept eight, carried a crew of six and was anchored
for the summer in the Monte Carlo yacht basin.

Ian, deeply tanned and blue-eyed, had a blond beard and
looked, to Jai Jai, like a Viking. He had the most beautiful
yacht, and after he and Jai Jai made love for the first time,
he said, "And now I have the most beautiful woman."

No one *has* me, Jai Jai thought, but she said nothing. If
Ian was happy with that fantasy, Jai Jai would do nothing
to destroy it. It pleased her to please.

Ian had always dreamed of being free. He was, he said, a
hedonist at heart, and there had been a long time when he
thought, in despair, that he would be trapped by life. In a
spasm of rebellion at the relatively late age of thirty-one,
Ian left a wife, a child and a place in his father's law firm
in Toronto, sold everything he could lay his hands on to
buy the *Bel Air* and live the life he had always dreamed of.
He planned to summer in the Mediterranean, winter in the
Caribbean, never again put on a suit or tie, never, in short,
do anything he didn't damn well please. He had plenty of
money, and that was what money was for, wasn't it?

His family made no attempt to stop him. His wife, with
the stubborn masochism sometimes found in women who
have been cruelly rejected, never stopped begging him to
return on any terms whatsoever. And his father, perhaps
even slightly envious, took the position that this was
"something Ian had to get out of his system" and that when
he had, it was perfectly clear he could come back and pick
up the pieces.

Not so Jai Jai. Ian played at passion; Jai Jai lived for it.
Ian was cautious; Jai Jai was reckless. Ian left his options
open; Jai Jai burned her bridges. She wanted to be a
woman without a past, ageless, timeless, existing only in
the present.

"No. You can't do this," said Maggie Blythe in the
spring, earlier that year. Jai Jai was engaged to Maggie's
son, and the wedding was less than a week away. "Every-

thing's planned," she said as if, at this late date, it were an argument that would change Jai Jai's mind.

Jai Jai was just twenty at the time, and on her left hand was an eight karat square-cut diamond ring. She and Maggie Blythe were standing in the conservatory of the Blythe mansion in Grosse Pointe, and the wedding presents, arranged by category—silver, crystal, linen—were displayed on long felt-covered tables temporarily erected for the purpose. Jai Jai was to marry Sam Blythe III that weekend in a wedding Maggie had spent half a year planning. Three hundred guests had been invited, tents ordered, two bands, a string quartet and a middle-of-the-road rock group engaged, florists in the triangle formed by Chicago, Detroit and Pittsburgh bought out, a caterer engaged from New York, a gown designed in Paris and planes chartered to fly in guests from San Francisco, Houston and Boston. "You can't."

"Sam Three will be unhappy," said Jai Jai. She had met Sam Three that past winter in Georgetown, where she was living with her mother and where he was in his last year of law school.

Jai Jai's mother, whose practical, rather calculating approach to life was in direct contradiction to her dark, Gypsy-like looks, was thrilled. "Sam Blythe is stable," she kept saying in obvious reference to her own unstable husband, who, having lost another fortune, had, as he always had whenever he was broke, deserted them temporarily. "And he's rich and going to be richer."

"It will end in divorce," Jai Jai said that noon in Grosse Pointe. Jai Jai, who wanted to please everyone, wanted to please her mother. But she also wanted to live out the inner image she had of herself as larger than life, above and beyond the ordinary rules—an image her father encouraged because it was the image he had of himself. And she had, she thought, in Preston Cunningham met a man who was her equal. A man who would take risks for her, and ironically, she had met him at a prewedding dance at the Grosse Pointe Country Club. As Jai Jai and Maggie spoke in the conservatory, Preston's chauffeur was going back and forth up and down the stairs to Jai Jai's room, bringing down her mountain of luggage.

"Three hundred people," Maggie kept saying. "What am I going to tell them?"

"All ready, Miss Valerian," said the chauffeur, "whenever you are."

"Well, goodbye," said Jai Jai, taking off the ring and handing it to Maggie to give to Sam Three. "I'm sorry. But it's better this way. It really is."

"Sorry," repeated Maggie Blythe, her poise on the verge of deserting her, a poise that had remained unshaken through twenty-six years of marriage to Sam Two, whose factories supplied Detroit with pistons and carburetors. There had been White House dinners, teas at Buckingham Palace and an audience with the Pope. Sam Two's decade-long tangles with the Justice Department in an on-again, off-again monopoly action, Sam Two's years as ambassador to Guatemala, her own scandalous affair with Sam Two's best friend, and through it all, Maggie had preserved at least the appearance of poise with every hair perfectly in place, her pearls lustrous at the base of a throat gently firmed by a plastic surgeon in Rio. "Telegrams," she was saying. "I'll have to send telegrams. I don't have to give an explanation."

Jai Jai left quietly as Maggie was coming to the conclusion that a broken engagement was better than a divorce. The Blythes were a prominent Catholic family, and people would simply have to understand. It was one of those things.

It was only when Jai Jai was settled in the back of Preston's big Chrysler that she realized that in the entire blowup, which had begun the previous evening after dinner and in which Maggie and Sam Two had pleaded, threatened and reasoned with Jai Jai, never once had Sam Three's name been mentioned. Not once had it occurred to anyone to find out what Sam Three thought or felt. He wasn't even in Grosse Pointe; he was in Washington running an errand for his father. Poor Sam Three.

Preston Cunningham was waiting for Jai Jai in the presidential suite of the Ambassador Hotel in Chicago, where he was defending a prominent stockbroker accused of stabbing his wife and her lesbian lover, a socialite dress designer, to death in their penthouse apartment overlooking Lake Shore

Drive. It was the kind of case combining money, celebrity, sex and violence that had made Preston Cunningham the most famous trial lawyer in the country. He was as well known as a movie star, looked like one and encouraged the illusion by conducting trials as if he were the producer, director and star; the judge, jury and defendant merely supporting players. He was candid about his relationship with Jai Jai, flaunted it even, and her picture appeared as often as his in the circuslike press and television coverage which attended the trial.

It was hard to tell what shocked or fascinated people more: that Preston's wife, who was also his law partner, occupied another bedroom in the presidential suite of the Ambassador or that Preston Cunningham, whose father had been white, had a black mother.

Preston Cunningham and Sam Three were the opposite extremes of Jai Jai's emotional seesaw. With men like Sam Three, Jai Jai felt secure and in control, but in the end, she left because they bored her. With men like Preston, Jai Jai felt alive and excited, but in the end, she became terrified by the enormity of her dependence on them and exhausted by her desperate need to keep them totally bewitched, totally enslaved, totally fascinated.

Just as Jai Jai had left Sam Three, Preston would leave Jai Jai and teach her a lesson in vulnerability, which, resonating with the painful memories of her father's periodic desertions, changed Jai Jai, she thought, for life. She would promise herself that she would never again get involved with a glamorous man. It was a promise she would break when she met Alexander Raimont.

Ten days after Preston had successfully defended the stockbroker, he went to Paris to address a group of European trial lawyers. The eyebrow-raising ménage—Jai Jai, Preston and Preston's wife, Delia—installed themselves in a suite in the Plaza Athénée, and it was Preston who first introduced Jai Jai to the international rich. He took her to dinner parties in *hôtels particuliers* on the Ile St. Louis, where butlers in white gloves served poached fish to women wearing cabochon sapphires the size of walnuts. He took her to a big party at Maxim's, where a *baronne* in a celadon green Dior dress introduced her to sophisticated and distinguished men who kissed her hand and women who asked the secrets of her beauty.

Preston's wife, Jai Jai felt sure, must be terrified of losing him. A formidable lawyer, Delia Cunningham was a most unformidable person. Barely five feet tall and weighing barely ninety-five pounds, she wore unbecoming harlequin-shaped glasses that slid down her nose, used no cosmetics with the result that her skin, brownish-black in hue, tended to be both oily and ashy, dressed in somber clothes that seemed to be a full size too large. The two women, sharing a hotel suite and a man, maintained a cordial, polite and careful distance, as if following by unspoken agreement the advice of some Emily Post of sexual competition.

On the morning of the day they were to leave Paris, Preston told Jai Jai that they were finished. It had been nice, but it was over. He used short, declarative sentences.

"No, no," said Jai Jai. She thought he must be mistaken. Everyone in Paris had admired and desired her. Everyone.

"There's another woman," Preston said.

What other woman? When Jai Jai walked into a room, other women faded.

"Someone else," Preston said, not sure that Jai Jai had heard. "It's as simple as that."

"Someone else?" Jai Jai repeated his words. How could he have met anyone else? She'd been with him constantly. "Who?"

"Delia," he said. Preston handed Jai Jai a return ticket and ten one-hundred-dollar bills. The ticket was good for a year. She could use it. She could cash it in. The choice was hers.

Preston and Delia left the suite, he carrying an elegant, thin crocodile attaché case, Delia with a bulging, pebbly cardboard lawyer's briefcase, the edges worn, the handles frayed. He was leaving her for his wife.

It became more real to Jai Jai when the bellboy came to pick up the five pieces of luggage, four of them Preston's, one Delia's, waiting in the foyer of the suite. Delia was with the bellboy; Jai Jai wondered if she had forgotten something.

"Every time he has a big case he falls in love," Delia said. "As soon as it's over, he falls out."

"This has happened before?" It had been so special for her; she had imagined it was as special for him.

"And it will happen again," Delia said calmly, having the last word.

Jai Jai had felt so special. Delia's words made her feel ordinary. She hated the feeling and tried to displace the hatred to Delia. She feared she would never feel special again.

For three days Jai Jai stayed in the suite, ordering from room service—malossol caviar, lobster soufflé, pâté of thrush—charging every luxury to Preston, thinking the phone would ring, imagining that he personally would present himself at the door. Jai Jai invented the dialogue, sometimes bitter, sometimes rueful, sometimes even humorous, always ending with a passionate reconciliation. But he didn't call, didn't materialize on the doorstep, and Jai Jai finally came to terms with it. She decided, there in the Plaza Athénée, that she would never again be the one who loved, who wanted, who needed. She would allow herself to *be* loved, *be* wanted, *be* needed. Above all, she would always be the first to leave.

When a Brazilian playboy offered her a lift to Monte Carlo, where he planned to enter a backgammon tournament, Jai Jai cashed in her ticket and accepted the offer.

On the day months later in Bequia when Peter Cameron came out to the *Bel Air*, Jai Jai was ready to leave. Life on *Bel Air* was indolent, luxurious and glamorous, and Jai Jai was dying inside. Ian loved her; he worshiped and adored her and told her so constantly. What Jai Jai had left out of the equation she had formulated in the Plaza Athénée was that in the end, she became bored with the love of men who worshiped her. The presence of a second lover had helped for a while, but the fantasy was more exciting than the reality. Jai Jai was disappointed to learn that a *ménage à trois* can be as domestic as marriage. When Peter asked if Jai Jai would be at the Frangipani that evening, he made it clear he was asking on behalf of Alexander Raimont. Jai Jai said yes, she was planning to be there.

Later, as she dressed, she mentioned it to Dante.

"It's hard to understand. He owns two dozen hotels, has thousands of employees and millions of dollars—and he sends someone else to deliver the invitation."

"*I* understand," Dante said, pressing the white Indian cotton dress Jai Jai planned to wear. "The richer they are, the more powerful they are, the more afraid they are of rejection."

It was a perceptive observation, and Jai Jai wondered, but did not ask, how Dante had realized it. Dante Mascheroni, from a vaguely aristocratic, periodically rich, periodically broke Piedmontese family, was Jai Jai's personal servant and mirror image. They had the same amber hair, olive skin and green eyes. They weighed the same, a hundred and eight pounds, had identical twenty-two-inch waists, wore the same shoe size, seven and a half and the same dress size, six. They had met earlier that summer in St. Tropez. Jai Jai had been having morning coffee alone at a front table at the Sénéquier when Dante, wearing only skintight leopard-skin jeans and a cheap wristwatch, got out of the passenger side of a silver Mercedes, which immediately drove off. As he attempted to walk away, he stumbled and fell into Jai Jai's table, upsetting her coffee. He began to apologize and ended by accepting her invitation to join her.

He became her confidant and her companion and eventually, wanting to contribute in exchange for his support, acted as her maid. Having learned from the on-again, off-again servants employed by his mother during her rich periods, Dante knew how to use French chalk so that fine clothing never had to be dry-cleaned, knew the proper temperature at which to press silk, hand polished leather with real bone until it had a mirror finish and could lengthen a hem so that the old line never showed. Jai Jai had never, since they had known each other, mentioned the deep, fresh scars and burns that crisscrossed his torso, back and front, that morning in St. Trop. He always appreciated that, and he had developed such a loyalty to her that his identity merged with hers. Jai Jai Valerian wasn't like other women. She wasn't like other people. Dante would have died for her, and he wondered if there was a man good enough for her—including Alexander Raimont.

When Peter Cameron told Alexander what he wanted to hear—that, yes, he'd see her that evening—Alexander was disappointed. Part of him wanted to fall madly, passionately, even dangerously in love. Whenever he met a new and beautiful woman, he always allowed himself the fantasy that this one would be the one to make him act on the reckless, passionate feelings he had but always rigidly controlled. Now, with the word of her availability, Alexander felt a sharp letdown, a downswing of disappointment. She was too easy, too available, another Instant Girl, available for a night, a week, available for whatever Alexander wanted on whatever terms. He thought he might not even bother to make love to her. Just go through the motions, pay for her drinks and send her back to the *Bel Air*.

∾ TWO ∾

Like Aristotle Onassis, Alexander Raimont believed that the man who could count his money was not a rich man. By his own standards, Alexander was a rich man.

His was not a rags-to-riches story. The son of a Bucks County neurologist of French Huguenot extraction with a talent for real estate and a mother of Russian ancestry who never denied the peasant in her, Alexander lasted through one year at Columbia P&S, his father's school, until his phobia about disease and death won over his desire to follow his father's footsteps. Among his father's properties was an inn in Lambertville, dating from the Revolutionary War, and during his thirteenth summer, when he worked there as a bellboy and lost his virginity to a Penn State freshman waitressing for the month of August, Alexander found the enduring passion of his life and the basis of his fortune. Because he hated and feared death, time too was his enemy, and in a hotel where life went on twenty-four hours a day, time did not exist.

The summer he dropped out of medical school, with money borrowed from his father, Alexander bought a run-down hotel in Condado Beach, spent two years turning it into a showplace that earned a profit and, without a backward glance, sold it for two million dollars cash and a five-million-dollar mortgage to a Kansas City-based chain with plans for offshore expansion. It was absolutely typical of Alexander that he could turn his back on something that had obsessed him for two years and never again think of it. He had a talent for shutting doors to the past and no talent whatsoever for nostalgia.

In the years that followed, Alexander amassed his fortune, which was held through five separate companies. Raimont Resorts owned resort hotels in Marbella, Cannes, Palm Beach, Montego Bay and Maui. Raimont Hotels owned skyscraper hotels in Milan, Rome, Geneva, Madrid, Quito, Frankfurt, Brussels, Dallas and Atlanta. Raimont Management managed hotels in North America, South America, Europe and the Orient for other owners on a fee basis of five percent of gross revenues plus ten percent of net profits. Raimont Development, with its own engineering, construction and financing departments, was exclusively concerned with the acquisition, construction and development of new properties. Raimont Travel owned and operated travel agencies in major American, Canadian and European cities, and at one time Alexander Raimont had owned controlling voting stock in Pan American World Airways. His fortune, now uncountable, was in his unconscious mind big enough and powerful enough to defeat time. Money, to Alexander Raimont, was immortality.

No one knew how rich Alexander Raimont was, and no one except the people who knew him personally knew what he looked like. No photograph of him had ever been published and none existed. The terms of his insurance forbade photographs, and when he was insured in 1969 for one billion dollars, every photograph and negative of him in existence were destroyed. His generosity was legendary, and he had once been called the Sigmund Freud of tipping by an associate who noted that Alexander Raimont had taught him how to use a tip as reward, weapon, promise, penalty, punishment.

He had once, it was said, destroyed an entire country in the Caribbean. Angered by the unending greed of the prime minister of a picturesque but desperately poor island-country who had appropriated carpeting ordered for the hotel's reception room for his own house and the house of his sister and who had, despite repeated warnings by Alexander, continued to take a percentage of every financial transaction connected with the building of a resort that would bring tourist dollars into the country, Alexander had simply pulled all his experts off the job and left, taking all the architects' and engineers' plans with him, leaving the island with a seventy-five-million-dollar International Monetary Fund debt, which it had no way whatsoever of repaying.

Alexander Raimont had an absolute phobia about death and age. No one knew how old Alexander Raimont was, and that included Alexander Raimont. He had willed himself not to know and removed the traces. He had had his birth certificate removed from the Bucks County files. Each of his wedding licenses (there were three) showed a different birthdate. State Department passport records showed contradictory information. He never wore a watch. Meetings began when he arrived and ended when he left. He hated weekends, holidays and time zones and did not permit them to exist. He took pleasure in reversing the seasons, skiing in New Zealand in August and swimming in the Seychelles in January. He controlled time by obliterating it and death by denying it. He did not attend his own father's funeral. Instead, that same week, using money as his weapon against death, he concluded an enormously complex, enormously profitable arrangement to develop twenty-five hundred acres fronting the Pacific in Baja, California.

In what he said was an effort to protect his mother, Alexander saw to it that the details of his father's death were never made public. Only the immediate family knew that one fine June morning, after a swim in the pool Alexander had given him that year for Christmas, Dr. Lucien Raimont went into the bathroom in the pool house, held a .32 caliber pistol to his temple and pulled the trigger, using the surgeon's hands that had saved lives to take his own.

There was no apparent reason for Lucien's action—no fatal disease, no financial problems, no legal problems, no devastating loss of love. His suicide was incomprehensible. It was ironic that a check for two hundred and fifty thousand dollars from Alexander happened to be in Lucien's mail that day. It represented his share of the profits on the sale of a hotel in the U.S. Virgin Islands. Alexander, a supreme realist about everything else, believed that money was magic. If his father had opened his mail before his swim, then, Alexander believed, he would not have taken his own life.

The rich are different in a thousand ways. It is not the things money buys that makes the difference; it is the freedom. Freedom from and freedom to. Freedom from the prisons of suffocating jobs and unhappy marriages. Freedom from geography and freedom from time. There is the freedom of choice, a sense of infinite possibility. The freedom to indulge or deny, to work or not to work, to play or not to play, to hurl oneself into life or to withdraw from it. The freedom to build and the freedom to destroy. The freedom to give and the freedom to take. At different times in his life Alexander Raimont had made all the choices. Money made him invulnerable; money was his shield. He was a man of a thousand faces, each one sincere, each one deceptive.

He had married three different times for three different reasons: once for social position; once for sex; once for dynasty. His first wife, the mother of his daughter, was a Baltimore debutante of impeccable American ancestry. Now married to the heir to a vast chemical fortune, who, like his father before him and *his* father before him, had never worked a day in his life, Brooke Lynwood Raimont Grey Vanocur lived a responsible, simple life, gardening in the morning and attending to philanthropic and charitable work in the afternoon. In the evening, wearing a nightgown and robe, she often dined off a tray presented by a uniformed butler in front of a television set. Andrea, his second wife, was the mother of his son. He had divorced Brooke to marry Andrea, an Italian socialite with bohemian tastes and assertive sexual appetites, who stunned him by leaving him for a temperamental but untalented theatrical producer. Liliane, his third wife, was the daughter of a fabled Swiss hotel family. Through her family, Alexander bought substantial Swiss holdings not normally available to outsiders and a hotel management school, which he subsequently sold to a German chain. Liliane, a clotheshorse, lasted longer than her predecessors because she shared his laissez-faire attitude toward marriage. She lived in a small palace in a park near Lausanne. Four bedrooms had been converted into closets, and Liliane changed her clothing three times a day, although on many days she saw no one but her hairdresser and head gardener. When she and Alexander were in the same place, they were faithful to each other, and when they weren't, they weren't. Married, they saw less of each other than many divorced couples and then usually on ceremonial occasions.

Alexander's wives—and his mistresses—had all chosen to be with him. All had the right to leave him. His children, tied to him by blood, did not have the same choice. The paternal role with its implications of age, continuity and mortality never attracted Alexander, and he rejected it. His rejection of the role confused his children into thinking he rejected them, and they reacted differently. Alix, his daughter by Brooke, thought that if she could become like him, she would earn his love. Sergei, his son by Andrea, thought he should compete with him, but he was afraid— afraid to win, afraid to lose. Sergei was a poor little rich boy playing in the world's golden sandboxes.

Alexander, accustomed to controlling things and people, could not control his children, just as he and all his money had not been able to buy his father's life.

The history of resort development is a history of the ideal place plus infusions of money and imagination. Miami Beach was more or less Florida swamp until, in the early years of the twentieth century, landfill was trucked in to permit the construction of big, beachfront hotels to serve a northern population who had the money, in those innocent, boom years, to escape for a few weeks the snow and ice of New York, Chicago, Philadelphia and Boston. Acapulco was a tiny, lazy fishing village with thatched huts and naked babies on a gorgeous Pacific beach until, in the glittery twenties, jaded travelers with sudden money to spend discovered the morning beach, the afternoon beach, the cliff divers of El Mirador, orchids and royal palms and the sunsodden tropical dream that *mañana* never comes. Sardinia was a windy, granite island populated by shepherds and bandits until the Aga Khan built the yacht basin at Porto Cervo and developed the Costa Smeralda to take advantage of a twisting coast of dramatic seaswept coves and powdery beaches. The Club Méd combined a new concept of ease and informality with Rothschild and Agnelli money to build vacation villages in Greece, Spain, Africa, the Pacific and the Caribbean—using the attitudes and life-styles of a postwar generation to build an empire.

Bequia, thought Alexander Raimont, had the potential to become a new destination for Caribbean travelers bored with Puerto Rico, Jamaica, Nassau and the Bahamas. Right now, as the foundations for the Bequia Raimont were being poured, it was a series of problems to be solved.

Transportation. There was no airport. Not even a strip. Except for the picturesque mailboat which also carried people, goats and chickens from St. Vincent, there was no way to get to Bequia except by private means. A ferry service would have to be provided, and Alexander was negotiating for a boat ferry and an air ferry via seaplane.

Construction. Bequia had none. Everything—cement, mortar, nails, hammers, drills, generators, plumbing and electrical supplies—would be shipped in. So would equipment and most furnishings—freezers, refrigerators, restaurant-sized stoves, bathroom fixtures, mattresses, springs, lamps, ashtrays, towel racks and clothes hangers.

Maintenance. Once the hotel was built, everything to keep it running—light bulbs, vacuum cleaners, toilet paper, facial tissues, dishes and silverware, soap and detergent, mops and sponges and brooms—would have to be continually inventoried and shuttled in.

Publicity. Almost no one had heard of Bequia, and that included travel professionals. Travel agents would be flown in. Travel writers invited, celebrities entertained. Advertising and promotion would have to begin from zero.

Profits. Once the hotel was built—and current estimates came to forty thousand dollars a room plus a half million dollars for landscaping and roads—the Bequia Raimont would not be expected to show a profit for three years. With good luck, it might break even in the fourth and return a profit in the fifth. Investors—a Canadian bank, an English insurance company anxious to get pounds out of Great Britain and a Wall Street venture capital firm—

would all be looking over Alexander's shoulder, nervous, as investors tend to be, over their investments.

Meanwhile, there was the Frangipani and the girl. As Alexander dressed, it occurred to him that he had forgotten to ask Peter what her name was.

The dockside bars of the West Indies—the Frangipani in Bequia, the Cobblestone in St. Vincent, the Mermaid in Carriacou, the Nutmeg in St. George, Grenada—are, all by themselves, worth the journey. Like their cousins in Kenya, the white hunters' bars, they are pickup places, social head-quarters, news central, information booths, post office and telegraph offices, in short, the nerve center of the permanently-in-transit charter-boat trade. Local special-ties—conch chowder and conch seviche, calalu soup, rum punch and Red Stripe and Carib beer—plus that interna-tional staple the cheeseburger are the food and drink of life. Everything—short of murder and public copulation—goes. The cast of characters represents the entire range of human fact and fantasy. There are yacht owners and yacht bums, college professors on two-week bare-boat charters, odd couples with unpublishable biographies, locals, both black and white, tourists and temporary residents, diplomats, ty-coons, philosophers and media celebrities, politicians with mistresses on the public payrolls, not to mention older men with younger women and older women with younger men, couples, trios and quartets with polysexual inclinations, Anglican priests who have long since stopped resisting the temptations of the tropics, bigamists on the lam, financiers en route to Costa Rica with the swag, Nazis relocated in the Argentine on offshore R & R. Paul Newman, one mem-orable night, waded ashore to the Frangipani, and Princess Margaret and friends stop off there on the way to Mus-tique.

The Frangipani has seen and heard one (at least) of ev-erything, and even so, now and then, they still talk about Jai Jai, who certainly knew how to make an entrance.

Ian McKenzie needed freedom, and he needed to punish himself for his need. When the summer ended, the *Bel Air* left Monte Carlo and sailed for the Grenadines. As geogra-

phy changed, Ian changed. In the South of France he had
been lighthearted about his poetry.

"What kind of poetry is it?" Jai Jai had asked, impressed
when Ian showed her some published poems.

"Obscure," he had answered.

"I don't understand it," Jai Jai said after she read a few
of the poems.

"That's OK," said Ian. "I don't either. I *told* you it was
obscure." They both laughed.

Now, in the West Indies, where there was space and
tranquillity and little distraction, he became obsessive,
working every day with felt-tipped pens on enormous pads
of blank paper. There were few words in his poems, and
they were spread out widely on the page. Ian said that the
spaces between the words were more important than the
words themselves. He compared his poems to the plays of
Harold Pinter. "Pinter uses silence. I use space." At every
port Ian would mail off envelopes to poetry journals. When
the big sheets would come back with letters of rejection,
some encouraging, some merely printed forms, he became
enraged.

"No one understands me" was the theme of his tirades.

"You *said* your poetry was obscure," Jai Jai said. Only
this time he didn't laugh.

Ian began to brood about money, although checks from
Toronto arrived the first of every month. He felt guilty, he
said, about his wife, his child and his parents, and the very
least he could do was make the *Bel Air* pay for herself.
Against Jai Jai's wishes, he put her up for charter; whoever
had sixty-five hundred a week and a desire to cruise the
Grenadines was acceptable to Ian. That included J. Anson
Herron.

J. Anson Herron had been profiled in *Fortune* and in the
Sunday *New York Times* business section. Son, it said, of a
North Carolina gentleman farmer, Anson Herron had
made a fortune in Sun Belt real estate, in Oklahoma oil and
gas and in banking. He was a complex mixture of good
guy/bad guy. He had been fined by a West Virginia court
for bribery in an attempt to deregulate natural gas prices,
was rumored to have access to Mafia money and was currently under indictment for land fraud in Georgia. He was
the South's largest contributor to the United Negro College

Fund, had donated a costly, sophisticated CAT Scan to the neurological department of a Durham hospital, and his employees enjoyed not only his policy of paying ten percent higher salaries than his competitors but the benefits of generous medical, retirement and educational funds established by him.

Anson Herron arrived in St. Vincent with three very young, very pretty women. He called them all Mary. In his dark, well-cut tropical suit, Anson Herron, who had often been told that he resembled Gregory Peck, looked like a gentleman criminal. He seemed sensual, tender, greedy.

Jai Jai, who liked to say she feared nothing, was rather afraid of Anson. "He's a killer," she told Ian that night.

"You're being dramatic," he said.

"I'm afraid of him. Did you notice his hands? There are scars all over the backs of them. Those hands frighten me." Jai Jai didn't add that they also excited her.

"Go to sleep," Ian said, turning away from her.

"What are you doing with him anyway?" Anson asked Jai Jai. He was referring to Ian. They had just finished a picnic lunch on a cay off Cannouan Island—broiled native langoustes with butter and lime juice, sliced tomatoes and white wine. "He's a nice kid, but you're in different leagues."

"We've been together for a while," Jai Jai said. They had left the others and were walking down the beach, blinding white, the sand hot from the sun.

"And you're happy?"

"Most of the time."

"Don't kid me," he said. Jai Jai shrugged and let the silence drag until he became uncomfortable. "I could make a big difference to you."

"Really?"

"The difference between a man and a boy," he said.

"I don't think you know who I am," Jai Jai said, irritated at his inflated self-esteem.

"Who are you?" he asked.

"Not one of your Marys," she said. "I'm superwoman. Wonderwoman." Then, as if to prove it, she waded into the transparent water and began, with powerful strokes, to swim out to the *Bel Air* in a demonstration of her strength and independence.

A literal man, accustomed to getting his way with a blunt approach, he watched as she swam, not understanding what had angered her. Then he turned and slowly walked back to rejoin the group.

Two days later Jai Jai found ten one-hundred-dollar bills in her lingerie drawer. For a moment she was reminded piercingly of Preston Cunningham. Then her feelings turned to anger, furious at the thought of Anson Herron pawing through her belongings. She found him on deck, a glass of Jack Daniel's in his hand.

"I gather this is yours," Jai Jai said. She held the bills out to him, thinking he would take them.

"They're yours," he said. "If you're a good girl."

Ian and the three Marys watched as Jai Jai thrust the money toward him and he held his hands up out of her reach. He danced away from her, managing to keep his balance despite the motion of the boat, teasing her, forcing her to move closer to him, and just when she was close enough to put the bills into his shirt pocket, he backed off tantalizingly out of reach. Abruptly Jai Jai stopped playing his game. Instead, looking straight into his eyes, she raised her right arm straight over her head, slowly and very deliberately opened her hand and let the wind take the bills and flutter them into the sea.

It wasn't Anson who spoke, but Ian.

"What the hell did you do that for?" he asked. No one paid any attention to him. Anson Herron smiled, understanding finally what he had failed to understand on Cannouan Cay. That night Jai Jai permitted him to share her bed.

Charter-boat clients customarily make a one-way trip downwind from St. Vincent to Grenada. The yachts return empty on the sail back upwind—a sail that can be choppy and wet. Anson left the three Marys, disappointed that there had been no duty-free shops on the yachtsman's islands of the Grenadines, in St. George, the pretty capital of Grenada. He had decided to make the return trip on board the *Bel Air.*

Ian was happy, he said, for the unexpected money. Anson was excited by his new conquest; he had been accustomed to girls named Mary, not to royal princesses. Jai Jai thought that two lovers might bring her back to life. Ian, a strong lover, was not passionate. Anson, passionate, was unimaginative. Jai Jai wanted both of them to make love to her at the same time. Both refused, angering Jai Jai with their conventionality.

Ian and Anson shared Jai Jai, imposing on her their ideas of fair play. One night Ian slept with her, the next Anson. That way each could think that she was his exclusively. Neither knew that when Ian's hands were on Jai Jai's breast, she imagined Anson's mouth hot on hers, and when Anson's weight pressed on Jai Jai, she imagined Ian's tongue on her thigh. Being worshiped by two men, if only in her fantasy, made her feel twice as desirable, twice as powerful, twice as beautiful.

When Jai Jai walked into the Frangipani, Anson, dark and dashingly sinister on one arm, Ian, blond and virile on the other, Alexander Raimont forgot that he had been disappointed, forgot that he had been indifferent, forgot that he was just going to go through the motions. His desire—for a woman, a hotel site, an automobile, a painting, a building—increased in geometric proportion to the degree to which it was coveted by others.

He knew when to wait, and he knew when to act. In the beginning he waited and watched, in the group but not part of it. The cast of characters gathered in the small thatched-roof open-sided bar that evening was, for the Frangipani, ordinary. There was a suntanned woman wearing diamond bracelets, accompanied by a much younger man, who lit, among other things, her Marlboros; an amiable homosexual couple from Philadelphia who had read about Bequia in a gay magazine; the heiress to a Colombian coffee fortune, accompanied by her ten-year-old niece; an alcoholic political writer from the Washington *Post*, who announced between his fifth and sixth rum punches that women—his wife, his ex-wife and his live-in girlfriend, to be precise—were ruining his life.

The conversation and the laughter rose and ebbed in the rhythm characteristic of parties everywhere. Jai Jai was conscious of Alexander, conscious of being watched. She laughed, she smiled, she spoke only a little, never quite closing her mouth entirely. She was being admired and desired, and she abandoned herself to the sensation. She, too, knew when to wait and when to act.

Just before midnight, as the group was breaking up, Alexander Raimont left. He walked out of the circle of light and disappeared into the black, warm West Indian night. Jai Jai was surprised at the sharpness of her panic. She had been so sure of his interest. Had she somehow been wrong? Had her instincts failed her? Had she somehow lost her power?

Then, suddenly, Alexander Raimont was standing just behind her chair. He was so close to her that she could feel the warmth of his body and smell the scent of his skin. He smelled clean and very healthy with no cosmetic scent to hide the odor of human skin. She looked up at him, into Tiffany-blue eyes, expecting to see desire, surprised, instead, to see gentleness. It was not a quality she would have associated with him.

Without a word he held his hand, curled into a loose fist, over hers. Instinctively she opened her hand under his, extending her palm. In a slow trickle Alexander Raimont poured a handful of shiny pebbles into her outstretched hand. Borrowing words from Charles MacArthur, he spoke to her for the first time.

"I wish they were emeralds."

Jai Jai closed her hand around the pebbles. They were still warm from his touch, and she felt their warmth throughout her body. It was as if she were touching him.

"I have to go," she said. She didn't understand why he had waited so long to make his approach, and she wanted to make him pay for it. Ian and Anson were waiting impatiently a little distance away where the floor of the bar area met the white beach.

"I don't know your name," he said. His voice was as calm and unhurried as if they had the whole night ahead of them.

"Yours is Alexander," she said. "Alexander Raimont."

"Jai Jai! Come on!" Ian called to her.

"J. J." Alexander repeated. "Is that short for something?"

"Jai Jai!" Anson called this time, impatient, used to being obeyed. She looked over at them. She wanted to go. She wanted to stay.

"My mother's name was Jacqueline. My father's name was James. I was named for them. For their love," Jai Jai said. "They thought it would last forever."

"Will you have lunch with me tomorrow? Dinner?"

"Jai Jai!" Ian was angry now, and Jai Jai responded to his anger. She got up. Standing, she was almost as tall as Alexander.

"The emeralds are beautiful," she said. "May I keep them?"

He nodded, and she left quickly, before he could say more. Jai Jai disappeared out of the pool of light of the Frangipani with her two escorts into the black West Indian night. The small plank dock was only a few steps from the bar, and their voices as they got into the dingy, the splash of oars as they rowed back to the *Bel Air* carried clearly over the water. Alexander stood and listened until he could no longer hear a sound.

The bar was deserted now, and Alexander crossed through it and out the opposite side. He walked up the steep hill to the large, attractive suite of rooms he had reserved for his use in Bequia. Built in West Indian style, they had thatched double-height cathedral ceilings, windows with wooden shutters but no glass, and a wide veranda running across the front of the structure. The rooms were furnished with rattan chairs and tables and lacy, khus-khus rugs, locally woven, dotted the terra-cotta tile floors. Clean white mosquito netting was suspended like a flower from the ceiling over the bed. He undressed and, naked, went out onto the veranda and looked out over the harbor. It was dark, the lights on the *Bel Air* off. The brilliant constellations of the southern skies glittered indifferently, casting a cool light over the black, shiny water of the harbor. He wished she were with him, but he had been afraid to ask. He didn't want her to think he was lonely.

◈ THREE ◈

"Where's the *Bel Air*?" Alexander concealed the unexpected panic he felt. It was six A.M., and the big yacht was gone.

"St. Vincent," Peter said. It was the next stop upwind. Peter wondered but did not ask what had happened last night. The last thing he had seen was Alexander pouring pebbles into Jai Jai's hand. Although they had not touched, the erotic aura was so apparent that Peter, a conservative fourth-generation Bermudian of reserved British ancestry, turned away, embarrassed. Now he held the Riva to the dock, expecting Alexander to get in.

"Just a moment," he said, and went to the small office of the Frangipani and telephoned Barbados Air Charter to order a seaplane for noon. As the Riva headed toward Grand Anse, Alexander wondered why he always knew what he thought immediately but always knew what he felt too late.

"Morning, Mr. Raimont. . . . Nice morning, Mr. Raimont. . . . Moving right along, Mr. Raimont. . . ." Here in the West Indies, where machinery is scarce and human labor plentiful, much of the work of construction is done by hand—mixing, hauling, pouring, smoothing. Bequian laborers, black and white (descendants of the Scottish settlers of earlier centuries), greeted Alexander, who in turn responded.

"Good morning, Tyler . . . William . . . Bailey. . . . Everything all right? . . . Have everything you need? . . . Watch that line, it's not plumb. . . ." The men worked, sweat shining on their backs even in the very early morning sun.

Alexander knew the names of the people who worked for him, the names, often, of their wives and children, facts about their health, abilities and problems. He established scholarships for their children and provided specialized training, yet Peter sensed that they had no existence for him beyond the moment of the actual encounter. Peter, who had worked for Raimont Development for a dozen years, had once, by coincidence, been passing through the Miami airport at the same time as Alexander. He went over to greet him and realized, to his amazement, that Alexander simply did not recognize him out of context. Peter reminded him of his name and of the fact that he had paid for years of costly rehabilitation therapy for his son, who had been paralyzed from the waist down in a freak water skiing accident. Alexander smiled politely and asked how his son was, remembering that the boy's name was Johnny.

Alexander Raimont was one-of-a-kind in other ways. Although he had children in their twenties, he didn't look much more than thirty-eight, possibly forty. Peter had heard rumors that he had had his face lifted and that he spent several weeks a year in a youth clinic in Switzerland, but he had no idea of whether or not they were true. What mattered to Peter was that Alexander Raimont was a one-of-a-kind man to work for.

As interested as any builder in keeping costs as low as possible, Alexander had an aesthetic sense that made him unusual. Most developers put up the biggest, cheapest structure possible in the quickest amount of time. Not Alexander—and that was what set Raimont Resorts apart.

Before he put a line on paper, Peter spent weeks at the Grand Anse site, sleeping in a lean-to on the beach, walking the property over and over, taking notes about the angle of the sun as it crossed the skies, the direction of the prevailing breezes, the rise and fall of the tide, the configuration of the property, the difference between daytime and nighttime temperatures. Structures would be designed and placed to take maximum advantage of the breeze, to avoid hot spots, to place windows so that the views, beautiful both out across the sea and looking back toward the steep, green hills that rose from the beach, would be advantageously framed. High ceilings would maximize air circulation, and generous overhangs would provide both shade and protection from rain. Local materials—rush, rattan, bamboo thatching, stone and gravel from West Indian quarries—as well as local craftsmen and labor would be used wherever possible. The object was to build a fifty-five-room hotel in West Indian style that would blend into the site with provision made for future additions and expansion.

Gradually the design evolved. The entrance would be open front and back, and a garden of tropical foliage and flowers would flow in and through with neither physical nor visual interruption. A hexagonally shaped dining room, open on all sides, set on a high elevation would have romantic views from every table. A series of thatched rondavels with two double rooms and baths that could be either closed off separately or open for parties and families would be spotted along the property. Guests, upon opening the doors of their rooms, would find themselves directly on the beach. None of the tall palms or sea grapes that dotted the property would be touched—they provided natural shade and cooling.

Now the hotel, which had existed only in Peter's imagination, was beginning to be real. He and Alexander walked along the beach as foundations for the rondavels were in different stages of work.

"The permit to bring in the kitchen equipment has come through," Alexander said. One hundred eighty thousand dollars' worth of freezers, refrigerators, stoves, sinks had been held up in Barbados pending local government approval to import the equipment tax-free. The arrangement had been agreed to because the local government was anxious to participate in the expanding tourism economy of the eastern Caribbean.

"That means it will be here the day after tomorrow," Peter said.

Alexander nodded. Normally it was a long half-day voyage from Barbados, but in the West Indies things functioned (if they functioned at all) West Indian time.

"And that cement is dangerously near the high-tide line."

"I'll have it moved back," said Peter, agreeing. In Italy a hotel workers' strike was raising havoc with the Milan and Rome hotels; in the United States Raimont Travel was negotiating a merger with a large communications complex; in Montego Bay occupancy had fallen to an alarming thirty-two percent in high season owing to the economic and racial tensions that erupted in periodic violence. Tourists were staying away from an island whose entire economy depended on two sources: tourist spending and the mining of bauxite. Every one of these problems demanded the full-time attention of Raimont executives, lawyers, controllers and managers, yet Alexander concentrated on the details of construction in Bequia as if it were the only thing on his mind. The ability to narrow his focus to one problem at a time without the fragmentation of his concentration was, Peter thought, one of the secrets of his success. It was an ability Peter had tried, but failed, to imitate. He simply was unable to be that single-minded.

Just before noon Alexander asked Peter to run him back to the Frangipani. It was odd that a man of Alexander's competence could neither drive a car nor run a boat. As the Riva rounded the turn into the harbor, Alexander told Peter he would be leaving Bequia. At the small plank dock the pilot of the seaplane was waiting. Peter waited as the plane took off, knowing that at that moment Bequia ceased to exist for Alexander.

The Cobblestone, on quayside in Kingstown, the capital of St. Vincent, is a two-century-old stone building which served in earlier times as a sugar warehouse. Foot-thick stone walls, graceful brick archways and narrow, shaded paths wind through the complex which has been divided into shops, a bar, a restaurant and a small hotel overlooking the harbor. The *Bel Air* rested at anchor, only its crew aboard. Alexander looked into the bar, an English rural dream, dark and publike, set down in the dazzling Caribbean. Ian sat with other skippers, comparing chandler's prices up and down the Grenadines, trading information about secondhand sails for sale and horror stories about demanding, impossibly neurotic clients. Alexander walked on, through the inner garden and back toward the shop selling Swiss watches, English china, German cameras and French crystal. He found Jai Jai sitting on a bench, alone and self-possessed. She looked up at his approach and, if she was surprised to see him, didn't show it.

"I didn't want to lose you," Alexander said. "It was too hard to find you."

"All you know about me is that I like emeralds," Jai Jai said and smiled. He couldn't see the expression in her eyes, hidden behind dark sunglasses. He knew more, much more, about her: the way her breasts looked; that she traveled with two lovers on a luxurious yacht, that she could make his fantasies come true.

"I didn't know I was looking for you until this morning," Alexander said. "I know what I want, but I don't know how I feel."

"That's a sad thing to say," Jai Jai said. "For a man who can have everything."

"Including you?"

"Not as easily as you imagine," she said.

He adored her for being difficult.

"I like what you're wearing," he said. Jai Jai had on white linen trousers, old-fashioned linen that creases, and a navy blue polo shirt. A man's flat gold watch with a crocodile strap was on her wrist. She wore no jewelry and no makeup except for an apricot-tinted lip gloss. She was very beautiful. "I like clothes that wrinkle. They seem very alive."

"I'm afraid of you," Jai Jai said abruptly and out of context.

"Why?" Very gently. Gentleness, in a man who could have, truly, whatever he wanted, was a gift beyond price.

"Not you, really," she corrected herself. She was thinking of Preston. Whatever Preston had meant to her, Alexander symbolized the same passions, only amplified to infinity. "I'm afraid of the way I'll feel about you. I'm afraid I'll lose control of myself."

"I won't let you be afraid," he said, and she knew he had the power to stay her fear. That power was what she feared. It was also what she wanted.

"Did it offend you that I sent Peter?" He seemed to care deeply that he might have angered her.

"It made me like you. It made you seem approachable," said Jai Jai. "I realized you were worried that I might not accept your invitation. You seemed human for the first time." Jai Jai's hair, dark when wet, was the color of amber when dry. Now, in the midday sun, it shone gold and tortoise.

"Will you have dinner with me?" Alexander asked, knowing she had the power to hurt him by refusing and

choosing, deliberately, to allow her that power. It was
risky, dangerous, thrilling. He waited for her answer.

"At the Cobblestone?" Ian was there. Anson was at the
Mariner's and would leave the next day. Not that it mattered. They were already in an unremembered past that
had stopped existing when Alexander Raimont had first
spoken to her of emeralds.

"Anywhere you like," Alexander said.

"Anywhere?" Jai Jai asked. When he nodded, she told
him where, and he adored her for that, too.

Ten hours later they dined at the Coq Hardi, in Bougi-
val, eleven miles outside Paris. Jai Jai's only regret was the
Bel Air. As the seaplane took off, Jai Jai looked down, and
her last sight of the *Bel Air* was as she lay quietly at anchor, remote, graceful, peaceful. She would miss the *Bel
Air* as much as she ever missed anything. Jai Jai was wearing the same clothes she'd worn that day in St. Vincent
with the addition of a navy blue cashmere blanket from
Alexander's plane as a shawl.

"Tomorrow you'll go shopping in Paris," Alexander had
said when they left St. Vincent. "I want you to get everything brand-new."

"I'll give my clothes to Dante," Jai Jai said. Dante liked
wearing Jai Jai's clothes, and she liked to see him in them.
It was as if there were two of her. Jai Jai had boarded the
seaplane with only her passport and a small brown and
white striped Bendel's cosmetic bag for her Laszlo. At
Seawell Airport in Barbados, they changed to Alexander's
Learjet Intercontinental 36, a model of which hangs from
the ceiling of the bar at New York's "21." The one-and-a-
half-million-dollar plane was Alexander's office and the
closest thing to home. It enabled him to go not only when
he wanted but to more places—the Lear gave him a choice
of an additional two thousand airports not served by commercial carriers. The interior fuselage was divided into an
office equipped with dictaphones, a Xerox machine and a
telex; a tiny but complete galley with a microwave oven
and a trash compactor and a bed-sitting room with an ad-
joining bathroom. The plane was fueled and waiting for
their arrival and, as soon as the tower gave clearance, took

off, banking west to east, flying away from the sun into the night.

Alexander and Jai Jai made love for the first time in the master stateroom, a chamber of masculine luxury in peanut-colored leather and stainless steel. They left the curtains open—at forty thousand feet, there was no one to see—and the setting sun shaped into circled squares by the rounded edges of the windows traced patterns of thin orange light on their naked bodies. Jai Jai was surprised that Alexander's armpits were shaved. She had never known a man to do that.

As a lover Alexander was very free, no caress offended him or seemed strange to him, and his hands and his body and the way he used them were of a wonderful warmth. He had, however, one sexual aversion, amounting almost to a phobia: Although he kissed every intimate place of Jai Jai's body, he would not kiss her on the mouth, and when she tried to kiss him, her mouth open on his, he turned his head away, moving his mouth away from hers, and whispered, "No."

Jai Jai thought she had somehow misunderstood, and when she tried again in the course of their passionate lovemaking to kiss him, he forcibly pushed her mouth away from his.

"Please don't," he said. "I don't like that," and Jai Jai, hurt, never tried again to kiss his mouth. It was strange and disturbing to make love to a man who refused to kiss and be kissed in an ordinary way. It robbed the act of intimacy, and Jai Jai, afterward, always had a worried, empty sense of having been cheated.

Jai Jai was the first physically strong woman Alexander had ever been to bed with, and her strength and the way she used it were something beyond his imagination. Highly developed control over her vaginal walls allowed her to tease, grasp and release his penis with exquisite precision. Her strong legs allowed her to control the force of his thrusts and the depth of his penetration even when she was beneath him. The physical nuances seemed to him infinite, and the novelty of being in bed with a woman who was almost his physical equal held him in thrall. Her strength was the essence of her mystery, and he was fascinated with it.

A man obsessed by physical health, he was impressed by the elaborate series of exercises she performed daily, a combination, she told him, invented by herself, of Royal Canadian Air Force routines, barre exercises from a ballet class she had attended in Georgetown and strength exercises with ankle weights, followed by a workout with five-pound barbells taught her by an Olympic boxing coach who had explained that female hormones prevent the development of bulging muscles. She had dropped yoga from her routine when a gymnastic teacher in Rome told her that yogas, while limber, had no strength. Yoga, he said, stretches the muscles but does not contract them, and it is the alternation of stretching and contracting that produces muscular strength.

"Strength is beauty," Jai Jai said. "Physical strength and psychological strength."

Alexander had never thought of that. He would have said that strength was unfeminine. He found that the opposite was true. It was Jai Jai's strength—physical and emotional—that was her hold on him. Her strength made his strength more valuable, just as her extravagance made his riches more valuable.

"You'd leave me if I displeased you," he said. He had admired the way she'd left her previous lovers. She'd shown no sentiment and no guilt, and when he asked her about them, she dismissed his questions. "It's not important," she had said. Alexander had always resented women who used sentiment and guilt as instruments of emotional blackmail. Jai Jai, he sensed, would never resort to those familiar, contemptible weapons. In her way, she was as ruthless and selfish as he was, and finding in her his emotional mirror image excited and awed him. "Of course, I intend only to please you."

He encouraged her greed and applauded her extravagance. The more she spent, the more he admired her. Money, he believed, was to be used. The more it was used, the more valuable it became to him because the more it was used, the more it bought, the more it resembled life to him. He equated her financial extravagance with her sexual extravagance, and he wondered what it would be like to have a baby with her. It had been years and years since he had thought of having a baby, a new life.

"Very few men could afford you," he said. His pride, usually carefully concealed, was obvious. "And fewer men could satisfy you."

"Only you can," Jai Jai answered. "Only you."

What money represented to Alexander, sex represented to Jai Jai. To her, sex was not part of life, it *was* life. It was existence itself, the only tangible proof of her desirability, her very being.

She was on better terms with her body than any woman Alexander had known. She liked to be naked and spent hours in front of a mirror, examining her body, absorbed in narcissistic pleasure. She bathed three times a day, stroking body lotions on afterward, touching perfumed oils— patchouli, sandalwood, ilang-ilang—to the amber-colored pubic hairs, holding cold cloths to her nipples so that they would be erect under thin crepe de chine garments. She touched herself constantly, unconsciously stroking a thigh, cupping a shoulder in a hand, caressing a breast, touching an ankle or a wrist, smoothing her already-smooth hair. She was a connoisseur of erotic sensation. When they made love, they gave themselves up to every kind of voluptuous pleasure, crossing and recrossing the invisible borderlines where pain and pleasure merge and intermingle. It sur- prised him that the one thing she would not do was mastur- bate. He had asked once, desiring to watch her, and she had refused.

"Why not?" She, who had never drawn a sexual limit, was doing so now.

"I don't feel as beautiful when I make love to myself as I do when a man makes love to me."

"Even if I watch? Even if I admire?"

"Even then."

It was as close as she could come to admitting that her beauty—spectacular as it was, commanding admiration and attention—depended on others. No mirror could replace the look of desire in a man's eyes, and Jai Jai, like a drug fiend and his drug, was addicted to desire in larger and larger doses. She went to dinner parties and receptions, the ballet and the theater, balls and cocktail parties, caring only to see desire and envy in the eyes of others. She de- voted her existence to the maintenance of her beauty and its adornment, and with Alexander's money anyone and ev-

erything she needed were at her disposal. She searched the
world for salves and unguents; if she heard that the best
shampoo was made in a Nepalese village and that the pure-
ness of the mountain water at that high altitude was the
reason, sherpas were dispatched to bring back a sample.
When a famed beauty of a certain age told her that the best
manicure was given by a mulatto girl in a hairdresser's in
New Orleans, she had the girl flown to Paris. And thus her
rooms became cathedrals to the worship of her beauty.
Dressing tables and bathroom and closets were stocked
with Egyptian mud from the banks of the Nile River to
whiten the skin, Indian kohl to cleanse and make up the
eyes, bars of solid ambergris from the souks of Beirut to
scent lingerie, Swiss-manufactured infusions of licorice, tam-
arind, cassia, camomile and senna to purify the intestines,
cakes of jeweler's rouge to buff the nails, volcanic pumice
to soften the skin, black toothpowder from Ceylon for the
whitest teeth, organic facial vinegar to normalize the skin's
ph balance, sprays of Evian water to set the makeup,
double-distilled witch hazel to reduce puffiness around the
eyes. Jai Jai had only to want something—raspberries out
of season, carved cinnabar bracelets, a museum-quality
Fortuny dress—and it was hers. With Alexander, Jai Jai
had become an empress.

Empresses never have to choose. Empresses can have all
of everything they want. Narcotized by satisfied greed—
sexual and material—Jai Jai forgot only one thing: Empresses, too, have feelings. Jai Jai, who had everything,
wanted more.

"Is he wonderful?" It was the first thing Dante asked
after inspecting the splendor of the Plaza Athénée suite
with a gold door Alexander had arranged for Jai Jai. Dante
had flown in commercial from Barbados two weeks after
Jai Jai had left, treating himself in the meantime to Bain de
Soleil and shared pleasures of the flesh with a Hungarian
(of course) who had sold his wife's jewels to buy himself a
house in the Sandy Lane enclave. Dante reported that Ian,
after a three-day drunk, announced that he was selling the
Bel Air. J. P. Morgan had been right, after all. If you have
to ask how much it costs, you can't afford it. Ian had
asked, and only later had he found out that he couldn't

afford the *Bel Air*. As someone else once said, a yacht is a
hole in the water you pour money into. He was returning,
with a certain relief, to Toronto, his wife, his child and his
place in his father's law firm. Anson had simply disappeared, along with a pretty Canadian girl he'd picked up at
the Cobblestone and promptly named Mary.

"He's very mysterious," said Jai Jai. "I've never seen
him sleep."

"A lot of people can't sleep with someone else in the
room," Dante said. He knew that Jai Jai thought that except for exercise, sleep was the key to beauty.

"And he's always alone. He doesn't even have a regular
secretary. He borrows secretaries from whichever office
he's in. He doesn't depend on anyone. Every successful
man I've ever known was surrounded by people—Anson
talked about his lawyers, his business partners, his golf
cronies; Preston had his wife, who was also his law partner,
as well as a whole staff of lawyers to do research and draft
the briefs; Sam Blythe had a retinue of vice-presidents, yes-
men and assorted flunkies, not to mention Sam Three. Not
Alexander Raimont." Jai Jai, who rarely drank, was sipping
champagne she had purposely allowed to get flat. The bub-
bles, she was convinced, caused bloating.

"He's got you," Dante pointed out.

"But I haven't got him," Jai Jai said. "That was my big
mistake. To let him know that I'm his. He's only interested
in what he hasn't got or thinks he can't have."

In the beginning Jai Jai had gone everywhere Alexander
did. He traveled constantly, using Paris as a base, occupying a suite across the hall from Jai Jai's. He flew to Brussels, Milan, Rome, Madrid, London. It was not unusual for
him to attend three meetings in three different countries in
one day. Jai Jai flew with him, quickly accustomed to the
luxury of private jets, fueled and waiting; she accompanied
him in silent limousines to various hotels, office buildings,
banks and brokerage firms. She shopped or went sightsee-
ing while he attended to his business.

Jai Jai knew nothing about his business, and he never
spoke about it. It was impossible for her to tell whether
things were going well or badly from his behavior. He gave
no clues. She had never seen him irritable, elated or angry;
occasionally he would betray impatience by compulsively

asking what the time was. He always seemed calm, reasonable and unhurried. The overriding impression he left with others was one of invulnerability.

He made no attempt to hide Jai Jai's existence, but neither did he flaunt it. When appropriate, she attended parties and dinners and receptions with him, her role entirely accepted in the sophisticated circles in which he moved. She once asked about his wife.

"We have an arrangement," he said. "When we're in the same city, we're faithful to each other. When we're not, we're not."

"Do you always have a mistress?" Jai Jai, who was rarely curious about other people, was insatiably curious about Alexander.

"From time to time," he said. He never evaded a question, but he never told her as much as she wanted to know.

"I don't know what he's like," Jai Jai complained to Dante. "And I don't know how he feels about me. He's never told me that he loves me."

"You've only got everything," Dante said. "Don't tell me you want love, too."

"Yes," said Jai Jai. "I want love, too."

"God! How middle-class can you get." "Middle-class" was the worst epithet in Dante's vocabulary, second only to "bourgeois." "The next thing you're going to want is marriage."

"I'm a woman," Jai Jai said. "Why not?"

"Don't ask for more than you can have."

"I don't know how to live any other way." Jai Jai finished the champagne and poured more.

"Do what you have to do," Dante said. "But don't say I didn't warn you." He watched her for a moment. "And no more champagne. Your skin will get blotchy."

The next afternoon Jai Jai went shopping. She bought three furs—a fisher coat, a sable pea jacket and a mink sweater lined, collared and cuffed with cashmere. Alexander rewarded her with a pair of diamond studs for her ears.

"You're the most extravagant woman in the world," he said to her as he gave her the studs. "I'm absolutely in awe of you."

"I'll never take them off," Jai Jai said as she fastened

them. They were the first gift Alexander had ever chosen for her, and she interpreted them as a sign that she was special to him. "I adore them," she said, admiring them in a mirror. "I promise I'll wear them always," she said, crossing her heart.

Jai Jai kept her promise, and Alexander promptly forgot all about it. He did not remember until two months later, in June, when he saw her naked on a beach in Mexico, naked except for the earrings. She was married to Sergei by then. They had eloped and were living in Mazatlán, where Sergei was making another attempt to become an heir worthy of his inheritance. Sergei Raimont had the qualities of a talented businessman—he knew when to be cautious, he knew when to take a risk, he had grown up in the hotel business and knew it in his bones, he had studied the theory and practice of business at Harvard and he had grown up understanding the power of money: when to spend it; when to withhold it.

What stopped Sergei from being richer, more powerful than his father was a secret sickness, a sickness Sergei perceived as shame. Periodically, for no reason he could ever understand, he would become seized by crippling depressions, so severe that he had several times tried to take his own life. He had carefully hidden the secret suicidal desperation from his father and, indeed, from almost everybody, including himself. Because when Sergei felt good, he felt better than anyone else: more energetic; more enthusiastic; more efficient; more magnetic.

But Jai Jai would not learn Sergei's secret until that summer. Right now, in April in Paris, less than three months since their meeting in Bequia, she knew that Alexander had begun to tire of her. The gentleness that had been so unexpected disappeared; sometimes he was brusque and impatient with her; other times he was indifferent except for the moments he desired her. He made love to her with his hands while he cradled a telephone on his shoulder and talked business to Dallas, Hong Kong or London. He gave her a dress from the couture which had been originally ordered by Liliane, who decided she was bored with it even before the atelier could finish it. When Jai Jai resented the gift, Alexander became angry with her and refused to speak to her for several days. He traveled as ceaselessly as ever, but now he left Jai Jai behind more and more often. She wondered if he had a new mistress in another city, but she was afraid to ask because she didn't want to hear the answer. Jai Jai had the same eerie sensation Peter Cameron had: that when Alexander wasn't physically in the same room with her, he literally forgot her existence.

What Jai Jai didn't know was that just as Alexander Raimont associated money with eternal life, he also identified emotion with death. Alexander Raimont did not know how to drive a car; he would not even sit in the front seat of a car. He was afraid. He had an image of what he would do, of what he would be unable to stop himself from doing. He would press his foot on the accelerator and go faster and faster until he was soaring and flying and free; until he had no thoughts, no consciousness, no control; until he had only feelings and *was*, eventually, only feelings. Then he would be unable to stop himself from going even faster while he spun the wheel, crashing the automobile, smashing himself, his body, surrendering, feeling death, irresistible, uncontrollable. He was able to repress that image when he was awake; in years past it had been the one and only dream he ever dreamed. A dream of ultimate freedom inevitably followed by a horrible, fatal smashup in which he could feel the pain, the suffocation, the tearing of limb from limb, the struggle of his lungs to get oxygen that wasn't there, the impotent final flutters of his heart. He would wake up drenched in sweat, unsure of whether he had screamed aloud or only in his nightmare. He had learned, years before, that if he took a Seconal, he never dreamed, and so every night in secret, ashamed of his dependence, he took a Seconal and slept an artificial sleep without dreams.

Jai Jai made him feel the way he had once felt in his dreams—free, as if there were no limits, no boundaries, that with her he would go faster and faster, deeper and deeper, until speed and control had no meaning and he would eventually, compulsively be powerless to resist the smashup, the inevitable destruction, the irresistible fatality. The paradox, the insoluble, terrible, compelling paradox he found himself in was that he desired the freedom, that he passionately wanted to obliterate the limits and that with Jai Jai he would go faster, higher, beyond every limit, every boundary. What he feared was that if he did, he would die.

Jai Jai was afraid, too, desperate and panicky. It was the fear she had confessed to Alexander in St. Vincent: the fear he had promised he would never let her feel: the fear that if she loved him, he would leave her.

It was a fear she had learned as a child.

James Valerian had made three fortunes, and he had lost three fortunes. When he had money, he would come home to his wife and to his daughter. Every day would be Christmas, filled with love and excitement, attention and presents. Jai Jai had a small heart-shaped diamond on a gold chain when she was eight and a white ermine coat when she was eleven. Just when Jai Jai had begun to trust her father enough to love him, he would leave. One day the money would be gone, and so would her father.

Money was love. It was the central fact of Jai Jai's early life. With Alexander, she had found both, and she was terrified now of losing both. This time, she feared, there would be no next time.

The more indifferent Alexander became, the more desperately Jai Jai wanted him. In Bequia, she had known instinctively how to interest him. Now, in Paris, her instincts did not desert her. It was a lucky coincidence, she thought, that Sergei Raimont, in the middle of a love affair violently opposed by his father, was so obviously attracted to her.

She had no way, of course, of knowing that one day she would save Sergei Raimont's life—literally.

✤ FOUR ✤

Sergei Raimont had everything to live for. He was young, twenty-six; exceedingly rich, the beneficiary of the incomes from three trust funds established by his father under the advantageous tax laws of Monaco, Liechtenstein and Hong Kong; good-looking, a Tiffany-blue-eyed replica of his handsome father and, unlike his father whom many feared, universally well liked. Everyone said, meaning it as a compliment, that Sergei was so unpretentious, so down-to-earth that no one would ever know that he had a dime to his name. Sergei had everything to live for, and two times in five years he had tried to kill himself.

The first time, when he was twenty-one, there was no apparent reason. It happened at the end of his first year at Harvard Business School, where he had gone, as his sister had, in an attempt to get his father to pay attention to him. He chased girls and footballs, diagrammed decision forks and event forks, knew the difference between capital-intensive businesses and labor-intensive businesses and was conscientious about handing in detailed case analyses every other Saturday at Baker Library. The summer stretched ahead emptily. No one expected anything of Sergei, and Sergei expected nothing of himself.

On the third Tuesday night in May he swallowed an entire bottle of four-hundred-milligram Equanil, the property of a roommate whose connections with a pharmaceutical company allowed him to obtain drugs, quasi-legally, in wholesale quantities. The roommate did a brisk resale business, thus paying for the maintenance of his quirky but beloved Porsche 914. Tuesday night happened to be inventory night, and the roommate realized what had happened before Sergei even had a chance to fall asleep. Sergei's stomach was pumped, he visited a Boston psychiatrist, who told him he was depressed, something Sergei already knew. The incident was hushed up and six weeks later almost everyone, including Sergei, who said he wasn't really trying anyway, forgot the whole thing.

Everyone, that is, except the psychiatrist. When Sergei skipped two appointments in a row and was reported by Harvard to be in Europe for the summer, the psychiatrist called Sergei's father. It took three calls to locate Alexander Raimont—one to his Manhattan office, which referred him to a Montreal number, which referred him to a Brussels number. Alexander, at a Common Market conference, refused to believe the psychiatrist, refused to believe that Sergei had really tried to kill himself. He said that if Sergei didn't want to keep his appointments, it was up to Sergei, and in any event Sergei was in Europe, healthy and well and having a good time. He, Alexander, had seen him four days before and saw no reason for concern.

The psychiatrist's nurse was shocked that Alexander Raimont refused to believe that Sergei had tried to commit suicide and didn't think that Sergei ought to be treated for his depression. The psychiatrist wasn't. Parents frequently found it impossible to believe that their children might be suicidal, and since depression was an emotional disease, not a physical one, it was difficult for people to believe that it *was* a disease and that it could be treated. What did puzzle the psychiatrist was the nature of Sergei Raimont's suicide attempt.

"Women use pills, men rarely do," he said. "Women tend to use suicide as a desperate means of communication, the well known 'cry for help.' Men more often really intend to kill themselves. Men use guns; they jump from high places. Men are violent; women aren't. Sergei Raimont used pills."

"Why?" asked the nurse.

"I don't know. I was hoping the father could give me a clue. Unfortunately he didn't. Or couldn't," said the psychiatrist. "And unfortunately unsuccessful suicides generally try again."

But Sergei didn't try again, not for a long time, because that summer he met Britta Sundsvall. Britta, at thirty-one, was ten years older than Sergei. She had been married twice and divorced twice. After her first divorce Britta remarried immediately. After her second divorce she swore she would never marry again.

"It's too painful. I'm a monogamous woman in a promiscuous world," she told her friends, who found it difficult to believe her. Britta's cool blond hair and cool blue eyes contradicted a voluptuous body and a generous spirit. When she met Sergei Raimont, they found they each wanted the same thing: a permanent relationship with no formal ties.

Britta's first divorce, from a Swedish bureaucrat, was quiet and amicable and went almost unnoticed even by the principals. Her second divorce was a scandalous entertainment, served up by gossip columnists for the delectation of readers starved for vicarious thrills. To Britta, it was ugly and humiliating, and it left her scarred.

Teddy Hales-Warrington's appeal was his eccentricity

and outrageousness. He made a point of announcing publicly and frequently that he planned never to do one useful thing during his entire lifetime. He could afford it, he went on to say, because one of his ancestors, by raping the Midlands right at the beginning of the Industrial Revolution, had made a fortune in the manufacture of tweeds, woolens and cashmeres that would survive even Teddy's most determined assaults on it. At the height of the fuel crisis Teddy chartered a jet to fly his polo ponies to Deauville for a Sunday afternoon meet. He gambled—and lost—a Mount Street house worth a quarter of a million pounds one night at Crockford's. Three nights later at the same table at the same club with the same Iranian opponent he won back the house plus a teen-aged Iranian girl. When he and Britta married, they went to live on a farm in Devon, and for six months, just long enough for Britta to become pregnant, they played country squire. Britta, lazier, stayed in Devon, while Teddy, quickly bored, went up to London, where he found a challenge that intrigued him: the seduction of both members of a lesbian couple who had been together for eight years. Teddy had an astounding success: He managed to sleep with both of them on the same weekend in the same bed. The story, oddly, had a happy ending for Teddy. After his divorce from Britta he married the prettier of the two women; they had three children and lived happily and, as far as anyone knew, monogamously ever after. Teddy became a model husband and father, and most surprisingly, in a story filled with surprise, he went to work. The bank that administered his trust fund took him on as a junior partner, and eventually Teddy Hales-Warrington became a member of the board, a voice of restraint and an authority in financial matters.

The ending for Britta was far less happy. Not only did she lose her husband (which, from a certain point of view, may not have been such a big loss), but she lost something far more valuable: her confidence that her life would, without her doing anything about it, be a happy one. She, in fact, lost her innocence.

The first year after her breakup with Teddy, Britta was numb and celibate. She left her child in the care of a Swedish nursemaid and relinquished all attempts to direct her own life. She traveled mindlessly to familiar places, to London, to Gstaad, to Cannes, going through the motions of a social life and at night drinking white wine until she could sleep. In the second year her desolation began to lift, and she began to care about herself. She initiated a rapprochement with her father, who had not spoken to her since her divorce from Teddy. Emotionally unable to move back to Sweden, she bought a spacious flat in the Rue Jean Goujon in Paris and became her father's hostess, an unofficial representative of the Sundsvall Mills in Western Europe. She had grown up with the steel business and knew, by osmosis, the terms, the problems, the personalities. She entertained businessmen, engineers, salesmen, government functionaries; she reported back to her father gossip and rumors and relayed, in turn, opinions and comments of his. She was able to arrange introductions and, now and then, was even paid for the value of her connections. Britta was not fascinated by steel, business, profit or money, but she found that she was now interested in something outside herself. More than that, she felt a sense of confidence that comes from being able to take over one's own life and to contribute, in some way, to the larger world.

When Britta first met Sergei Raimont, she was beginning to be at peace with herself. She was at a point in her life when, after two failed marriages and the resultant despair, she liked herself again. She met Sergei, oddly enough, in her own apartment. Some steel people from Turin were in Paris on the way back from Pittsburgh, and Britta invited them over for a drink. They arrived with platters of couscous from a Moroccan restaurant and Sergei Raimont, a B School friend of one of the Italians. They ate the dinner, Mideastern style, sitting on pillows around a low coffee table and drank lashings of Algerian wine. At two-thirty in the morning the evening broke up gaily and tipsily.

When Britta woke the next morning, with a slight hangover, her first thought was of Sergei Raimont, and her next a great sensation of relief that he was gone. That he hadn't spent the night. That she wouldn't have to make any decisions about him.

That evening she dined with two Bulgarians, representatives of that government charged with the procurement of foreign steel. Like many of the representatives of Communist governments Britta had met, they wanted only the best.

They wore suits tailored on Savile Row (suits they did *not* bring back on their visits home), gloves handmade in Venice and soft hand-cobbled shoes. They dined at Maxim's, demanding a table on the Rue Royale side, and, like caricatures of bloated capitalists, ordered champagne in magnums and golden malossol caviar and left tips lavish enough to be considered vulgar by the waiters, who accepted them with a smile. The evening ended at eleven-thirty. The two Bulgarians went off to meet a pair of expensive whores in the sixteenth arrondissement, and Britta, declining their offer of a lift, went home alone.

Britta rang the concierge, and as she waited for her to unlock the stout wooden doors to the inner courtyard with an ancient key that looked more suited to the locking and unlocking of dungeons, a dark limousine drew up and Sergei got out and dismissed car and driver.

"I was afraid you'd come," Britta said. She was taken off guard and blurted out what was really on her mind.

"And I was afraid I wouldn't," he said.

They spent the next three days exploring each other's bodies and souls. What made them irresistible to each other and impossible for each other was that they were both fragile, patched-up people who shared the same strength and the same weakness: an unusual vulnerability.

For the next three years they were inseparable. Sergei moved into Britta's flat. It was the first time in his life that he had a sense of home. His father refused even to own a house, saying that his business was the hotel business and that living in hotels, owned by him and owned by others, was part of doing business. Sergei's mother and her producer-husband were gypsies, shuttling among London, New York and Los Angeles and occupying a series of rented and borrowed apartments and houses. Britta and Sergei made no attempt to conceal their liaison, introducing each other to their families, defying the violent disapproval of both fathers. Now and then they spoke of marriage.

"She's too old for you. Too experienced," said Alexander, who spelled out what he could and certainly would do in the event that Sergei actually went ahead and married Britta. Alexander hoped that one day Sergei would take over Raimont; meanwhile, his only source of support was the three trust funds Alexander had set up for him, trust funds of which Alexander was trustee and trust funds which were, if Alexander so decided, revocable. If Sergei married Britta, Alexander would cut him off.

"But she makes me happy," Sergei replied.

"That proves it. Not only is she too old for you; you're too young for her. Adults are responsible for their own happiness. Only children depend on others for happiness. Whatever *that* is." Alexander was convinced that Britta was interested in Sergei because of the Raimont money. Alix tried to plead Sergei's case with their father, but he brushed her aside when she pointed out that Britta, an heiress herself, was hardly to be accused of mercenary motives. Alexander was obsessed with the idea that his children would fall prey to fortune hunters; it was an *idée fixe* with him, and nothing could budge him from it. The situation drifted on unresolved because Sergei did not want to defy his father, whom he loved, and because Alexander, a man of almost legendary generosity, could not bring himself to act on his threat. Ironically, it was Britta's father who broke up the affair.

Bertil Sundsvall didn't threaten. He acted. A wintry man nearing seventy, he was a millionaire many times over, who accompanied his annual one-hundred-dollar Christmas gifts to his children and grandchildren with a stern, frightening lecture on the virtues of thrift, the evils of indulgence and hideous tales of sudden loss owing to improvidence or extravagance of any kind.

Bertil had never forgiven his three daughters for being girls. They were a bitter disappointment to him in every way. Not one of them had provided him with a son-in-law who could help run and eventually (for Bertil was a realist and did not flinch from the realization that his eventual destination would be the grave, from which remote place he intended to control the lives of his inheritors) take over the Sundsvall steel mills, established by Bertil's grandfather in the third quarter of the nineteenth century and run by Bertil's father before him. Solveg, the eldest, called herself a Marxist and taught political theory in the University of Copenhagen. For a decade she had lived with but never married a fellow professor, also a Marxist. They lived in a penthouse in a glass apartment building overlooking the Tivoli Gardens and spent summers in Calabria renovating a former stable, adding electricity, plumbing, a sophisticated stereophonic sound system and a heated swimming pool. Neither of them seemed to find the slightest inconsistency between their avowed political beliefs and the fact that it was Solveg's income, an income derived from the fruits of capitalism, not their university salaries, that permitted them their enviable life-style.

The youngest daughter, Harriet, had worked as a stewardess for SAS and, at the first opportunity, married a pilot, a handsome, sensuous and dour Swede. She lived a suburban life outside Stockholm with her five children and a husband who appeared only infrequently. She disliked both her sisters, disapproving of their lives, and refused to visit when either of them were home since she was on speaking terms with neither.

His middle daughter, Britta, was in Bertil's eyes, to be perfectly blunt, not much more than a tramp. Twice divorced in a family that had never had one divorce, she had been carrying on openly with a boy, a playboy, ten years her junior. Sergei Raimont had no home, no roots, no job, no profession. His personal habits enraged Bertil. He slept until noon and at four o'clock in the afternoon, still in pajamas, would be leisurely reading the newspapers. Britta's son, Bertil's grandson, was left in a Swiss boarding school, his education left to Catholics, a fact that horrified Bertil, himself a Lutheran and an atheist simultaneously. As for Britta's contributions in Paris, Bertil denigrated them. Being a hostess was not, in his eyes, the same as getting up and going to an office every day.

When Britta announced that she and Sergei might marry, Bertil said nothing. Instead, he made two telephone calls, one to his lawyer and one to his bank, and a week later Britta received a letter from her father, typed by his secretary with carbons to the lawyer and banker, informing Britta that the income she had received since her eighteenth birthday would cease immediately.

"What am I going to do?" asked Britta. Her childhood had been shriveled by her father's haughty coldness, and now even when she was a woman, he had the power to wound her with icy rejection.

"We'll live off my money. I have plenty," Sergei said. "It's no problem."

But it was. Their relationship, which had been so happy, began to change, and Bertil finally got what he wanted as he intended to all along. It wasn't the money—there *was* plenty—it was what the money meant. To Britta. To Sergei. Britta had never depended on anyone. Sergei had never had anyone depend on him, and neither knew how to handle it. Sergei was generous but erratic, and Britta, who had a monthly income to do with as she pleased, never knew how much he would give her or when. She hated to ask for money, didn't know how to do it, and every time she did, it ended in a fight.

"I just gave you five hundred dollars. What do you do with it? Eat it?"

"That was three weeks ago," Britta would say and then would explain where and how she had spent it—food, the hairdresser, taxis, clothes, the cleaner, the monthly phone, gas and electricity bills. Britta had never had to account for herself to anyone, and she resented it enormously. The age difference which had worked for them began, subtly and then not so subtly, to work against them.

Older woman/younger man. Older man/younger woman. Lovers like to say that age difference doesn't matter. They are lying. Perhaps not consciously, but nevertheless lying. Britta and Sergei never lied. From the very beginning it was the difference in age that attracted them to each other. Britta lavished a kind of boundless, uncritical maternal love on Sergei that she had never expressed even to her son, who had been brought up, as she had been, by nurses and governesses. Sergei, the victim who suffered most from the unpredictability of his erratic moods, achieved an inner stability with Britta that evened out the wild pendulum swing of his depressions and elations. Unlike his passionate, tempestuous mother and his remote, powerful father, who confused him by spurts of attention and indulgence alternating with periods of preoccupied indifference, Britta was constant, uncritical, utterly dependable. Britta mothered him. There was nothing wrong with it. Nothing neurotic. Nothing destructive.

"Baby, baby," Britta would say, cuddling him.

"Am I your big baby?" Sergei would ask, knowing the answer in advance.

In a sex-obsessed world that counted, compared and measured orgasms, Sergei and Britta admitted that sex didn't matter that much to them. What did matter was affection, hugging and kissing and cuddling each other by the hour. People enjoyed seeing them together because they were so affectionate with each other, always a head on a shoulder, a hand on an arm, his on hers, hers on his.

When Britta asked Sergei for money, he could no longer be her baby. And when that happened, Sergei's old vicious cycles began again, this time more extreme than they'd been in Cambridge. He would spend days in bed, not eating, too depressed to get up, too fatigued to bathe and dress. He would think about suicide and wonder if he could find the energy to kill himself and wonder, if he could, if it was worth the effort. Britta would know he was coming out of it when he'd appear in a robe and sit in the living room and read all the newspapers for the days he'd been what he called "in retreat." And she would think him better, although exhausting to be with, when he would wake with bursts of energy and optimism. He would get wildly creative ideas for business ventures and spend hours on the phone with classmates from the B School about implementing them. He would call his father with ideas for new hotel sites, with ideas for reorganizing the five Raimont companies, and he would talk about what he would do when the day came that he would be the sole master of the Raimont fortune. He needed no sleep in his bursts of energy, and when he wasn't on the telephone, he would go on shopping sprees, buying everything in sight in quantity. Once he ordered a dozen shirts from Turnbull and Asser but was too impatient to choose colors and patterns.

"I can't waste the time," he told the amazed salesman in an irritated, impatient voice. "You pick them."

And then he marched out to take Britta for tea to Fortnum's where he walked out a moment after ordering because the waitress, he said, was taking too long to serve them. As his energy gathered momentum, the fuse on his temper grew shorter. Everything angered him, irritated him. Nothing happened fast enough for him. He once forced Britta to get out of a taxi and walk in a violent rainstorm because the taxi was going too slowly for him. The whirl would continue until the outer world abraded his inner world, and exhausted, he would fall back into withdrawn depression.

Sergei's advances into life and withdrawals from it, erratic, violent and unpredictable, ended by killing Britta's feelings for him. It was a murder he didn't regret, he said. And he acted as if he meant it until his sister, Alix, who had remained friendly with Britta despite the breakup, told him that Britta was going to get married.

Austrian and Hungarian titles, except for a certain few, are taken seriously only by headwaiters. Russian titles may be fact or fiction, but bearers of them have created a new career category: the professional prince. English titles, whether hereditary or lifetime peerages, carry a certain distinction, and French titles, which speak of kings and high civilization, are, among those who know and care about such things, highly regarded.

Prince Pierre-Gilles de Lalande-Dessault had, at the age of forty, never been married. Neither homosexual nor neuter, he was, as the French say, "serious." He had a degree in political economy and as a counselor of foreign affairs had spent a dozen years on the Ivory Coast, served as a specialist in African affairs at the United Nations, both in Paris and New York, and was the author of a voluminous, now-standard text, *Economie Politique*. When Britta met him at a cocktail party in Paris the winter of her final break with Sergei, P.-G., as he was called by his friends, had been newly appointed a vice-president of a multinational corporation.

P.-G. was tall, too slender. His years in Africa and the atabrine he took to combat the malaria he had contracted there gave his skin a saffron tone, striking with dark hair and light-hazel eyes. P.-G. was the interesting type, not uncommon in Europe but unusual in the United States, the businessman-intellectual, and he had, surprisingly, an excellent sense of humor. His courtship of Britta reflected his character; it was serious, patient, tender.

At first Britta thought she would never be interested in him. Like her father, he was a businessman. Like her father, he tended to take things seriously. As time went on, Britta discovered he was also different from her father. Different in ways that mattered: He was capable of passion for things other than money; he had little interest in controlling the people around him; he was generous, both emotionally and financially. Ten months after they'd met, on New Year's Day, P.-G. gave Britta an old-fashioned perfect-cut diamond ring that had belonged to his grandmother. They would marry in April. In Neuilly-sous-Clermont, in the eighteenth-century house, not quite a château, in which P.-G. had spent his childhood. Meanwhile, Britta was living in P.-G.'s Paris apartment. Sergei, when Alix told him the news of Britta's forthcoming marriage, had not seen or spoken to Britta for more than a year. Which did not prevent him from reacting with possessive jealousy.

"Impossible!" he said. "Does she think she can just discard me like yesterday's newspaper?"

"But Sergei, *you* left her," Alix pointed out in that reasonable tone, a carbon copy of their father's. They were in the library of Alix's Belgravia house. Sergei had been working in the Raimont London office, living with his sister and her husband since he'd slammed the door and walked out on Britta. "You said you didn't care if you ever saw her again."

"I didn't mean it, and I don't know how you could have thought I did." Sergei could make paradoxical statements sound like basic common sense.

"I believed you. Britta believed you. Everyone believed you." Alix did not point out that the reason he was in London, drawing a salary from Raimont Management, was that their father also believed him.

"I don't understand how people can be so unperceptive," said Sergei. "Everyone knows how I feel about Britta. Yale told me I was making a mistake to give her up." Yale was Yale Warrant, Alix's husband. Sergei got up and began walking toward the stairs.

"Where are you going?"

"To Britta."

"Oh, Sergei."

The next morning he flew to Paris, where Britta was living with P.-G. in his top-floor apartment on the Ile de la Cité with its enchanting view of the Seine.

"It's me," Sergei shouted through the door. He was ringing the bell with his left hand, knocking on the door itself with his right. "Your baby."

"Oh, Sergei," said Britta, echoing Alix, as she let him in. "It's over. It's in the past."

"It's the present and the future, too," said Sergei. "For me and for you, too. For us. You'll see."

The ring on her left hand, her presence in another man's apartment—it wasn't real to Sergei, and because it wasn't real to him, he acted as if it weren't real to anyone else. He moved into his father's permanent suite in the Plaza Athénée, across from Jai Jai's suite, and, excited, began to think of ways in which he might please Britta. With Jai Jai's advice, he sent a gift every day, a gift he and Jai Jai would pick out together: a necklace of lapis and gold beads; handmade crepe de chine lingerie; four rock-crystal teardrops; a set of fine white handkerchief linen bedsheets with matching pillowcases. Britta returned everything.

"I won't accept anything, Sergei. Please stop sending things." Britta had come to dread the ringing of the doorbell every morning at eleven, knowing it would be Sergei, wanting to know how she had liked his latest gift, wanting to take her to lunch, wanting to go riding in the Bois. Wanting to know if she'd been pleased. Wanting to know if she'd go to Corfu with him, to the West Indies, to the Seychelles. Wanting, wanting, wanting. Britta felt threatened and guilty and overwhelmed by the endlessness of his wanting.

"I want you, Britta. I'll do anything you want me to. I'll be anyone you want me to be. Just tell me what you want."

Britta couldn't bring herself to say the words, so Sergei said them for her.

"I'll go away if that's what you want," he finally said in March. His passionate second courtship had begun the month before. Britta nodded. When he had first left her, she had entertained fantasies of hurting him. Of revenge. Now that they had come true, she found she had no taste for cruelty.

"Please, Sergei. It would be better."

He left quietly, giving Britta a false sense of security.

Pierre-Gilles, a Catholic, and Britta, a twice-divorced Lutheran, were married civilly, the ceremony performed by the mayor of Neuilly-sous-Clermont. Pierre-Gilles' mother —his father was dead—was so happy about the marriage— she had begun to abandon hope that her son would ever marry—that she gave Britta the mahogany chest of crested silver from which the princes de Lalande-Dessault had dined for more than a century and the address of the only silversmith in Paris to be entrusted with the task of polishing it and utterly ignored the difference in religion, saying that such prejudices were *pas moderne*. Two of Pierre-Gilles' aunts, on his father's side, one a spinster, one a widow, disagreed violently and boycotted the wedding, which they called heathen.

Bertil flew in from Stockholm and smiled his thin, frosty smile. He had got what he wanted—the end of the affair with Sergei Raimont—and received an unexpected bonus, an event which made him, always a value-conscious businessman, exceedingly happy. Pierre-Gilles was the kind of son-in-law fate seemed to have denied him. So pleased was Bertil at the prospect of a candidate to run the Sundsvall Mills that he gave Pierre-Gilles shares in the company, the first outsider so honored.

Britta's sisters attended the wedding—under protest. P.-G.'s title offended Solveg's Marxist sensibilities, and Harriet's comment, spoken loud enough to be heard by all thirty guests who witnessed the actual vows, was: "I wonder how long this one will last?"

Attendance at the wedding was as far as both sisters would go. Both refused to stand up for Britta, and when, at the last moment, Britta asked Jai Jai to attend her, Jai Jai, who had become friendly with Britta during the six weeks of Sergei's second, impassioned courtship, agreed.

The squabbles and discontents diminished into insignificance at the wedding itself. The air at mid-April had the first warmth of spring. The skies were cloudless. Sycamore, elm and ash trees had turned the tender green of spring, and white and yellow narcissus and jonquil bloomed in

newly green grass. The willows fringing the banks of the
stream that ran through the property, forming, at the foot
of the garden, a reflecting pond, bent sinuously to its glassy
surface. Britta's first wedding had been a somber Lutheran affair in Stockholm with her father gloomily keeping
count of the quantity of champagne consumed by the
groom's relatives. Her second marriage had been accomplished in Spanish by a bored functionary in the same
courthouse in Mexico City in which she had, moments before, picked up her divorce papers.

In the months before her third marriage Britta realized
that all the things she had always said had no importance
for her—stability, her father's approval, a husband's protection—mattered. At thirty-five, after two rebellious marriages and the long, scandalous and exhausting affair with
Sergei Raimont, Britta felt at peace. She was too down-to-
earth to delude herself into the poetic notion that she was a
bride for the first time, but she did feel that this marriage
would be the one that counted.

The reception, to which the entire village of Neuilly-
sous-Clermont had been invited, was held outdoors. Servants offered champagne, put down by Pierre-Gilles' father
in the year of his birth for his wedding day, while Britta
and Pierre-Gilles and their surviving parents formed a
short receiving line that was completed by the two atten-
dants. Jai Jai for Britta and Pierre-Gilles' best man, his
cousin, an agent for a group of winegrowers of the Lower
Rhône and Upper Provence.

Britta, busy accepting the congratulations, best wishes
and kisses of the guests, did not see Sergei Raimont as he
walked up from the pond, past the latticed gazebo toward
the groups of people drinking, talking and laughing on the
lawn. Jai Jai saw him first, and it was Jai Jai who saw the
gun. Sergei, formally attired for the occasion in white tie,
tails and a top hat, stopped in front of Britta, took her left
hand with its gold wedding band in his almost as if to kiss it.

"I have no reason to live," he said in a pleasant, conversational tone. "This is goodbye. I intend to kill myself."

It happened almost instantaneously. As he spoke, sunlight glinted off the oily blue-black metal of the gun, and
Jai Jai, moving swiftly and decisively, taking him off guard,
held his arm with her left hand and, with her right, twisted

the revolver forcibly from his grasp. It fell soundlessly to the lawn, and those nearby, not knowing what had happened, gasped at the sight of Jai Jai's violence and Sergei's surprised curse. As he bent to retrieve the revolver, Jai Jai kicked it out of his reach with a gold-sandaled foot. Pierre-Gilles picked up the weapon and, concealing it with a handkerchief, went to the potting shed, where he turned it over to the chief of the gendarmerie, who had come as a guest. Jai Jai, putting one arm around Sergei's waist and using the other to support him, steered him across the flagstone terrace, through the first floor of the house and out the front door to the graveled circular driveway, where she put him into her car and drove south to Paris.

They drove silently through the deep woods and misty river valleys of the department of the Oise, through rural countryside that had attracted gardeners and huntsmen and, in their turn, Romantic poets in the late nineteenth century and Impressionist painters of the early twentieth century. Rural tranquillity gave way to the suburbs of Paris, dreary and uniform as such suburbs are the world over, and then to the fringes of the city itself, in a perpetual state of construction. Cement mixers rumbled, and Oriental laborers worked by hand with shovels and picks. Jai Jai always wondered where they had come from. Vietnam, perhaps, refugees from a ruined country rebuilding the nation that had helped make them refugees in one of the endlessly self-repeating cyclical ironies of history.

It was sad, and nothing about it ever seemed to change. Jai Jai was always touched by the sentiment and always drove past quickly, not wanting to be touched by a situation she was powerless to change. Neither of them had spoken, and Jai Jai was first to break the silence. They had paused for a red light when the thought had abruptly occurred to her.

"You weren't really going to do it," she said. It was a statement, not a question.

"How did you know?" Sergei was surprised at Jai Jai's observation. He had always felt that Jai Jai barely knew he was alive.

"I don't know, but I did."

"Let's let it be our secret," Sergei said, and they laughed together. Sergei looked at her as she laughed, unaware of being watched. She was so beautiful she hardly seemed real. But then, his father's taste had always been impeccable.

The next morning, after a night of caresses, they agreed to marry.

PART TWO

POOR LITTLE RICH GIRL

May 1976

∾ FIVE ∾

Alix Raimont felt the tranquilizer begin to work as the headwaiter showed her into the executive dining room of the Raimont London office on New Bond Street. The day before Cartwright Dunne, head of the Raimont European operations, had invited her to lunch; he had, he said, something to ask her. As Alix took her place at the big mahogany table set with two Madeira linen place mats, she was depressed and uneasy. She and her husband had had another fight. It had been about Sergei and Jai Jai. This time Alix, who usually avoided confrontations with her glamorous husband, as she did with her powerful father and unpredictable brother, had felt strong enough to oppose Yale, and she had won.

Yale had wanted to give them a wedding in the library of their—*her*—Belgravia house. Alix had refused, absolutely. She had known of Jai Jai's affair with her father; when she heard that Jai Jai and Sergei were to marry, she felt a terrible premonition, a sense of disaster. Her father and her brother had always had a loving, competitive and tempestuous relationship, but it was Jai Jai Alix feared. Not that she felt Jai Jai was consciously malicious or intended evil, but worse, Jai Jai was careless about other people's lives. Jai Jai exuded Scott Fitzgerald's vast carelessness, a carelessness that allowed her to smash things and people and then retreat, untouched, indifferent, into her own preoccupied narcissism.

Alix knew about Jai Jai's casually broken engagement, about her abandoning not one but two lovers in Bequia without a backward glance; now, after an affair with her father, Jai Jai was marrying Alix's brother. Alix's husband, always angrily aware of his father-in-law's antagonism, wanted to strike back by hosting the wedding. Alix found herself in the situation that had dominated her life caught between the conflicting desires of rich, powerful men used to having, always, whatever they wanted. When she married Yale and stopped working at Raimont, Alix thought she had removed herself from their battles; now in London, in the spring of 1976, she was back in the middle.

"I've spent too much of my life caught between my father and my brother," Alix said. "If we give Jai Jai and Sergei a wedding, I'll be caught again."

"What do you mean, caught? Your father is giving Jai Jai an emerald necklace for a wedding present. *He* doesn't object," Yale had said. "Why should you?"

"It's dangerous. It's emotional dynamite, and it's decadent," Alix said, "and I don't want to be part of it."

"You sound like Queen Victoria," said Yale. "It is not decadent. It's sophisticated. You live in a sophisticated world, *very, very* sophisticated, and you refuse to admit it."

It was not the first time they had argued about sex in their six years of marriage. One evening in San Lorenzo another couple had invited Yale and Alix to bed with them. A foursome, they had called it. Yale had wanted to; Alix had refused. Another time, in New York, at a party in a SoHo loft decorated with the latest in industrial chic, the entertainment had included a live sex show imported from Eighth Avenue, currently a fashionable amusement. Alix had left alone; Yale had stayed until the party broke up at nine the next morning.

It had been Yale's idea to host the wedding. He wanted to stage-manage a spectacular. After all, a great beauty was marrying a great heir. It was the stuff dreams, Yale's dreams, were made of. The entire situation, with its delicious sexual undertones, fitted his idea of what the sophisticated, international rich were all about.

"Your notions of sex come from the Dark Ages," Yale had told Alix, not for the first time.

"They come from knowing my father—and my brother," Alix said. A triangle in which the same woman slept with father and son had an explosive potential that poets and playwrights since Sophocles and Euripides had understood. "I don't want to be involved in a classic tragedy."

"It isn't exactly the first time a father and son have been attracted to the same woman," Yale said. He cited the scandal-shrouded private life of an extremely well-known and extremely rich Greek. He mentioned an actress who had had an affair with an important European politician, a head of state, and subsequently had married his son. For a third example, he referred to a charmer on the international landscape who had divorced her husband to marry his father. "What are you going to do, Alix? Stick your head in the ground and pretend it isn't happening?"

"It doesn't have to happen with my blessing. And it certainly isn't going to happen in my house."

"The rich girl has spoken," Yale said. "And what rich girls want, rich girls get."

Alix had resisted using the fact that the house they lived in was hers, chosen by her and paid for with her money, until it seemed it was the only way to win the argument. She was very conscious of Yale's sensitivity to the difference in their finances. He was a poor millionaire, and she was a rich millionaire—those were Yale's own words—and once upon a time he had joked about it. This morning was one of the rare times Alix had used her money to get her way. Yale had often criticized her for her reluctance to use her money to get what she wanted. "That's what money is for," he would tell her, "to get what you want." But now that she had done it, it was a mistake. Yale had stormed out of the house, slamming the door behind him.

Now, after a morning of shopping and the hairdresser, Alix's tensions had yielded to chemistry, and she paid full attention to Cartwright's words.

He told her that Sergei wanted to make the first Raimont investment in Mexico at Playa Sol, a one-and-three-quarter-mile-long crescent beach, south of Mazatlán on the coastline shared by Acapulco, Puerto Vallarta and Manzanillo. Sergei foresaw Playa Sol as a future Acapulco, and he wanted to bid on behalf of Raimont Development. Playa Sol was a short hop from the large population centers of California and east to Texas and New Orleans, and the Barragan participation would provide guarantees of favorable Mexican government involvement.

Alexander disagreed. Cartwright listed his reasons: New resorts going up at Cancun and Ixtapa, Cabo de San Lucas, the new thirty-three-million-dollar Las Hadas and two Club Méditerranés, one at Careyes, another at Punta Nixuc, as well as major renovations being undertaken at Puerto Vallarta and Acapulco, would make too many rooms available at one time. There was no way the existing tourist economy could fill them, Alexander argued. In addition, said Cartwright, Alexander worried about the devaluation of the peso, which would make building expenses unpredictable and uncontrollable. Father and son were in diametric disagreement.

"Sergei is going ahead anyway. He went to your father for financing," Cartwright said. "He refused."

An emerald necklace, on the one hand, Alix thought, the refusal of financing on the other. Alix wondered how her father really felt about Sergei's marriage. As usual, he was sending mixed signals.

"Sergei and Paolo Barragan have formed a partnership. They've raised twelve of the fifteen million they need," Cartwright said. "They're looking for another three. Sergei asked me to ask you if you would speak to your father, try to get him to change his mind."

"Why doesn't Sergei speak to him?" Alix asked, knowing it wasn't a fair question. Her father and her brother were alike in so many ways. They were both cowards about face-to-face confrontations, and for as long as she could remember, she had been the mediator in their quarrels, whether it was over a five-dollar raise in allowance when Sergei had been ten or over a business disagreement now, more than a dozen years later. Alix agreed to speak to her father, though, because she found it impossible to refuse Sergei.

"But I don't think it will do the slightest bit of good," she cautioned. "You know my father, once his mind is made up. . . ."

"Sergei will appreciate it, I know," said Cartwright. A Swiss-trained hotelman, Cartwright had managed the Raimont European division since Alix had been a child. His Mayfair apartment and Cotswolds farm had been Alix's "home" in Britain, and as a girl she had called him Uncle Cartwright.

The rest of the lunch passed with conversation about the Arabs' purchase of the Dorchester, the outlook for the pound (improving—slowly), the prospects for the English tourist economy (very good since the relative weakness of the pound against other currencies made food, accommodations, shopping and entertainment in London a bargain). When lunch was over, Alix asked if she could use a telephone . . . privately. Cartwright showed her into his office and, leaving her alone behind his big desk, shut the door as Alix dialed.

Alix Raimont was a plain girl in a world of glamorous men and beautiful women. Her childhood had been a fairy tale; Jansen of Paris had decorated her nursery; Dali, who had painted the murals for the dining room of a Paris hotel her father owned, had painted yellow elephants and rose-colored lions for her; the movie stars, millionaires and politicians who came to court her father oohed and aahed over her first steps and earliest words, praised the arabesques she learned in ballet class and hung the paintings she did in nursery school in their homes and offices.

She was shy and lonely, insecure and, on occasion, imperious. She worried about her hair, which had a tendency to be unmanageable, and was self-conscious about the glasses which she had to wear as a child and which later were replaced with contact lenses. She wanted more than anything to be loved for herself, not for her money.

Alix Raimont had an accent in every language: Her English sounded British to Americans and American to the English; her French had her grandmother's Russian *r*; her German the Alsatian inflection of a tutor; her Spanish the Castilian lisp of the Madrid school for the sons and daughters of noblemen she attended the year she turned ten. Her first words were neither "mama" nor "dada" but "byebye"; her parents traveled so much that Alix's nanny was always prompting her to wave and say "byebye."

She was comfortable everywhere and at home nowhere. Her mother, from an extremely rich, extremely conservative and very social Philadelphia family, had been married three times, and so had her father. She had had, in the course of her twenty-six years, four stepbrothers, two stepsisters and one halfbrother, Sergei, whom she considered a full brother.

Until Alix married Yale Warrant and bought her house in Belgravia, she had never thought of any one place as home. On her eighth birthday her father had given her a dollhouse; only it wasn't a house, it was a hotel. It had furnished guest rooms and suites, a restaurant with miniature crystal chandeliers, a bar with tiny glasses suspended from an overhead rack and tiny bottles with minuscule labels lined up in front of a mirror, a reception desk with a tiny guest register with real registration forms with spaces for names, addresses and passport numbers; across from it was a stand for the concierge, and in proper uniforms, there were one hundred staff members: maids and valets, waiters and maître d's, bellmen and porters, a manager and an assistant manager, garagemen, housekeepers, dishwashers, painters, janitors, gardeners and telephone operators.

Alix had always been a good girl, anxious to please her busy and sought-after parents. She was tormented by a feeling of inadequacy as a child, sure that she would never grow up to be important enough for her father to pay attention to her or beautiful enough for her mother to be proud of her. To please her mother, she became immaculately well groomed and made a point of never leaving her bedroom unless she was completely dressed and freshly made up; to please her father and because she found she loved it, she worked.

In Alix's earliest years, her grandmother, her father's mother, Tatiana, had influenced Alix more than anyone else—more than her mother, her father, her governess. Tatiana's parents had left Russia during the Revolution and moved to Paris, where her father, a lawyer in the service of the czar, worked for a while as a doorman in a Pigalle nightclub until he could qualify for the French bar. Tatiana remembered being very poor, so poor that the family ate day-old bread, and when there was no money for even that, they drank warm water to assuage their hunger. After school Tatiana worked in a laundry. She was too young to work with the enormous vats of soap and water that were agitated by hand with long wooden paddles but not too young to do what the proprietress, Madame Poilaine, called "delicate work." Tatiana pressed miles of beribbonned, beruffled underwear worn by fine ladies of that era with heavy flat irons warmed to different temperatures on different parts of the cast-iron wood-burning stove.

Tatiana had met her future husband, Lucien, half-Russian, half-French, from a respectable bourgeois family at one of the frequent teas served nostalgically from huge samovars that had, like the people who owned them, made their way across Europe. Lucien was in conflict with his family, who wanted him to go into practice immediately and cater to the fashionable nervous diseases of the time, to the neurasthenics given to fainting and weakness and vapors. Lucien wanted additional study. He wanted to be a surgeon. Surgery might cure or it might kill, but surgery had results that could be seen and measured. Treatment of nervous ailments at the time consisted of retreats to the spas of Evian-les-Bains and Baden-Baden and, as far as Lucien could see, accomplished nothing. Tatiana encouraged Lucien to pursue his desires, and they put off their marriage until he could afford to support his young wife. Despite the rigid disapproval of Lucien's mother, a tiny, formidable woman who drank tea laced with Ricard, whose licorice smell Lucien would forever associate with her, he and his wife, with the clouds of world war in the distance and a baby on the way, daringly moved to America.

When Alix was a child, Tatiana lived in the Bucks County stone farmhouse she and Lucien had bought when he first began to make money. She had a gift for horticulture which she used both commercially and experimentally. She had a big herb garden, and she sold fresh herbs in season to markets nearby and dried herbs by mail all year around. Lavender and mint and camomile and basil and oregano and dill were tied into bunches and hung upside down to dry from the beams of the cool dark barn that had sheltered cows when the property had been a dairy farm. She worked with the county agriculture department to develop a hybrid blueberry that bore twice each summer: in late June and then again in early August. She also helped develop a disease-resistant strain of potato and a variety of frost-resistant green bean.

It was Tatiana who had instilled in Alix the importance of work. "Work and love; love and work," she would say. "They are the two essentials for a happy life. For men and for women. One without the other is only half a life."

It had never occurred to Alix that she wouldn't work. In her early years, playing with her dollhouse/hotel, she had dreamed she would work for Raimont, and for a time she did. The summer of 1960, when she was fourteen, Alix spent with her father. Everywhere he went, she went, and it was the happiest summer of her life. He took her to con-

struction sites, to executive meetings, to conferences of
travel and resort associations at which he spoke. He—and
she—had liked the idea of the image they presented. Like
Marjorie Merriweather Post, whose own father had taken
her to meetings of the board of Postum before she was ten
and who said years later in recollection, "I loved it," Alix
loved it. After meetings, in the back of her father's limo, he
would ask her about what had been said and encouraged her
to ask about what she hadn't understood. That was the same
summer that Alexander, at the time heavily involved in airport construction, was building an addition to Barajas airport in Madrid. He took her to a bulldozed strip where
new cement was being poured, and with a stick, Alix wrote
her initials and the date in the not-yet-dry concrete. Forever after, when she went through Barajas, she always had
a warm, secret glow at the thought that somewhere in the
huge airport the initials scratched by a little girl with her
father proudly looking on still existed. For the next nine
years, until she was twenty, Alix spent summers working with her father and, by that time, had a deep
knowledge of his business. He taught her the value of a
dollar; he taught her when to sacrifice an immediate profit
for an eventual greater profit; she learned to read a balance
sheet and, eventually at Harvard, how one was put together; she became comfortable with men; with accountants and lawyers, architects and businessmen, professional
hoteliers with professional charm and tough building con-
tractors with a different kind of rougher charm, she could
talk as comfortably to a busboy as to a president of a large
corporation. She learned phrases of Turkish from the Turks
who immigrated on work permits to find work in Germany
when the Frankfurt hotel was built; she learned a few
phrases of Tagalog when she spent time in the Philippines
with her father looking into a project that never came off;
she knew that sand and stone were bought and sold by the
yard, an amount equal to twenty-seven cubic feet, that the
lodging industry's traditional occupancy goal was seventy-
five percent, that the basis of costing estimates was calculated on a per-room dollar amount. Those summers, close
to her father, were the only times Alix could remember not
feeling lonely until she met Yale. She wanted to continue to
work, and although her formal education had been sketchy,

with tutors and a series of boarding schools in her earlier years followed by one year at the University of Geneva, she was permitted by a special arrangement to attend the Harvard School of Business, where she took WAC (Written Analysis of Cases), MERC 1 (Managerial Economics, Reporting and Control) and HBO (Human Behavior in Organizations). She got her highest grade HP+ (High Pass Plus) in HBO and her lowest P (Pass) in the complicated, precisely diagrammed Decision Problems of MERC 1.

At twenty-two, after her first year at Harvard, filled with enthusiasm and armed with projections showing cash savings, improved service and, eventually, a profit increase of one percent a month (twelve percent a year), she suggested that the computer system that made and confirmed worldwide reservations in Raimont Hotels, in Raimont Resorts and in hotels managed by Raimont be linked to the computer networks of the major airlines. At the time it was an untried concept.

Sergei criticized the suggestion. "The start-up costs are prohibitive," he said, "and besides, the airlines will never agree."

"But it will save money in the long run," said Alix, "and it will provide convenience to the traveler. People will be able to make and confirm travel and room reservations simultaneously."

The argument went back and forth, and Alexander refused to intercede. He considered conflict and competition between Raimont executives creative and treated his children the same way he treated his employees.

Alexander, although he tried to conceal it, loved Sergei more but depended on Alix more. Both children sensed how he felt, and the irony of their lives was that Alix longed to be uncritically loved while Sergei longed to be relied and depended on. Alexander's dream was that one day Sergei would run Raimont while Alix would marry Paolo Barragan, son of one of his longtime business associates, and thus bring into the family a husband whose financial resources matched the Raimonts' and whose background in the hotel business would make him an ideal son-in-law. The trouble was that Sergei, charming and magnetic, was erratic and temperamental, while Alix, less superficially charming, had the inborn talents of a hotelier and the discipline Sergei lacked.

Just as Alix had, Sergei began to work at Raimont during the summers of his midteens, and from that early date, the patterns that would eventually lead Alix to withdraw from Raimont were established.

One summer Sergei worked in the New York office mailroom, a way to acquaint him with the personnel and functions of all departments. One Monday he did not appear for work. Nor did he call. Alexander and Alix, frantic with worry, hired private detectives, who finally found Sergei on Thursday. He was in a friend's cottage on Martha's Vineyard. He was alone, neither drunk nor drugged and unharmed. He had no explanation for his failure to return to work on Monday except that "he was depressed and didn't feel like it." Although Alexander had been at first relieved when Sergei was found unhurt, he became furious later and showed his fury characteristically by refusing to speak to Sergei. Sergei, complaining to Alix that he was fed up, left New York, joined a friend on his parents' yacht in the Aegean and partied the rest of the summer away. Alix stayed on in New York and worked and couldn't help feeling hurt at the way her father seemed to take her for granted while he couldn't hide how much he missed Sergei.

After Sergei's first year at Harvard, Alexander organized a three-day meeting of all Raimont executives, American, Asian and European, at the Raimont/Maui, to introduce Sergei. At four on Friday, the first day of the meeting, there was to be a formal meeting at which Sergei would be formally presented. It was to be followed by a cocktail party, a luau and Hawaiian entertainment. At four o'clock twenty-five key Raimont people were assembled in the conference room. At a quarter to five Sergei sauntered in. Men of fifty years who earned six-figure salaries were not amused, and although eventually Sergei charmed them all, Alix was hurt and angry that she, who had helped prepare the data for her father's introductory speech, went unthanked while her father fumed and worried over Sergei.

As time went on, Alix found herself in an impossible situation: As her father depended on her more and more, Sergei became more and more resentful of her, and the more resentful he became, the more he rebelled at working and the less he did. In turn, Alexander depended even more on Alix, and she, in turn, began to resent Sergei. She felt that if he were more reliable and disciplined and did his share of the work, she wouldn't bear the brunt of her father's almost inhuman demands and frequent impatient outbursts. Sergei accused Alix of trying to push him out of his rightful place at Raimont, and his resentment and anger had already reached the boiling point when she suggested the linkage of computer systems.

"If Raimont goes ahead with this idea, I quit," Sergei told his father. "It will show that you have no respect at all for my opinion and judgment."

The look on her father's face told Alix all she needed to know about the anguish he felt at being put into a position of having to choose between his children, and to avoid a showdown in which no one would win, Alix withdrew the suggestion and, after dropping out of Harvard and leaving Raimont, moved to New York City and began to live the life of a jet-set heiress. Alix was given too much money and nothing to do except spend it; she filled her days with shopping, lunches, parties and, finding herself nevertheless restless and bored, took some courses at Columbia. Because HBO had been her favorite and best class at Harvard, she signed up for two psychology courses and, through a chain of circumstances, met Yale Warrant, the man she would marry against her father's violent opposition.

Yale Warrant's entire life had been a love-hate relationship with the rich. He had grown up with them but not of them. His father had been the son of a Forest Hills pharmacist. Eddie Warrant could not remember when he had not been on a tennis court. The West Side Tennis Club was four blocks away, and after school young Eddie retrieved balls, warmed up club players and got to know the pro. In exchange for being ball boy during lessons, the pro coached Eddie, who had a steady, well-balanced game: a strong serve; a decent volley; a good passing shot; a reliable backhand. Eddie Warrant could have been an outstanding competitive player. What stopped him was that he had no instinct for the kill. Nevertheless, Eddie Warrant made the junior Davis Cup team.

In those years tennis was a gentleman's sport, and Eddie, who couldn't afford equipment, court time, lessons, lodging and travel, found, as did others in his circumstances, a sponsor. Phillip Noyes, an investment banker, was looking for a hobby; what he found was Eddie Warrant. Eddie was appreciative of Phillip Noyes' help and made returns on his sponsor's investment by, one year, winning the junior grass court championships.

Phillip, who had retired from the investment firm he had cofounded, Noyes, Lea, was delighted, and as time went on, he and his wife, who had lost both sons in World War II—one in the Aleutians, one in a fighter plane over the English Channel—virtually adopted Eddie. Phillip and Margaret Noyes divided their time between an estate with a croquet lawn in Locust Valley and a pseudo-Spanish Colonial mansion in Palm Beach, and so, eventually, did Eddie. He lived in their guest cottages, played gentle doubles with his benefactors and his friends during the day and gin rummy with them at night. Whatever dreams he may have had of the center court at Wimbledon gradually receded, and Eddie, in time, replaced the retiring pro at the West Side Tennis Club and, at the suggestion of Phillip Noyes, a member of the board, also became pro at the Everglades Club. Thus, winter and summer, Eddie Warrant's life moved in synchronization with the lives of the very rich.

By the time he was twenty-eight, good-looking with a perpetual tan and sun-bleached hair, he had developed the social skills to alleviate the deep boredom known only to the very rich. In earlier centuries Eddie would have been a courtier, existing to distract, amuse and cater to the whims and caprices of the nobles to whom he was a sworn liege. In the democratic twentieth century Eddie had other functions. One was as escort to the daughters of the rich. He went with them to debutante parties, masked balls, champagne picnics, weddings, birthday parties and graduation dances. If the service happened to include sex in well-appointed beach cabanas or in the back seats of rakish convertibles, Eddie was, after all, a young and virile man.

Eddie knew his place. Never did he aspire to an ambitious marriage, and when he did marry, at the age of thirty, he chose the perfect wife. Beatrice Powell was a social secretary to a midwestern meat-packing heiress, who wintered in a hundred-room mansion on the sea so palatial that upon her death it was willed to the government of the United States of America, a gift which was eventually refused. The maintenance on Las Olas (The Waves) ran to three-quarters of a million dollars a year, a sum politically embarrassing and impossible to explain to voters struggling to keep up car payments.

Beatrice ran the mechanics of Madame's life. She kept three separate cross-referenced card files (one for Palm Beach, one for Chicago, one for Bar Harbor) with names, addresses, telephone numbers, birthdates, anniversaries and, where appropriate and it almost always was, notation of divorces and remarriages. Included on another set of cards (The Party File) were detailed menus, the wines and years of vintage, color snapshots of the table, recording silver and china service, table linens and floral decorations or centerpieces. In addition, the gown and jewelry worn by Madame on each occasion were meticulously noted.

It was Beatrice, not Madame, who gave the butler daily instructions, delivered Madame's compliments if she was pleased and criticism if she wasn't. Beatrice underlined newspaper stories so that Madame's daily reading would be made easier. She kept a constant supply of best-sellers, rented prints of new and favorite old movies, catalogued and inventoried Madame's gem collection and kept the insurance on it updated as fluctuations in jewelry prices affected their value. Beatrice worked with curators who purchased art and antiques on Madame's behalf, making certain that Madame was never overcharged and didn't miss anything either at auction or through a dealer that properly belonged in Madame's collections. She met weekly with Madame's accountant and banker to go over the household bills: meats and fish, groceries, hardware, maintenance and staff salaries. Eventually Beatrice had her own staff of two.

When Edward and Beatrice met, at a party at Madame's, they recognized in each other their destined alter egos and, six months later, were married in the ballroom of Madame's Lakefront Drive mansion. As a wedding gift Madame and the Noyeses each gave the identical gift: the three-thousand-dollar tax-free one-time-a-year gift permitted by the Internal Revenue Code.

When, a sedate two years later, their son was born, they

named him Yale in memory of the Noyeses' elder son. They chose to have no more, realizing that while one child was an ornament, two children would inhibit their freedom to pursue the way of life they borrowed but did not truly share with the very rich. Yale's playmates were the children of the very rich, the heirs and heiresses to third- and fourth-generation trust funds. Unlike his father, who lacked a killer instinct, a drive to compete and excel, Yale burned. He hated the rich, and he wanted to be one of them. He envied them, and he wanted to punish them for the corrosiveness of his envy.

He kept his feelings to himself and thought of himself as a secret adversary with dreams of conquest, a spy in the corridors of the rich. He went to St. Marks, Mr. Noyes' prep school, and to Princeton, Mr. Noyes' beloved alma mater, the expenses in both instances paid for by Mr. Noyes. Yale went from Princeton to Wall Street and a junior job waiting for him at Noyes, Lea, where he attended the blue-chip portfolios of widows and orphans. He was responsible, conservative, conscientious and bored. He drank weak tea served by uniformed Irish maids in the dark Park Avenue apartments of old ladies who worried about their A T & T, sent dividend checks to rebellious heiresses living on communes in Wisconsin, reinvested dividends for those clients who lived on the interest on interest. He hated every minute of it and was so good at it only because he knew it wouldn't last forever.

Yale was appreciated at Noyes, Lea and was assured, over and over, that he had a "future," unspecified, with the firm. Yale appeared to appreciate the promise and never once betrayed the fact that he didn't plan to wait around to find out what that future might be. When Phillip Noyes died, at seventy-six, of cancer of the liver, his will left ten thousand dollars to his godson, Yale Warrant. It was, as Yale had known it would be, exactly an appropriate amount. Contrary to newspaper headlines, the rich do not leave fortunes to outsiders no matter how fond of them they might have been. To the old-line rich, money is to be protected, hoarded and, above all, kept in the family, as many sons- and daughters-in-law have, to their shock and surprise, learned too late. Although ten thousand dollars was a token compared to the fifty-five-million-dollar estate left by Phillip Noyes, Yale did not dwell bitterly on the disparity. Instead, because of his good relations with banks that valued him for the large portfolios he was entrusted with, he was permitted to borrow eighty percent of the ten thousand dollars. Thus, with a stake of eighteen thousand dollars and the ability to trade without paying a broker's commission, Yale began to buy and sell for himself, as aggressive with his own money as he had been conservative with the money of others.

In the bull market of the sixties Yale consistently outperformed the Dow. His abilities did not go unnoticed on the Street, and in the sincerest compliment of all, other brokers asked him to handle their own trading accounts. Yale wanted to make a million dollars by the time he was thirty. At twenty-eight, the year he met Alix, he was on schedule.

New York's Metropolitan Club at 1 East Sixtieth Street was founded in 1891 by, among others, J. P. Morgan. The building itself, designed by Stanford White, is a Manhattan landmark. The empty cobblestone courtyard, standing in the middle of prime East Side real estate, gives the best clue to its members' wealth. Only the rich can afford to own land in the middle of valuable real estate and then indulge the luxury of letting it stand idle.

Everyone has problems. The trust departments of banks are no exception. Their problems are the fairly obvious ones that come from handling large amounts of other people's money. Two examples will suffice.

It is far from uncommon for women who have worked for years with their husbands building up a business to find, upon their husband's death, that his estate has been left in trust. The widow, with thirty years of experience in business, now finds herself with a new partner: a fresh-faced twenty-five-year-old with a brand-new MBA. The potential for conflict and resentment is obvious.

The resentment can work the other way around. Imagine a young, ambitious banker who worked his way through college now administering an eight-figure trust the beneficiary of which is someone his own age whose only problem in life is whether to ski in Gstaad or Aspen. The bank's problem is to make sure that the young banker does not take out his resentment in his handling of the trust assets.

It was thus that the trust department of the MetroBank commissioned a behavioral study of the relationship between the members of trust departments and the clients they served. One of the consultants to the psychological research firm the MetroBank hired was a professor at the Columbia Graduate School of Psychology; one of his students was Alix Raimont, who as a trust beneficiary was happy to assist him, hoping to find in the process some understanding of her own position.

Each of the brokerage houses that traded accounts for MetroBank was invited to send a representative to the meeting at which the research report would be presented. The meeting was held in a second-floor conference room at the Metropolitan Club, a large room, square in shape, with a fireplace big enough in which to park a Jeep, four duplex windows overlooking Central Park at treetop level and a rectangular conference table set with water carafes, yellow legal pads and freshly sharpened pencils. Noyes, Lea elected to send Yale Warrant, one of its brightest young men, to the conference.

∽ SIX ∾

"Women think too much about love and not enough about money. Men think too much about money and not enough about love," read Alix, quoting the psychologist Martin Wagner, as she concluded reading the part of the research she had prepared for the report to the Trust Department of the MetroBank and its guests. She put down the file cards which contained her notes, and before she could sit down, Yale Warrant spoke.

"Would men be able to make more money if they thought more about love?" he asked. Everyone in the room laughed. The meeting was drawing to a close, and the mood was relaxed.

"Perhaps they might be happier with the money they already had," said Alix, and the men in the room laughed again and applauded her quick riposte. When the room quieted down, the head of the research company summed up by saying that research had shown that fear—fear manifested as lack of interest, fear manifested as hostility, fear manifested as withdrawal—was the underlying problem facing trust departments. The report recommended financial education, closer contact with beneficiaries and frequent updates of portfolio positions as steps the bank might take to improve relations between the department and the people it served. The meeting broke up, and cheese straws and tiny glasses of sherry were served.

"Touché," said Yale, handing Alix a glass and referring to their exchange.

"Do you think the report is going to help?" Alix asked, aware of Yale's dark-blond sun-streaked hair and navy-blue eyes. Only his mouth, almost embarrassingly sensual, saved him from being too handsome.

"It's going to be a struggle. If you only knew how many times women have told me that their mind freezes when they look at figures or that they can't, simply cannot, balance a bank statement, you'd know what a problem it is. They think we're magicians or witch doctors. Half the time they're in awe of us, and the other half they're convinced we're cheating them," he said. He sipped his wine. "How did you get interested in finance? It's unusual for a woman." His directness surprised her and put her at ease. She wondered if he connected her name with Raimont Hotels and Resorts. Sometimes people did; sometimes they didn't.

"I saw my first balance sheet when I was eleven," she said, aware that, very slightly, she was bragging, wanting to separate herself from women who held themselves aloof from financial matters.

"And did you understand it?" Yale asked, teasing her.

"Not then but soon after," Alix answered with her characteristic seriousness. "My father explained it to me. He always said that money had no sex."

"I disagree," said Yale. "There's nothing sexier than money. It's what makes the world go round." Alix felt suddenly embarrassed at the discussion of sex, even though she had inadvertently given Yale the lead, and she was uncomfortably silent for a moment.

"It used to be love that made the world go round," said a man standing nearby, who had obviously overheard the exchange. He was a broker from one of Noyes, Lea's competitors, a former all-American, now, in his mid-fifties, still at playing weight and proud of it. "But I guess those days are gone forever."

"I hope not," said Yale, looking straight at Alix, who, to her chagrin, blushed. "And you're wrong, Alix, about men not thinking enough about love. I think about it all the time."

"When I was your age, I used to fall in love every month," said the all-American. "The only problem was that my wife always objected."

He had intended it to come out as a hearty salesman's punch line. Instead, midway through, reacting to Alix's expression, his tone changed, and it came out sad and poignant. He sounded like a lonely man living a life of regret. He was embarrassed at the private, unintended revelation.

"It wasn't funny," he said in apology and then disappeared.

"Do psychology students always get intimate confessions?" Yale asked. "Or is it just you?"

The meeting had dispersed, and the room was three-quarters empty. Alix and Yale left together, and she never replied to his question. People—except for her own parents—had confided in Alix for as long as she could remember, and the sympathetic quality about her that invited confidences from friends and strangers was one of the things she liked most about herself. Oddly, though, she would not admit it. She was afraid of pride, afraid that admitting something she valued would be to risk losing it.

As Yale and Alix reached the sidewalk, the skies, which had been overcast all day long, opened up. The rain was torrential, like a jungle rain in South America, and instantly, as it always was in New York, every single taxi in the city immediately disappeared. Alix and Yale stood in the shelter of the overhang of the club, waiting for the rain to subside. Alix was attracted to him and, because of it, nervous.

"Can you have dinner with me?" Alix asked in a voice

that was familiar to Yale. It was a rich girl's voice. The rich, Yale had noticed, were always very sure about what they wanted and not at all shy about asking for it.

"I have a date," Yale said. He'd been seeing a model, a girl with the face of an angel whose celestial looks sold perfume, silk lingerie and expensive cosmetics.

"Oh," said Alix, disappointed.

"But I'll break it," Yale said, immediately comfortable with Alix. Like his ex-wife, a California heiress, like all the rich Yale had grown up with, Alix did not bother to hide behind conventional façades of politeness; she was candid and straightforward about her feelings. Her answering smile was a reward in itself.

The rain had abruptly run its course, dwindling to a drop here and there, and in the southern sky the sunset was already beginning to break through. Violence in New York isn't confined to the streets; the weather, too, is violent. Taxis reappeared as instantly and magically as they'd disappeared, and they flagged one immediately. Alix's choice was the Four Seasons, where she was known. Sometime during the dinner Yale realized that he wanted Alix. At first he'd been impressed by her. He'd realized—although he did not show it—exactly who she was as soon as she was introduced at the Metropolitan Club meeting. Then, during dinner, finding her impressively knowledgeable and intelligent, he realized that in addition to being impressed, he was genuinely attracted. By an agreement that did not need to be spoken, Yale took her home.

Alix lived on the forty-ninth floor of the Olympic Towers on Fifty-first Street and Fifth Avenue. Expanses of bronzed glass framed a view west over Rockefeller Center to the Hudson River and south over St. Patrick's all the way to the twin Trade Center towers. The apartment, staffed by a Scandinavian couple, was utterly contemporary; built-in banquettes lined the solid wall areas and plump hassocks on casters rolled wherever one wished. Everything was covered in off-white artists' canvas. There was a large square glass coffee table, several large trees in tubs dramatically lit from below and simple matchstick blinds at the windows. A huge blue Albers was the only art in the room and the only art the room needed. The apartment was both luxurious and restrained. It seemed to reflect Alix perfectly. Yale complimented Alix on her apartment, and she thanked him. There was a moment of uncomfortable silence. Suddenly Yale spoke. "Do you want me to stay?" he asked, touching her hand.

Alix nodded, and then she said, "I don't do this every night."

"I know."

"I just wanted to make sure you understood that." She led him through the apartment to her bedroom, a white and apricot room with a view of the city that sparkled like a diamond necklace below. It occurred to him as they began their first embrace that Alix Raimont, more than anyone he had ever known, cared that she not be misunderstood.

OCTOBER 1950

When, in her mind's eye, Alix pictured herself as a child, she saw herself as small and alone. When she was four, she was living in a big house on Sutton Place, and every morning her father's New York driver, Mr. Gordon, waited with a big limousine to drive her to school. At that time, when her father's business was in a decade of explosive growth, he was at home even less than usual. Alix saw her mother infrequently, although they lived in the same house. Brooke Raimont stayed in her bedroom until it was time to dress for lunch. Her bedroom was her office, and she stayed on the telephone all morning, buying tickets to her friends' charity balls and fashion shows and selling them tickets to hers in the ritual quid pro quo of the rich, social and charity-minded.

Sometimes, as a surprise, Alix would ask her mother's maid, a Colombian woman, a fine seamstress named Estella, if she could "help" carry in her mother's breakfast tray—always the same, China tea and an English muffin. Her mother would be propped up on pillows, big square European ones, wearing a pastel bed jacket, her hair brushed and held back with a matching ribbon. Always, a cigarette, an unfiltered Camel, smoldered in Brooke Raimont's hand—she was a three-pack-a-day chain smoker—and ashes dotted the sheets and blanket cover.

"Try not to grow up," Brooke would tell her daughter.

"I'll try, Mummy," Alix would answer, sensing her mother's sadness, although not understanding it and trying to make her happier with her agreeable response to an impossible suggestion.

That year her parents divorced. Neither her mother nor her father told her what was happening. She found out by accident from her mother's maid.

"Estella, what is it?" Alix spoke in Spanish, pointing toward the huge moving van parked in front of the house. "Are we moving?"

The maid's brown eyes avoided Alix's. She looked embarrassed and uncomfortable, but Alix wouldn't go away. Estella finally said, in Spanish, "Your mother is moving."

Alix had been halfway to nursery school when it began to rain and Alix asked to return home for rubbers and a raincoat. The big car had traveled two blocks north from Sutton Place when Alix asked Mr. Gordon to return home. (Alix called her father's driver "Mr." because it was one of her mother's rules. Her mother had rules for everything, including the treatment of servants. It was proper to ask a maid to draw a bath, but, one must wash the bathtub afterward oneself because it was disgusting to have a servant clean personal mess; money must never be discussed in front of servants, nor was it proper to joke with servants; a cook was never to be interrupted; servants' children must be treated politely; a servant's mistakes should be pointed out firmly but always in private—they were rules Alix would remember her whole life the way other people remembered multiplication tables or nursery rhymes.)

A big Morgan-Manhattan van was parked in the limousine's usual place at the curb. As Alix walked the few steps to the front door, two men moved out a large cardboard wardrobe. Alix didn't understand. She was accustomed to moving but always in certain cycles throughout the year—in June to Darkharbor, at Christmas to Palm Beach, Easter to Mill Reef—but this was October, the middle of the school term.

"Then I must be moving, too," Alix said to the maid.

"It's not my place," said Estella. "I'm the maid of your mother. You must ask her." She turned her attention to the moving men, directing them to take care.

"Thank you, Estella," Alix said in the automatic politeness so inbred, but she felt that something terrible was happening. She willed herself not to cry and went to her mother's room, the first door opposite the elevator on the third floor.

Her mother was at her dressing table, a cigarette smoldering in a small crystal ashtray, fitting pearl earrings to her ears. Alix asked her mother what was happening.

"He's divorcing me," she said.

Alix gazed at her mother. There was a long, sad silence.

"He's married to his business," her mother said. And then added in the one and only crudity Alix would ever hear her mother utter. "He wants to marry that bitch. Well, I just don't care anymore."

Her mother took a long drag on her cigarette. "He's going to have to pay for the privilege. Then he can do whatever he pleases." It was not the first time Alix had heard talk about the relationship between love and money. Many of the children she went to school with had divorced parents, and at an early age they already were familiar with alimony, settlements and lump-sum payments.

"I wish you didn't have to get divorced," Alix said.

"Dear, be realistic. We're not like other people."

"Why not?" Alix asked. "Why can't we be?"

"We have too much freedom," her mother said. And then she got up and put on a velvet blazer. She looked just as if she were going to one of her lunches. "He's an alley cat," she said. "And I don't want to talk about it anymore."

She picked up her handbag and left the bedroom, leaving Alix alone. Alix had always felt sorry for children with divorced parents. Now it was happening to her, something between her parents that excluded her. It was the beginning of her deep sense of loneliness and exclusion. Because her parents thought it would be best for Alix to stay in a familiar house and go to a familiar school, Alix remained in the Sutton Place house with her governess, a cook, butler and two maids until the end of the school term. Three weekends a month she saw her mother; on the other, her father.

Three months later, the divorce final, both her parents remarried within a week of each other, and Alix went to both weddings. Her mother married Slade Grey, a gentleman rancher, at his place near Scottsdale. Her father's marriage took place at his lawyer's Mount Kisco house. Slade

Grey had four children—three sons and a daughter—from his previous marriage. The youngest was ten years older than Alix, and they immediately took out their resentment toward their new stepmother on Alix. They made fun of her accent, which they considered affected, and of the fact that she rode eastern instead of western style, and they terrified her with alarming stories of the dangers of rattlesnakes.

Her father's new wife, Andrea, was a socialite/bohemian who had brushed education at Sarah Lawrence, who ate organic vegetables before health food became fashionable, wore spangled gypsy clothes and tightly wrapped turbans before *they* became fashionable and used enormous quantities of patchouli to state her presence. One of the first things she told Alix was that she was not to blame for the breakup of her parents' marriage: that Brooke Raimont and Slade Grey had been having an affair for almost a year before Andrea ever met Alexander. She overwhelmed Alix with extravagant declarations of affection and spontaneous hugs and kisses and five months after the wedding had a baby boy.

She explained the difference between mere stepsisters and stepbrothers—the children of her stepfather by his previous marriage—and Alix's new half brother.

"You and Sergei have the same father. It's a blood relationship, and you must love him as much as a full brother." Andrea had a holy faith in love that never deserted her through three husbands and countless lovers.

An arrangement was made for Alix to divide her time equally between her parents. Like a package, she was flown around the globe according to a timetable negotiated by her parents' lawyers. She eventually learned to ride western style, to shoot rattlesnakes with a .22 and to love Sergei like a blood brother. She never learned, though, not to be lonely. It was hardly surprising, therefore, that her first experience with sex had more to do with loneliness than love or passion.

CHRISTMAS 1964
AIR FRANCE FLIGHT #103
JFK/ORLY

Christmas night. He was the only person in the first-class section, and as he waited for the plane to take off, he was looking out the window. It was a drizzly night; the tarmac was just wet enough to reflect the lights of the service vans, catering trucks and fuel equipment. A silver Rolls pulled up to the stairs leading to first class, and she did not wait for the chauffeur to come around and open the door. Alix was wearing black, a black silk shirt and black trousers. A sable polo coat was left casually open, and although it was night, she wore dark glasses. Since she maintained wardrobes around the world, she had only a handbag, a soft sporty style swinging from a shoulder strap, a January issue of *Vogue* and a battered plain briefcase. He wondered who she was.

When the stewardess served the champagne, he took his glass and walked to the first row, where she was sitting. He asked if he could join her, and as she nodded yes, he wondered if she were crying behind the dark glasses. They were the only two passengers in the first-class section.

He cannot decide whether or not she is crying. As they sip the wine, they begin to speak. He tells her that he is American, born and bred in California, but that he has lived and worked in Paris since graduating from Stanford. He is a businessman, an importer and exporter of commodities, although at one time he wanted to be a writer. It was a romantic notion, he says, the kind of a thing you admit only to strangers on airplanes on Christmas night. She wonders if he regrets not following his original ambition.

"No," he says. "No regrets. I wanted to be like Hemingway. At that time everybody wanted to be like Hemingway. It was a young man's fantasy."

It would be hard to imagine a more un-Hemingway-like man. He is of medium height, thin and delicately boned. He is wearing a well-cut suit, and his hands, clean and fine, are nicely manicured. He has a sad, sensitive expression. He thinks the same of her. Poor little rich girl, he thinks.

Dinner is done; the jet races through the night. It is dim in the cabin. They speak softly. She tells him that she has just come from her annual holiday visit to her mother, now married for the third time, in the Maryland countryside. She tells him that her mother seems wounded by life. She describes a Christmas Eve open house at which her mother

very politely greeted the guests and then retired to her
room, where in a robe she ate her usual small dinner off a
tray. She tells him that the conversation she is having with
him, a stranger, is more intimate than any she has ever had
with her mother. Her mother believes that talking about
feelings is bad manners. They speak softly, close enough
now so that he can smell her hair.

"Were you crying?" he finally asks.

"Only inside," she answers.

"Why?"

"Because I'm alone."

"Everyone's alone," he says. "Everyone's always alone."

She doesn't answer. Moments pass, and then they kiss.
Softly. Then not so softly. He wants her. He wants some
indefinable something. He has always wanted something.
He is married, not happily. He put his hand on her throat
and up into the warm, shiny hair. He is excited, tender,
and she begins to weep. He wonders why but does not ask.
She does not seem given to self-pity; perhaps it is her age.
She is so young, eighteen, perhaps. He holds her, strokes
her. They make love in the deserted, curtained-off section
of the jet. After, he holds her. Gently. He holds her until
she falls asleep. He holds her in his arms across the Atlantic. It is better than sex. The feeling lasts longer.

At Orly another limousine is waiting on the tarmac.
She gets in and is swallowed up in its large interior. She
looks very small against the enormous car, the big Air
France plane, the terminal building in the currently fashionable brutal style of architecture. She is lost from his
sight as the chauffeur closes the door. The car starts and
disappears slowly into the gray early-morning fog. She is
gone.

He turns and walks across the strip toward immigration.
It is impossible to tell from looking at him how moved he
is, how evocative the sight of a girl in black wearing dark
glasses will be for him as long as he lives.

Alix is on her way to Venice to spend the New Year
with her father and Andrea. She has no way of knowing
that they will tell her that they plan to divorce.

Alix will add up the divorces: her mother and father;

her mother and her first stepfather, Slade Grey; her father and her first stepmother, Andrea. She wonders with a terrible anxiety whether her mother and her second stepfather will divorce, and she wonders if her father has already chosen a third wife.

She wonders if she will ever be able to marry without a sense of doom.

∾ SEVEN ∾

1970–1976

Yale and Alix were both outsiders. The difference was that Yale flaunted it and Alix tried to hide it.

"You act as if you're ashamed of who you are," he told her early in their courtship. He noticed that she rarely spoke about herself and was almost overly careful never to demand special treatment. She said she missed working but was afraid to reenter the intensely competitive atmosphere created by her father and brother and to expose herself to the emotionally bruising situation.

"If I were you," said Yale, "I'd try everything. At least once. As for working, I don't understand why you miss it. I work only because I have to. When I get my millions, I intend to quit and devote my life to pleasure. You don't know how to enjoy what you have."

"Perhaps you're right," Alix said. Yale had made her aware of how serious she was. Once, looking at a photograph album, Yale had pointed out that in none of her photographs was Alix smiling. Sunning on a yacht, in ski clothes with goggles pushed up into her hair, formally dressed at a grand ball, sipping lemonade at a tennis finals in Wimbledon, Alix Raimont had the same, serious expression. "I would like to have more fun . . . perhaps you could teach me."

"It's not at all hard once you get the hang of it," Yale said. "And I think I would make a good teacher. A loving teacher," he said. Yale's New York friends were fashionable people, models, artists, performers, who set styles, being avid to be the first to do and wear the latest. They were in perpetual motion, on a dance floor, going from party to party, being photographed, admired, emulated. They seemed bright, gleaming, glossy, as if freshly minted for each evening of pleasure, and Alix found their pursuit of excitement exciting. She began, to Yale's pleasure, to smile.

"Your smile is the most beautiful smile in the whole world," he would tell her. Alix Raimont's smile transformed her; it brought blood to her face, color to her cheeks and light to her eyes. When he saw her smile, Yale felt that he had created her. "Smile your beautiful smile for me," he would say, and she would obey, happy to please him, happy because he made her happy. Since meeting Yale, Alix had forgotten her loneliness. He lavished attention on her, calling her constantly when he wasn't with her, anxious about her comfort, solicitous about her preferences. He went with her when she bought clothes, met her when she was finished with the hairdresser. Whenever she went somewhere without him, he insisted she call him to let him know she had arrived safely; he telephoned her first thing when he woke and last thing before he fell asleep. Not only did Yale obliterate Alix's loneliness, but he refused to let her spend any of her own money when they were together. When she took a taxi, he gave her the fare, and when she went to the ladies' room, he gave her the tip; at a newsstand, at a florist, buying ice cream in Central Park, he paid. He bought her presents, costly and cheap, but always chosen with only her in mind, constantly. He made her feel loved, and as Yale intended, Alix fell madly in love with him.

Alix wanted Yale to move in with her. He refused. It was the shrewdest thing he could have done. She was, after all, a rich girl used to getting what she wanted. He refused to keep even a razor and clean shirt at her apartment, and although they saw each other every night, he kept his small Fifty-seventh Street apartment, and after making love to her and holding her in his arms until she fell asleep, he left her quietly and went to his own bed. When she woke, he would be gone, and she would be, as she had been so often as a child, alone and feeling deserted. It was Alix, finally, who brought up the subject of marriage, and it was she who proposed to him. She was twenty-three then and just eight months had passed since she left Raimont.

"I'd like to marry you," she said.

"But your father doesn't like me. He thinks I'm after your money," Yale said. Alexander had made his disapproval perfectly clear both in words and behavior; on the occasions at dinner, at a party, at Alix's apartment, when the two men met, Alexander was only just very barely polite. Yale had been married briefly once before, to a Southern California real estate heiress whose brother had been his Princeton roommate, and Alexander, who had always feared that Alix, particularly shy and vulnerable, would be an easy target for a fortune hunter, told her that Yale was a man with a *penchant* for heiresses, a man who was incapable of loving her for herself. Additionally, Alexander had a husband picked out for Alix: Paolo Barragan, heir to a fortune at least as large as the one Alix would inherit and a man, therefore, accustomed to money, who knew how to handle it, who could help Alix preserve and increase her assets, not drain them. Alix and Paolo had known each other since they had been children, and whenever her father said something about her marrying Paolo, Alix always had the same reply: "I like Paolo, I don't love him." Alexander felt he could afford to be patient. A Raimont-Barragan marriage seemed so right, so logical he never doubted it would happen.

"He'll change his mind once we're actually married," Alix said to Yale. "My father is very realistic and would never resist a *fait accompli*."

They were married simply and privately three months before Alix's twenty-fourth birthday in 1970 by a Manhattan Supreme Court judge in his chambers, and when Alix called her father after the ceremony, expecting to receive his forgiveness and good wishes, she was shocked when he lost his temper and, a man who never raised his voice, screamed at her over the telephone.

"How could you do this to me? I can't understand it!" he yelled. "You were always such an obedient child. I'll never forgive you for this, Alix. You've stabbed me in the back."

He threatened to cut off her trust funds, although he could never quite bring himself to do it. However, he had been planning to give her a hotel—the resort in Maui—as a birthday present, and as soon as he hung up, he called his lawyers and ordered them to cancel the papers transferring ownership from Raimont Resorts to a new company he had formed of which Alix was to be the sole stockholder.

Alix hung up, shaken. In the most difficult business dealing, during the periods of his divorces, she had never once, privately or publicly, heard her father raise his voice; if anything, the angrier he became, the quieter and more ominously reasonable his words and tone became. He had never, never screamed at her, and she trembled; her hands trembled outwardly, and, inwardly, something in the middle of her seemed to have collapsed. She had the horrible, overwhelming feeling that she had made a terrible, irrevocable mistake.

"Are you all right?" Yale was alarmed. Alix had turned pale.

"He was furious," she said. "I've never heard him like that. He threatened to cut me off."

"It will be all right. He needs time to get used to the idea," Yale said, using the arguments Alix had used with him. His first father-in-law had threatened to cut off his daughter, and for as long as Yale could remember, in the privileged, private rooms of Palm Beach and Oyster Bay and Newport, being cut off was the first threat uttered by every parent whose child had rebelled or disobeyed.

"Do you think so?" Alix asked. Her father had withdrawn his love, and he threatened to withdraw his money. The situation was unimaginable to Alix. "I've never heard him sound like that."

"He'll come around," Yale said confidently. He had been able to win over his first father-in-law, and he was certain he would win over Alexander Raimont. After all, Alexander Raimont was wrong about him: He was not a fortune hunter, and he did not intend to touch a penny of his wife's money. In fact, if Alexander bothered to check, he would learn that Yale had come out of his first marriage poorer than when he had gone into it; he had never touched his first wife's money, not a penny of it, and had, in fact, during the two years their marriage lasted, paid for everything at a time when, as a young broker, he really couldn't afford his wife's extravagances. "He just needs time to get used to the idea," Yale said. "After all, I'm not a criminal. You didn't run off with a murderer."

Alix looked at him and smiled, but the smile was more bravado than sincerity. Then Yale asked, very seriously, "You're not sorry you did it, are you? You're not sorry you married me?"

"No," said Alix. "I just wish. . . ."

"Just wish what?"

"That my father was like other fathers . . ." she said, knowing, as she said it, how impossible a wish it was.

After a three-month honeymoon that took them around the world they moved to London. To Alix, an international commuter since childhood, it mattered little where they lived; to Yale, his ambitions ignited by marriage, it meant everything.

He was attracted by the opportunities created by the differences between American and British financial law. British laws, unlike American laws, do not require that banks separate their commercial banking arms from their trust operations, and no law specifically forbidding insider trading exists in England. Yale's plan could be put into operation only in England; on Wall Street and in other major financial centers the kind of freewheeling moves that attracted Yale were prohibited by far more constrictive banking and securities regulations. With banking and corporate contacts carefully established and nourished during his years at Noyes, Lea, Yale's impact on the London scene was dazzling, the get-rich-quick dream come true.

Yale had already proved that he could get rich buying the stock of companies. He decided he could get even richer buying the companies themselves, and that decision was the basis of his London strategy. He hired away the head of research at Noyes, Lea and a young, aggressive floor trader, a Princeton classmate, from a big, retail brokerage firm to execute the actual purchases. Warrant Ltd.'s first acquisition was a manufacturer of department-store display fixtures whose principal asset was real estate—primarily a warehouse just off Southwark Bridge on the south side of the Thames. The warehouse was promptly sold off, and the proceeds were used to buy a company that made inflatables, specifically life jackets and rafts, and from that beginning Yale continued the chain, selling the assets of one company to help finance the acquisition of others.

Yale had become richer—in three years Warrant Ltd. controlled assets worth twelve million four hundred thousand pounds—faster than he had imagined. His uncanny ability to spot undervalued, asset-rich companies, an ability he attributed to the superior talents of his research department, made him a financial superstar and Warrant Ltd. became the place talented young men with the "wrong" accents from the grimy industrial cities of the Midlands, the slums of Liverpool and the ethnic porridge of Marylebone could circumvent the old-boy network that had excluded them from the centers of finance. Sons of cabinet-makers and factory workers could now calculate, through an investment trust set up by Warrant for its executives, their earning in capital gains rather than the pay packets of their fathers' generation.

In late 1973 Yale decided that the future direction would lie in merchant banking and in that year concluded a merger with Charlton, Dover, a firm with a far less conservative image than, say, Hambros or N. M. Rothschild. The new company was called Warrant, Charlton, Dover, and it put Yale into another league, giving him access to financing on a multiplied scale, as well as privileged relationships with the client companies counseled by Charlton, Dover. The new firm, upon the completion of the merger, promptly moved into ultramodern offices in a Park Row skyscraper. The move underlined the separation which Yale had always felt from the rest of the world and which, as he had always known, would be his greatest strength.

Like the conservative corporate lawyer in his pin-striped three-piece suit who fondly remembers a boyhood dream of being a forest ranger, Yale now remembered his early ambition to make a million dollars by the time he was thirty with a mixture of indulgent affection and wonder at how naive he had been. At thirty-four he was well on his way to his first ten million.

"You see how wise you were to marry me?" Yale would ask affectionately.

"Yes, I had no idea . . ." Alix would answer, and she cared not so much about the money as about his pride in earning it and her growing confidence that he had not, after all, married her for her money.

"Oh, you must have, you must have known deep down that I was a wonder." The financial press referred to Yale as a "wonder boy."

"And a magician," Alix would add in an exchange that had become a loving ritual. Yale was also referred to as a "financial magician."

It would be unfair to Yale to say that he had married Alix for her money. On the other hand, she would not have been who she was without money, and without it and its effect on her, Yale would never have been attracted to her.

It is true that everything changes after marriage, and the marriage of Yale and Alix was no exception. What happened in the early years of their marriage was that Yale, who had seen Alix as a prize to be conquered and had carefully calculated his conquest, fell madly in love with her once she was his wife. The shrewd suitor became a man bedazzled. He thought she was wondrous, and he became fascinated with everything about her. She was, to him, an exotic and rare species, and he became a scholar of her quirks and habits.

She was, for example, a wonderful driver. Her shyness and awkwardness disappeared behind the wheel. She drove very expensive sports cars very well, with passionate concentration and a sense of abandon controlled by an edgy discipline. She and her powerful cars seemed to share the same nervous system. Her touch on the accelerator was the touch of a lover; she heeled and toed the brake-accelerator with Formula One precision, up- and downshifting in perfect synchronization with the rpm's. On a hairpin curve on a mountain corniche or on the entrance to a highway, she invariably entered corners on the inside and came out of them on the high point of the apex while maintaining road speed more steadily than any driver Yale had ever ridden with.

At first, Alix's total inability to park bewildered Yale. She, who could do anything with an automobile, could not punch it into a parking slot. And her inability didn't bother her. She'd leave forty thousand dollars' worth of hand-tooled machinery every which way against the curb. It took

Yale months to figure it out. It was the rich girl syndrome: She had never learned to park because she'd never needed to. There had always been someone to do it for her: a garage attendant, a chauffeur, a doorman. And it never occurred to her to worry about the safety of her expensive, jazzy cars. Whatever went wrong would be fixed. It was the kind of confidence and carelessness that only money—lots of it for as long as anyone could remember—could buy.

There were other manifestations of the rich girl syndrome: Alix did not know how to buy a theater ticket or an airplane ticket because whenever she wanted one, she called her father's office and it was done for her. She had never returned anything to a store or gone to pick up anything; a maid or chauffeur did it for her. She did not receive bills or pay them; the bank that handled her trust accounts did. When she wanted wine or liquor, she did not go to a liquor store; instead, the sommelier of one of her father's hotel dining rooms made the selections for her and had them delivered. She never ordered groceries because her housekeeper did it for her on the telephone, and Alix found going to a supermarket an exotic treat. She had never ridden on a bus, picked up dry cleaning, gone to a sale, waited for a plumber, flown economy or stood in line. She never went into a bank; every Monday someone from her father's office would drop off an envelope of cash to see her through the week.

She was, Yale learned, addicted to the telephone. She used long distance so casually that Yale, who thought he could be impressed by nothing, was impressed. She would call a Dallas department store to order sheets she'd seen in a catalogue; a coachworks in Milan to order a custom basketwork body for her car like one she'd seen parked in front of Hermès in Monte Carlo; a smokehouse outside Budapest to order specially cured bacon. She called her brother at least once a week wherever he was, and she called her father, although he remained rigidly opposed to her marriage, once a week wherever *he* was. She telephoned her mother and grandmother, whom she called Grandmère, constantly and had several close women friends with whom she gossiped for hours long distance. Her shyness disappeared over the telephone, and Alix became direct, intimate, intense, silly, frivolous, philosophical and, on occasion, libelous.

Behind the wheel of a car and over the telephone Alix Raimont became a different woman: confident, strong, assured. In person, at dinner parties, balls, social events, she retreated into an awkwardness that was almost painful, and no matter how much Yale complimented and encouraged her, Alix seemed to stay split into two women: the one on the telephone; the other in a drawing room.

Marrying her was the best thing he'd ever done, and Yale never understood the compulsion that drove him constantly to risk the marriage and finally to destroy it.

Yale grew richer, faster than he could have imagined. He was particularly proud that he had done it himself. He had not asked for or received help from Alexander; he had not used his wife's money or connections. When Alexander was in London, Yale made a point of entertaining him lavishly, of putting his own car and driver at Alexander's disposal, of going to every possible length to prove that he was his equal. His efforts were rejected by Alexander, and Yale knew that there was widespread gossip that Alexander had offered Alix a million dollars to divorce him. The gossip was true; the offer had been made not once but several times—the first coming upon their return to London from the honeymoon—and each time Alix had turned her father down. It increased her commitment to Yale and to her marriage, and despite gossip and the unending temptations of the easy and sophisticated world in which they lived, the marriage lasted.

Their sixth anniversary coincided with Alix's thirtieth birthday in the spring of 1976, and it was Alix's husband, not her father, who gave her a lavish party. In every way possible the party was Yale's proof to the world that he had an identity and a success entirely separate from the Raimonts'. Five hundred, a cross section of international party people, financial and business wizards, the higher-level Raimont and WCD executives were invited. Alexander, to Yale's delight, accepted the invitation and brought Jai Jai, whom he had met the month before; Brooke and her current husband flew in from Delaware to celebrate her daughter's birthday; Sergei and Britta arrived from Paris, and father and son did not speak to each other the entire evening—Sergei was threatening to marry Britta despite Alexander's disapproval—and the fact that Alix had married Yale gave Sergei courage in his defiance.

The party, given in Claridge's, a hotel chosen by Yale because it was *not* owned by Raimont, was a coup for Yale. "The whiff of scandal" attracted an Emma Soames column in the *Evening Standard*, William Hicky of the *Express* loved it and speculated about whether or not Sergei would marry against his father's wishes and Nigel Dempster of the *Daily Mail* commented that the most beautiful women on both sides of the Atlantic had attended the party and that, of those, the *most* beautiful was Jai Jai Valerian. Only "Jennifer's Diary" omitted mention of it, Betty Kenward being in Venice at the time for the coming-out party of a young and lovely *principessa*.

It was a splendid party of champagne and caviar, dancing and flirting; it was said that several affairs had begun, and one ended, and there was even a story that a divorce resulting from a passionate embrace in the cloakroom just off the Dover Street entrance was directly traceable to Yale's party. At midnight Yale gave Alix her present: a pair of ruby earrings weighing thirty karats.

"One for each year," he said as she opened the jeweler's box, and Alix's thanks were lost in the music, the crowd, the gaiety. The party and its glamorous guests were extensively photographed, and Yale noticed that in the magazine and newspaper coverage not one picture of Alix appeared, even though the party had been in her honor. Every layout, however, featured a photograph of Jai Jai, splendid in a pleated cloth of gold Fortuny dress.

It was the first time Yale's name had moved from the financial pages to the social pages. He craved the glamour and the attention, and he wanted more.

"Dear, you know I never ask personal questions," Brooke said the day after the party, "but isn't it time you and Yale started a family?" Alix's mother was to return to Maryland, and Alix had invited her to tea before she left. They were in the second-floor library, the smallest, coziest room in the house, and as the sun went down, it turned the cream and navy room almost gold. Brooke was proud of her daughter for having created a stable-seeming life. She knew from her own experience as the daughter and wife of rich, powerful men used to having their own way in everything that it could not have been easy.

"Soon," said Alix, uneasily. "I'm not *that* old yet." As she spoke, Alix dropped a silver teaspoon to the carpet, and she bent to pick it up.

"I don't intend to pry," said Brooke, uncomfortable as always at intimate conversation. She had been brought up to believe that it was impolite to ask personal questions, and it was difficult for her, even with her own child, to bring up anything personal, even though she had felt the lack of intimacy in her life and felt certain that Alix, too, suffered from the sense of isolation and loneliness it produced. Rich people, Brooke thought, grew up with the luxuries of distance and space, but distance and space when translated into emotional terms exacted a penalty in terms of loneliness. She continued, "You've been married six years now. . . ."

"Yale doesn't want to have children," said Alix, surprising Brooke by her willingness to continue the conversation. "He says it's not chic."

"And you?" asked Brooke.

"I'd like to have a family," said Alix. "But not now. Not until Yale changes his mind, not until my father changes his mind about Yale." Alix put the teaspoon on a plate, and while they waited for the butler to bring another, Brooke ventured another question.

"Is your marriage"—she paused, searching for the word—"satisfactory?" She had noticed the sad look in Alix's eyes as Yale had danced with every beautiful woman at the party and most of all with Jai Jai.

"I think so, particularly considering what you once told me: that we're different from other people, that we have too much freedom," said Alix. "It's just that I wish—" She stopped as the butler knocked, then came forward with the teaspoon and left the room, leaving the two women alone again. "I wish Yale would stop competing with my father. I wish my father would accept the marriage. No matter what I do, one of them is angry." The situation, Alix thought sadly, was similar to the one in which she had found herself when she and Sergei both had worked for Raimont.

"You have to think of what will make you happy, Alix," Brooke suggested. She surprised even herself by advocating self-interest. She had been so wounded by selfish men that she had rigorously avoided even the appearance of selfishness in herself and had brought up her daughter always to think of the other person first. She wondered, now that Alix was a woman, if she hadn't been too successful and if Alix wouldn't be happier if she thought more often of herself.

"Yes," said Alix, smiling slightly. "Perhaps I should think of myself. I would love to have a baby. Perhaps if I just go ahead and get pregnant, Yale will change his mind. And my father might like being a grandfather," she said. "What do you think?"

Brooke didn't want to dash the hopes she had perhaps inadvertently helped raise, but she didn't want to lie either. In the rigid code with which she had been brought up, Brooke prided herself on never lying, never cheating, not even if no one would ever, ever find out. She really didn't know how Alexander would react. On the one hand, he had such a phobia about age and all clues to it; on the other, it was *human* to want grandchildren. . . . Brooke just didn't know how he would feel, and that is what she told her daughter.

"I don't know how your father would react," she said. "He's very mysterious. I never understood him."

"I don't understand him, either," said Alix, the smile gone now. Then she asked, "Do you think anyone understands him?"

"No," said Brooke, finally. "How can anyone understand a man with a billion dollars to hide behind?"

The conversation and the questions it raised stayed in Alix's mind. Strictly speaking, she had been telling the truth when she told her mother that her marriage was satisfactory, but more profoundly, Alix wasn't sure. It seemed to her that as time went on, she and Yale more and more wanted different things out of life: She wanted stability, permanence, a family; he wanted excitement, novelty, glamour. He wanted to go everywhere and do everything;

Alix, who in the course of simply growing up, had already gone everywhere and done everything she wanted to do, was concerned mainly in finding a happy way to coexist with the three men who dominated her life: her husband; her father; her brother.

As she dialed Yale's number from Cartwright Dunne's office, Alix thought she had been wrong in refusing to give Jai Jai and Sergei a wedding. Perhaps, she thought, by doing so, she might be able to please all three of the men in her life: to show Sergei that he had a sister who cared for him (she could imagine how hurt he must have been by their father's rejection of the Mexican deal), to include her father in her life (after all, he had given Jai Jai a fabulous wedding present, so whatever had happened between Jai Jai, Sergei and Alexander must have been happily resolved) and to please Yale, who wanted so badly to assume a position of importance among the powerful Raimonts.

"I want to apologize for this morning," Alix began when Yale came to the telephone. "It was generous of you to offer to have the wedding at home. I think you were right, and I was wrong. I'll call Sergei. . . ."

"It's too late."

"Too late?"

"Sergei's already married. He and Jai Jai eloped," Yale said. "They got married in Gibraltar. A telegram came to the office."

"What should we do?" Alix was hurt that Sergei had informed Yale first, but it was typical that he'd let her find out indirectly.

"Do? I don't know about you, but I plan to celebrate," Yale said, and hung up.

Yale had been thinking about calling Oliver Holborn for a long time. Every time he had come close to it he had put it off. He wanted to be careful about it. He wanted everything to be perfect, and he had waited for the exact moment. What moment could be better, he thought, than a wedding which evoked thoughts of love and sex and erotic adventure?

Yale wanted to make love with someone new, someone beautiful, someone young. He wanted to do things he had never done before. He dialed Oliver's elegant red-brick house in a cul-de-sac in Kensington and made an appointment for later that afternoon. Oliver Holborn, it was said, always had the newest, youngest, most beautiful boys in London.

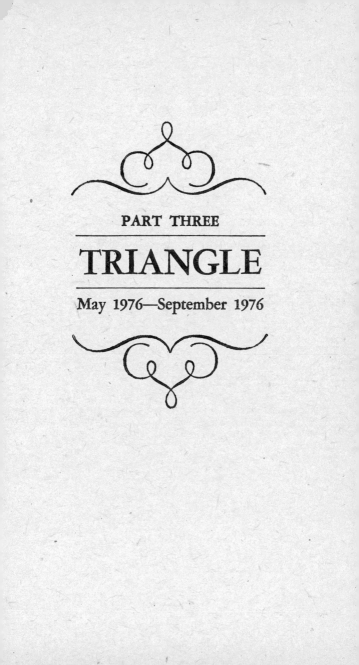

PART THREE

TRIANGLE

May 1976—September 1976

⚦ EIGHT ⚦

There are very few places in the world from which two continents can be seen. Istanbul is one. It is pleasant to sip a raki on the restaurant terrace of the Topkapi Palace at sunset and watch the waters of the Bosporus turn gold, the shores of Asia to the east, those of Europe to the west. Gibraltar is another. A garrison basically, important for its strategic value, it is a British enclave carved out of the tip of Spain. The profile of its rock fortress is world-famous; the colony of wild Barbary apes—a mangy bunch—is a major tourist attraction. On a clear day the view from the top of the rock accessible by cable car is everything. On one side is Europe; on the other, Africa. There is a spectacular panorama of the brown and green plains of Spain with the snow-capped Sierra Nevada in the background and the blue waters of the Mediterranean lapping the shores of the Costa del Sol in the foreground. Across the strait stretches the northern coast of Africa with exotic, sophisticated Tangier, its surrounding beaches, broad as meadows, and, looming in the distance, the Atlas and Rif mountains.

Sergei and Jai Jai paid no attention to the view. With Dante as a witness, they were married civilly by the marriage registrar on May 10, 1976, four months after Jai Jai had met Alexander Raimont in Bequia. Sharing a bottle of champagne afterward, Sergei was surprised at how good he felt.

"I feel wonderful," he kept saying. "I can't believe it."

"You sound so surprised," Jai Jai said. In marrying her with his father's approval, he had conquered his father without having to run the risk of defying him. He was having his cake and eating it, too, and Jai Jai couldn't imagine his feeling any way other than wonderful. "How did you *think* you'd feel?"

"I don't know what I thought," Sergei said. "But I feel wonderful, just wonderful. This is the best thing I've ever

101

done in my whole life." He smiled at Jai Jai and signaled the waiter for a second bottle of champagne. "We could honeymoon in Tangier," Sergei said. Car and passenger ferries made the two-and-one-half-hour trip several times daily. "We could go to the Casbah and sip mint tea and watch the world go by."

"I want to send my mother a cable," said Jai Jai. The red Her Britannic Majesty's mailboxes dotted along the streets made Jai Jai think of her mother, a widow now, still living in Georgetown.

"Will she be upset you and Sergei eloped?" asked Dante. "Was she looking forward to being mother of the bride?"

"She and my father eloped. She'll just think it's a family tradition," said Jai Jai. "Which by now I suppose it is."

"What about your parents?" Dante asked Sergei.

"I don't know where my mother is," he said. "I spoke to her last month. She was in London with Jules. He's trying to get the U.S. rights to some esoteric new play that just opened in the West End. He's still trying to make money with art." Sergei's put-down of his stepfather was blunt.

"It's been done, you know," said Dante. "Turning art into money. Duveen, Picasso, Dali. . . ."

"Not by Jules," said Sergei. "Anyway, I'll cable them in New York and London. The news will catch up with them sooner or later. And I'll cable Alix and Yale."

"What about your father?" Dante knew that Alexander Raimont had been talking about giving Sergei and Jai Jai a lavish wedding almost as if he were the father of the bride, not the groom.

"He won't give a damn." Sergei drained the tulip-shaped glass.

"That's not true," said Jai Jai. The expression on Sergei's face was carefully blank, concealing from her whatever hurt he felt.

"He's in Lausanne," said Sergei. "I'll wire him at the Beau Rivage. Did you know that he doesn't even stay with Liliane? Hasn't for years."

Jai Jai didn't know and was careful not to reveal it.

"Separate residences, separate cities. That's not my idea of marriage," he said, taking Jai Jai's hand and kissing her fingers. "We're going to be together. All the time."

"All the time," said Jai Jai.

They had not been apart for more than an afternoon since the day—Britta's wedding day—eight weeks before, when they had begun their love affair. It was emotionally charged and sexually charged, intense and consuming, and if there was an element of the rebound—Sergei from Britta, Jai Jai from Alexander—it served only to intensify an already intense attraction. Both of them knew from the very beginning that this was no brief interlude, no casual, ships-that-pass-in-the-night romance. There had been no official proposal; the inevitability of marriage was accepted by both of them—and everyone who knew them—without discussion. They were perfect for each other: Jai Jai, young, beautiful, yet sophisticated and experienced; Sergei, adoring, attentive, free.

"I didn't know what was going to happen to me until I met you," Jai Jai said. She was twenty-four and already thinking about age. Ian, playing at freedom, wasn't for her; neither were the Prestons and Alexanders of the world—glamorous, self-absorbed, competitive—nor Sam Three, dutiful, rich, yet provincial. "I was beginning to think there wasn't anyone for me."

"I knew what was happening to me," said Sergei, "and it wasn't good. I need you. Need and want."

And Jai Jai, who needed to be needed and needed even more to be wanted, fell deeply in love with Sergei, who reflected back to her her best image of herself.

"I love you," Jai Jai would say, "and I love the way you make me feel."

Sex—insatiable, inventive, demanding—was the key. Sergei's affair with Britta had had an element of comfort that had muted the importance of sex; with Jai Jai there was a tension, an electricity that transformed him into a being possessed and obsessed by eroticism. In bed with a beautiful woman—a beautiful woman who had been his father's mistress—Sergei found the key to his identity, to an individual existence that did not depend on his father's money, power or influence. Sergei could not keep away from Jai Jai, and Jai Jai, who defined her beauty in terms of her desirability, responded, goading them to higher plateaus of lust. The avidity with which their eyes and hands devoured each other was embarrassing to other people. Even Dante commented.

"Jai Jai, you're *lewd*," he said. "You two really ought to control yourselves in public. You're indecent."

For an answer Jai Jai told him to draw her bath.

"Put in plenty of Stephanotis," she added. Stephanotis was Sergei's favorite Floris scent. And Dante, whose choice of sexual partners had been known to include members of the animal kingdom, pursed his lips in a parody of shock and went off to draw her bath at the temperature (100 degrees F; 37.7 degrees C) she insisted upon.

Jai Jai had had an affair with Alexander, and now she was carrying on with his son. Dante thought it was glamorous. Ultraglamorous.

He wouldn't have missed it for the world.

"I'm going to make my wish come true," Alexander told Jai Jai as soon as he knew she planned to marry Sergei, "and give you emeralds. For a wedding gift."

Alexander had been out of Paris—in Bequia, Atlanta, Montreal, Tunisia—almost the entire time of Sergei and Jai Jai's love affair. When they told him they planned to marry, he said he was very happy, very pleased.

"I'm glad it ended this way," he told Sergei. "I don't have to tell you how I felt about Britta. But it's over. I'd like to give you a big wedding. Anywhere you and Jai Jai want."

There was no indication by word or tone that Alexander Raimont was anything but an ordinary, prospective father-in-law, approving of the girl his son had chosen. Jai Jai was in Alexander's past, and because the past didn't exist for him, he assumed it existed for no one else. Sergei, however, was acutely aware of the past, of Jai Jai and Alexander's relationship, and although he had asked, even begged, Jai Jai to tell him the details, she had refused, just as she had refused to tell Alexander about Ian and Anson.

"I don't think it would be . . . well . . . appropriate for you to give us a wedding," Sergei said, enjoying the novelty of rejecting his father.

"Whatever you wish," Alexander said in the deceptive way he had of appearing never to resist, never to disagree. "What do you plan to do once you're married?"

"I'm going ahead with the Playa Sol development. Paolo is a codirector of a Fonatur study group, and they're ready to begin," said Sergei. Paolo was Paolo Barragan, the man Alexander had wanted for a son-in-law. Fonatur (Fondo Nacional de Fomento Al Turismo), the two-hundred-fifty-million-dollar trust established by the Mexican government to fund development of tourist facilities, was the agency that had turned Cancun from jungle greenery into an eighteen-hotel resort in only a few years. Its massive study of Playa Sol had been completed, and it was ready to bring bulldozers and cranes, tractors and cement mixers, engineers and urban planners to the twenty-five-hundred-acre parcel fronting on the Pacific.

For years Playa Sol had been a sleepy village of fishermen and their families. Only a few knowledgeable tourists knew about it, and they kept the secret to themselves. As the Fonatur study showed, Playa Sol had almost no rain, almost no clouds between November and May. It was completely clear two hundred days a year; the median temperature was eighty degrees. Topographical analysis detailed the lovely ocean views, the elevations of the hills and the configuration of the beige beach, and a study of the existing facilities showed the state of everything from sewerage (virtually nonexistent) to movie theaters (there were none—seats were put up in the open air and the film was projected on the side of a building wall).

The first step would be the construction, funded by Fonatur, of the infrastructure: sewage; electricity; telephones. Next would come hotels, houses and, to make the resort competitive with other Mexican facilities, a Robert Trent golf course. The investment—in the hundreds of millions of dollars—was calculated to be a sound one on the basis of a Fonatur project begun in the late sixties in an effort to convince the Bank of Mexico that tourism held the greatest potential for hard-currency return on investment. Figures showed that from 1960 to 1971, the year the study was completed, tourism in Mexico had tripled and that while Mexico's economy had grown only five to six percent a year, tourism was expanding at a rate of eleven percent. Alarm at the northward flight of the peso and the results of the Harvard Business School graduate-directed statistical analysis produced a massive program of building along the thousands of miles of Pacific, Caribbean and Gulf of Mexico coastlines. Cancun, Ixtapa, Cozumel, Las Hadas in

Manzanillo, Careyes, Puerto Vallarta and the isolated rocky tip of Baja, California, all shared in the swift expansion, and even Acapulco, doyen of Mexican resorts, benefited via low-cost housing, a new sewerage system, reform in the police department, the licensing of taxi drivers to curb abuses and a program to combat pollution in beautiful Acapulco Bay.

The governor of the state of Sinaloa, where Playa Sol is located, was anxious for his state to share in the jobs, prestige and economic rewards of a major development. As part of its master plan, Fonatur would establish training units for hotel workers: people who wanted would learn to be carpenters, masons, electricians, firemen, health workers, chambermaids, clerks, bookkeepers, waiters, busboys, switchboard operators, waiters and barmen. The development of Playa Sol would bring it and its citizens into the prosperous twentieth century.

"It could be interesting," Alexander said, "but there are pitfalls." He had never done business in Mexico, although at one time he had bid on but lost out on the site on which the pyramid-shaped Acapulco Princess was eventually built. "There's a real danger of overdevelopment in Mexico, and if you *do* go ahead, you'll have to move quickly," he added. A Mexican law, passed to prevent land speculation, which historically proceeds in a boom-to-bust pattern like that of Florida in the twenties, stipulates that land, once purchased, must be built on within thirty days.

"I know," said Sergei. "Jai Jai and I are going in June."

"About the emeralds . . ." Alexander began, but Sergei wasn't listening. He was accustomed to his father's habit of never commenting on Sergei's plans. Sergei never knew whether his father viewed him or his plans as insignificant or as disturbingly competitive. If Sergei had been less resentful of Alix, he would have learned from her that Alexander treated her in the same confusing and contradictory way.

Sergei was enough of a realist to know that Paolo had called him, in part, because of the Raimont name. The Raimont name had been the most important emotional fact of Sergei's life—sometimes benevolent, sometimes malevolent—always there, hovering, substituting its existence for

Sergei's own. His occasional dream, like his sister's, had been to be somehow anonymous. But anonymity wasn't the answer either; he would have to give up too many privileges, too many open doors, too many luxuries—the kind money would buy and, more important, the kind it wouldn't. The Raimont name had always been Sergei's double bind: It was hard to live with, yet living without it was unthinkable. Somehow, somewhere, between the Raimont name and the Raimont millions, Sergei Raimont had been lost.

When he fell in love with Jai Jai, he felt newly found. Jai Jai, so desirable, Jai Jai, who could have had anyone she wanted, had chosen him and, in doing so, had given him a self-assurance he had never had. With that self-assurance Sergei could do anything—even build a fortune that would make him his father's equal. All along, Sergei had had the talent, the education, the experience. All he had lacked was the motivation. Jai Jai had provided that.

His father was giving Jai Jai emeralds. One day, he, Sergei, would give her the world.

"I don't want an old lady's necklace," Jai Jai told Alexander, "something that's going to sit in a bank vault three hundred sixty-four days a year, waiting for someone to give a grand ball." She had been looking at Van Cleef and Cartier, Boucheron and Bulgari and hadn't seen anything she liked. Everything looked stiff and old-fashioned to her, as if the designers were so intimidated by the value of the stones they were working with that their reverence interfered with their creativity. "I want something I can wear with sweaters, too."

"I'll send you to Elie Koster," Alexander said. "He'll know what to do."

"Will you come with me?" Jai Jai was looking forward to picking out her emeralds, Alexander with her, admiring and interested.

"I don't know anything about jewelry," he said.

Jai Jai knew better than to press. Like so many others, she had learned that Alexander rarely said no in so many words. On the other hand, nothing in the world could make him do something he didn't want to do. He was generous with money, stingy with time.

Elie Koster's office was in a fin-de-siècle *hôtel particulier*, a building so beautiful it had been declared a national monument. The entrance was directly on the Place Vendôme, diagonally across from the Hôtel Ritz, and through an archway that led into a charming courtyard, the building, hidden from view of passersby, was guarded by two ferocious stone lions. Elie Koster's office, directly at the head of a flight of broad marble stairs, was perfectly square, a room generous in size and exuding a sense of calm and tranquillity in its balanced symmetry. The polished parquet floor, an antique Ushak in pastel, luminous colors, a marquetry desk with ormolu mounts purchased at the Hôtel Drouot transmitted a sense of quiet luxury in which every wish seemed capable of immediate fulfillment. A large window with a rooftop view of Paris had sheer white curtains which admitted a clear, true north light. Jai Jai sat in the client's chair, facing M. Koster, who sat behind his desk.

"I once saw a photograph of Chanel climbing a tree at her country house. She was wearing a sweater and flannel trousers, and ropes of jewels were around her neck. What I'd like is something like that—elegant, yet casual, luxurious, yet modern."

"M. Raimont gave me one instruction only: that the necklace must be emeralds." Elie Koster was a portly Dutch Jew, now a naturalized citizen of France. He wore the traditional oatmeal-colored jeweler's smock, as immaculate as a surgeon's operating gown, over his street clothes. A loupe on a black silk cord hung around his neck.

"To match my eyes," Jai Jai said, quoting Alexander's words to her.

"Emerald beads," he said, extracting one from a drawer in his desk with a pair of jeweler's long, thin tweezers, "are even rarer than cabochon stones." Beginning to visualize a necklace, taking into account his client's age, her description of the kind of necklace she wanted and the fact that M. Raimont had said that price was of no concern, he began to speak. "I suggest we string emerald beads as if they were pearls. To separate the beads from each other and to set them off, I would like to insert diamond rondels between each bead."

In his late sixties, Elie Koster found his passion for gems had increased, not diminished, in the more than five decades he had worked with them daily, starting as a boy, apprenticed to a cutter in his father's Amsterdam firm. Elie's specialty, the specialty in which the firm of Koster Fils had made its reputation, was in colored stones: rubies; emeralds; sapphires. Colored stones had depth, fire, passion; colored stones could be carved, and their flaws made them more rather than less interesting. Diamonds, thought Elie, while beautiful, were icy, frigid, forbidding.

"The best emerald beads come from Colombia," he went on. "Since we have to bore a hole through the emerald itself to string it, we are dealing here with the most extravagant use possible of one of the rarities in the world of fine gems." As he spoke of the difference among various stones, Elie withdrew unset samples of each with a pair of long, thin tweezers. He told Jai Jai to place the gems on her skin so that she might choose which tones were more flattering to her coloring since a necklace, unlike a ring, is worn directly against the skin.

"We will find pure jade-green beads," he said, "to match your eyes." Emeralds with a yellowish cast, beside being less valuable, were also less flattering.

Elie showed Jai Jai how to examine a stone, holding each to the true north light streaming in from the window and then under an electric light. He pointed out to her the nuances of shade and clarity, depth and tone.

"What we will make is a thirty-inch-long rope," he said, sketching on a pad. "We will make it so that you can wear it at its full length or so that you take it apart and wear it as two strands that will fit at the base of your throat." As he sketched and spoke, he made a mental list of the dealers in Geneva, New York, Antwerp, Amsterdam, London and Hong Kong he would call on to assemble the three-karat beads he had decided would provide the perfect proportion to the length of the necklace and the physical size of the client. Too large beads could overwhelm a woman; too small beads could look insufficient.

"This necklace will be one of a kind," he said. "Emerald beads are so rare that once I acquire enough to make your necklace, there will probably not be enough left in the world to make another. Not to mention, that even if I could afford to make another, almost no one alive could afford to buy it."

"Oh, M. Koster, I can hardly wait," Jai Jai said. When she had first seen him, she felt no confidence that he could translate the necklace in her mind into reality. He was short and plump, and he had an air about him of almost terminal fatigue. He seemed to her the tiredest man she had ever encountered. As they spoke, and she described her horror of the stiff settings and unimaginative design with which most fine gems were burdened and he seemed intuitively to understand her, she began to warm to him. Then, as he patiently explained to her the difference between a fine gem and a not-so-fine one, as he handled them, appearing to derive as much joy from them as if he were seeing them for the first time, she began to like him. He no longer seemed a plump, exhausted man; she felt that he was a kind man with a unique passion, and she forgot her initial impression to the point that she was unable to remember it. "How soon will I have it?"

"Be patient. It will take time just to gather the beads," he said, escorting her to the steel door of his otherwise-elegant office. "You should have your necklace in, perhaps, eight months."

"Oh," said Jai Jai, unable to conceal her disappointment. She felt like a child on Christmas Eve, unable to contain her excitement and greed.

As Elie Koster extended his hand to open the complicated lock custom-made by a Belgian locksmith for ultra-security, his shirt cuff rode up, and Jai Jai noticed something she hadn't seen before. On the inside of his forearm, on the delicate thin skin of the upper wrist, in dark-blue ink, was tattooed a number. He responded to the direction of Jai Jai's eyes.

"Auschwitz," he said.

"I'm sorry," Jai Jai said. "I don't know what to say. I'm humiliated about my greed. And to think what you have suffered."

"Don't be. I was greedy, too. Greedy for life. I thank God for my greed. It was the reason I survived. A fat Jew, one who lived among many thousands who died."

There were tears in Jai Jai's eyes as Elie Koster shut the heavy door. She stood alone on the landing for a moment. Jai Jai was a connoisseur of emotion, attuned to the nuances of feeling, elevating feelings, her own feelings and her reactions to them, to the status of an art. She reacted to the poignant disparity between the luxury Elie Koster traded in and what must have been the scars inflicted by the past—scars that didn't show in the brilliant depths of rubies and emeralds and sapphires.

As tears welled in her eyes, she was also aware at how much was missing, how barren it had seemed, when she had gone alone to select her extraordinary gift. How different the experience would have been with Alexander there, interested, discerning, excited. Instead, it had been lonely. Did he make everyone feel lonely? Or was it just her? With an effort of will, Jai Jai collected herself, descended the staircase and crossed the Place Vendôme to the Ritz, where she was meeting Sergei for a drink. Over kirs, they planned their wedding.

Gibraltar is dusty, forlorn and vaguely exotic with its string of tacky Indian stores and population of bored soldiers. Its lenient marriage laws have made it a reverse-chic destination for eloping couples. No blood tests are required and, under certain conditions, no residency requirement. Jai Jai and Sergei had obtained a governor's special license and would not even have to spend the night there. They flew in single and flew out, later the same day, married.

"It wasn't very glamorous. Are you sure you don't mind?" Sergei was slightly drunk from champagne and stumbled slightly as he boarded the plane for the flight back to Paris. The ceremony, which had taken place in a bureaucratic setting, had had all the glamour of applying for a driver's license. "Are you sure you wouldn't have liked a real wedding with flowers, music and a thousand guests?" His anxiety to please her was touching.

"Not at all," she reassured him. She was, she felt certain, the most unconventional woman in the world. The elopement to seedy Gibraltar appealed to her sense of intrigue and romance. After all, her parents had eloped to Elkin, Maryland, hardly a town known for its aesthetic appeal. "In fact, it was perfect. I adored it," she said, smiling as she thought of the rumpled official who had married them, a man who looked more suited to running a gas station than joining people in eternal wedlock. Then she added, in further reassurance, "And I adore you."

That night, after a champagne dinner at Maxim's, they returned to Jai Jai's suite at the Plaza Athénée and found that it had been transformed. The rooms were filled with white flowers, only white: there were what seemed to be fields of freesias, a dozen branches of orchids, tubs of rare African lilies and crystal bowls in which floated waxy gardenias with their ravishing scent. All had been sent by Alexander, whose personality invaded and dominated the room which his bouquets had turned into a fragrant bower. It was impossible to be in the suite and not be reminded of him by three of the five human senses: sight; scent; touch.

In bed, a little later, Sergei was unable to achieve an erection. He blamed it on the champagne.

∾ NINE ∾

"Where did you learn to shoot?" Dante asked. He and Jai Jai were taking target practice at the Balboa Club, a private club of impeccable luxury on Gaviotas Beach, devoted primarily to hunters and fishermen. The club boasted, among other attractions, a private duck hunting preserve. Two American tourists had been kidnapped and raped as they drove south on the international Highway 15, which runs from Nogales, Arizona, to Guadalajara and, en route, passes directly by Mazatlán. The story, sensational and terrifying, had produced shock waves through the Mexican tourist industry, as well as among expatriates living there. It caused husbands and fathers to fear for the safety of their wives and daughters. Sergei had given Jai Jai a .22 and insisted she practice.

"My father taught me when I was a child," Jai Jai replied. "My father had a business associate in St. Louis, and in the fall they went duck hunting. Blinds were built in the marshes on the banks of the Mississippi. I begged and begged and made a real nuisance of myself until, when I was ten, he let me go with him.

"We'd get up at three in the morning and put on so many layers of clothes it was hard to move, and at four we'd be in the blinds. It was cold and wet, and it would still be dark. The men drank hot coffee laced with brandy out of thermoses. My father allowed me to taste if I promised not to tell my mother. And we'd wait, silently, in the cold.

"The dogs could sense the ducks before we could see them. They'd go stiff, and their hair would stand on end. I always thought it was like goose pimples on human beings. The flock would appear. You could hear them before you could see them. The noise of their beating wings seemed loud in the silence of dawn, and as they appeared, we'd shoot. My father taught me to move the barrel of the gun with the arc of flight and to pick out one duck from the mass and aim only at it and always to aim just a little ahead of the target bird. 'Squeeze the trigger,' he'd tell me. 'Never pull.'

"As abruptly as the reports of the guns started, they'd stop, and there'd never be that predawn silence again. The men would begin to talk and laugh and joke about each other's hits and misses. The dogs would retrieve the fallen birds and the gamekeepers would gather them into big canvas sacks and take them to be drawn and hung. There was a big lodge, it seemed enormous to me then, made of logs, and it had a stone fireplace that reached from floor to ceiling, and we'd go back there and get out of our soggy, cold clothes, layer after layer, and by the time we had changed a huge breakfast would be waiting: pancakes and eggs and bacon cured in local smokehouses. Freshly squeezed orange juice, thick slices of homemade bread toasted in big ovens and pitchers of milk studded with thickly clotted cream from the nearby dairies.

"When my father was rich, he was a wonderful father," Jai Jai said. It was the most Dante had ever heard Jai Jai speak of her childhood. "It wasn't like this," Jai Jai added. "Hot and oppressive. It was fun. Life used to be fun."

When Jai Jai married Sergei, she thought that her life would stay the same but better. It never occurred to her that she would be a prisoner. Of a country. Of a house. Of a man.

Mexico was exotic and seductive and frightening. There were layers and layers, of Olmec, Aztec, Mayan, Zapotec and Mixtec superimposed on by the conquistadores and, on top of that, the influence of the *norteamericanos*. The primitive and the sophisticated coexisted and struggled, and something merged indistinguishably. The rites of the Roman Church, the racial memory of blood sacrifice, old women walking on bare, bloody knees over meters of rough stone to holy shrines, Montezuma and Carlotta and the goddess of earth and death, Coatlicue, adorned with a necklace of human hands and human hearts and garbed in a dress woven of snakes, fiestas and piñatas, Indians with flat, impenetrable eyes and businessmen emerging from brand-new Mercedes, *banditos* riding down from the central mountains, the tradition of macho with its abhorrence/attraction and unspoken homosexual content—they were all still there as if time had no meaning: Mexico's wealth and poverty—both material and cultural. The fabled mines of La Nevada and Santa Eulalia, where a silver so pure came from the earth that it required no refining, gold from Guanajuato, oil from the eastern provinces which had made Tampico into a brawling, rich city, the copper canyons of Chihuahua, marble, lapis, obsidian and rose quartz from the bowels of the earth extracted by men who could neither read nor buy food enough to keep them and their families healthy. Advanced architecture and science, the calendar containing the Aztec markings for time and the elements, sculpture, painting and priests to proclaim the religions that possibly predated Christianity and, as part of their priestly function, to interpret the still-quivering intestines of animal and human sacrifices.

Jai Jai was attracted, then frightened and subsequently bored as she became a prisoner in her house. In the beginning she had the habit of going to the main square of Mazatlán, of wandering through the big open markets, where piles of golden mangoes and fish still wet from the sea were on sale, where old women sold gnarled roots with no names to cure diseases with no names, where plastic pails and spools of thread, peas and bananas, and bouquets of parsley, oranges and limes and bits of colored ribbon, rusted pop-bottle tops, ancient Mexican comic books, used nails, baskets of every size and shape, live poultry, cheeses wrapped in palm fronds, vinyl boots and leather sandals—where everything imaginable was set out for sale. Cobblers, seamstresses, tailors, makers of leather belts and vests, jewelers, proprietors of tortilla stands, bakers, and magicians all plied their trade in full view. Beggars, scabrous, blind, crippled, silent unlike the beggars of the Middle East, their hands extended, were part of the market. Jai Jai always gave to a little boy, seven perhaps, who carried his hideously deformed brother—or perhaps it wasn't a brother—on his shoulders, his burden and, at the same time, his source of wealth.

When she tired of the market, she would walk down to *malecón*, the seawall, and watch the traffic in the busy industrial port. Freighters from Hong Kong, Manila, Yokohama brought in manufactured goods from the Far East: industrial machinery, trucks and autos, chemicals, electrical components and consumer goods—television sets, radios, stereos, calculators. The big gray ships, bulky and awkward in the water, would make the return trip laden with foodstuffs and agricultural goods—chicle, cotton, sugar, coffee, shrimp—as well as valuable minerals and metals: copper, sulphur, silver, tin, iron and zinc. Huge commercial fishing boats with processing and freezing plants on board, carrying Japanese, Russian and Scandinavian crews, plied the rich waters. Here and there, dotted between the big commercial vessels, were the powerful private fishing boats, Hatteras and Chris-Craft, equipped with tuna towers, sonar, radar and sophisticated communications equipment, docked for provisioning and marine repairs before returning with their sportsmen owners for the big-game fish of the Pacific: marlin; tarpon; sailfish.

Jai Jai, used to the pleasures of the *Bel Air*, the easy luxury of the Plaza Athénée, to lingerie of crepe de chine and a social life which guaranteed attention and admiration, fitted in nowhere. She was warned by Sergei and Paolo to stop her wanderings in town, and she didn't resist their advice. Mazatlán in July was no tourist center, and the sight of a lone white woman was subject to misinterpretation. Jai Jai was frightened by the looks she drew, although so far no one, however bold his eyes, had spoken to her or touched her. For the first time in her life her beauty was becoming her enemy. She spent almost all her time at home with only Dante and the shy, impassive Mexican maids for company.

She was bored and lonely. There was something for everyone in Mazatlán—the proposed hotel for Sergei, sailors' bars on the waterfront for Dante—and nothing for her. It was July now, very hot and very humid, and even swimming, which Jai Jai disciplined herself to do daily for the sake of exercise and her body, was no surcease. The Pacific was highly saline and very warm, and because of the extremely high humidity and total lack of breeze, the salt water never dried on her skin. It had an unpleasant viscosity, and swimming in it was like swimming in blood.

They were living in the biggest house in the best neighborhood, rented for a year, from a former vice-president of Mexico. Large and spacious, built around an inner courtyard, as Mexican houses often are, it had a spectacular view. Set high on a hill, the house had a view of the city of Mazatlán spread out below and the Pacific Ocean stretching outward into infinity. The sunsets were ripe and gorgeous, gold and orange, and the garden within the courtyard was lush with jacarandas and wild orchids, with scented night-blooming jasmines and red and purple bougainvilleas. The house was beautiful, and to Jai Jai it was a prison. She was starved for attention, for love. Her marriage was a fraud. Her husband was, most of the time, impotent.

In the beginning he blamed his failure on drink, fatigue, business worries. Then he refused to admit that it was a failure, insisting that his inability was actually normal. "All men go through these phases," he'd say. Then he began to blame Jai Jai. He told her she was too demanding, that her appetites were excessive and abnormal. He was angry at her for her desire for him and punished her by refusing to touch her. And finally, he refused to speak about it at all, acting as if falling asleep next to the untouched body of his beautiful wife were perfectly natural.

In the first three months of their marriage they made

love five times. Each time it was Jai Jai who made the initial approach. And it was Jai Jai's tenderness, passion, patience and skill that permitted Sergei to act like a man, a husband, a lover. He hated her for it.

In the second week of the marriage his love turned to rage, and after she had caressed and loved him and his passion was spent, he got off her and methodically broke every bottle of scent on her dressing table. He cut himself on the shards of glass, and his blood, diluted with Joy, stained the marble floor. Wordlessly he left her bedroom. The next time, once he had finished with her, he told her that he felt like pissing on her; then he stood up and struck her, a blow directed to her breast that glanced off her shoulder. It didn't hurt her so much as it confused and, ultimately, terrified her.

She didn't understand what she had done to earn his anger and his contempt. "Sergei, what's happening to us?" she asked. "Is it something I did? Is it my fault? Is there something wrong with you? Something the matter that I don't understand?" She wanted a reason, an explanation. She would have accepted any explanation, any criticism. "I don't understand what's happening, what's gone wrong."

"Jai Jai, if you don't understand," Sergei said the only time he ever even permitted her to bring up the subject of his violence, "I'm not going to explain it to you."

Sergei didn't understand what was happening to him. When he told Jai Jai that he wasn't going to explain it to her, what he was really saying was that he couldn't explain it to himself.

"You're depressed," the psychiatrist in Boston had told him. It had been years ago—at the beginning of the summer. Beginnings, Sergei thought, should be full of promise, of choices, of opportunities, and all he had felt was a confused panic that had turned into depression. "Depression is a disease," the psychiatrist had gone on to say, "a disease that can be treated."

"But I don't feel depressed anymore. I feel good." Sergei was telling the truth. The suicide attempt had been his way of hitting bottom. Now, two weeks later, he felt better, so much better that he couldn't believe that it was he who had swallowed all those pills; it was someone else, someone he didn't know. "Anyway, I'm not going to try anything again. I have more willpower than that."

"Sergei, willpower never cured what you've got. It doesn't even do much good for things far less serious." The doctor thought of people who'd been trying to lose ten pounds for ten years with willpower, people struggling to give up smoking who stubbornly insisted that "all" they needed was willpower. Willpower, in his opinion, was the prescription ordered by those who didn't need it.

Depression was a disease, and doctors could describe and treat it, like many diseases. There was argument and uncertainty about what caused it: Was it biochemical, psychological or genetic in origin? Depression, whatever its causes, was the number one reason people sought psychiatric help, and it was one of the conditions that could be effectively dealt with—in earlier years by electric shock, more recently with chemotherapy.

"The irony, Sergei, is that when a depressed person feels depressed, he is anxious for treatment—you yourself came freely to consult me—but when they feel better—which may or may not be the 'up' part of a manic-depressive cycle—they don't feel they need any further help." Even as the doctor spoke, he felt he had lost Sergei Raimont.

Now, years later, Sergei called a Mexico City jeweler and ordered a jade and gold pendant suspended from a silk cord which Jai Jai had once admired. He made up his mind that he would never strike her again. He was horrified and humiliated by what he'd done. Of course, he never said so to Jai Jai in so many words. He thought that promises made a man seem weak. What if, for some reason beyond anyone's control, a promise was broken? No. Instead, he'd give her the expensive gift. It would say what he wanted to say better than any words could.

No. Sergei didn't understand what was happening to him, and it wasn't his fault. It was, in fact, part of the frustration and tragedy of the human condition—the inability to see the threads that weave the fabric of our lives. The color and pattern are too distracting as we stand in the middle of them, dazzled and confused.

Sergei didn't understand that, to him, beginnings and endings were dangerous. Once at Harvard, the beginning of summer. More recently the ending with Britta. And now there were *two* beginnings at once: a new marriage and a new hotel. And there was one more thing Sergei didn't see: that suicide is violence turned inward and that what can be turned inward can also be turned outward.

Instead, he believed in willpower, and when his father, who had finally agreed to assist him with the three-million-dollar loan, came to Mazatlán with several engineers and financial men to give help and advice on the project at Playa Sol, Sergei invited his father to walk with him and Jai Jai to the private beach where she went for her daily morning swim. Jai Jai swam nude, as she always did, and while she did, Alexander and Sergei stood on the beach watching her and discussing Playa Sol: acreage; cost; payback. When Jai Jai finished swimming, she emerged from the sea, her wet hair sleek to her head. As Sergei handed her the oversized white terry robe in which she wrapped herself after swimming, the diamond studs which Alexander had given her flashed in the brilliant Mexican sun.

"Aeromexico is overhauling its reservations system, computerizing it," Alexander said, continuing the conversation with Sergei, appearing not to notice Jai Jai. "But they have a long way to go." It was no accident that Aeromexico was referred to as Aeromañana.

Whatever Alexander thought or felt about Jai Jai, naked under the undersized robe, his diamonds in her ears, he gave no sign of it, and as the three of them returned to the house, Alexander mentioned that Pepe Barragan was giving a party that evening in Cuernavaca and invited them to accompany him. Sergei declined the invitation but urged Jai Jai to go.

"You deserve a good time," he said and kissed her goodbye.

When, as a reward for his conquest of Mexico, the king of Spain offered Cortes his choice of any part of his conquered land as personal property, Cortes chose Cuernavaca. In 1530 Cortes had a governor's palace erected there, and it still stands today, with its famous Diego Rivera murals, at the side of a small plaza. Since Cortes, every one of the rulers of Mexico, emperors and presidents, dictators and revolutionaries, has had a residence there. South of

Mexico City, situated at a height of five thousand feet
above sea level, the climate is semitropical. It has been described as perpetual spring. An hour from Mexico City on
the super-highway, two hours on the "old" road cut into the
mountains and through pine forests, it is a spectacular
drive, rising to ten thousand feet, then dropping in breath-
taking curves down to a five-thousand-foot plateau. As one
leaves Mexico City, the snowcapped peaks of Popocatepetl
and Ixtacihuatl loom far off in the distance and then disappear from sight until, dramatically, just outside Cuernavaca, Popocatepetl reappears, this time rising steeply dead
ahead. Like Southampton to rich New Yorkers, Cuernavaca is a weekend retreat and resort for the *capitalinos*.
And like Southampton, Cuernavaca is social, very, very social.

"It's like being back in civilization," Jai Jai said, glowing
in a slender white silk column and diamonds. The invitation read for ten P.M. At the fashionable hour of eleven-
thirty she and Alexander entered the walled hacienda. The
party was just beginning to begin, and gaiety sparkled in
every corner of the house, built like the houses of ancient
Rome, as Mexican houses so often are, looking toward an
atrium. Hundreds and hundreds of candles provided the
only sources of illumination, and they sparkled on the
fountains and reflecting pool of the garden, on the fine collection, housed in immaculate glass cases, of pre-Hispanic
silver, on the jewels at the wrists, throats and fingers of the
women. Musicians, mariachis alternating with a soft-pop-
rock band played continuously, and an enormous buffet of
food, including a whole *cabrito* roasted that day in an open
pit, offered Mexican specialties—tortillas in every incarna-
tion from taco to enchilada, chiles, *huachanango* cooked
with tomatoes and peppers and onion in the style of Vera-
cruz, pink Gulf shrimp and an array of *dulces*—as well as
imported delicacies—caviar in the original blue Iranian
tins, beef from Argentina, bread from Poilane and sweet-
meats from Fauchon.

The providers of all this plenty and pleasure were Maja
(pronounced Maya) and Pepe Barragan. Maja, a fabled
beauty, had been at one time Mexico's most popular movie
star, and Pepe, educated in the United States, as so often
upper-class Mexicans are, was an international financier,

referred to in the financial press as "The Rich Billionaire" to distinguish him from lesser billionaires. His interests— real estate, mining, petrochemicals, shipping, construction, insurance and savings and loan associations—touched every major landmass on earth save the Arctic and Antarctica. There were office towers and mining in seventeen states of the United States, agriculture in Canada and Venezuela, financial services in the United Kingdom, France and Switzerland, shipping in Taiwan, Korea, Singapore and Japan, real estate in Hawaii, Australia and New Zealand, oil refining in Indonesia, housing in Nicaragua, South Africa and two of the Middle Eastern emirates. Neither pursued by neurotic demons like Howard Hughes nor a highly gregarious extrovert like Onassis, Pepe Barragan was— except for an amazing penchant for making money—a perfectly normal man, likeable, generous on a personal level, politically conservative and salty-tongued in six languages. He and Maja had been married for twenty-seven years, happily, and had three children, two boys, of whom Paolo was the elder, and a girl, all of whom worked in some aspect of their father's businesses. They were happy people, their home was a happy home and the party was a happy party.

"You're beginning to enjoy yourself," Alexander said as they danced in the courtyard, the stars and the velvet sky the only ceiling.

Jai Jai sensed that he was aware of something about her, but she did not reply. She continued to dance.

Jai Jai had said nothing about Sergei; nothing in the world would have made her utter a syllable. She didn't understand what was happening to him, but even though she didn't understand, she felt compassion for what he must have felt. Compassion, sympathy and love. Along with the fear, the terror, the feeling she had been cheated. She felt everything all at once—one feeling mixed with another, feelings sliding into and out of each other like the shards of colored glass when a kaleidoscope is turned, feelings sometimes dissolving into each other like red ink into water, sometimes remaining separate but intimately congruent like colored grains of sand in a clear glass jar. But whatever was happening to them, whatever was going wrong, it was her secret. She was a good actress. Not a good actress, a great actress, and no one knew. Not Dante. Not the maids. Not Paolo. No one knew; no one suspected.

No one except Alexander.

"You're so beautiful, so very, very beautiful," he said, and he drew her closer into his embrace as they danced. "You deserve only tropical nights and the light of the southern stars reflected in your hair."

Jai Jai drew closer to him, not hearing his exact words but reacting to their sense, to the tone of his voice. She had forgotten so many things in Mazatlán. She had forgotten what it was like to be rich and to enjoy it. The rich don't wait. That afternoon Alexander's car had taken them to the airport at Mazatlán. His plane was serviced, fueled, waiting. Because of his importance to international travel, he—and his party—were extended courtesy of the port wherever they traveled. He traveled on diplomatic status: Customs were waived; passports and other travel documents, prestamped. The rich didn't stand in line, didn't have bags opened, didn't have to answer questions about the duration and purpose of their journey. The rich were different, and in Mazatlán with Sergei, Jai Jai had forgotten what it was like to be different, to be special, to be privileged. To have the illusion always and the reality frequently of being able to have and do anything.

Now, dancing with Alexander, feeling the warmth of him and smelling his smell, the scent of perfectly, newly clean skin so reminiscent of the night they'd first met in Bequia, Jai Jai remembered.

She seemed less perfect and therefore more human and more desirable. Alexander had noticed a difference in Jai Jai as soon as he'd first seen her four days ago, but what the difference was eluded him, tantalized him until the moment, early the day before they'd left for Mazatlán, she'd emerged naked from the Pacific, glistening wet from her morning swim, the diamond studs he'd given her when they'd been lovers refracting the colors of the spectrum in the sunlight. She seemed, for the first time since he'd met her that winter, vulnerable, touchable. As soon as he realized what the difference in her was, he put it from his conscious mind. But the desire was something else. It was

something he could no more control than he could control
the need of his lungs for oxygen or for his heart to beat.

"It isn't only me," he told Jai Jai at some unknown hour
in the pink marble guestroom Pepe had once told Alexander to consider "his." "It's you, too."

"It's us," said Jai Jai. "The two of us."

"I love you the way I always wanted to love a woman,"
said Alexander. He was in her. She abandoned herself to
his strength and then countered with her own the way she
had always instinctively known to respond to him.

"I love you," he said. "Madly, passionately, dangerously."

And that night, for the first time, he kissed her deeply on
the mouth, opening his on hers, pouring himself into her.

∾ TEN ∾

A week later Jai Jai returned to Mazatlán. She had telephoned Sergei from Cuernavaca, from the pink marble
bedroom, Alexander on the bed beside her.

"I'd like to go to Mexico City to do some shopping," she
told him. She expected him to explode, to demand she return immediately. She knew his temper, feared it. Half of
her hoped for his anger, more than hoped, invited it, in
fact.

"Have a good time," he said. "Buy a lot of pretty things."

"Your father is going with me," she said, *telling* him.
Drawing a picture. Increasing the risk, pushing it to the
edge. She wanted him to stop her.

"Call me," was what Sergei said. "Every day."

She spent the week with Alexander in Pepe Barragan's
house facing Chapultepec Park, an elegant house, European in style, rather like a chic *hôtel particulier* at a fashionable address in Paris. Alexander spoke of marriage.

"You'll get an annulment," he said. "I can arrange it."
He talked on, making plans for the future. Now that he
knew what he wanted, all that remained were the mechani-

cal problems of solving the details. He planned his life as if he were planning a business deal. It was a delicate situation, but not unheard-of. Jai Jai didn't interrupt him or stop him; neither did she encourage or discourage him. She felt her fate lay outside her control. She welcomed her destiny, whatever it was, welcoming, even, her sense of passivity, abandoning herself to her inability to change or influence it. She savored the comfort of powerlessness.

The night she returned to Mazatlán her husband came to her bed, no longer impotent, a strong, demanding, insistent lover. That night was the wedding night they'd never had. Sergei was ardent and tender, and Jai Jai fell in love with him all over again, and her fear of him and disappointment in him dissolved in the passion she once again felt. Sergei never once asked her where she had been or what she had done.

"Not once? Not a word?" Dante asked the next day.

"Nothing."

"Maybe he thinks what he doesn't know isn't going to hurt him."

"He has to guess," Jai Jai said. "He's not naive. He knows about Alexander and me. . . ." She shrugged. She didn't know what Sergei thought or suspected or felt, only that he desired her. Sergei was as enigmatic about his deepest feelings as Alexander was candid—once he knew what they were.

"The question is," Dante said, fixing a gold earring to his left earlobe, "is how long can this go on?"

"Forever, I hope," said Jai Jai. "Why not?"

It went on for almost two months. Every other week, Alexander would come to Mazatlán, spend a day with Sergei at Playa Sol and then take Jai Jai away—to Puerto Vallarta, to Acapulco, to Cozumel—for two or three days.

In the very beginning every time she returned to Mazatlán she returned afraid. But whatever she feared—and the fear, although always violent, was nonspecific—never happened. Instead, upon her return she found her husband restored to her. He never questioned her, never accused her, and secure in his desire, she fell in love with him each time all over again, just as, when she was with Alexander, she loved him, forgetting Sergei.

For Jai Jai, it was the best interval of her life. The two men she loved loved her. And when Jai Jai was loved in the ways she needed to be loved, then she loved herself. As for the future, she never thought about it. For Jai Jai, the future, like the past, was an abstraction with no reality.

Jai Jai's forever ended when she realized she was pregnant.

"You're pregnant," Sergei said when he realized she had skipped two periods. "You could have told me. Or did you tell *him* first? Am I supposed to be the last to know?" It was perfectly clear to both of them who Sergei meant when he said *him*.

"Sergei . . ." Jai Jai said, not knowing how to finish the sentence she had begun. She was confused. Sergei had been her accomplice in adultery. It had been Sergei who had suggested the trips to Acapulco, Cozumel, Puerto Vallarta. He had encouraged them, had encouraged Alexander and Jai Jai. Sergei had, Jai Jai realized, rediscovered his manhood after she'd spent the week in Mexico City with Alexander. And Sergei was always most potent, most ardent the day of her return. He needed his father, needed to be in competition with him, to be a man. But the competition had to be a silent one, a secret shared by the three of them, a secret secretly acknowledged but never openly expressed.

Jai Jai didn't know quite what to say, but it didn't matter because before she could continue, Sergei hit her twice, hard, on the face. Red, burning marks flamed up. Involuntary tears of pain appeared in her eyes. "Please don't." All the fears of him she had pushed aside now rose to terrify her.

"Whose is it?" They were in their bedroom, a large square room at the opposite side of the house at some distance from the servants' rooms. It overlooked the Pacific Ocean on one side and, on the other, opened onto the inner courtyard. All the windows were open to catch any night breeze and the scent, sweet and seductive, of night-blooming jasmine hung in the heavy, humid August air. Sergei, who usually drank only moderately, poured aged amber tequila into a pebbled squat green Mexican glass until it was half full. His hands shook, and the bottle clattered against the lip of the glass. In two swallows he drained the tequila and poured more. "Tell me. Goddamn it, Jai Jai. Whose is it? His or mine?"

Sergei's rage seemed to have expanded him physically. His skin seemed stretched, filled with it, as if inflated by it. His body seemed to occupy more space, to fill the room, pushing upward and outward, until it burst through the walls, the floor, the ceiling. His voice was flat, ugly, uninflected. His rage filled the room, leaving no space for Jai Jai.

"You encouraged us, Sergei. You pushed me at him," Jai Jai said, unaware that she wasn't responding to his question, aware only of her fear of him and the feeling that as long as they kept talking, nothing terrible would happen. "You encouraged us, Sergei. Your father and I—"

Before she could finish, Sergei had opened the carved wooden doors of a Mexican colonial piece, elaborately carved and surmounted with heavy cast-iron hardware, that served as a night table and withdrawn from it the pistol that was kept there. When they had first moved to Mazatlán, Jai Jai was upset by it. Sergei told her that in Mexico it was not unusual to keep a weapon. As far as she knew, he was right. Paolo had confirmed it to her when she had asked, and among the amenities in Pepe Barragan's guest rooms, along with scented soaps and thermoses of chilled mineral water, were cleaned, oiled, loaded pistols.

Sergei balanced it on his open palm, weighing it, as if weighing a decision. He drank the rest of the tequila in the glass, then, with great force, smashed it to the terra-cotta tiles of the floor.

"You bitch," he said in that ugly, uninflected voice. "I'm going to kill you," he said, and he fired. Jai Jai moved blindly, instinctively, out of the way of the path of the bullet, picked up the bottle of Cuervo, now half empty, and swung, aiming for Sergei's hand, wanting to knock the gun from it. He caught her arm, stopping it in mid-arc. Then he forced her arm down and around, twisting it up behind her back. The bottle fell from her immobilized hand to crash to the floor, and the smell of tequila mixed with the scent of jasmine and blood where Jai Jai had cut her bare feet on the shards of glass.

They both were wet with sweat, fear, rage, panic. Sergei was behind her now, his hand slippery on her wrist, forcing it upward, hurting her. They stood that way for a moment, rigid, unmoving, neither wanting to be the first to relent. Then, suddenly, Jai Jai felt the length of Sergei's body against her back. His erection was enormous.

"Let's," he said.

"You know I want you," Jai Jai said. "I always want you."

There was, that time for the first time, magic in the combination of his body and her body. It had never been like this for them. Consumed with hatred, they abandoned themselves to the act of love. Jai Jai wanted to dominate him, him to dominate her; she wanted to make him beg for her, to cry for her, to force her to feel that he loved her. She wanted him to force his love on and up and through her. To fill her up with it. Sergei wanted to kill her. To make her come and then kill her with the gun he had placed on the night table for that purpose.

Sensation overwhelmed them. They surrendered themselves to the warmth that was welcome even in the oppressive heat, to wetness that electrified even in the suffocating humidity. Jai Jai felt like the woman she wanted to be, the most loved, the most desired, the most precious, the most beautiful woman in the world. And Sergei felt like the man he wanted to be. Strong and powerful. Stronger and more powerful than his father. The impotence that had haunted him even when he was strong was washed away in a new confidence born of passion.

They moved together, obeying dictates that originated deep and uncontrollably within their central nervous systems, involuntary reflexes inaccessible to their wills or wishes. Messages received by the threadlike dendrites that branch out from the cell nuclei and then transmitted by synapses and sent along in turn to other dendrites by nerve fibers called axons produced the symptoms of sexual excitement in Sergei and Jai Jai, as the same processes of biology do in all humans and, indeed, in the most primitive of vertebrates. The irresistible impulses of the involuntary nervous system caused erection, lubrication and ballooning of the vagina, acceleration of the heartbeat and dilation of the pupils of the eyes. Said to be located in the sacral segments of the spinal cord and brain stem, these nerve centers serve the parasympathetic nervous system and are as instinctive as breathing. The centers serving orgasm, however, are said to be found in the cervicolumbar cord, are sympathetic in nature and therefore can be willed, postponed, denied.

It was Sergei who first restrained himself, holding back by an exercise of his will, until Jai Jai had had her first orgasm. He always made her come first; it had been part of their sexual ritual, a ritual agreed upon a long time before without any words being spoken. And he was on top, another part of that ritual. He thrust himself into her, harder and harder, violently and harshly, punishing her until she reached a second climax. Only then did Sergei allow himself to lose control. Jai Jai felt the searing hot rush inside her, feared wildly that he might have scalded her, and with no sense of making a conscious decision, she decided *yes.* She would do it.

It was difficult to move with his weight pressing her down into the bed, but she got her arm free, and she reached out to the night table. The pistol, the way it felt to her touch, was an unexpected, pleasant surprise. The metal butt felt cool and dry in her sticky, sex-sweaty palm. *Yes,* she thought. *Now.*

The thought that was going through her mind as she murdered her husband were the words of her father recalled from a long time ago in the cold early-morning darkness of a duck blind. He was teaching her to use a gun.

"Squeeze the trigger. Don't pull. *Squeeze,* Jai Jai."

And she squeezed it, exerting equal pressure from her index finger on the front of the trigger and at the back of the butt, tightening the crotch formed by the base of her thumb and the palm of her hand.

When, later on, she would remember it, she could remember the deliberate strength with which she had squeezed the trigger. What she could not remember was the noise. It was, in her memory, like a scene from a silent movie. She could not remember the sound of the gunshot; she could not remember the sound of her own scream.

Dante had been awakened by the first shot and had gone out to the courtyard, curious and only slightly afraid. By the time he placed the location of the noise Jai Jai and Sergei were locked in their violent embrace, and Dante, surrendering to his voyeuristic impulses, watched as the bottle slid from Jai Jai's hand. He was still watching when Jai Jai reached out for the gun. By the time, a few moments later, she knocked on his bedroom door he was back in bed, pretending to be asleep.

PART FOUR

LIAISONS DANGEREUSES

September 1976—December 1977

∾ ELEVEN ∾

Jai Jai got away with it. There was no trial, no public scandal. Officially, there was no crime, no punishment. Gossip followed Jai Jai wherever she went. It added to her mystery, her glamour, her allure, and the rumors were that Jai Jai's freedom had cost Alexander Raimont eleven million dollars.

"Oh my God, he's dead. Sergei's dead. Oh my God!" Jai Jai was hysterical, incoherent. She burst into Dante's room, naked, blood on her breasts and shoulders and arms. Her entire body shook, and her hands and upper torso jerked in spastic dysrhythm.

Dante brought her a Valium and a glass of mineral water. Taking the glass with a jerky, uncoordinated movement, she spilled its contents once, then a second time. With the third glass of water, she was finally able to swallow the drug. Dante held out a wet washcloth; Jai Jai looked at it blankly, and Dante, realizing that she didn't know she was covered with blood, wiped it, still wet and sticky, off her body. When she was clean, he handed her one of his cotton nightshirts and finally had to help her slip it on. Her entire body was ravaged with uncontrollable spasms, and Jai Jai was unable to breathe. With silent, wrenching gasps, she collapsed on the bed, desperately trying to get oxygen into her lungs. The effort to breathe left her unable to speak, and as she struggled, Dante placed a telephone call to Alexander Raimont's suite at the Hotel Inter-Continental in Manila, where he was addressing a meeting of the Pacific Area Travel Association. In Manila, across the international date line, it was already tomorrow. When Alexander came to the telephone, Dante told him that Sergei was dead.

"Dead." Alexander Raimont repeated the syllable as if it were an unfamiliar word from a strange language.

"I'm sorry, terribly sorry," said Dante, instinctively reverting to the ritual phrase of condolence. Dante remembered when his twin brother had died in an automobile accident on the *autostrada* between Milan and Rome. At the funeral in the small church where Dante's parents had been married and where Dante and his twin, Virgil, had been baptized and received their first communion, relatives and friends, villagers and tradespeople all had used the same phrase: "Terribly sorry." It had been fitting; it had said all there was to say. Now Dante found himself saying it to Alexander Raimont. "I'm terribly sorry."

"Dead," Alexander repeated, using the repetition to help make it real. He did not question Dante; he accepted the fact of Sergei's death as soon as Dante reported it.

"Yes," said Dante.

"How?" Alexander asked. "What happened?"

"A gun . . . Sergei's gun," Dante began. When he realized he was being evasive, he stopped and began again, forcing himself to be direct. "Sergei and Jai Jai had an argument and Jai Jai—" Suddenly he looked at Jai Jai crouched on the bed, her body still ripped by violent shudders, and the shocked look on her face turned to horror as she realized what Dante was about to say, as she realized that somehow Dante had been a witness. She reached ineffectually for the phone, trying to take it from Dante, and they exchanged a long look and Dante began a third time. "Sergei and Jai Jai had an argument, and Jai Jai picked it up . . . it was on the night table—"

"Oh my God," Alexander said, and then, as Dante began to speak again, cut him off. "Not on the telephone." Jai Jai had killed Sergei, and Alexander knew instinctively and intuitively that it had to do with him . . . with him and Jai Jai. Immediately comprehending the potential dimensions of the scandal, he thought of what could be done to avert it, of protecting Jai Jai and the Raimont reputation.

"What are you going to do?" asked Alexander in a careful, neutral tone. He wanted to know what side Dante would be on.

"Whatever you tell me," said Dante, without having to think about it. Dante had always been an outlaw; his loyalty was to people, not abstractions.

"Thank you," said Alexander. Then: "How is she?"

Dante looked at Jai Jai. She had finally caught her breath, and still crouched on the bed, the horror of what she had done flooding over her, she began to scream. Long, bloodcurdling screams. Dante never had to answer Alexander's question. Alexander could hear the answer himself.

"Call a doctor. Get her calmed down," said Alexander. "I'll order a plane. I'll be there. And, Dante, don't let her speak to anyone. Not a soul."

"I'll stay with her," said Dante. He was about to hang up when Jai Jai reached for the telephone again. She had stopped screaming; she wanted to speak to Alexander. Dante handed the telephone to her, and hoarse from screaming, she held it, unable to speak.

"Jai Jai?" Alexander said, his voice perfectly audible on the long-distance connection. "Jai Jai?" He had heard the screams; now he heard silence. "Jai Jai! Jai Jai!"

"Alexander," she finally said, her voice choked and sounding strangled. The initial shock had begun to recede just enough for Jai Jai to be panicked at the thought of what she had done and what might happen to her.

"Listen to me carefully," Alexander said. His tone was efficient and impersonal. "Don't see anyone. Don't talk to anyone until I get there."

There was another long silence. "Do you understand?" Alexander asked. "Jai Jai, do you understand me?"

"Yes."

"Yes, what?" Alexander, at a moment of intense crisis, thought coolly and logically. He wanted Jai Jai to repeat his instructions, to make certain that Jai Jai understood and would obey.

"I won't see anyone. I won't talk to anyone until you come," she repeated, grateful to have someone tell her what to do.

"Good," said Alexander, about to hang up.

"Is that all?" Jai Jai asked suddenly. His directions seemed so simple in the face of the enormity of the events. He sounded so impersonal, so businesslike.

"Yes, that's all for now," Alexander said. "Now hang up."

"Alexander?" Jai Jai sounded panicky. "Alexander!"

"Yes?" He was annoyed. He had a series of phone calls to make before he could board his plane.

"I love you," Jai Jai said.

She held onto the telephone, waiting for his response, waiting for him to tell her that he loved her. There was silence. Finally, Alexander spoke. "Jai Jai, hang up. Dante needs the telephone."

Numbly she obeyed. Why couldn't he have told her that he loved her; why did he always have to withdraw when she needed him most? There was a long moment before Dante picked up the receiver to call the doctor, and Jai Jai looked at him, afraid to meet his eyes. "Are you going to tell," she asked him, "everything?"

"I'm going to tell whatever will help you," he said.

"Yes, of course," said Jai Jai. "I know you will." Then, without protest, as she always had, Jai Jai let the men around her determine her fate.

While Dante called a doctor in Mazatlán and asked him to administer a sedative to Jai Jai, Alexander began a series of telephone calls: Alix and Yale in London, Tatiana in Southampton, Andrea in East Hampton, Liliane in Lausanne. He told everyone the same thing: that there had been an accident in Mazatlán and that Sergei was dead. He gave no details because he had none, and he asked everyone to come to Southampton, where Sergei would be buried next to his grandfather.

Then he called the vice-president of Mexico to ask for help and the best criminal lawyer in the world to ask for advice. The vice-president in his Zona Rosa hideaway, about to begin a second session of lovemaking with his young and beautiful mistress, expressed first his shock and then his condolences. Then, offering to do whatever he could to be of assistance, the vice-president gave Alexander Raimont the name and number he needed. He then asked Alexander to wait a quarter of an hour before calling Inspector Rodríguez of the Mazatlán police so that he personally, the vice-president, could speak with the inspector.

In that quarter of an hour, Alexander called the twenty-four-hour number of Preston Cunningham and Associates and received a referral number in Palm Springs. Alexander knew about Jai Jai and Preston, and he cared—he had once made a childish, destructive, ugly scene over Jai Jai's affair with Preston—but Alexander Raimont was a man who never let his personal feelings interfere with business decisions, and the death of his only son was no exception. "Mr. Cunningham, this is Alexander Raimont," he said. "I'm calling on behalf of my daughter-in-law. You knew her as Jai Jai Valerian. . . ."

Deep in sleep next to his wife of twenty-three years, the mother of his four children, Inspector Gilberto Rodríguez answered the telephone before it could ring a second time. The telephone, dusted daily and kept next to the inspector's side of the big marital bed, was a symbol of status, of how far he had come in the world. Born into extreme poverty, Gilberto Rodríguez, an ascetically slender man of medium height with high Indian cheekbones punctuating the flat planes of his face, had, despite the prejudice against him for his Indian blood and as a result of nineteen years of diligent work and careful relations with all those around him, risen in police ranks until he headed the department in Mazatlán. In just a little while he could retire with full pension.

"Inspector Rodríguez, this is . . ." the caller began, and Gilberto Rodríguez recognized the name as that of Mexico's vice-president. Gilberto felt, as he always did when speaking to his superiors, the familiar mixture of pride and antagonism: pride that he was on speaking terms with important people and antagonism at their authority over him.

One of a family of eleven children, four dead, seven still living, Gilberto's father had worked on a plantation harvesting bananas with a machete. It was brutal, punishing work with only a very few pesos a week in payment. Life would have been the same for Gilberto had it not been for a Catholic school and a priest who perceived qualities in the boy and educated and encouraged him, raising his expectations and helping him to realize them. The priest arranged the scholarship at a college in Hidalgo State, and Gilberto, the eldest, was the first of his family to escape the fields; he had, in his turn, encouraged his younger brothers and sisters. Two of his sisters worked in a Catholic hospital in Colima, one of his brothers was also a policeman and another a nightwatchman in a shoe factory. The other children hadn't escaped. They lived, as their parents had, in a shack of tin siding and tar paper with a dirt floor by the side of a canal in the once-proud city of Zempoala. Gilberto rarely returned to Zempoala because he was reminded too vividly of how narrow his own escape had been and how poverty and hopelessness waited indifferently and patiently for him, for his smallest mistake.

"There's been a tragedy," the vice-president was saying, "in the big house on the hill." Gilberto Rodríguez knew, of course, who Alexander Raimont was, and he listened as the vice-president told him that Señor Raimont himself was on his way to Mazatlán, where he and his family would extend every cooperation to the police. He, the vice-president, knew his confidence would not be misplaced when he assured other high government officials that the legalities would be strictly observed without offending the already-bereaved family.

Inspector Rodríguez carefully assured the vice-president that he personally would handle the entire matter, but equally carefully, he made no promises about not offending. When, within the quarter hour, the telephone rang again, Inspector Rodríguez had already formed the phrases of his condolences to Señor Raimont, as well as the words informing Señor Raimont that it was his obligation, his duty, to make a thorough and complete investigation.

In Mexico City the vice-president, his telephoning finished, looked over at his mistress. She had fallen asleep and looked innocent and untouched as she breathed serenely and dreamed sweet dreams. For a moment the vice-president considered awakening her and then decided not to. The loss of an encore to one night's pleasure was little enough to give up when he thought about how a man who had lost his only son must feel.

Dressed in his newest uniform and accompanied by two deputies, Gilberto Rodríguez was the first to enter the bedroom since Jai Jai had left it just about one and one-half hours before. Without touching anything, Gilberto observed the body on the bed and knew that ballistics would only confirm in dry statistics, in numbers, percentages, graphs and charts, what was obvious to the naked eye: that Sergei Raimont, a right-handed Caucasian of approximately thirty years of age, had died from a bullet which had entered the right temple at point-blank range, sliced off the top third of the skull and exited at a point just under the left ear. The bullet, only slightly misshapen, lay in the rumpled tangle of sheets.

Inspector Rodríguez ordered fingerprints to be taken and ordered a police photographer to take the usual photographs, all in keeping with strict police procedure. The bloody detritus that had once been a skull, the right arm still bent, the gun nearby on the bloody sheets, sperm drying in the area adjacent to the male organ—it was strange, Gilberto Rodríguez thought, how the body involuntarily asserted life even at the moment of death. On the basis of what he had seen, Gilberto Rodríguez concluded, although the police were only to investigate, not conclude, that Sergei Raimont, for whatever reason, had taken his own life.

As he was leaving the room, Inspector Rodríguez noticed something he hadn't noticed before: In the wall, almost hidden by a shadow cast by a beam, lodged another bullet. He immediately ordered photographs taken of it and then its removal to the safe in headquarters as evidence. Inspector Rodríguez wondered about the second bullet. Had Sergei Raimont, like many suicides, lost his courage at the last moment and deflected the aim of the gun the first time and, only on the second attempt, successfully taken his own life? Or had he shot at his wife? Or had his wife shot at him? Was there more to the death of Sergei Raimont than met the eye?

As he walked through the long halls of the large, luxurious house, Inspector Rodríguez thought about Jai Jai Raimont. He had seen her many times, walking through Mazatlán, always alone. She was an extremely beautiful woman, extremely desirable, and it had struck Inspector Rodríguez as strange that she was alone so much of the time. She could not have been very happy. Inspector Rodríguez wondered what really went on behind the walls of the biggest house in the best neighborhood in Mazatlán. There were many questions he would have to ask the lovely young widow.

Alexander Raimont's chartered 747 flew the nine thousand miles from Manila to Mazatlán in just under sixteen hours. He went first to the undertaker's, a whitewashed building with red and purple bougainvilleas climbing its façade, where, in an air-conditioned and velvet-draped room, he viewed the body of his son. He then went to the house where his son had lived and died.

"How is she?" Alexander asked as Dante opened the door to him. Whatever he felt at the sight of his dead son did not yet show.

"Heavily sedated," said Dante, himself exhausted.

Alexander Raimont was immaculate and unrumpled in a dark suit of tropical worsted, although his eyes were ringed and smudged with fatigue.

"Has she seen anyone?"

"Only the doctor," said Dante. An Inspector Rodríguez had asked to interview Jai Jai but agreed that he would have to wait until the sedation wore off. "Rodríguez had been back twice. I can't keep putting him off. He's extremely suspicious, and I don't blame him."

"You've done a good job. When he comes back, Jai Jai will have to see him," said Alexander.

"She keeps asking for you. She wants to see you," said Dante. Jai Jai had, in fact, been obsessed with seeing Alexander, had, in the moments she was awake and coherent, asked for him over and over. *Is he here yet? Is he here yet?*

"In a moment," said Alexander. He drew Dante into the small den and shut the door behind them. He declined the offer of a drink but asked for a glass of iced tea and then sat behind the desk, motioning Dante to take the chair to the right of it. "How did Sergei die?" he asked, speaking in a quiet, intense tone.

Dante wondered what to say.

"Tell me the truth," Alexander said. "Whatever it is."

"Are you sure?" asked Dante. He wanted to protect Jai Jai, and he wanted to spare Alexander.

Alexander nodded. "First of all, for myself. I want to know how Sergei . . . how my son . . . died." As he said the words, Alexander wondered how many times he had called Sergei "son." Not enough; not nearly enough. Then Alexander continued, "I can't bring back the dead, but I can protect the living. I need the truth," he said, "in order to lie."

Alexander paused, then added, taking Dante into his

confidence in a way he rarely took anyone into his confidence, "If I have to lie, I will."

"I know." Dante nodded. "I understand." Then he began. "I was asleep. I heard a shot, and I went out into the courtyard. The lights were on in the master bedroom. Jai Jai and Sergei. . . ." Dante paused, continued. "Sergei had a gun. They were fighting for it and then . . . it turned into an embrace. Sergei said he wanted her and—"

"And?" asked Alexander, unflinching, wanting to hear, needing to know. "And?"

"She said she wanted him, too. They made love. I watched." Dante was deeply ashamed; then he collected himself and forced himself to go on. "I watched. I shouldn't have but—" He searched for a way to explain his behavior.

"Go ahead."

"They finished. They had *just* finished. Suddenly Jai Jai moved, and I heard the shot. I saw—" He was about to say that he had seen Sergei's head explode, but he couldn't.

"Yes," said Alexander, reacting to Dante's inability to put the bloody details into words. "She shot, and then?"

"I don't know why, but I ran back to my room. I don't even remember doing it. I just know that suddenly I was back in my bed. Jai Jai burst into the room, I pretended to be sleeping. I felt guilty. Responsible," Dante said. If he had not encouraged Jai Jai in her reckless affair, if he had not thought it glamorous and daring, perhaps Sergei Raimont would still be alive.

"Does Jai Jai know you saw . . . everything?"

Dante nodded.

"Does anyone else know? Except me?"

Dante shook his head. "No. No one."

Alexander nodded. For a long while he said nothing. A question tried to come to him from the bottom of his mind, but the more he tried to concentrate on it, the more it eluded him. There was something he wanted to ask Dante. It was his fatigue, he thought, that stopped him from thinking clearly. He was frustrated by his mind's failure and for a moment sagged back into the big leather desk chair. Then he sat upright and asked if the lawyers had arrived.

"Several hours ago," Dante said. "They're in the sunroom."

Alexander rose, and Dante spoke again. "Will you see

Jai Jai now? She's desperate to see you." Dante wondered whether or not Alexander knew she was pregnant.

"In a moment," said Alexander, and went down the cool dark corridor toward the sun-room.

All that money, all that power, thought Dante as he watched Alexander leave, and he was unbelievably good-looking, too. Like a blond panther. He was absolutely the sexiest man Dante had ever seen, and the most mysterious. No wonder he drove Jai Jai crazy with frustration; there was absolutely no way to tell what he thought or felt.

∾ TWELVE ∾

Alexander Raimont believed in paying for advice. When he planned a hotel, research teams spent thousands of hours surveying air-passenger traffic in and out of the proposed location, the number of existing and projected competing rooms and their current and projected occupancy rates. Population statistics, commercial and leisure activity, prevailing labor costs, projected growth rates, traffic density, highway, rail and air access, infrastructure costs where relevant, real estate values and taxes, availability and cost of mortgaging, construction estimates, decorating, maintaining, repairing and replacing costs, restrictions and variances in local zoning ordinances were gathered, fed into computers, analyzed and, with the guidance of every bit of available data, Alexander and the Raimont executives made decisions involving millions and millions of dollars.

Faced with a personal catastrophe, Alexander responded as if he were faced with a complex business decision. He wanted all the facts, specific information about the ultimate upside and downside risks, the possibilities for action and the consequences of each type of decision. Just as he contracted with the most highly regarded research and marketing organizations, so he wanted the best legal advice. His New York lawyers, Cartwright Dunne and Pepe Barragan all had come up with the same name: Preston Cunningham and Associates. The associate, everyone told Alexander, was Preston's wife, Delia. Brilliant, incisive, a genius at trial strategy.

Since his brief affair with Jai Jai two years before, Preston Cunningham, with Delia pulling the strings, had had a string of dazzling successes. He had defended a former Las Vegas croupier, who had been accused of poisoning three wealthy widows after marrying them and getting them to change their wills in his favor; a movie starlet, accused of stabbing her married lover to death in the sauna of their Malibu hideaway after an argument over his attentions to a newer, younger girlfriend; and a Nobel-prize-winning geneticist, who had run over a colleague in the parking lot of a Cambridge laboratory when the colleague had threatened to make public the fact that most of the basic experimental work had been done by graduate students.

Preston Cunningham had been located in Palm Springs, where he was taking a golfing vacation with his wife, who accompanied him everywhere. A plane had been chartered to pick up the couple, fly them to Mazatlán and wait, fueled and cleared, for the next eventuality. When Alexander entered the sun-room, Preston was at the window wall, gazing out at the gardens below and the Pacific beyond; his wife was seated on a long sofa, legal papers spread out on the coffee table in front of her. The introductions were made quickly.

"My son is dead," Alexander Raimont began. "He died . . ." he began, then stopped and rephrased his thought. "His death was—"

"Don't," cautioned Preston, putting up his hand and stopping Alexander. "I know that he's dead. I know that the circumstances are complex. I prefer to hear what happened from his widow. I believe she was a witness, the only witness. Is that correct?"

Alexander nodded. Without saying a word, he had told his first lie.

"After I speak to her," Preston continued, "I'll take statements from servants et cetera if it seems necessary."

Alexander nodded. "I want to know precisely what our legal position is," he told Preston, "and I want to know precisely what our alternatives are."

"We will be able to give you that information," Preston

said, "after we interview the widow." Delia, still on the
sofa, nodded silently. She had said nothing once the introductions had been made.

"I understand," said Alexander. Then, rapidly, client and
lawyer agreed upon the fee. The initial payment would be
considered a consultation fee; if there were a trial, the fee
would then be considered an advance against an additional
fee. When the discussion of money was over, Alexander
told Preston that his daughter-in-law would be in momen-
tarily. He excused himself and left the sun-room to head
toward the bedroom where Jai Jai had been secluded. After
Alexander had left the room, Delia spoke for the first time.

"I notice you never call Jai Jai by her name," she said.

"Naturally," said Preston. "Our 'thing' was over a long
time ago."

"It's interesting," said Delia, pointedly, "that our client,
Mr. Raimont, never called her by her name either."

"So?" asked Preston.

"So . . ." answered Delia enigmatically, and turned
back to the papers, which were the ballistics reports prepared overnight by the Mazatlán Police Department. Interesting, Delia thought, there were traces of gunpowder on
Sergei Raimont's hands.

"You're here," Jai Jai sobbed as Alexander entered her
room. "I'd thought you'd never come. You're here. It's
been so long." Jai Jai had been weeping softly all night
long; at the sight of her lover she began to cry, although
she had thought there were no more tears left to be shed.
She crossed the room and went to him, asking without
words to be embraced. Alexander put his arms around her,
and even in her horror at what she had done, Jai Jai was
aware that Alexander's embrace was the embrace of a father, of a priest, of a physician. It was not the embrace of
the man who had been her ardent lover.

"Shhh, Jai Jai," he crooned, patting her shoulder in the
timeless gesture of comfort. "Try not to cry."

"Don't leave me," she said, "don't leave me," putting
into words her greatest fear. Her father—and ever since—
the men she loved more than she loved herself had always
left her. "Don't leave me. You won't leave me, will you?
Promise?"

"Jai Jai. Jai Jai," Alexander repeated, realizing that his saying her name calmed her. "Jai Jai," he said, rocking her gently, wiping her tears with a big linen handkerchief, holding her as tenderly as he would a beloved child. "Jai Jai."

Jai Jai leaned into him, trying to melt her body into his, trying to merge and become one with him, trying to evoke the response, even in the midst of shock and horror, that she needed: a man's emotional response to a woman. Desire. Need. Lust. She failed. Alexander continued to hold her, comforting, attentive, detached until, superficially at least, she was under control. Then he began to talk to her. She was terrified that he was going to accuse her of murdering Sergei.

"Preston Cunningham is here," he began. At the mention of Preston's name, Jai Jai turned white, the blood visibly draining from her face. Alexander Raimont was a jealous and violently possessive man, traits he rigidly concealed because he thought them signs of weakness. The one and only time he had ever lost control was when he found out about Preston. It had been at the Plaza Athénée when they'd returned to France from Bequia. Preston's photo had appeared on a French newscast, and Jai Jai had mentioned that she had known him and had, in fact, stayed with him at the Plaza Athénée on the floor just below Alexander's suite. Alexander had suddenly switched off the television set and blocked its screen with his body.

"What did you do that for?" asked Jai Jai.

"It never happened," Alexander said.

"Yes. Here in the Plaza Athénée. Downstairs," said Jai Jai, who should have recognized the tight rage on Alexander's face but didn't, perhaps because she'd never seen it before.

"Get out!" he said in a low snarl. "Now."

"Why? Why should I?" Jai Jai was confused. She didn't know what she had done wrong.

"I don't care what you did and who you did it with before you met me, but I don't want to hear about your goddamn lovers. Now get out of here." His snarl had turned hoarse.

"The other night you asked me to tell you," said Jai Jai. Alexander had asked her to tell him about the other men she'd made love to. There hadn't been many, but she'd left out Preston, perhaps because he'd left her and she still stung from the desertion.

"That was the other night. Now get out." His voice was almost a scream, just barely under control. He had her by the arm, pushing and pulling her to the door. In lounging pajamas and a robe, Jai Jai found herself in the corridor with nowhere to go except a Raimont courtesy suite across the hall. It was empty, and Jai Jai had it to herself. Being alone in a luxurious Plaza Athénée suite evoked painful memories of the days after Preston had so coldly left her. For two days Jai Jai neither saw nor heard from Alexander; on the third he appeared in the suite and said, curtly and without meeting her eyes, "You can come back."

Jai Jai returned to him, and the incident was never referred to. Alexander was excited by her affairs with men he considered no competition. Preston, as brilliant and important in his field as Alexander was in his, was something else, a competitor, an equal, and Alexander was murderously jealous of men he considered a threat. Now Alexander had called Preston; Jai Jai didn't understand why.

"It's all right," Alexander said, remembering the same scene. "It isn't important now. We need him. This"—he couldn't bring himself to use Sergei's name to Jai Jai—"this situation is . . . complicated. I don't know where we stand legally. Preston wants to talk to you."

"Why? I don't understand."

"If there's a trial, he'll represent you," said Alexander.

"Trial?" Jai Jai seemed to shrink physically. In the long night she had wondered how she would live without Sergei, where she would go, how she would be able to survive knowing she had done what she had done; she had wondered about her relationship with Alexander: Would he accuse her and desert her? Would they remain lovers? Never once had the thought of a trial, a judge, a jury, prison, execution—oh-my-God-what-did-they-do-to-people-in-Mexico—ever crossed her mind. "No!" she screamed.

"Please, Jai Jai, calm yourself," said Alexander, stroking and petting her. "Please. You must speak to him. You must tell him what happened."

"Why don't you tell him?" Jai Jai asked.

"I wasn't there," Alexander said simply.

There was a silence. And then Jai Jai spoke, softly. "Alexander, don't you want to know what happened?"

"Dante told me."

"I know," she said. "But don't you want to know *why*?" Jai Jai touched his arm, facing him. He refused to meet her eyes, and he turned away from her as she spoke. He didn't want to hear her side of it; he didn't want to feel any sympathy.

"I was terrified of Sergei," she began. "He used to hit me, to hurt me. I never told you. How could I? I was afraid of him, afraid that one day he'd lose control. . . . He'd always be remorseful. He never said anything, but he'd bring a gift, he'd be sweet and very loving and each time I thought it would never happen again.

"Then, last night, it happened. He lost control. He said he'd kill me. He had a gun. Alexander, he shot at me. I'm alive because of luck," Jai Jai said. "I could be the one who's dead." She paused, out of breath, waiting for Alexander's sympathy.

He loved his son with the unreasoning, uncritical love of a father; he loved Jai Jai with the passionate, incendiary love of a man on fire. The two feelings could not coexist, and just as the two people who evoked them had been driven to murder, the violence and impossibility of Alexander's emotions consumed each other, and he appeared to feel nothing.

As she waited, Alexander realized what it was he had been trying to think of earlier when he'd spoken to Dante. The first shot. Who had fired it? What about it? Now he knew the answer: Sergei had tried to kill Jai Jai. Alexander was devastated by the death of his son; now he imagined how he might have felt at the death of his mistress. Jai Jai, as she had so many times, gave up waiting for a reaction from him, and she continued.

"Somehow, I don't know how, we made love; only it was like making hate, and I knew he was going to kill me. I sensed it. I knew it," Jai Jai said and paused for a moment. "I shot him," she said. "That's all. I shot him."

Jai Jai once again waited for Alexander to react. He said nothing. He didn't even move. Jai Jai waited for something, an accusation, an expression of disgust, a slap, something, anything human. There was nothing, nothing at all. Finally, she could bear it no longer. "Say something, Alexander. Say something!"

He turned slowly to her, finally meeting her eyes. "What do you want me to say?" he asked in the saddest, gentlest voice she had ever heard. The son he loved was dead. The mistress he would never stop desiring had killed him. "Jai Jai, what on earth do you want me to say?"

She was immediately sorry, not that she had told him what she had done, he already knew, but for demanding a response when there was nothing to say. Nothing. She looked at him, thinking how much she loved him and how much she had loved Sergei and wondered why it couldn't be easy. Love should be easy, but in Jai Jai's experience it never was. It was always mixed with the anxiety of anticipated loss, the need to seduce and fascinate, the constant competition of who loved whom the most.

"Don't you want to know what we fought about?" asked Jai Jai.

"I know," said Alexander, shaking his head. It had been about him and Jai Jai—Sergei had found out. "I know what it was about. I don't want to hear it."

"You don't know," said Jai Jai.

"No?" Alexander was surprised.

"Alexander, I'm pregnant," Jai Jai said, speaking as gently as she could. "I'm pregnant, and I don't know who the baby belongs to. You or Sergei."

"Oh, my God," he said, "oh, my God." And he came to her as she had come to him, to be held and comforted, to be relieved of an unbearable pain.

Jai Jai held him closely, understanding now that their positions had been reversed why there had been no passion in his earlier embrace. Now, in Mazatlán, he was a father who had lost a son first and a man who loved his mistress last. Just as Alexander had held her as if she were a child, Jai Jai now embraced him as if he were, not her lover, but her child. Then, after a long while, he gently disengaged himself from her arms.

"Jai Jai, the police are waiting. They're suspicious and angry. Preston and Delia are waiting."

"Should I tell the truth?" Jai Jai asked. She would do whatever he told her. Anything and everything.

"Yes," he said, and added, knowing perfectly well that

he had one set of rules for himself and another for the rest of the world, "there's no point in paying for advice and then lying."

"Jai Jai, what a tragedy. It must be terrible for you," Preston murmured, shaking her hand warmly when she entered the sun-room. "I'm so sorry, so sorry."

Jai Jai responded to the warmth of his greeting, thanking him, and looked to him for protection when Delia cut her off in mid-sentence.

"You made love to your husband. You took a gun from the night table and then you shot him," she said as coldly and as accusingly as a prosecuting attorney. "Didn't you?"

"It wasn't like that," Jai Jai began evasively.

"Answer," ordered Delia. "Did you or did you not shoot your husband in cold blood?"

"I shot him but not . . ." Jai Jai began. "No, no," she said realizing what she had admitted. "He threatened to kill me. He did. He did. He shot at me."

"You *did* pull the trigger, did you not?" Delia pressed, unrelenting, thinking that if Sergei had shot at her, it would explain the traces of gunpowder; it would also buttress a plea based on self-defense. "Well, didn't you kill him?"

Jai Jai turned to Preston, looking for help, for guidance. He gave none.

"Just answer the question," he said, turning in that phrase from drawing-room condolences to criminal lawyer.

For the next hour Delia and Preston cross-examined Jai Jai. They alternated role of friend and enemy; they confused her, caught her in contradictions and inconsistencies. They made insulting innuendoes, damning references to her past, to her morals, to her affair with Preston, and by the time Delia, acting on her hunch, accused her of having an adulterous affair with her father-in-law, Jai Jai was too exhausted, frightened, confused, hysterical to deny it. They'd made her sound to herself like a whore, a slut, a woman who'd cold-bloodedly murdered her husband after an argument over her love affair with her wealthy father-in-law.

"What's going to happen to me?" Jai Jai asked. It was the first time she'd seen the consequences through others' eyes, and the thought of what might happen to her chilled her.

"I don't know," Delia said, coldly, and in those moments she had repaid Jai Jai for the injuries she had suffered when Jai Jai had, for a time, taken away her husband. Jai Jai looked at Preston, hoping for reassurance.

"Wash your face and comb your hair," he said. "You're going to have to answer the same questions for Inspector Rodríguez in a few moments."

"There are four possibilities. Murder is the first," said Preston. "Jai Jai shot him, and she admits it." Preston and Delia had gone into the same small library where Alexander had spoken to Dante earlier, and again Alexander sat behind the desk, while the lawyers occupied twin chairs in front of it.

"And what are the other three?" asked Alexander.

"Self-defense. He threatened to kill her. She says he shot at her, and she killed him in self-defense," said Preston. "The third: a fatal accident. Specifically, Jai Jai did not *know* the gun was loaded. Fourth: suicide."

"Suicide?" Alexander, shocked, had an involuntary memory of his father's death, the pool house, the check in the morning mail. Then he remembered a Boston psychiatrist he'd refused to believe, and he remembered asking Sergei if what the psychiatrist had said was true and Sergei, laughing and in a good mood, assuring him that the psychiatrist was taking the melodramatic playacting of a college boy too seriously. Sergei had made it easy not to believe the psychiatrist. What father would take the word of a stranger over the word of his own child? "Jai Jai pulled the trigger," Alexander said. "Not Sergei."

"It doesn't necessarily matter *who* pulled the trigger. If it can be shown that one, the victim had a history of previous attempts and two, he goaded another person into killing him." Preston stopped and looked at Delia, who cited a specific example. It had taken place in California.

"The deceased had been restrained from jumping off a roof, gone home and, that night, provoked a violent argument with his wife, threatened her with a knife, and in the struggle she killed him with a kitchen knife. The jury on the basis of psychiatric testimony ruled the death a suicide. The phrase he used was: suicide by another's hand." Delia finished her recitation, and Preston took up where he had left off.

"From a lawyer's point of view, this is a fascinating case," said Preston.

"And from a practical point of view?" asked Alexander.

"From a practical point of view, it's a disaster," said Preston. "This is a Catholic country; they practically invented macho—they're not going to be terribly sympathetic to a woman who shoots her husband after making love to him, a woman who has been committing adultery with her father-in-law. In addition, Jai Jai is a terrible witness: She changes her mind, says one thing and then another, she's easy to bully, she's confused and she tries to please whoever questions her. She may be lying, and she may not be, but I can tell you one thing: A judge and a jury are going to think she's lying.

"Furthermore," Preston went on, "no matter what verdict you get, the circumstances are open to so many interpretations that there will certainly be appeals and undoubtedly reversals in higher courts. Basically, what you have is a juicy sex-and-murder scandal and enough ammunition to keep it alive for years."

"What's your advice then?" Alexander asked Preston. "What would you do if you were me?"

Preston turned to Delia, and so did Alexander.

"If I were you?" the small black woman asked, aware of the infinity of impossibilities that separated her from him and appreciating the unconscious humor in his question.

"If you were me," said Alexander.

"Bribe. Lie. Threaten. Get the whole thing buried," said Delia. "And then get Jai Jai the hell out of Mexico."

"You're right, of course," said Alexander, and he thanked the Cunninghams for their help. He waited patiently while they sat in on Jai Jai's interview with Inspector Rodríguez. When it was over, Alexander asked the Cunninghams how it had gone.

Delia rolled her eyes.

Preston spoke. "You have money and power. You're going to need them."

Alexander walked the two lawyers to the door, where a Raimont car waited to take them to the airport for the flight back to Palm Springs. Preston had missed two golf lessons and would include their cost in the bill he submitted to Alexander Raimont. As they settled back in the car, Delia spoke.

"It's early," she said, "but I guarantee you one thing: Jai Jai Raimont is pregnant."

Preston looked at his wife, surprised. Then he thought over what she had said and commented, "Good. If she comes to trial, it'll help us get sympathy for her."

"You're not thinking," said Delia. "She was sleeping with both of them. I'll bet you a lobster dinner she doesn't know whose it is."

Preston had the charisma, and Delia had the brains, and Preston admitted it. He looked at her with amazement, realizing that, of course, she was right. "Sympathy? She'll be lucky if the judge and jury don't lynch her. No wonder you told him to get Jai Jai the hell out of Mexico." Then he chuckled and said, "Well, she can be sure of one thing anyway: It'll be white."

Delia joined in. A long time ago she had set the limits to Preston's extramarital behavior: He could do whatever he wanted as long as it was with white women. Delia wasn't afraid of them.

Alexander Raimont was too rich to have to bribe, too powerful to have to threaten. In a long meeting with the vice-president of Mexico, the minister of tourism, Inspector Rodríguez, Pepe and Paolo Barragan, an agreement was reached. It was based on a juxtaposition of interests: Alexander wanted to avoid a trial and the attendant scandal; the Mexican government wanted the three-hundred-fifty-room hotel Sergei Raimont had been building.

Pepe and Paolo agreed to remain in the original partnership and continued to oversee the day-to-day on-site construction. The vice-president and minister of tourism were all for dropping all official inquiries, particularly in view of the fact that none of the people involved was a Mexican citizen. Only Gilberto Rodríguez demurred; he was extremely conscientious and proud of his reputation and that of his department. He pointed out that a suspicious death had taken place in his jurisdiction and that it was his duty to investigate. Finally, one memory and one argument changed his mind.

The memory was of Sergei Raimont driving through Mazatlán in an air-conditioned burgundy-red Mercedes that
had cost more than Gilberto's father had earned in a lifetime. The car was constantly parked illegally, and none of
the tickets were ever paid. Sergei Raimont's indifference to
authority had been a constant irritant to Gilberto Rodríguez, and personally he had no sympathy for the young
man.

The argument was about the jobs the hotel would create.
Gilberto thought of Zempoala, of people who went hungry
because they had no money for food, who died because
they could afford no doctor, no medicine. If Gilberto ignored the death of one spoiled young man, he could help
change the future of hundreds of young Mexicans. When
Gilberto thought about it in those terms—one death for
hundreds of jobs—he realized that he had, really, no choice
and, in fact, wanted none.

It was agreed that the circumstances surrounding Sergei
Raimont's death were endlessly arguable and that a trial
would be expensive for both sides, time-consuming and undoubtedly inconclusive. In exchange for agreeing not to try
Jai Jai, for sealing the police files and for officially listing
the cause of Sergei Raimont's death as accidental, Alexander Raimont agreed to provide the financial guarantees
that the hotel begun by his son and not yet even a fourth
finished would, in fact, be completed. That guarantee, in
the form of performance and completion bonds, cost Alexander Raimont eleven million dollars.

Thirty-six hours after Sergei's death, his body was on a
Raimont jet bound for Southampton, New York. During
the eight-hour flight, Alexander Raimont sat alone in the
curtained-off private compartment writing in longhand on a
yellow legal pad. Just as he expressed every other emotion
with money, he expressed his reaction to Sergei's death
with money. He directed his Zurich bank to transfer one
million dollars to an account in the name of Dante Mascheroni, and he drafted a new will, leaving everything he
owned to Alix. As coexecutor with Alix of Sergei's estate,
Alexander authorized a one-hundred-thousand-dollar-a-
year income to be paid to Jai Jai until her remarriage, if
any. The remainder of Sergei's estate amounting to a

hundred twenty-five million dollars, the total assets of three trust funds originally established by Alexander, reverted on Sergei's death to him, and he arranged to have them transferred to Alix at the time of the final accounting of the estate.

Jai Jai, in the passenger compartment with Dante, was exhausted but fought off sleep because of the nightmares that, unbidden, invaded it. Nightmares that began with kisses on the mouth and ended with a scream.

∽ THIRTEEN ∾

Sergei Raimont was buried next to his grandfather in a family plot in a graveyard dating from the eighteenth century in a secluded corner of Tatiana Raimont's Southampton estate—forty acres of ancient oaks, a thirty-five room red-brick colonnaded mansion built by an investment banker as a summer cottage before the crash of '29 and bought by Alexander for his mother the year before his father's death from the estate of the banker's grandson.

On the grounds were a greenhouse, stables, and ring and bridle paths, a pool, tennis courts, a croquet lawn, garaging for six automobiles, sheds for the storage of lawn and garden equipment, a generator shack that provided the estate with its own electric supply and a pump house that supplied water from an underground freshwater spring. The estate was utterly private and as self-contained as a small country. It was isolated from the outside world by an ivy-covered brick wall and a manned guardhouse controlling access to the driveway on one side and by three thousand miles of the Atlantic Ocean on the other.

The simple funeral service was held in total privacy, conducted by a local Episcopalian minister and attended only by the immediate family. Alix had flown in from London with Yale; Andrea and Jules had driven in from East Hampton, where they were spending the summer in a rented angular glass beach house they couldn't particularly afford; Liliane had come in from Lausanne to be with Alexander; Tatiana, erect though frail, crippled with arthritis, stood unsupported at the gravesite. None of the Raimonts cried, and even Andrea, highly emotional and melodramatic by temperament, watched dry-eyed as her child was buried.

Only Jai Jai wept. Silently, steadily tears fell unchecked down her face. She remembered only the good times with Sergei—the secrets they shared, the time he had filled their swimming pool with gardenias for her, the way he held her *after* they'd made love, all the times he'd made her promise she'd never leave him and made her seal it with a kiss. She looked desolate and several times seemed almost to come to the point of fainting. Dante stood by her side throughout the brief service, holding her arm, her only companion.

When the reading of the Twenty-third Psalm was finished, signifying the end of the service, Jai Jai walked unsteadily toward the edge of the grave and with graceful, elegant gestures slipped off her gold wedding band, slid it through the black-ribbon place marker of the Bible she carried and tied it to one of the handles at the head of the coffin to be buried with her husband for eternity. Her gesture touched Yale. He thought it romantic, heartbreaking, memorable.

He looked at Alix, her face somber, her eyes hidden behind large sunglasses, and he wondered if she would ever make a dramatic gesture like Jai Jai's. He decided that she wouldn't, although he wished she would. He remembered the first time they'd met Jai Jai. Sergei had brought her to London to meet his sister and brother-in-law. It had been in April—when Jai Jai and Sergei had just fallen in love. . . .

Jai Jai and Sergei had arrived for the weekend in a Raimont limousine. Another limousine followed with Jai Jai's luggage: two large suitcases, a ballgown-length garment bag and a makeup case the size of a small trunk. The makeup case attracted Alix's attention, and she complimented Jai Jai on it and asked where she had bought it.

"I bought it at an auction in Paris," Jai Jai said. "It once belonged to Coco Chanel."

"It's extraordinary," said Alix. And Jai Jai opened it to

show Alix the inside. The inside of the case, made of baby crocodile, was crimson suede and marquetried rosewood. Silver-stoppered lead crystal bottles and jars held lotions, creams, foundations, rouges and powder. Silver-backed hairbrushes occupied specially fitted sections, and concealed was a locked strongbox for jewels. "It's hard to believe people once traveled like this," Alix said, thinking of airline allowances and the difficulty of finding porters. "You need a separate employee just to carry it."

"*You* could travel that way," said Jai Jai, surprised at Alix's envy. One day Alix Raimont would be one of the richest women in the world. She could travel with mountains of baggage and armed guards to protect it if she wanted. "I'm surprised you don't."

"I'd feel ostentatious," said Alix. "It would embarrass me."

Jai Jai had thought she would be intimidated by Alix Raimont, and she was disappointed not to be. Jai Jai was used to the company of women as glamorous and narcissistic as she was. She liked long lazy chats with girlfriends about where to buy bikinis that really fitted (some liked the ones made in the South of France, others swore by a man in Acapulco who mailed anywhere in the world); discussions of Laszlo versus Sartin versus Cyclax; praise for the best haircutters in the world—Roger Thompson in New York and London and Jean-Marc Maniatis in Paris; the exchange of names of dermatologists, exercise gurus, masseurs and gynecologists. Jai Jai wanted Alix to like her, just as she wanted everyone to like her, but she found she had nothing to talk to her about, that they had nothing in common, and she ended by feeling the disdain toward Alix that beautiful women tend to feel toward plain women.

The weekend passed quickly, Sergei quite obviously a man enchanted and madly in love and Jai Jai, complaisant, sweet-tempered, self-involved.

"What did you think?" Alix asked Yale when Jai Jai and Sergei returned to Paris after dinner on Sunday.

"Sergei's in over his head," Yale said.

"And Jai Jai?"

"Dazzling. Nothing less than absolutely dazzling," he said. And then, without stopping to consider his words he added, "I wish you were more like her."

There was a pause, and then Alix replied, "I know you do."

There was no more mention of Jai Jai until their argument over having the wedding in the Belgravia house. Now, five months later, Sergei was dead. As Alix and Yale entered Tatiana's imposing house after the funeral, Yale remembered the intensity of his attraction to Jai Jai the first moment he'd met her. At the time he'd done nothing about it. Now, when she was newly bereaved, under mysterious circumstances that only added to her allure, Yale wondered why he had been so punctilious. He had got everything he'd ever wanted. Why not Jai Jai?

Alexander Raimont did not attend the funeral of his son, just as he had not attended the funeral of his father. While the service was being held in the old cemetery, Alexander met with three lawyers from the estate department of his New York law firm to discuss the new will he had drafted on the plane trip from Mazatlán to New York. Four pages long, it would replace his former will, a document bound like a book that ran a hundred and twelve pages. Sergei had always resented the old will because it left everything in trust, giving Sergei and Alix large incomes but no power, no responsibility. Alexander had not known until Sergei was dead how much he had loved him. He had never shown his love; never known how to. It was too late to change things with Sergei; it wasn't too late to change them with Alix.

Alexander directed his lawyers to translate his wishes from his simple draft into proper legal form. He gave the lawyers a Xerox of his handwritten pages, keeping the original for himself. He intended to give it to Alix personally.

"I can't wait to get out of this house," Jai Jai told Yale after dinner on the day of the funeral. She felt numb and emptied by her tears, deserted and abandoned by Alexander. She had found out that Alexander had already left Southampton for Manila. He had not even taken the time to say goodbye to her, although she knew he had spent the afternoon with Alix. "It makes me feel insignificant."

"I know what you mean," Yale said. "I feel the same

way." They were alone in one of the living rooms, everyone else having retired.

The house, renovated and furnished by Tatiana, reflected her taste and generation. It had the ambience of a grand European residence, its furnishings including a suite of fauteuils signed by Jacob and made for Marie Antoinette and, in the grand entrance hall, a priceless quartet of Rembrandt portraits. The size of the rooms diminished people, and the perfection of the furnishings and housekeeping—perfectly polished silver, glossy parquet, absolutely fresh flowers in Meissen and Chi'en containers, dazzlingly clean windows, rich lacquer chinoiserie cabinets on gilded seventeenth- and eighteenth-century stands—made human beings seem, by comparison, imperfect.

"I never realized housekeeping was an art," Jai Jai said. Dante had pointed it out to her. He had said that it reminded him of his mother's houses when his father was in his rich periods. Jai Jai recalled Alexander's giving a lecture to a hotel executive once in Madrid about how to clean a room. He had been displeased at the conditions of the guest rooms in a Raimont-operated hotel on the Paseo de la Castellana. "From the top to the bottom," he told the manager, "from the top to the bottom." Alexander then went on to describe exactly how each room should be made up: The beds were to be stripped first and allowed to air while the trash was emptied and the bathroom cleaned. The beds were then to be remade, always leaving the open ends of the pillow slips to the outer corners on a double and to the left as the guest faced the headboard on twins. Moldings were to be dusted first, followed by pictures, tables, bureau tops, lamps and so on. Last of all, in line with the top-to-bottom rule, so that dust would be picked up by subsequent steps in the cleaning, the carpet was to be vacuumed from the farthest corner to the door. A guest entering the room, Alexander had stressed, should have the impression that it had never before been occupied. At the time Jai Jai had been amazed by Alexander's attention to the minutest details of housekeeping procedures. She realized, now that she was in his mother's house, that he must have absorbed that knowledge as indelibly as he had learned his own name and how to spell it.

"The rich," Jai Jai said, quoting Dante, "really understand maintenance."

"And silence," Yale added, somewhat theatrically. Tatiana's spacious rooms were hushed, the ticking of delicate French clocks muted by densely knotted Aubusson and Savonnerie carpets.

"I didn't think people lived like this anymore," Jai Jai said. With her ultrafashionable clothes, she felt out of place and even slightly vulgar. Alix, whose dress was usually so understated as to be invisible, was one of the few people not to be swallowed up by her grandmother's opulent rooms.

"I grew up with people who lived just like this," Yale said, telling Jai Jai about Phillip Noyes and Madame. "I vowed I'd live like them one day. Now that I can almost afford it, it's out of style." He laughed at the irony, and so did Jai Jai. For a moment they felt relaxed and unguarded, and then their laughter in the tragic circumstances and cathedral quiet of the formal house embarrassed them, and guilty conspirators, they stopped.

"What are you going to do"—Yale paused, searching for a way to end the sentence without mentioning Sergei's death—"now?"

"Wait for my baby to be born," Jai Jai said, and her eyes flooded with involuntary tears, not of self-pity, but of agony.

"Poor Jai Jai," said Yale, who had not known she was pregnant. He tried to comfort her with an embrace. Jai Jai was not comforted, but she did not push him away.

Alexander Raimont was a man who had many secrets from himself. He did not understand what drove him, and he had no need to. He had used money to replace emotion and had done it for so long that he was a stranger to his own feelings. Always driven by what he didn't have, when he met Jai Jai in Bequia, he felt empty, lonely, dead. It had been a long time since he had been stirred by passion. He desired it; he feared it. He desired her; he feared his desire.

The moment he saw her at the Frangipani with two men, he wanted her. He did everything he could to possess her and, then, having succeeded, grew frightened of his feelings and dealt with his fear by tiring of her. His interest reawakened, more fiery, more consuming than before, only when she married his son, when, by ordinary conventions, he could never possess her again. But ordinary conventions did not apply to Alexander, had never applied to him. His money had been earned by his defying conventions, and the more money he had, the more freedom he bought from conventions. When Sergei encouraged Jai Jai to go to Pepe Barragan's party with Alexander, Alexander, who had never needed to deny himself anything, did not deny himself Jai Jai. In August, he had brought up the subject of divorce with Liliane.

"Absolutely not," she had said. They were in St.-Jean-Cap-Ferrat in the house Liliane rented every year, in the gazebo in the rose garden. The roses of midsummer were lush and full, their scent perfuming the air. In front of them, beyond the blue swimming pool with its blue and white changing pavilion, dazzled the Mediterranean. White sails dotted the blue water, and from far off came the sound of powerful speedboats, followed by graceful water skiers.

"I've met someone . . ." Alexander began. He burned for Jai Jai. He had lost her to Sergei. Now that he had broken every taboo to have her again, he wanted to possess her absolutely. Once, several years before, New York City's Plaza Hotel had been for sale, and Alexander had wanted it desperately—for its prestige, for its aesthetic value, for its real value. It was one of the most desirable properties on earth. Alexander had gone to Manhattan to bid against a big American hotel chain. The bids were comparable, but the deadline day had fallen on a minor holiday—in New York, a bank holiday. Three top men from the competing chain had chartered a plane, flown to Boston, where the banks were open, arranged financing and, that same day, before the five P.M. deadline, had returned to New York and the Plaza Hotel was theirs. In the next five years Alexander had offered three times to buy it, and three times he had been turned down. It was one of Alexander Raimont's rare business misjudgments, and he ached for the Plaza the way, that summer, he ached for Jai Jai.

"You've met other someones," said Liliane with more confidence than she really felt. Alexander's infidelities, although she tried to be sophisticated and worldly about them, hurt her. "Someone is no reason."

Liliane remembered, and so did Alexander, another

someone in the decade of their marriage. Just as each of his wives had been different from the others, so was Jill Laurel different from all his wives. Jill Laurel was the travel editor of a Chicago newspaper, an American career woman, a brand-new kind of woman for Alexander. He discussed business with her, a novelty to him, and she was, unlike other women he had known, independent. He never knew when he called whether she would be home or not or even, if she were, if she would be free to see him. She had a busy, interesting life that had nothing to do with him.

Jill fascinated Alexander, and for a while he wanted to marry her. The affair had lasted for more than two years and had finally ended for a number of reasons: her constant travel, his constant travel, Liliane's refusal to agree to a divorce and, most of all, Alexander's realization that although he was attracted to Jill's independence, ultimately he wanted women who depended totally on him. But that was the ending. In the beginning of the fascination with Jill, Alexander had wanted a divorce just as now, desperate to possess Jai Jai, he raised the subject again.

"I'd like to be free," he said.

"You are free," replied Liliane sadly.

"Not to remarry."

"I refuse to discuss divorce," said Liliane. "You'll get over this . . . someone . . . too."

No, thought Alexander, I won't get over this someone. I won't get over Jai Jai. Desiring his own son's wife made him feel totally alive. He would not "get over it."

Alexander did not, however, pursue his conversation with Liliane at that moment, although he did not intend to let the matter drop. Even seized by forbidden passions, Alexander Raimont was a realist. If, in fact, he did come to the point of insisting, Liliane's lawyers would make a divorce costly—so costly that even Alexander would feel it—and although Jai Jai was worth whatever it would cost, he did not intend to pay a penny more than he absolutely had to. In addition, he was afraid that if he insisted on a divorce too vehemently at this early date, Liliane would let her curiosity get the better of her and ask who her rival was. In the past she had never asked. She had told him why: She didn't want to know. Knowing would hurt more than not knowing. If she didn't know, if it wasn't a real person with a real name, she could pretend it wasn't really happening.

Although Alexander was excited by the shocking and scandalous circumstances surrounding his affair with Jai Jai, he knew perfectly well that Liliane would be utterly horrified and would never consent to a divorce. For those reasons, Alexander decided to drop the issue of divorce for a while. He would bring it up again. But he never did.

A month later Sergei was dead, and so were his feelings for Jai Jai. If it hadn't been for the baby, Alexander tried to tell himself, he would never have seen her again.

During her pregnancy Alexander treated Jai Jai with a detached kindness and disinterested protectiveness that undermined all sense of her own desirability. His behavior toward her was impeccably thoughtful and totally sexless. She would hardly believe, when he left after a visit to inquire about her health, diet, habits of rest and exercise, that he was the same man who had once desired her so passionately.

"Perhaps it's because I'm pregnant," Jai Jai had said to Dante in an attempt to explain to herself Alexander's sexual indifference toward her. "Perhaps he'll want me once I've had the baby."

"Perhaps," said Dante, not really understanding heterosexual attraction, their erotic behavior as enigmatic to him as he imagined homosexual desire was to straights. Jai Jai had gained very little weight, and pregnancy had given her features a lush softness and her skin a glow she had never before had. "You look more beautiful than ever," Dante said, sincere in his compliment and wanting to reassure her.

"Has he said anything to you," Jai Jai asked, "about how he feels toward me?" Jai Jai meant Alexander. Jai Jai, who could love herself only when she was being loved, was frantic to know what Alexander felt about her. Since the accident in Mazatlán (which was how Jai Jai referred to it in her own mind) Alexander had refused all her attempts at intimacy—sexual or conversational. Dante had spent more time with him than Jai Jai had, and Jai Jai was jealous of their relationship. Alexander, who had always felt uncomfortable around homosexual men and who had once fired his first wife's butler because he found him too effeminate, had developed respect for Dante because of his cool and efficient behavior in the critical hours following Sergei's death.

Dante, too, had changed. Always flamboyant, always in search of conventions to break, he no longer wanted to shock for the sake of shocking. He had thought of leaving Jai Jai, but Alexander had asked him to stay with her through the birth of the child, and Dante, who had an extremely strong sense of loyalty, had agreed. Once the baby was born, though, Dante promised himself that he would create a life that had more substance than the endless pursuit of self-gratification. In Mazatlán he had seen where self-indulgence ended, and he had learned from it. He knew that people would find it hard to believe, but he was basically a nice person. He wanted to be good, to be kind, to be caring; he wanted, if he could have it, a happy ending for himself.

"Alexander doesn't care about me. He sees me only because of the baby," said Jai Jai. "He doesn't care if I'm dead or alive."

"He got you out of Mexico safely. He bought you this apartment," Dante said, gesturing at the luxurious rooms. "He gives you anything you want—furs, jewels, clothes. What more do you want?"

"Love," said Jai Jai, echoing an earlier conversation. "Or even hate. If he hated me, he could love me again."

She waited for Dante to make a comforting reply, to reassure her, to soothe her anxiety. When he didn't, she supplied one herself. "He loved me once. He'll love me again. I'll make him love me," she said.

Jai Jai spoke with a bravery she didn't feel. His indifference was crushing her. Against his indifference she had no weapons.

Jai Jai's daughter was born in March in the fashionable American Hospital in Paris. She named the child Jacqueline after her mother, and it was the only decision concerning the baby Jai Jai was allowed to make. Every other decision was made by Alexander, who paid the same kind of detailed attention to Jai Jai and the coming baby that he lavished on the acquisition, construction and running of one of his hotels. The baby was born in Paris because Alexander wanted it to be. He bought an apartment on the elegant Avenue Foch, and Jai Jai and her baby would live there; he staffed it, had the head of the decorating department of his French company decorate it, hired a baby nurse only after interviewing eight candidates sent to him by an exclusive Anglo-French agency, personally selected the obstetrician, a distinguished man who had attended the births of the children of the shah of Iran, and even specified the airy corner hospital room Jai Jai was to occupy.

Alexander stage-managed the birth so that by the time Jai Jai's confinement had come, it had acquired the trappings of a royal accouchement. The room Jai Jai occupied had been redecorated as far as the hospital rules allowed. The walls had been painted a soft apricot, hospital furniture had been moved out and replaced with antiques of Alexander's choice and hospital linens had been replaced by flower-printed sheets and towels from an elegant shop on the Avenue Montaigne. Stacks of glossy magazines from New York, Paris and London and the newest fiction and non-fiction best-sellers were attractively arranged in baskets and on tabletops. Tubs of spring plants—tulips, freesias, lilies of the valley, azaleas, and narcissus—reminded Jai Jai painfully of her wedding night.

The birth itself was entirely normal, healthy, uncomplicated. The emotional events surrounding it were not.

Alexander Raimont was Jai Jai's first visitor. He, who never carried anything, not a briefcase, not a raincoat, not an envelope, arrived with both arms full. He set a terra-cotta pot of white orchids on the table next to Jai Jai's bed and handed her a package the size of a thick paperback book, wrapped in a fine quality handmade rag paper the faint creamy color of eggshells and tied with twine the color of straw. He had even thought to bring a pair of small gold scissors.

"Open it," he said, standing by the bed. He never sat when he could stand. It made Jai Jai nervous as if he couldn't wait to leave her. It lent an edgy air to their meetings, and whenever he sat down, Jai Jai always took it as proof of her desirability. It was one of the wordless competitions between them that gave their affair such an irresistible electric undercurrent.

Jai Jai clipped the twine, unwrapped the thick paper

wrapping. A simple box of dove-gray suede lined with white doeskin held a dazzling necklace of emerald beads separated by diamond rondels.

"It's incredible. Beautiful," said Jai Jai, picking up the necklace and caressing the jewels with her fingers, running them sensuously through her hands. The workmanship was so flexible that the sinuously strung beads moved more like fabric than stones mined from the earth. It was everything—and more than—Jai Jai had imagined when she had described to Elie Koster her heart's desire. She had been greedily impatient for her gift and had thought about it often. Then, one weekend in Acapulco, Alexander had said that Elie had obtained the first of the beads, had shown them to him and that they were everything, green velvet fire, that emeralds should be. But after that Alexander had never mentioned the necklace again, and Jai Jai had never asked, queries about gifts offending her. Now, here, after the sequence of unimaginable events, here they were. Perhaps, Jai Jai allowed herself to think, he does love me, does want me.

"Please put them on for me," Jai Jai asked, holding the necklace out to Alexander. She leaned forward and lifted her hair from the nape of her neck. She expected to feel his fingers on her hair and at the back of her neck, a touch that would lead to a caress, and she was surprised when she didn't. Instead, Alexander crossed the room and brought her a hand mirror from her makeup table.

He held the mirror while Jai Jai, turning the necklace back to front, clasped its complicated safety catch herself. Instead of feeling treasured, Jai Jai felt as she sometimes did with Alexander, the most excluded at the moment she expected to feel closest. Jai Jai arranged the necklace, admired it in the mirror and made herself smile. "It's the most beautiful necklace in the world. Thank you." Alexander watched her watch herself, and the look in his eyes was as admiring and detached as if he were viewing a painting he admired but didn't care to buy.

"Shall I ring for the baby to be brought in?" asked Jai Jai, wanting to be close to him, wanting to touch him and be touched by him.

"Please," said Alexander, "although I saw her before I came in."

"And?" Jai Jai was surprised that Alexander had already seen Jacqueline, but she realized she shouldn't have been surprised by anything Alexander Raimont did.

Jai Jai thought her baby was the most beautiful baby in the world. Her hair was the same tawny color as Jai Jai's, she had Jai Jai's emerald-green eyes and her head was oversized in proportion to her narrow-boned body. Jai Jai was anxious to hear what Alexander thought.

"She has a Raimont face," Alexander said. "A Raimont mouth and Raimont hands."

There was a knock on the door, and a nurse came in with Jacqueline, drowsy, wrapped in white swaddling. She went to the bed, intending, as usual, to hand the infant to its mother. Instead, Alexander held out his arms and took the child from the nurse.

"I'll hold her," he said. The nurse left the room.

"I'm amazed," said Jai Jai. "I never imagined you holding a baby." Alexander did not answer.

"Liliane will be here later," he said. "And so will Alix and Yale. And Dante asked me to ask if there's anything special you'd like him to bring."

"Nothing," said Jai Jai, "but thank him for asking." Alexander moved, about to leave. Jai Jai wanted him to stay. "What about the necklace?" she asked. "What should I do with it?" Jai Jai didn't want to part from her necklace—a sign perhaps that Alexander still loved her even though he wouldn't say so—but she didn't want to have it when Liliane and Alix arrived. She didn't want them to be jealous of her.

"I'll take it back to the vault," Alexander said, taking the necklace and returning it to its box. "When you leave the hospital, go to the Morgan, the bank next door to Van Cleef and Arpels, and give them your signature. All you'll need to do is call them whenever you want to wear it."

"Thank you, Alexander, for the necklace," Jai Jai said. "Thank you." Then she asked the question she would have given anything—even her emerald necklace—not to have asked: "Do you love me?"

Alexander rang for the nurse, waited in silence for her return, surrendered Jacqueline to her and, without in any way having touched or kissed Jai Jai, wished her a pleasant day. He left Jai Jai alone in her luxurious room; alone with the question she wished she had never asked, alone with the question he never answered.

Much later, when all the visitors had left, Jai Jai rang and asked to see Jacqueline. She wanted to be alone with her baby.

"I'm sorry," said the nurse. Jai Jai thought she seemed somewhat uncomfortable.

"It's too late?" Jai Jai asked, thinking there might be some hospital rule about hours she was unaware of.

"Mr. Raimont asked that we bring the baby from the nursery only when he himself is here," the nurse said, unable to meet Jai Jai's eyes. After an awkward pause she asked if there were anything else Jai Jai wanted.

"No," answered Jai Jai, thinking of all the things she wanted but couldn't have. "Nothing, thank you."

The nurse bade her goodnight and left, closing the door behind her, leaving Jai Jai by herself. Her baby, Jai Jai realized, was not even her baby. Jacqueline was a Raimont baby. That made all the difference in the world, and there was nothing she could do about it.

∾ FOURTEEN ∾

In June, Jai Jai and Yale began a liaison. In July, Yale and Alix separated. In August, Jai Jai and Yale reinvented glamour.

In August in St. Tropez pleasure is measured by the degree of abandon. The quest for it occupies twenty-four hours a day: around the Byblos pool or in its bar decorated with real leopard skins; in the villas of movie stars and dress designers, businessmen and playboys; at quayside, where the gleaming yachts are separated by meager inches separating one teak-decked beauty from the next; at the Mouscardins, the Sénéquier or discos, which rise and fall in style as quickly and predictably as the sun rises and sets.

Coexisting with the fashionable frenzy are the open-air markets, under traditional large square umbrellas, where the produce of Provence—black olives, white cheeses, red tomatoes, green peppers and beans and bulbs of garlic with white, mauve-streaked papery skins, vats of golden-green olive oil and the morning's catch, *oursins* and mussels and the tiny crabs called *favouilles* and all the ingredients for a fine bouillabaisse, *rascasses, girelle, congre, vive* and *rouget*, are kept wet and colorful in the shade by the black-garbed Frenchwomen who, like generations before them, have pursued a living geared to the sun, the soil, the sea, exempt from the fads and fashions that have transformed St. Tropez from a simple fisherman's port to one of the most famous summer resorts in the world.

Jai Jai and Yale had taken a villa in the enclave between the citadel and the port. Situated on a hill covered with wild thyme, the view from the bleached-wood deck surrounding the pool was a panorama of whitewashed houses with terra-cotta tiled roofs and, beyond, the long arm of the Mole Jean Reveille guarding and half-embracing the small harbor. Dante, wanting to leave his old life but not yet having found a new one, accepted Jai Jai's invitation to be their houseguest. Jacqueline, now five months old, cared for since birth by Alexander and Alix, was in Southampton for the summer with her nurse, Miss Cooper, an English-woman of middle age, who ate oranges, neatly arranging the peels in ashtrays for the maids to discard, while reading the novels of Barbara Cartland in her free hours. Jai Jai and Yale, now living openly together, installed themselves and their wardrobes in the villa and began a month of entertaining and being entertained.

The summer of 1977 had for Yale and Jai Jai an F. Scott Fitzgerald splendor. The luxuries of time and money and the company of stylish companions seemed untouched by memories of blood and premonitions of punishment. Jai Jai and Yale together achieved what separately neither had quite been able to achieve: They became people other people imitated. When Jai Jai wore gold high-heeled sandals with a bikini at noon, she launched a style that crossed the Atlantic and was worn the next summer at American beaches by women who had never heard of her. Yale's habit of pouring only one round from a bottle of Dom

Pérignon '69 and discarding the rest appeared in print in London and New York. While it never appeared in print and while no one could afford to imitate it, their custom of making love to each other while Jai Jai wore her fabulous emeralds was gossiped about.

"Is it really true?" asked Mignonne Mireille, a film actress known for her intelligence and business acumen, as well as for her cat-shaped eyes and ballerina's legs. "That she keeps the emeralds on while they . . ."

"Absolutely," said her companion, Paul d'Arches, her former lover and then as now her all-time best friend. "Dante told me that Yale had shown him the marks on his body."

"How very erotic," said Mignonne, who had an unconscious habit of sucking on the eight-karat diamond ring her last husband had given her, "how very decadent."

"Don't take the emeralds off," Yale had said early in their liaison, and Jai Jai, her child an ocean away, her lover gone, was sad beneath her smile.

It was nine o'clock in the morning on a June day in the Belgravia house. Alix was in Maryland, and they had the house to themselves. Jai Jai and Yale had been up all night at a masked ball, and Jai Jai had worn her emeralds that night for the first time. Cole Whitelaw's intention had been to duplicate the Beaux-Arts balls of Paris in the fifties, and the ball had been a great success. Cocaine had been passed on black Lalique mirrors, Russian vodka was mixed with French champagne to make a drink of Cole's own devising and marijuana and hashish cigarettes were rolled in gold-tipped papers stamped with the initials which Cole incorporated in his designs. A sound system as elaborate as any installed in a disco was turned up so loud that the leaves on the hanging plants vibrated with the pulsing sounds of hard rock.

They had come to revel, to see and be seen, to have their existence noted and validated. There were society beauties in thousand-dollar dresses, rock stars in glitter makeup and punk chic, men and women and boys and girls of uncertain sexuality who lived to be where the action was, investment bankers drawn to the lights, show biz agents, managers, performers, the fashion Mafia, designers, manufacturers, editors and publicists, writers, reporters, photographers and, wraithlike, a young man, slender as a skeleton, considered the best lighting designer in the world who varnished his nails green and swallowed Quaaludes with Campari. The party was lavishly photographed and described in gossip columns on both sides of the Atlantic. People who only read about it would think they had missed something.

It was the kind of party Alix and Yale would have fought over. He would have wanted to go; she would have wanted to stay away, and however the conflict would have been resolved, neither would have been happy. There was no such conflict with Jai Jai; in the months following Jacqueline's birth Jai Jai was driven by a compulsive restlessness, a need to be in constant movement, an appetite for unceasing distraction. Their affair, begun within two months of Jacqueline's birth, had made them automatically notorious and had attracted to them a group of people, rich, fashionable, rootless, restless, creative or desiring to seem creative, who admired their flouting of the rules, their stylish conduct of an international scandal. Admiration and envy fueled Jai Jai and Yale, and they were conspirators with a delicious secret. Yale was beginning to find out what he had always secretly suspected: that once he had enough money and once he had met the right people, he could invent a new self. That new self, to which nothing was impossible and for which no boundaries existed, became the grand obsession of his life and, eventually, the sole focus of his existence.

Jai Jai had worn her fabulous emeralds for the first time at the masked ball, and they had attracted attention, envy and admiration. Now, the next morning, Yale, wanting somehow to celebrate his new self, told her to keep the emeralds on.

"I want you to wear them," he said, "while I make love to you."

So naked, except for two hundred and fifty thousand dollars' worth of emeralds, Jai Jai looked into her lover's eyes, smiled and invited his caresses. By the same night all London knew of Yale and Jai Jai's latest extravagant fantasy. Yale, unable to keep a secret, had confided in Cole Whitelaw.

In the beginning, the liaison was known to only a few, but like the ripples caused by a stone thrown into still water, the knowledge and the gossip spread. In classic fashion, Alix, Yale's wife, was one of the last to know. Alix found out from Corinne de Sancheval, who had debated with herself and finally decided that Alix would hear it eventually and that it would be better to hear it from a friend than an enemy.

It was well known that Corinne de Sancheval had once been a Yakov mistress, not at all a past to be sneered at, for the Yakovs, one of the oldest, richest Jewish mercantile families in Europe, were noted for the high personal qualities of the mistresses they chose and the generous way they treated them not only during the course of the affair but afterward as well. Attractive apartments were purchased in the mistress' name, and the furnishings were elegant and expensive. There were gifts of jewels and stocks and bonds, as well as bank accounts into which monthly sums were deposited. No Yakov mistress was ever put into the position of having to ask for money. In addition, the financial advice and guidance of the Yakov banks were available both during and after the affair.

Corinne was the daughter of a prosperous *haut bourgeois* family from Touraine. In the summer she turned twenty, Corinne was vacationing in Biarritz with a school chum, properly chaperoned by her friend's older married sister, when she caught the eye of Esau Yakov, then in his early thirties and in the process of being groomed by his uncle to take over eventually as head of the Paris branch of the Yakov family. Quite properly, as such things go, Esau entertained Corinne and her friend at teas and dinners and, when assured by Corinne that his attentions were not offensive to her, went to her father and proposed the terms of a liaison. The father, being both French and practical, after consulting his lawyer, consented, and Corinne moved to Paris under the protection of Esau.

The affair stood the place of a finishing school, turning Corinne from a well-bred young lady from the provinces into a graceful, stylishly turned-out Parisienne. In the course of her affair with Esau all of Corinne's most attractive qualities—an innate kindness, a sweetness of character and a compassionate intelligence—were heightened, while her less attractive qualities—a certain humorlessness and a youthful predisposition toward self-centeredness—were muted and even, to an extent, overcome. By the time, four years later, the liaison had run its course Corinne had become a most elegant, most desirable woman.

Her marriage to Raoul de Sancheval, a union blessed by Corinne's parents, her lover, Esau, and the church itself, was to begin happily and become, over the years, a source of joy to husband and wife and to everyone fortunate enough to meet them. Raoul de Sancheval had established in the late 1950s one of the first public relations firms in France. In fact, in the press he was referred to as the man who had introduced modern public relations to Europe. Raoul, son of a Paris businessman, had gone to the Columbia School of Journalism, where he had found that his journalistic talents lay in the feature area rather than in so-called hard news. He found it difficult to write a lead with the who, what, when, where and why. But human interest, the so-called soft news—interviewing personalities, celebrities and wives of politicians, social events, commencements, publicity stunts, fashion shows—came easily to him, and he invariably got the highest grades in his class in feature writing. Raoul's real talent, his real interest, was in people, and that talent became the basis of his business. In America, in the 1950s, the dollar-and-cents value of skillful public relations had already been established; in France at that time public relations was virtually unheard of. Raoul, a Frenchman, knew that his idea of starting a public relations firm in Paris was sure to be a struggle, but he missed France and was convinced that eventually the French would come to see the merits of the service he offered.

In the beginning Raoul's only clients were the European subsidiaries of American companies, and even they were difficult to enlist since if they wanted European public relations, they tended to prefer setting up their own public relations divisions. It was a struggle to convince them that a European understood Europeans best, but after several lean years Raoul had a small but choice list of American clients. Gradually they were joined by French companies, and Raoul's stubborn persistence was rewarded.

Raoul's marriage to Corinne in the mid-sixties brought

him not only an excellent wife but also a superb business partner. Unable, to her great sorrow, to have children, Corinne went to work with her husband, and the company and its clients and their increasingly wide circle of friends and acquaintances had lavished on them the care and affectionate attention Corinne would have given her children. Corinne brought to the company a talent for thoughtfulness and an instinctive understanding of how to make people feel relaxed, desirable and important, while Raoul had a gift for presenting to the public the best face his clients had to offer. Together Corinne and Raoul prospered, although they never became rich, never really caring about amassing money. They lived well, though, and went and were welcomed everywhere.

Their relationship with Raimont began in 1967, when they handled European publicity and public relations for the opening of a Raimont hotel in Marbella. Travel editors and writers, the fashion press, feature editors, magazine and newspaper reporters and journalists, a variety of celebrities and titled and conspicuous jet-setters were invited to the opening of the hotel, and thus, attention and positive coverage were assured. The Marbella Raimont became a place to go and a place to be seen, and Raoul and Corinne became, as a result of their effective work, European press and publicity representatives for all the Raimont chain. Whenever any of the Raimonts were in Paris, Raoul and Corinne entertained for them, and a personal as well as a business relationship developed. Raoul, in age between Sergei and his father, was close to both, while Corinne, about a decade older than Alix, shopped and lunched with her and grew very fond indeed of her. Corinne was, therefore, placed in a difficult situation over the weekend in June when Yale Warrant arrived in Paris and invited Corinne and Raoul to dine.

"Alix and I have just separated," he said. "There's someone I want you to meet."

Corinne had not known of the separation and wondered why she was hearing it from Yale rather than Alix. Nevertheless, she agreed to meet Yale and his new friend at Maxim's, the highest-profile restaurant in Paris and a particular Raimont favorite. Whatever Yale was doing, he was not keeping it a secret.

Corinne was shocked that Yale's new friend was Jai Jai. No introductions were necessary. Corinne, who thought she had seen everything, who thought nothing could shock her, was shocked. She had first met Jai Jai when she had been Alexander's mistress. Then, when Jai Jai had married Sergei, Corinne had entertained for them in Paris.

Corinne had, at the time, admired Jai Jai—certainly for her great beauty but even more for the sure way she had become the mistress of a rich and powerful man and then made a dazzling marriage to his son and heir. It was the plot of a fairy tale, a very sophisticated fairy tale, and if Jai Jai had, in fact, been shrewdly calculating, her demeanor, pleasing and unpretentious, revealed no hard edges of ambition. Now, seated across a dinner table from Jai Jai in her latest role as Sergei Raimont's widow and Yale Warrant's mistress, Corinne was shocked and slightly afraid of her. For a moment Corinne had an impulse to get up and walk out. She resented being put in the middle of an impossibly embarrassing position. She decided against it; she had no taste for a public scene. She was also, she admitted to herself, curious.

"Why did you invite me," asked Corinne, "and here of all places?" She gestured at the beautiful room, the elegantly dressed diners, many of whom she knew.

"People are going to know soon enough that Alix and I are divorcing," said Yale. "Jai Jai and I are getting married."

"Hasn't this happened very fast?" asked Corinne.

"We knew how we felt about each other for a long time," said Yale and then, turning to Jai Jai, added, "haven't we?"

She did not answer with a word, simply with a nod.

"Aren't you going to wish us well?" Yale asked Corinne. He could not keep his eyes off Jai Jai; he kept turning to look at her as if he were afraid she would suddenly no longer be there. Corinne was disconcerted; Yale was talking to her, but she felt he was not really even at the same table with her; he was somewhere else, somewhere with Jai Jai, somewhere with his dreams of Jai Jai.

"I don't know what to say," said Corinne candidly. The usual wishes for a happy future seemed grossly inappropriate.

"She's extraordinary, isn't she?" asked Yale, apparently oblivious to Corinne's discomfort.

"Yes, beautiful," said Corinne. Whatever had happened to Jai Jai did not show; she was more magnetically lovely than ever, her green eyes glittering in smoky depths, her chiseled bones underlying her broad forehead and slanting cheekbones; she was perfectly made up, but it was impossible to tell what was makeup and what was the gift of nature. Jai Jai's hair had gold highlights in the flattering restaurant lighting, and later, when Corinne tried to remember what she had worn, she couldn't. Whatever the dress had been, it had been so chosen as to disappear from memory, leaving only the haunting afterimage of Jai Jai's extraordinary beauty.

"We were shocked by Sergei's death, Raoul and I," Corinne said, feeling that letting Sergei's death go unmentioned would have been unforgivably cold even though she had heard all the gossip surrounding those moments in Mazatlán, gossip that called it suicide, gossip that called it murder, gossip that said that Alexander had killed his son, that Dante had done it, that Jai Jai had done it, that a Mexican whore had done it, gossip that raged on and on. "Everyone who knew Sergei still grieves for him."

"I received your note of condolence," said Jai Jai. "It meant a great deal to me."

"Raoul and I are very sad," Corinne said and, wanting to change the subject to something neutral, spoke of the violent controversy in Paris over the design of the new Pompidou art museum, the Beaubourg. The conversation remained resolutely impersonal until coffee was served.

Dinner ended, and while Corinne and Jai Jai waited for Yale to retrieve their wraps from the attendant, Jai Jai said to Corinne in a soft voice, "Please don't think I'm terrible."

"I don't know what to think," Corinne said.

"I can't help myself. I'm a victim," Jai Jai said. "A victim of victims."

Yale returned with their wraps before Corinne could respond, and the exchange was cut off. Jai Jai's mysterious words haunted Corinne. She couldn't sleep that night. She didn't understand what Jai Jai meant by saying that she was the victim of victims, nor did she understand why Yale and Jai Jai were deliberately behaving in a way that would attract envy and resentment. Didn't she understand that envy could be dangerous? And didn't Jai Jai and Yale understand, whatever they wanted, that they were publicly humiliating Alix and Alexander, who was still supporting Jai Jai? Didn't they realize that with the rich there was no way of winning?

∾ FIFTEEN ∾

"I'd like to watch you with another man," Yale told Jai Jai one night in August in the moments before they surrendered to sleep. "I've been thinking about it for a long time."

"We promised we'd always tell each other everything," Jai Jai said, not revealing how she felt, a technique she had learned from Alexander.

"I'd like to watch you with Paul. I've already suggested it to him," Yale said. "How do you feel about it?" They had also promised each other that one would never impose his or her wishes on the other without his or her consent.

Jai Jai remembered her long-ago fantasies about Ian and J. Anson Herron on the *Bel Air*. It had been only two summers ago. It seemed to her a lifetime. Now, in St. Tropez, those fantasies could come true, and Jai Jai was reluctant.

"Jai Jai, you haven't answered. How would you feel about it? Not a threesome. Just the two of you."

"I'd like to, Yale, if it would please you," Jai Jai said finally.

"Only if it pleases you as well," Yale said. "Tell me it would make you happy, too."

"Yes," Jai Jai said, and wondered why she was lying. Perhaps it was only half a lie.

Yale chose Jai Jai's lovers, and at first Yale merely watched. In time, it seemed normal to him to kiss and caress Jai Jai at the same time her lovers did because watching them excited him, too. In doing so, Yale unavoidably touched them. In the beginning the contact of Yale's hand with a man's arm was a brief accident, a fleeting touch followed by an immediate pulling away. It had been more than a year since he'd made love to a man. After a few visits to Oliver Holborn's, Yale had stopped. What he told himself was that he was bored and disappointed. What he feared was that if he continued, he'd never be able to stop.

"Don't fight yourself," Roman Bartok said one evening toward the very end of August, and he put his hand over Yale's and held it to him. "The real sin is resisting your own sensuality."

Roman Bartok was a propagandist of bisexual chic, a regular on the St. Tropez-Beverly Hills-Gstaad circuit. His memoirs, four volumes of them, of his erotic life had been hailed by contemporary critics. Roman wrote in English, his adopted language, and his volumes were translated into all the major European languages, as well as Japanese, where each volume had been a greater best-seller than the one before. He wrote exclusively of one subject—his own appetites—and in doing so, had become a hero of both avant-garde intellectuals and large numbers of more ordinary readers, who, if only in their fantasies, wanted to achieve the same degree of personal freedom Roman celebrated in his life and work.

A short, slight, elegantly put-together man, Roman was exceedingly vain of his physical appearance and spoken of as much for perfection of proportions and grace of his movements as for his ordinary literary gifts. Lying on a sofa in a Charvet robe, he dictated five hours a day Thursday through Saturday to the British secretary who had worked for him since the success of his first volume of memoirs published fourteen years before. Through his own earnings, the gifts of admirers, some of whom had been lovers, some of whom hadn't, and through shrewd investments in real estate and stock markets, Roman Bartok, son of a schoolmaster, a boy who had grown up in the hills of Czechoslovakia fifty kilometers west of the Ukrainian border in an agricultural village where white sheep and dappled cows grazed on green hills in a timeless bucolic dream, was a millionaire in half a dozen currencies. The fear that haunted him was that he was not an artist but a fraud, and he lived in terror that his secret would somehow be revealed and the audience that worshiped would then revile him. A spiritual descendant of D. H. Lawrence, Roman Bartok believed that erotic pleasure was the only purpose in life because only through erotic pleasure was man able to conquer the knowledge of the inevitability of his own death. Eros and Thanatos, he preached, were all that mattered. And Eros and Thanatos were the names he had given to the two Persian cats he kept as pets. It was considered daring, the very essence of chic, just as Roman had intended.

Roman encouraged Yale to explore his impulses rather than suppress them. "There are only two possibilities," Roman would say. "If you don't love, you die."

At first Yale would make love to Roman only when Jai Jai was there. And at first it was apparent that Yale preferred Jai Jai's regarding Roman an accessory but not a principal to their lovemaking. Then gradually it became clear to all of them that Yale preferred Roman. Jai Jai, who had always imagined that being made love to by two men at the same time would make her feel more of a woman, found that the opposite was true. She felt like less of a woman, and the more Yale insisted that he loved her, the less she liked herself.

Jai Jai had hoped that aura of glamour that surrounded her and attracted so much attention would attract Alexander, but apparently it didn't because she never saw him and only rarely spoke to him. When he did telephone, he spoke mainly of Jacqueline, of how quickly she was growing, how pretty she was, and now, exactly a year since Sergei's death, Jai Jai had almost given up hope.

She had flown back from the South of France in the beginning of September, from the Côte d'Azur airport in Nice to de Gaulle in Paris. She was crossing the arrivals terminal with Dante, Yale and Roman and two porters with four carts stacked high with luggage when she happened to look up, and there, coming at right angles toward her, was Alexander with three men who looked like business associates. They were deep in conversation when, at the same instant that Jai Jai had happened to look up, Alexander did, too. Their eyes met for a very long moment, and then, not having spoken a word to each other, they continued, each in a separate group toward the terminal exits.

The Rolls Yale had ordered was at curbside, and while the porters loaded the luggage, Alexander detached himself from his group and came over. He exchanged greetings with Roman, whom he had never met but whom he recognized from photographs. A man with money, Alexander admired people with talent. He was impressed by celebrities, particularly creative people who were talented, successful and rich. He barely acknowledged Yale's presence: he was pleased that Yale and Alix were separated, and he thought that in the long run, despite her temporary unhappiness, Alix would be far better off without him. Then, turning to Jai Jai, he said, "I've never seen you look so beautiful."

Jai Jai smiled her thanks for the compliment and then, the baggage having been loaded, disappeared into the back of the Rolls. She knew that she looked particularly well, tanned and rested after the month in St. Tropez. And she knew something Alexander had no way of knowing: that Yale and Roman were interested in each other, not her. But it didn't matter because from Alexander's point of view, it looked as if Jai Jai were again traveling with two lovers, and this time one was a rival and the other an international celebrity.

Jai Jai was not at all surprised when Alexander called later that week and invited her to spend the weekend with him on a friend's yacht anchored in Beaulieu. In fact, she had been expecting it.

Two people who cared only about the present, Jai Jai and Alexander were conspirators against the past, and they enjoyed a weekend of greedy pleasures—lovemaking, dining and drinking, swimming and sunning, shopping in the boutiques that ringed the Beaulieu yacht basin, gambling in Beaulieu's casino, smaller, less wedding-cake elegant, more casually intimate than Monte Carlo's—and never once referred to Sergei, to Mazatlán, to Yale, to Roman, to their chance encounter at de Gaulle. On Monday Jai Jai returned on a commercial flight to Paris, and Alexander went to Mexico City, where plans for the grand opening of the Raimont/Mazatlán Playa Blanca more than a year off were being made. The goal, from Alexander's point of view, was to outdo the successful opening the winter before of the Bequia Raimont.

"You were seen in Beaulieu," Yale said when Jai Jai returned to Paris. She had left for the weekend without telling him where she was going. "Britta and Pierre-Gilles were having lunch at the African Queen; they saw you boarding a yacht. I saw Britta last night at a dinner party. She said you looked very happy," Yale said. "You and Alexander."

Jai Jai was in her dressing room, an astringent clay mask hardening on her face preventing her from answering. The expression in her eyes showed acknowledgment, nothing more, nothing less, of Yale's words.

"We're going to the fragrance party tonight," Yale said, confirming an earlier appointment they'd made. Yale and Jai Jai's mail was filled with invitations. Every day they poured in, inviting them to cocktail parties, receptions, dinners, screenings, fashion showings, art openings, all the frenetic activity, private and commercial, that fills the autumn social calendars of *le tout Paris*. Jai Jai, imprisoned behind the mask, nodded.

"When will you see him again?" Yale asked, knowing Jai Jai couldn't answer. She permitted herself, so as not to crack the clay mask, only the tiniest trace of an expression, the merest hint of a smile, and she shrugged.

"Roman and I will pick up you and Dante at five-thirty," Yale said. Then, leaving her dressing room, he said, "Jai Jai, I really do think we ought to marry. It would be perfect, you know, the four of us . . . you and Alexander, me and Roman."

Alone, Jai Jai closed her eyes, covered them with cotton soaked in witch hazel to shrink the slight swelling that had surrounded them since the weekend. There was a split-second prickle of unshed tears behind her eyes. Dante had always told her she was an outlaw, and she had never thought so, but now she wondered. She lived in an apartment paid for by Alexander, wore clothes he bought and ate food he paid for. If he seemed only to want her when she belonged to someone else, perhaps she should marry Yale. . . .

The best thing about being an outlaw, Dante had always thought, was the freedom; the worst was the fear. A sexual outlaw, Dante had freedom of choice—of a young man for an encounter of the flesh, of an older man, riper, more experienced, as much or as little commitment as suited him at any moment. The fear was of growing old and undesirable, of ultimately losing the freedom. Lately Dante had begun avoiding the sun to preserve the youthful elasticity of his skin, undertaken stringent diets to combat a certain flabbiness and submitted to a regimen of vigorous exercise and deep massage for the sake of muscle tone. Dante had known too many desperate homosexuals, and he didn't want to become what he referred to bitterly as an old queen, drinking too much at night, shaking too much the next morning. He wanted, now that thirty-five was no longer a far-off impossibility, what he had promised himself in Mazatlán he wanted: to change his life.

Certain things had been obvious and easy. He had stopped going to the baths, steamy and anonymous, the same in Paris as in London, in Rome as in New York, and he no longer frequented gay bars in Pigalle, Chelsea and the West Village. He stayed away from Fire Island and Key West, Mykonos and Capri. He had no interest at all in changing his basic preferences—homoerotic preferences he had accepted and acknowledged since he had been twelve and enjoyed the advances of a professor of Romance languages from the university at Aix-en-Provence who was passing the summer at a rented villa near Dante's parents' house in Tuscany. Since that passionate twelfth summer Dante had concerned himself only with satisfying his immediate appetites; now, suddenly, he wanted to give rather than take, to build rather than enjoy and move on. The events in Mazatlán had profoundly affected Dante's outlook; there he had seen how far self-indulgence could lead, and it frightened him. Despite his flamboyant rebelliousness, Dante wanted to be a nice person.

He was intelligent, he knew, and energetic, and he needed a focus for his intelligence and energy. He was well traveled and well connected and well organized. He had quite a bit to offer but didn't know how to mobilize his assets, and it was in this nervous state of desiring change but not knowing how to achieve it that at the fragrance party he met Cole Whitelaw.

Cole was from a British family of intellectuals, public servants and clergymen. The Whitelaw family tree had had room for several distinguished but discreet pederasts. Cole was another, although, as he was fond of saying, he was hardly distinguished and most certainly not discreet. As a result of one of his more flamboyant seasons, his family had disinherited him. But that had been in his rebellious youth, and a reconciliation had been effected, although, to the enormous relief of both Cole and his family, he spent little time at the family seat in Yorkshire.

"At the age of three," he always said, "I rearranged the furniture in my nursery, and I've never stopped." A designer and decorator trained at the Royal Academy of Art, Cole had done set design, first for repertory companies in the provinces, then in the West End and still later on Broadway. From set design, Cole turned to interior design for friends and then for both private and commercial clients. He had won the commission to design the interiors of the Air France fleet and, with the help of an orthopedist, had designed a typist's chair that was used in offices throughout the world.

As a designer Cole had undeniable ability; as a businessman he was a disaster. He was the despair of his accountants, forgetting both to pay bills and to submit them; when he did charge, he tended to underbill since the selection of a fabric, the treatment of a window, the degree of cant in a chair back was as automatic to him as breathing and therefore, in his eyes, neither rare nor valuable.

"I've done one of everything," said Cole to Dante the night they met at a cocktail party to launch a new perfume (the bottle had been designed by Cole), "and I'm old, tired and broke."

"You don't expect me to believe *that*," Dante said. Cole, who was thirty-seven and looked twenty-seven, was impeccably dressed, as he always was. He was the kind of man, Dante thought, whose pajamas don't wrinkle.

"Then you should believe approximately half," Cole amended, "because approximately half is true."

"I haven't done half of your idea of half," Dante said.

"I've cultivated indolence, and I've ended up exactly where you have: old, tired, broke."

Cole smiled. "Let's have dinner," he suggested. "Perhaps two wrongs will, in this case, make a right."

Dante, accustomed to instant relationships with equally instant life spans, had never allowed himself the luxury of allowing time for a friendship to develop. He dined with Cole, lunched with him, went to the theater and ballet with him, and by the time he made love with Cole he knew him, knew his strengths and weaknesses. Cole was loyal, almost embarrassingly honest; he was impatient to a fault and had a quick temper, for which he made amends by equally quick apologies. He was more than generous—he squandered time, attention, affection and interest on those around him, and it was the first time Dante had enjoyed the pleasures of a generous companion.

"I'm beginning to think there might be a future for us," Cole said one day over a sandwich and coffee lunch in the small office he rented over a boutique on the Rue du Bac. "After all, you've put up with me this long, and I definitely am in need of help." In the months since they'd met, Dante had begun to impose a bit of order on the conduct of Cole's business affairs, straightening out his billings, collections and payments with the help of Cole's relieved accountant. He had even engaged a lawyer to inquire about the lack of royalties on the typist's chair patent. An orderly cash flow had begun to develop, and for the first time in Cole's life there was some semblance of stability in his business and personal existence. It had all been due to Dante, and Cole had appreciated it and thanked Dante.

"Cole, you know I wanted to do it. You know how I feel about you," Dante said. They had been together constantly except that Cole still kept his Kensington house and, in Paris, lived in a hotel room, while Dante, no longer living with Jai Jai on the Avenue Foch, had sublet a small flat in Montmartre. "Let's live together."

"I don't know . . ." Cole said hesitantly. He had said he wanted a permanent relationship, but now that Dante had put it into words, Cole felt himself pull back. It would be a major commitment, and Cole had always shunned commitment. To him, commitment meant growing up, and growing up meant getting old, losing freedom, being stale, boring, giving up the creativity that was more important to him than life itself. To Cole, making a commitment felt like the end of every thing, and he was afraid. He was torn between his feelings and his fears. He panicked and asked for time. "I need time to think."

"We're not getting any younger," Dante said, increasingly conscious of age, of lost opportunities. Dante thought of commitment not as losing but as gaining: stability, a center of life, security and freedom to grow and change with someone at his side growing and changing, too. He was disappointed that Cole was not as ready as he was to share a life. But he did not want to press him into a commitment until he was ready. Dante was particularly conscious that Cole, like everyone he knew at all well, homosexual or heterosexual, had been scarred in one way or another, was afraid in one way or another, even if the scars were well hidden and the fears invisible.

"I know," said Cole, also conscious of time passing, "but I've never lived with anyone. Part of me wants to . . . part of me is afraid." Cole paused. "Can you understand?"

"Of course," said Dante.

"You won't leave me, will you?" said Cole, suddenly anxious. "Just because I can't say yes right away?"

"No, I won't leave you," said Dante. He was very disappointed, but his feelings for Cole went deep. He was not about to throw them away because he didn't get what he wanted the minute he wanted it. "I'm not going to walk away."

Cole was relieved. He did not have to say anything; the expression on his face showed how he felt.

"Are you going back home to Tuscany for Christmas?" Cole asked. Dante's parents were still alive, and he was very attached to them.

"I do every year," said Dante. "I had hoped you'd come with me." Dante had wanted to introduce him to his parents. He had never done that. Although his parents certainly knew about his sexual preferences, they had long since accepted them, however reluctantly and unhappily.

"Roman Bartok has invited me to Cairo with him," said Cole, upset at having to reject Dante twice. "I've never been, and I'm looking forward to going."

"Then we won't see each other over the holidays," said Dante sadly.

"I've already promised I'd go," said Cole. He, too, was sad at the thought of spending the holidays without his lover. "And I want to go. I've always been attracted to Egyptian design. I thought I might get some ideas. I've been thinking of doing an Egyptian collection . . . furniture, perhaps, or fabric designs."

"It's a good idea," said Dante. As always, Cole was extraordinary in his ability to think of something new, something fresh. Dante was in awe of his creativity. It was getting late, and Dante put the paper wrapping from the sandwiches and disposable coffee containers into the trash. Getting up to leave, he said, "Merry Christmas, Cole. And I mean it sincerely."

"Merry Christmas," said Cole, and for a moment he had an impulse to tell Dante that he'd cancel Cairo, that he wanted to spend the holidays with him. But he wasn't ready to make that commitment. He wanted to go to Cairo, and what he finally said as Dante left was: "Let's have dinner the first night we're both back in Paris."

Dante walked the streets of Paris that afternoon with a happy realization that their relationship had come at lunch not to an ending but to a new kind of beginning.

In Cairo, the liaison that had begun in scandal ended in violence.

Istanbul merges East and West and is therefore partially accessible to Westerners. Cairo joins the Mideastern and African, the Mediterranean and the Nile, the cult of Isis overlaid with the worship of Allah. Its polyglot impenetrability causes Western visitors to feel isolated, threatened and free. Roman Bartok—attracted to Arab hospitality and cruelty, to the aura of fatalism and a tradition of funerary pomp, to the pervasive scent of rare spices, freshly ground coffee and the perfumes extracted from the flowers grown for that purpose in the Faiyum oasis gardens, the richness of the past and the fertile Nile Delta capable, with irrigation systems invented in antiquity, water wheels still drawn by oxen, of three harvests a year, contrasting with the poverty of a peasantry subsisting on onions, of Bedouins traveling from oasis to oasis, of beggars parading their afflictions in hopes of a coin—kept an apartment in Cairo. Located in a former royal palace between the British embassy and the El Tahrir bridge, Roman's top-floor apartment overlooked the Nile, where feluccas, the sailboats of Arab design, with their exotic, attenuated triangular sails, plied the brown waters of the river in maritime traffic as dense as the human traffic that thronged the streets and alleys of Cairo itself. Across the river, the view extended to the lush, green Tahrir gardens.

"There is nothing new in Egypt," Roman said. "Art, science, architecture—the Egyptians had it, or they invented it. They've seen it all before. Egypt is the only place I feel ordinary. Believe it or not, now and then, part of me craves ordinariness."

Roman invited Jai Jai and Yale to Cairo, and with Cole, they made a party of four. They had spent a night in Cairo and then in a Nile steamer had cruised to Luxor, formerly Thebes, capital of the ancient Egyptian empire. Roman himself was their guide to the Temple of Luxor, the open colonnaded court and pillared halls, the chapels of the gods and sanctuaries of the sun; he accompanied them to nearby Karnak, to the Great Temple of Amon-Ra built by the pharaohs of the Twelfth Dynasty and enlarged and splendidly adorned by the following generations.

" 'Only the grains of sand,' " Roman said, quoting Homer, " 'outnumber the wealth of Thebes.' You must imagine," Roman said, "what is no longer there: decor of gold and silver, gold plates on the gates glistening in the sun visible from afar, obelisks of pink granite and jewels both precious and semiprecious. You must imagine the scent of incense, visualize the gilded barques of the gods swaying on the shoulders of the priests and hear the sounds of the great masses seized by religious frenzy.

"History in other places is measured in centuries. In Egypt it is measured in millennia," Roman concluded. "And in Egypt, unlike the West, death is part of life. That attitude makes everything possible, nothing unforgivable."

But Roman was wrong, for it was in Cairo that the unforgivable happened.

In Cairo Jai Jai discovered the pleasures of concealment. She adopted the dress of Arab women and had made for herself robes and headdresses of fine white Egyptian cotton. Hiding her features, save for her eyes, outlined with kohl bought in a perfumer's in El Khalili, she moved silently, veiled, unobserved by others, yet able to observe as she pleased, unseen but seeing.

In Cairo, fifteen months after Sergei's death, Jai Jai was drifting—lonely and ashamed. She was the mother of a child she never saw; she was the mistress of a man who desired other men. She had seen Alexander twice since Beaulieu, and she was miserably aware that he never spoke of love, never kissed her on the mouth. When he made love to her, she felt he was following the dictates of a compulsion he hated but could not resist.

Dante no longer lived with her; by the end of August Jai Jai sensed his impatience to leave. He was living alone now in a sublet apartment, preferring to be alone rather than to be with her. It was a rejection that particularly hurt; if he had found someone else, Jai Jai might have understood. To be left for solitude was crushing. Not, in a certain way, that Jai Jai blamed him for wanting to leave her. She was an emotional chasm with nothing but a compulsion to be filled. It was an impossible demand to put upon a man who was a friend.

Jai Jai thought of Sergei and did not feel guilty. What she felt was worse: she felt empty. She needed to be paid attention to, to be desired and wanted. And everyone was ignoring her. Even, by now, Yale.

By late 1977 Yale Warrant was in trouble. In financial trouble and in sexual trouble.

Warrant, Charlton, Dover was in trouble. The shares, selling during the sixties at a high price/earnings ratio, had been dropping steadily on the London exchange. From a high of twelve pounds five the price of a share had declined to four pounds seven. Loan losses were running close to seventy million pounds, and the London Bank, which had granted WCD an advance facility the previous year of one hundred million, had been conducting a housekeeping. A team of accountants had been brought in at the demand of the bank to investigate the company's affairs. Their report was devastating: The banking unit, Yale's unit, had, they said, been run as an "in-house" bank which by the end of

November had advanced ninety-eight million dollars to companies in which WCD had an interest; the loan list, the accountants contended in particularly critical wording, consisted of a very small number of very large loans; further, they said, there had been a gross mismatching of maturity dates of assets and liabilities. They suggested the possibility, without accusing, that British law might have been broken with loans of WCD money to WCD-related companies to buy shares in the parent company. For the year, the accountants' report concluded, WCD had had a net loss of sixty-four million seven hundred thousand, almost twice as much as the thirty-four-million-two-hundred-thousand loss of the previous year.

Although the accountants' report stressed that there was no evidence that Mr. Warrant or any other of the WCD directors had derived personal benefit from any of the WCD transactions, it did make note of the fact that a house mortgage loan of three-hundred-fifty-thousand pounds had been made to Mr. Warrant for the purchase of a house in Belgravia.

The London Bank was pressing Yale's partners for his removal as president of the company before it would consider lending further sums. As the most highly publicized board member of WCD, Yale was the focus of the blame. Yale had at first turned down Roman's invitation to Cairo but had, rebelliously, decided to go. "They don't own me," he had said referring to his partners, the teams of investigating accountants and the bankers. "I didn't get rich to have to spend the Christmas holidays in London."

Once in Cairo, though, Yale was perpetually angry. He felt he had been cheated. "I should have sold my shares a year ago. I wanted to cash in then, but I let myself get talked out of it. I was worth millions. They promised me I'd be worth more millions if I held on. I shouldn't have listened."

Yale talked obsessively about money, about how unfair the criticisms of the accountants had been, about schemes to recoup his losses. He blamed Jai Jai.

"If it weren't for you and your extravagance, I could have retired and lived in luxury for the rest of my life."

Jai Jai learned not to respond to Yale's accusations because her responses, no matter how mildly phrased, drove

Yale into irrational, violent rages. The fact was that Alexander Raimont supported her and paid all her bills. Although he had never struck her, Jai Jai began to fear Yale just as she had feared Sergei, and she wondered what it was in her that drew passion, and its fiery companion violence, to her.

Financial pressures threatened Yale externally. Sexual pressure threatened him internally. It was becoming more and more difficult for him to maintain a façade of fashionable bisexuality as his desire became exclusively homosexual. That he had begun to prefer men to women did not disturb him as much as the dark enchantments his desires demanded. He could no longer control the morbidity of his needs and his inability to control them made him fear where they would lead.

He tried to conceal the change in him from Jai Jai, but her need for love and attention increased at the same rate as his physical distaste for her. At first she had liked, she said, the threesomes with Roman. She reveled in the attentions of two men at the same time. But gradually it became clear that Yale paid more attention to Roman than he did to her.

"I feel left out," Jai Jai had complained early that fall in Paris. "You pay more attention to Roman than you do to me."

"Jai Jai, your problem is that you're insatiable," Yale said. "You're just imagining it."

"I don't know," Jai Jai said hesitantly and then added, "perhaps you're right." She gave more weight to others' opinions of her than to her own feelings about herself and usually deferred.

"The one thing I have never experienced is death," said Roman, enjoying, as he always did, the impact of his most outrageous statements on his listeners. Jai Jai and Yale and Roman were spending the evening in an elegant brothel in old Cairo's Coptic district built over the site of the Roman fortress. The brothel, which Jai Jai had imagined would be seedy and depressing, was, in fact, as smart as the most luxurious nightclub in Paris or New York.

French wines and champagnes, *cuisine minceur*, pre-

pared by a chef hired away at an enormous salary from a
three-star Lyons restaurant, were available. Succulent vegetables and soft summer fruits, white peaches and tiny raspberries grown in the rich silty soil of the Nile Delta were
displayed in living still lifes on silver epergnes arranged on
buffets spread with starched white linen tablecloths. The
entertainment and the decor were the best Egypt's musicians and dancers, designers and architects could provide.
The walls were of blue-and-white faience tile in gorgeous,
intricate Arab designs; Oriental carpets in stained-glass colors made the floors soft and silky beneath the feet. Guests
sat on comfortable leather hassocks arranged around low,
round brass tables, and candlelight flickered through the
punched-out and filigreed openings of tin lanterns, casting
their illuminations in lozenge-shaped pinpricks of light.
Musicians played hypnotic, repetitive Arab melodies on
wind and stringed instruments whose names were unknown
to Jai Jai. A belly dancer, as graceful as a ballerina, as
seductive as a whore, performed steps perhaps choreo-
graphed two thousand years before to delight a pharaoh.
Now and then guests excused themselves to sample the
pleasures of the rooms upstairs. The unobtrusive traffic up
and down was the only sign that this was a brothel and not
simply an elegant and expensive nightclub.

"Shall I choose for you?" Roman asked Yale. With Jai
Jai's unspoken consent, Roman and Yale had begun to
speak as if she weren't present. It was comforting to Jai Jai
to have decisions made for her just as concealment in her
white robes was comforting.

"I'll go with you," Yale said. They rose, leaving Jai Jai
alone at the table. Just as they excluded her from the conversation, they excluded her from their bed, and Jai Jai was
relieved to be excluded. She sipped champagne from a crystal tulip solicitously filled by a waiter wearing a white mess
jacket and a red tarboosh. She had at first resisted the suggestion of a visit to a brothel, but Yale and Roman had
persuaded her that one had not truly experienced Cairo
until one had visited a brothel.

"I didn't think you were a puritan," Roman had said.

"I didn't think so either," Jai Jai had answered.

"There is a great deal to be said on behalf of commercial
sex," said Roman, habitually tending to intellectualize his

behavior. "After all, we pay to satisfy our other appetites. We buy food to assuage hunger, liquid for our thirsts, art to gratify our aesthetic hungers. Why shouldn't we pay to satisfy our erotic appetites?"

Roman's arguments were not, however, what persuaded Jai Jai to go to the nightclub. It was her fear, irrational and frightening to her, of finally losing Yale. Yale made all the superficial gestures of love and attention. Being with Yale gave her an existence and an identity. Jai Jai, who once had never doubted that she could have any man she wanted, now feared that if she lost Yale, she would never again see desire or even its counterfeit in a man's eyes. Yale wanted to visit the brothel; therefore, Jai Jai accompanied him, not wishing to offend him with her refusal.

Yale and Roman had been gone almost half an hour when Jai Jai began to look for them. The maître d', as handsome as a 1940s matinee idol, directed Jai Jai to the staircase leading upstairs. The soft white slippers of unborn kidskin which Jai Jai wore under her robes made no sound on the white marble stairs. At the landing, a woman, soignée as a vendeuse in a house of haute couture in Paris, sat in a dove-gray velvet Louis Quatorze chair in front of a delicate lady's desk also in the style of the first of the great Louises.

"*Je cherche M. Warrant*," Jai Jai began, instinctively using French.

"No names, please," the woman answered, in an upper-class British accent, making Jai Jai slightly ill-at-ease. "You need only describe the people for whom you look."

"Two gentlemen," Jai Jai began, wondering from the woman's discreet use of the noun "people" how many women patronized these upstairs chambers. She described Yale's clean-cut American looks and Roman, small, wiry, tense.

"You will find them in Ebony and Ivory," the woman said, consulting a list hidden in a book bound with watered silk the color of hyacinths and gesturing toward a corridor that led away at a right angle from the landing.

The white marble flooring of the landing led to a corridor carpeted in densely loomed navy-blue wool. Crystal sconces on cream moiré walls cast soft, flattering light, and Jai Jai saw that each doorway was inscribed with a name:

Attar of Roses, Sultan's Dream, Harem, Pasha's Delight. Just past a room called Thorn was Ebony and Ivory. Jai Jai knocked, and the heavy door with a large brass knob centered in its four panels opened.

The carpet of the hexagonal room was black; the walls were white. In each of the six corners of the room stood a blackamoor in white satin shirt and knee breeches holding a flaming torch. Torchlight was the only source of illumination in the room, and at first Jai Jai thought the blackamoors were plaster statues. A moment later, when her eyes adjusted to the light, she realized they were alive—boys of eleven and twelve participating in a living tableau. Jai Jai wondered where they had come from, what kinds of houses or huts, what remote villages, whether their parents knew and, if they knew, approved or disapproved.

In the middle of the room was the bed that had given the chamber its name. Made of ebony inlaid with ivory carved in intricate Oriental patterns, the bed was eight feet square and had a canopy of ebony and ivory mirrored on the inside. White sheets and black furs, currently tangled, dressed the bed.

Roman sat cross-legged at the foot of the bed, which had been brought from China, where in earlier centuries it had been used for groups of opium smokers, and watched, rather like a spectator, interested, yet detached, the scene being played out in front of him. Yale was crouched over a child. The child was splayed out on his stomach, and with his left hand Yale had pinned the boy's wrists to the sheet above his head. In his right hand, Yale held an ivory riding crop with a switch of black horsehair. The boy was making whimpering, frightened sounds as Yale moved roughly above him.

"Stop!" Jai Jai screamed. "Stop!" She moved swiftly toward the bed and, taking Yale by surprise and off-balance, pulled him away from the boy with such force that Yale had to struggle to prevent himself from falling to the floor. Jai Jai took one of the fur throws and spread it over the boy. By then Yale had recovered.

"Get out of here!" Yale struck the crop into the cupped palm of his left hand hard enough to make a sharp, cracking sound. His face had turned heavy with extra blood pumped forcefully into it, propelled by anger and excitement.

"Yale, you don't know what you're doing!" Jai Jai was horrified at him, at herself, at where their recklessness had led.

"I know exactly what I'm doing," Yale answered. He had been thinking for a long time of combining pain with pleasure. Tonight he had decided to act upon his fantasies.

"You're abusing a child!" Jai Jai thought of Jacqueline.

"Jai Jai, get out of here," Yale said, cold, furious, turning on her, the crop raised in his hand. Jai Jai looked at Roman.

"You'd better go," said Roman. "Come on," he said, getting up and taking Jai Jai by the arm.

"If I go now," Jai Jai said looking directly at Yale, who met her gaze without flinching, "you will never, ever see me again."

"Good," he said, "because if I ever see you again, I'll kill you." Then he removed the fur throw from the boy, resumed the scene he had been enacting when Jai Jai first entered the room. The last thing Jai Jai heard as she closed the door behind her was the sound of the crop striking flesh.

She left Cairo early the next morning.

"I don't blame Jai Jai for leaving," Roman told Yale much later that same evening. He had waited for Yale to return to the apartment, and they were having a final glass of date brandy together before retiring. It was dawn, and the sun was beginning to rise over the desert, turning it, for a few moments, into an illuminated fantasy of gold and rose. "You've gone too far."

"You're wrong," said Yale. Never overweight, he had lost fifteen pounds since leaving Alix; he was strangely thin, and his eyes glowed feverishly. He no longer looked like an all-American, Ivy League banker but rather like a man seized by an inner compulsion, like a mystic who has seen a terrible, irresistible vision. "I haven't gone far enough."

"Now you sound like me," said Roman. "Except that I know when I'm being shocking, and I don't think you do."

Yale didn't answer. He seemed to be in a reverie. He mused with serene anticipation of the boy he had selected as he left the brothel for his pleasure the next night and of the room he had reserved. Thorn.

Two days later Roman followed Jai Jai to Paris. Now that she was gone, he realized that he missed her.

Cole, who had left the group at Luxor, had journeyed alone through Egypt. He traveled by railroad, vintage American Chevrolets, camel and horseback to the oasis at El Faiyum, known as the Garden of Egypt, a provincial capital where peaches, tangerines, olives, grapes, and pomegranates prosper; where palms, tamarisks, eucalypti and acacias cast their precious shade; where, during the Middle Kingdom, the pharaohs of the Twelfth Dynasty built temples and pyramids and worshiped sacred crocodiles and where Cole fell in love with and bought the famous multi-handled dark-red spherical water jugs whose motifs he planned to use in the Egyptian collection. He traveled to Memphis, Saqqara, Dahshur, Asyut, Port Safaga, Marsa Alam and Suez.

By the time, a month later, he returned to Paris filled with ideas, anxious to work, he had made a decision: If Dante still wanted him, they would live together. Cole's journey through Egypt had been an inward as well as an outward journey. He had not said anything to Dante, but he had been afraid of what he would do in Egypt. Cole had always, in the past, been discreet at home; when traveling, he had had bouts of promiscuity that, in retrospect, had horrified him. He was afraid that in Egypt he would be unable to stop himself from going on a sexual binge. To his surprise, in a country that offered every kind of erotic diversion, he had not even once been unfaithful to Dante. What surprised Cole was that he had not even had to use discipline or willpower to stay away from available boys; he had not even been tempted, he had not desired them. He desired only Dante; he missed Dante fiercely both as a lover and as the one person with whom he wanted to share every aesthetic and pleasurable moment of his journey. Cole discovered, as he ended his Egyptian trip, that he had begun to think of commitments not as losing but as gaining. He wondered why it had taken him so long and so much unhappiness to realize it. He decided not to regret the past but to begin the future.

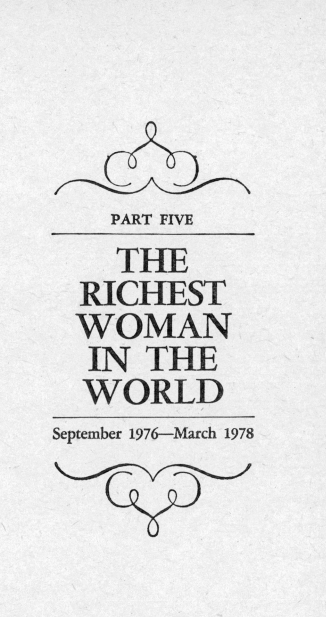

PART FIVE

THE RICHEST WOMAN IN THE WORLD

September 1976—March 1978

∾ SIXTEEN ∾

Sergei Raimont's death began a year of death for Alix. Later that same fall her mother died in a fall from her hunter, Galahad; that spring her marriage faltered; by summer it was dead. There were rumors that Alix had tried to commit suicide on the anniversary of Sergei's death and had spent several weeks in a psychiatric clinic in London. Although the family denied the rumors, they persisted.

"Do you really think it was an accident?" asked Alix. She and Yale were in Yale's car on the way to Heathrow, the September day bright, warm and sunny; an hour before, Alexander had called from Manila; Sergei had died in an accident, he had said. There were no details yet; he was on his way to Mazatlán; Alix should go to Grandmère's in Southampton, where the funeral would be held as soon as the body could be flown out of Mexico. "Or is that just Raimont PR?"

"Of course I think it was an accident," said Yale, surprised at the question, surprised at Alix's suspiciousness—very uncharacteristic of her. "Don't you?"

"I don't know. My brother has tried to kill himself three times," said Alix. She was calm. Yale thought she had not yet had the time to accept the reality of her brother's death. "In Cambridge. In Neuilly-sous-Clermont. And once in Southampton."

"Southampton?" Yale knew about Cambridge and Neuilly-sous-Clermont. "I didn't know about Southampton," he said. "Are you sure?"

"I was there," said Alix. Her eyes were dry. Yale wondered when she would cry, if she would cry. She looked into her ghostly reflection in the tinted green glass separating the back seat from the chauffeur, and she remembered. She had been eighteen, Sergei fourteen; it had happened on the first of August. Sergei's mother had taken him on a vacation trip through Canada for the last two weeks of July, and when it was over, he had got on the plane alone at Montreal for the flight to New York. Alix picked him up at the airport and drove him out to Grandmère's, where they would spend August. Alix had a Jaguar that year, British racing green, a birthday present from her father. She had loved that car, racy, sleek, powerful, but in the end she had been happy to sell it because its memories haunted her.

"How was the trip?" Alix asked Sergei once she had pulled out of the maze of exit roads from the airport and was on the highway, heading east. Sergei was in the bucket seat next to her. "Did you have a good time?"

"I wish I were dead." His tone was sullen, stubborn.

"Sergei!" Alix, taking her eyes off the road for a second, turned to look at her brother. He was not being dramatic like his mother; he was perfectly serious. "Sergei, don't say that!"

Sergei did not reply. "What happened?" Alix asked, unable to imagine something terrible enough to make her little brother want to die. "Nothing could be that awful."

"My mother doesn't love me," Nicky said. "And my father doesn't love me," he said, and then went on to tell the story. "The day before I left for Canada to meet my mother, our father took me aside and gave me two hundred and fifty dollars. 'Your mother doesn't know how to tip,' he said. 'She never leaves enough. Be sure you always add extra.'

"So I did; you know how he is about tipping. But you also know my mother—since she married Jules, she never has enough money, and being able to take me on a trip that she paid for meant a lot to her. She said she would finally be able to do something for me without the Raimonts' contributing one penny. She was very proud of that. Anyway, I got away with adding money without my mother finding out. Until Montreal. We had finished lunch in the garden restaurant of the Ritz-Carlton, and as usual, I waited until Mother had gone before I added a few dollars to her tip. Suddenly she returned to the table; she'd forgotten her compact. She saw the extra money. She yelled and screamed at me: I was a sneak, a typical Raimont, showing the world what a big shot I was with my lousy millions.

"Everyone in the garden stared. I was humiliated, and I wanted to die right there. But that was only the beginning. Once my mother's tirade was over, she took all the money I had left. For the rest of the trip she charged everything to my father, and she refused to tip.

"Then our father called me and in that controlled voice told me that I had hurt the Raimont name in its own business. He said he expected nothing from my mother, but he expected me to know what to do. My father wants me to be a man, and my mother wants me to be a boy. She's not talking to me, and neither is he. He just hung up the phone when I tried to explain. I can't please anybody, and if I were dead, I wouldn't have to try."

"Sergei, you mustn't talk like that," Alix said. Sergei was not making an empty threat; he was serious. "You know that Andrea's overdramatic and overemotional, and well, you know Daddy. Next week he'll buy you F.A.O. Schwarz, and the whole episode will be forgotten."

"But not forgiven," said Sergei, in the relentless voice he had been using.

"Suddenly Sergei grabbed the steering wheel and tried to hit another car," Alix told her husband as the limousine passed through the dreary London suburbs on the way to Heathrow. "Then he tried to steer into a bridge piling. He was trying to kill himself and me, too, if he had to. I struggled with him. The car veered from side to side; horns were blaring; we almost crashed. I managed to get control, and finally, Sergei just slumped back into his seat and gave up."

Yale thought of the way Alix kept her hands firmly at ten and two o'clock on the wheel in proper Grand Prix position. It must have saved her life when she was eighteen. Alix turned slightly in her seat to face Yale. Her eyes were still dry; the expression in them unreadable. "I've never told anyone about that," Alix said. "Sergei made me promise not to."

He was disturbed by the story Alix had just told him. A story about money and death that seemed almost an epitaph for Sergei Raimont.

"And your father doesn't know?"

"No," said Alix. "I never told him. I promised Sergei I wouldn't. And I know Sergei never did."

Yale wondered whether Alix's suspicions might be right.

Her grandfather had killed himself and now, perhaps, her brother. He knew what she was thinking: that a fatal taint ran in the family; that she might have inherited it. He felt profoundly compassionate toward his wife, and he put an arm around her and held her, comforting her as well as he could, loving her as much as he ever had.

As their plane crossed the Atlantic, a thought he couldn't drive from his mind obsessed him: He had always known that Alix would inherit two immense fortunes—her mother's and half her father's. And it had always been his goal to equal them. Now that Sergei was dead, she would inherit Sergei's share of the Raimont wealth. One day his wife would be the richest woman in the world, and no matter what Yale did now, he could never be her equal. And at the same time that Yale loved her and sympathized with her, he hated her and resented her.

Alix, in black from head to foot, heard nothing of the funeral service. She could not bring herself to look at the coffin; instead, she looked at Jai Jai. Alix could not let herself cry; instead, she watched Jai Jai cry. Alix wanted to make a gesture to show the loss, the shock, the grief she felt for her dead brother. Instead, she watched as Jai Jai removed her wedding ring, fastened it to Sergei's coffin, a symbol of their love forever to be buried with him. Alix wanted her father to comfort her; instead, he was in his library with his lawyers, as physically inaccessible as he was emotionally inaccessible. Alix wanted Yale to be by her side; instead, she watched as he expressed his condolences to Jai Jai and then walked with her on the slow, sad promenade back to the house.

Alix had lost her brother, her ally, the only other person in the world who understood what it was like to be the child of a man like Alexander Raimont.

When Alix returned to the house, she was surprised when the butler told her that her father wanted to see her in his study. Knowing his absolute aversion to emotional scenes, she had thought she wouldn't see him at all for a while, while he gave everyone time to adjust to Sergei's death.

"For the rest of your life you will hear rumors about your brother's death. I want you to hear the truth from me," Alexander began once the door was shut. In another surprising departure from his usual behavior he was not seated behind his desk; instead, he was on the leather Chesterfield and had gestured for Alix to sit next to him. "Sergei's . . ." he began. His voice broke, and he cleared his throat. "Sergei. . . ." He tried to speak again, and this time he was not even able to complete the name of his dead son. He began to cry, and most terrible of all was that there were no tears. His face was contorted, his mouth drawn back from his teeth, his eyelids blinking rapidly. A choking sound came from his throat. It was unbearable, and Alix wanted to touch him but didn't, knowing how much he disliked being handled. She waited until he was quiet.

"He did . . . what Grandpère did," said Alix in a soft voice; not quite a question, it was not a statement either. In all the years of her life she had never heard her father speak once of his father, and she was afraid she had gone too far.

There was a long pause, and finally, her father in a voice that sounded like the voice of a very old man said, "It's my fault. Sergei is gone, and it's my fault."

"No," said Alix. It had been unbearable when her father had cried without tears; it was unimaginable to hear him accuse himself. "It's not your fault. It can't be," said Alix.

Her father shook his head. His shoulders heaved with unshed tears. He tried to begin to speak again but could not.

"Daddy, I knew what happened . . . as soon as you told me Sergei was. . . ." She let the sentence trail off, not able to use the proper word, not wishing to use the polite evasion. She wanted to spare her father from his compulsion to tell her about her brother's death.

"Alix, Jai Jai and I . . ." Alexander said, finding a strength he had not known he had. "Jai Jai and I . . . were seeing each other. Sergei found out. . . . He had a gun. . . ." Alexander's voice broke again, and this time he wept, tears flowing down his face until it was as wet as if he had emerged from a swimming pool. He sobbed then for a while, vast, racking sobs that caused his entire body to react with spasms until the machinery of his body was exhausted and he quieted, weeping again, the tears slowly coursing down his cheeks. Alix waited until he was quiet, silently handing him tissues. "No one knows," he finally said when he could speak again, "except Dante, and he won't say anything."

"Neither will I," said Alix. "I promise. I will never tell anyone." It was the first confidence her father had ever told her; Alix would almost have given her own life for it not to have been that particular one. "I will never tell anyone."

"I know you won't," said her father. He looked exsanguinated, pale, gray beneath the perpetual suntan. Alix thought: He's going to die, too. It was a thought she had never had. She had never seen her father cry, and so she had supposed that he never did; she had never seen him defeated, and now she had; she had never seen him seem mortal, and now, suddenly, she realized that one day he would die.

"There's more. Jai Jai's pregnant," he said finally, his voice barely audible in the upholstered, carpeted, booklined quiet of the study, its luxurious appointments isolating its occupants from everything except the anguish they both felt. "The baby might be mine."

There was complete silence. Alix said nothing. There was nothing to say. Jai Jai and her father had been . . . seeing each other. Sergei had found out and . . . done what Grandpère had done. Alix understood why her father blamed himself. In his exhausted old man's voice, her father said, "I'm returning to Manila this afternoon. Before I go, I want to give you this." He handed her an envelope, an ordinary white nine-by-three envelope. Alix's name, nothing else, no address, no return address, was typed on the front. She began to open it. "No," said her father. "Don't open it here. I want you to read it carefully when you will be alone and undisturbed. It's important."

"Of course," said Alix and, in a spontaneous gesture, kissed her father on the cheek and left the room.

"I hate it here. I hate this house, and I hate this room,"

Yale said that night. The balance in Yale's love/hate relationship with the rich had already begun to change. He used the word "hate" three times in two sentences. Alix, numb with shock, did not notice, although later she would remember and realize its significance. It was after dinner but too early for sleep, and they were in Alix's room, the room that had been hers since she'd been a girl, the room they always used when they were in Southampton. "This is a room for a girl, not a woman. And this house, it reminds me of the Noyeses' house—it's too elegant. Too perfect. I hated it when I was a kid, and I hate it now."

"But you always said your ambition was to live like the Noyeses," Alix said. She had told Yale about the contents of the envelope her father had given her, shy, proud, excited, but ever since, Yale had been restless, pacing back and forth, unable to sit still, to read, to watch television, not wanting to talk to her. "You always said you wanted to live in a house just like the Noyeses' house."

"Not anymore," Yale said. "This life behind guarded walls is forty years out of style. No one lives like this anymore." To be out of date, out of style was as devastating an epithet in Yale's vocabulary as "middle-class" had once been in Dante's. "I'm going out for a walk."

"I'll go with you," said Alix. "I don't feel like being alone tonight."

"Please, Alix," said Yale. "*I* want to be alone. I don't like funerals, and I don't like their aftermath."

"Don't be gone long then," Alix asked, capitulating to his wishes, as she usually did.

"I'll see you later," Yale said, and he left her in the room, which she now looked at through his eyes.

The room had a four-poster bed, wide bay windows overlooking the treetops, beyond them, the swimming pool and pavilion, and beyond that, beyond the acres of lawns and old trees, she could just barely see the Atlantic Ocean. There was a fireplace on the wall opposite the bed, and one entire wall was floor-to-ceiling bookcases holding the books Alix had collected for years. There were the novels of Tolstoy, Balzac and Jane Austen, but they were far outnumbered by the words of nonfiction, all of them biographies, all devoted to two kinds of subjects: rich men and beautiful women. In addition, the shelves contained the elaborate scrapbooks Alix had made as a teenager to commemorate her summers. One at a Swiss summer school contained mementos of visits to chocolate and cheese factories, to châteaux and concerts, autographs of classmates from England, Lebanon, New Zealand, France, Spain and the United States, photographs of herself and a friend in new bikinis they considered daring, in formals they wore to a summer's-end dance and in jeans standing by the funicular that ascended an Alp whose name Alix didn't know. Another scrapbook was from the summer she had spent at her mother's white frame house in Darkharbor and contained stubs of ferry tickets from Camden to Isleboro, fragments of a lobster net, pressed yellow field daisies turned straw-colored with time, photographs of her and a boyfriend on bikes, on a picnic in the pine woods and on a sailboat coming in fifth at the Fourth of July race. It was these photographs that had once prompted Yale to comment on something Alix had never noticed: that in none of them was she smiling. A third scrapbook held the memories of a summer she'd spent in Manhattan working for Raimont first as a reservations clerk and then in the promotion department, helping assemble illustrated folders for her father's hotels with photos of the reception areas, restaurants, cocktail lounges and guest rooms. There were photos of Alix answering the phone, of her with her boss, the head of reservations, looking over the huge wallboard where reservations were kept track of on color-coded slips by an army of clerical workers, of her New York weekends at Southampton at Meadow Club debutante parties, at Herb McCarthy's, at a big charity party held under a tent on the grounds of the Parrish Museum.

The books and scrapbooks revealed Alix's past; the rest of the room revealed a woman who was still a little girl. The white wicker furniture, dainty sheets and eyelet covers, the phonograph with pop records from Alix's teenage years and the Raggedy Ann doll propped up in the corner of a settee stacked with ruffled pillows had not been changed from the time when the room had been decorated, almost fifteen years before, for a privileged teenager. The room had always been Alix's favorite of all the rooms she occupied around the world, but now, for the first time, it seemed too girlish to Alix. Yale had been, as he so often was, right.

Almost two hours had passed before Alix went down the curved, hanging staircase to look for Yale. She could hear his voice from the living room. Then, standing silently in the foyer at the foot of the stairs, Alix heard Jai Jai. She was saying something about housekeeping. Yale said something about the Noyeses', and they laughed. The tone was conspiratorial, and Alix, embarrassed at eavesdropping and not really wanting to hear, afraid they would talk about her, ran back up the stairs, its thick carpeting silencing her footfalls.

Everything had changed in her life, yet she felt, back in her room, the same feelings that had haunted her for as long as she could remember: She felt left-out, isolated, lonely.

Alone, Alix reopened the envelope her father had given her that afternoon. It contained three sheets of yellow legal paper clipped together with an ordinary paper clip. Alexander Raimont's elegant, cursive script covered the sheets. It was one of perhaps a score of times Alix had seen her father's handwriting. He usually communicated with her by telephone, telex or telegram. The few letters he had written to her when she was at camp or boarding school had always been dictated and typed. He never signed his own letters; a secretary did, circling her own initial to the right of Alexander's signature in standard office procedure. Alix had always wanted her father to write the way other fathers did, but she never said anything to him about it. She knew how busy he was, and she didn't want to add to his responsibilities.

Alix withdrew and unfolded the sheets of paper. The date was the date of Sergei's death, and the document was a will—a will Alexander had handwritten on the flight carrying Sergei's body back from Mazatlán. Alix read. Its terms were simple. It left everything—majority stock in the five Raimont companies owning or managing a total of fifty-one hotels with a total of seventy-five thousand employees on three continents, art and antiques, gold on deposit with Swiss and Hong Kong banks, stocks, bonds and certificates of deposit in the vaults of banks of a dozen countries, the ownership of mortgages totaling three hundred fifty-one million dollars payable over the next twenty-one years—to Alix outright.

The implications were overwhelming. Her father's previous will, as thick as a book, had left a series of interlocking trusts, organized under a Monegasque holding company, with minute instructions governed by page after page of dense legal terminology detailing powers and limitations on powers. Alexander's previous will had given Alix and her brother money but no power—something Sergei had always bitterly resented. This new, simple will gave Alix everything—the vast, uncountable fortune and total control over it.

Alix was terrified and overwhelmed by the implications of her father's will. It was too much: too much responsibility; too much power. Alix felt as if the entire world had suddenly fallen on her. She felt trapped and imprisoned and burdened. She felt unworthy and inadequate. She had always lacked confidence; now she was petrified and paralyzed. Compulsively Alix's eyes returned to the first page of the will and the four words with which it began: "To my beloved daughter, Alix."

It was the first time in her life her father had ever said he loved her. She should have felt better; instead, she felt worse. If Sergei were still alive, her father would never have written the will; he would never have written the words.

∾ SEVENTEEN ∾

In November, on the American holiday of Thanksgiving, August Vanocur, Alix's stepfather, called from Maryland with the news that Brooke had died six hours after a fall during a hunt. And Yale accompanied his wife to the second funeral of that autumn.

August Fish Vanocur IV had married Brooke when Alix was sixteen. Like his father, and his father's father before him, August Vanocur had never worked a day in his life. The family fortune, based on a variety of chemical patents used in the manufacture of aniline dyes, medicines and explosives, had grown steadily since it was accounted at eight million dollars in a Maryland surrogate's court in 1908. Gus lived in the horse country north of Baltimore in a stone house overlooking a green valley through which a river flowed, and when Brooke married him, she moved into his house, redecorated it in chintz, Sheraton and hunting prints in the style of a comfortable and friendly English country house. It seemed, finally, in this setting, reminiscent of the main-line childhood of which, over the passage of years, Brooke remembered only the happy times she had, after the glittering but formal marriage to Alexander and the marriage to Slade Grey in whose rangy, wide-open western setting she seemed invariably out of place, that she had found a marriage that contented her.

Brooke and Gus lived a healthy, quiet life, centered on the passing of the seasons—ice skating on frozen ponds, followed by drinks with friends in front of open fireplaces in winter; long walks and the fresh scent of wild lilacs in the spring, when deer visited the young green ivy beds near the house; swimming and tennis in the summer; and, in the fall, Gus' passion: fox hunting. He was Master of the Silverhead Hunt, riding out resplendent in a green coat with a gold collar, and owner of one of the few private packs of foxhounds in the country—seventeen and a half couples of crossbred Pennsylvania, Delaware and North Carolina blood. Although Brooke had ridden since she had been a child, she was accustomed to well-schooled horses and familiar bridle paths. The speed of the hunt, the runs over open country, the sharp sting on her face of the small stones and clods of earth raised by the flying hooves of the horses in front of her, the high jumps over stone walls, fences, gates, streams and fallen trees frightened her, and Gus had to use all his persuasiveness to get her to ride with the hunt.

"No one ever got killed during a hunt," he would say. "Half the time, not even the fox," he would add, making the hearty, simple joke so characteristic of him and the hearty, simple pleasures he so enjoyed.

Cautious at first and then with increasing pleasure, as her confidence grew and her fear receded, Brooke rode with the hunt, enjoying its rituals, its excitement, its sociability at the big hunt breakfasts and the sense of the passing seasons it represented, giving her a link to the earth and its fundamental rhythms. For the fourteen years of her marriage, Brooke rode whenever Gus did, her enjoyment in it almost equaling his.

The accident did not even take place at one of the high jumps Brooke had once feared so much. It happened on flat ground, as the hunt followed the hounds across a field of stubbly grown grass, already mown and stacked for hay. The last sound Brooke heard was a loud report that sounded as if a gun had gone off. Then, so fast she had no chance to react, Galahad, who had stepped into a hidden rabbit hole and broken a foreleg, went down, his forward motion abruptly stopped. Brooke was pitched forward off the saddle, her feet coming up and out of the stirrups, her body going forward with the speed of Galahad's gallop, and fell into the hard, almost-frozen ground. It was the kind of fall riders usually walk away from with a few days of painful bruises as a reminder, except in Brooke's case her head struck a rock hidden by the grass stubble at such an angle that despite the protective hunt derby she wore, her neck broke and the three vertebrae at the top of her spinal column were shattered. She never regained consciousness. The only comfort the doctors could hold out was that she had felt nothing, that she literally never knew what happened to her.

The Concorde London–Washington flight to her mother's funeral only two months after the London–New York flight to her brother's funeral had about it a sense of agonizing finality for Alix. She had lost her brother and now her mother. The loss of her mother was a devastating loss of equilibrium. Unlike the volatile, flamboyant Raimont men, Alix's mother was stable and emotionally dependable; she gave to Alix a reassuring center and the only real sense of permanence in a life characterized by impermanence.

When she had been a girl, Alix had thought her mother's "rules" stuffy and old-fashioned; as she had grown, she came to value them. If Alix had standards, moral and ethical standards, and she did, they were an inheritance from her mother, who believed that money and privilege demanded certain responsibilities, obligations and duties. With her mother dead, Alix had only her father, and since Sergei's death Alexander's behavior had been violently unpredictable. At times he showered her with love and attention; at others he seemed to resent her for being alive while Sergei was dead. Her mother's stable influence had been more important to Alix than ever, and now, suddenly without warning, her mother had been taken from her. Although Alix had not been able to cry at her brother's funeral, she had not been able to stop crying at her mother's. She *was* her tears; they defined her existence and her experience.

Gus was no help. Grief-stricken, he cried and drank, drank and cried. "She was the best woman in the world, the kindest, the most honorable," he kept repeating. "She was the best quality American. The very best, and now she's gone."

Yale was moved by Alix's grief, her profound sense of loss and abandonment. "It's unfair," he told her. "You've done nothing to deserve this much pain," he said. He tried to comfort her with attention, with kindness and gentleness, but there was nothing he could do to make her feel better because he was just beginning not to love her anymore. He tried to hide it and, for a while, succeeded. Distracted by grief and fear, she did not yet sense it.

Yale could not stop himself from feeling the way he did about Jai Jai, even though, awaiting the birth of her baby in Paris, she refused all his invitations. The woman he desired was in another city pregnant with another man's baby, he had committed adultery only in his imagination, yet Yale felt guilty and dishonest and shabby. He couldn't wait to return to London, where they could at least be able to resume the appearances of their old, familiar life. What he didn't know, couldn't know, was that he, that Alix would never again be the way they had been. Too much had already changed; soon everything would change.

On the flight back to London, Alix excused herself and locked herself in the lavatory. She wanted to wash her face and reapply her makeup; she thought it would make her feel better. She removed the small zippered case that contained her makeup from her handbag and opened it. On top of the lipstick, mascara, rouge and makeup brushes were a full vial of Valium and a full vial of Seconal. She had put them into her bag before leaving London for Maryland, and she had tried, with only fair success, not to think about their existence. Now she removed both vials and put them on the small, stainless-steel counter abutting the sink. It would be easy, she thought, and it was. Starting with the Valium, she swallowed the pills with water from a disposable cup. First one. A second, then a third.

She paused, as if suddenly understanding the consequences of her action. Was this how Grandpère had felt in the pool house? Was this how Sergei had felt in my car on the way to Southampton, in Cambridge, in Neuilly-sous-Clermont, in Mazatlán? Had they known how they would make other people feel? Her father had never spoken of his father, and Alix knew that the reason was that it was too difficult for him. In Southampton, with an effort of will that was visible, he had begun to speak of Sergei's death, a death Alix feared might destroy him with guilt and grief. By mutual agreement Alix and her father had never again spoken of Sergei's death; just as he could not bear to speak, Alix could not bear to listen. For a split second she thought of what would happen to her father if she . . . did as Grandpère had, as Sergei had.

Then, with quick gestures of her hands, before her resolution could waver, she dumped the contents of both vials into the toilet and watched as the blue, chemically treated water flushed them away. Alix refreshed her lipstick and returned to her seat.

"You were gone a long time," Yale said. "I was about to come for you. Is everything all right?"

Alix nodded. "I washed my face and redid my makeup. I thought looking better would help me feel better."

Yale didn't think she looked any different but didn't say so because he didn't want to depress her any further. She slept deeply for the entire flight, and Yale had trouble wak-

ing her when the plane landed at Heathrow. He was glad
she had been able to sleep. She had not been able to in
Maryland, and it was a way of forgetting, at least temporarily, what was happening to her.

Back in London, Yale threw himself into pleasure. Now
that he felt his fortune could never equal his wife's, he
seemed not to care about Warrant, Charlton, Dover. He
delegated more and more of his business to the bright
young men he had hired and trained. He immersed himself
in the London year-end social season; it was not unusual
for him to attend two cocktail parties, a dinner party and
the disco of the moment in one evening. He went to Paris
as often as Jai Jai would let him come. Lies—a conference,
a plant to inspect, a banker to meet, an investor to take to
dinner—became the dialogue of his marriage. He hated
himself for lying, and he turned his resentment over the
need to lie into anger at Alix. It seemed to him that she
forced him to lie, not that he did the lying. He was irritable
and cold toward her, filled with deep shame at his behavior. He preferred it when Alix provoked an argument; then
he could justify his resentment of her. Most of the time,
though, Alix did not question his lies, did not demand to
know what he was really doing, made no accusations and
initiated no scenes. She was exhausted all the time; she had
no energy, no interest in anything—even her husband's increasing estrangement. He was rarely at home, and Alix
poured out her despair, her thoughts of suicide to him in
letters she addressed to his office and mailed "Personal—
Confidential." He never answered them, but Alix continued
to write. It was the only outlet she had, and she thought
those letters were all that stood between her and death. On
the Concorde Alix Raimont had decided not to die, but
neither, back in London, did she have the desire to live.

Discarding the pills in the transatlantic flight had been a
melodramatic gesture. Cheap and theatrical. When she had
returned to the Belgravia house, the first thing she had
done was to flush away every pill, every prescription in the
house. It had been an act of bravado. Alix had lain awake
night after night with a crushing sense of burden and the
inescapable feeling that never could she be the equal of her

inheritances. She began to understand Sergei; she had even begun to act like him. She remembered his telling her how furious Bertil Sundsvall had been when he was still in pajamas at four in the afternoon and how he didn't have the energy to get dressed but no one understood. Now Alix was acting the same way, and she did understand. She was terrified of the future, and her terror robbed her of will, of desire, of energy. It would be easy for her to get more pills, as many as she wanted. Doctors, as Yale had taught her a long time ago, were just as impressed with money as most people; they would give her anything she wanted if she approached them the right way. All it would take would be a few phone calls; so far she had been able to stop herself from making them. She didn't know how much longer she could resist the temptation.

The tendency to self-destruction—Grandpère's fatal flaw, Sergei's fatal flaw—was also in her genes, and as Alix's depression grew, her ability to resist her fatal inheritance lessened. In the middle of December, Alix gave in. She dialed the number of the Harley Street internist who had in the past given her Seconal and Librium. She knew that he would give her more.

Alix was surprised that Grandmère's butler answered; then she realized that she had unconsciously dialed Grandmère's number. By the time Tatiana came to the telephone Alix was sobbing.

Tatiana flew to London the next day. When she saw Alix, she was shocked. Alix, always impeccably groomed, wore no makeup, and her hair, needing a shampoo, was held back carelessly with a rubber band. She wore, at four-thirty in the afternoon, a nightgown and robe. Her eyes were lusterless; her skin was muddy. She had lost an unbecoming amount of weight, giving her a strained drawn look.

"I know I look terrible," said Alix, aware of the thoughts going through Grandmère's mind. "But I don't care I just don't care. My brother is dead; my mother is dead. My husband no longer acts like a husband. Not that I blame him. I'm not acting like a wife."

Tatiana was angry at Alix for her self-pity, for blaming herself for Yale's behavior. "My husband is dead. My grandson is dead. I'm old. I'm going to die, too. You're young. Think of your father. Think of me. You're so selfish. A spoiled rich girl, Alix."

"Don't! Don't call me that!" Rich girl was the one criticism Alix could not tolerate. She could be called selfish, blunt, stubborn . . . but couldn't help it that she was rich. It wasn't her fault.

"And if you and Yale are having problems, don't take all the blame," said Tatiana. "And, Alix, you're not the only one who has suffered. Think of your father. Think of me. Think of the future."

"No I won't," said Alix, vehement again, angry again. "I won't. I can't."

Tatiana had known Alix was stubborn; it was one part of her character. But this came unexpectedly out of the depths of Alix's depression and mystified Tatiana.

"Why so stubborn?" she asked when suddenly Alix began to cry.

"I can't," Alix repeated. "I just can't do it. It's too much for me."

"You can't do what?" asked Grandmère. Other people had lost brothers and mothers; other people's marriages had gone through crises. Tatiana didn't understand the violence of Alix's reaction. "What's too much? Don't you think other people have suffered unfairly?"

"Hasn't my father told you?" Alix had turned cautious.

"Told me what?" Tatiana thought she knew everything there was to know: Sergei and Jai Jai. Alexander and Jai Jai. Jai Jai and her baby. What more could there be?

"When Sergei . . . died"—Alix still had difficulty saying the words because she inevitably thought of the despair he must have felt and compared it to her own—"my father changed his will. He left everything to me. Everything. Outright. There are no more trusts, no more foundations. It will be mine. My responsibility. It's too much. I can't do it."

Tatiana looked at her granddaughter, now beginning to understand what she had meant by too much.

"And now that my mother's dead," said Alix, "I have her estate. She was on the board of a hospital, a library and a performing arts center. She gave her time, and she gave her money. She wanted me to continue. I can't do it all. It's too much. It's too much for me. It's too much for anyone."

"But you'll have help," her grandmother said. "What does Yale say? He must have some ideas."

"He agrees. He doesn't think I can handle it either."

"That's not very constructive of him."

"I've always been alone," Alix said, "and now I'm more alone than ever. I feel crushed."

"Yes," said Tatiana, remembering times she had felt that way. "I understand." She thought for a moment and then asked, "Do the Raimont executives know of your father's intentions?"

"Not that I know of."

"Your father doesn't want you to walk in when he dies"— Tatiana did not flinch from the word or the thought; it was one of the many liberations of age—"and run a billion-dollar business without any preparation, does he?"

"I don't know what he wants," said Alix. "Sometimes he wants me to go to work for Cartwright," said Alix. "Other times he says no woman can handle a business that size and that he wants me to stay away and not get involved."

"And what do you want?" asked Tatiana.

Alix blinked. "I don't know."

It was Tatiana's turn to be surprised. "What do you mean you don't know?"

"Just that," said Alix.

"Why don't you know?"

"Because I'm afraid. I'm afraid if I go to work everyone will resent me. I'm afraid I'll fail. And I'm afraid if I don't go to work I won't deserve my inheritance, won't be worthy of it." Tatiana could hear Brooke's words echoing in Alix's words. "And if I work for Raimont, what about my mother's estate? She didn't just give money; she gave time. I don't know what I want because I'm terrified."

Her grandmother looked at her for a long moment and thought of the times when she was a girl, a refugee from czarist Russia in Paris, not knowing the language, eating day-old bread soaked in warm water because there was no money: and when her husband, even in the very prime of his life, went through periods of such inexplicable depression that he couldn't literally get out of bed; and when he had, finally, in the midst of one of those depressions taken his own life. She thought about terror: hers and his and their son's. Alexander's terror of death. And finally, she said, "But didn't you know, Alix? Everyone's afraid?"

"No, I didn't know," said Alix. No one around her *acted* afraid: not Yale; not her father; not even Sergei. Perhaps, she thought, they too were afraid in some invisible corner of themselves, in a secret chamber they carefully hid from her. The thought reassured Alix. Then she asked her grandmother a question: "What should I do?"

"Decide what it is you want to do, and then tell your father," Tatiana said. "Tell; don't ask."

Alix nodded. She realized that not only had she never *told* her father anything but that she had rarely even asked him for anything. She thought for a moment of all the hurt she had felt over his impersonally typed and signed letters and her fear about asking him to at least sign them himself. "It'll be hard," said Alix.

"What isn't?" said her grandmother, her matter-of-fact tone giving a sudden sense of perspective.

It would be nice to say that as a result of her conversation with her grandmother, Alix's depression vanished, her fear left and, with strengthened resolve, she began to dominate her own life. No one likes to admit it in the age of instant solutions, but everything takes longer than anyone wants to believe—recovery from an illness of the body; recovery from an injury to the soul.

It is true that her conversation with Grandmère helped Alix, but her inward recovery from her depression was slow and marked by frustration and unexpected setbacks. Gradually, however, she stopped dwelling on what had happened to her and how much she had lost and instead began to think about what she might do and be. Gradually her mentality changed from passive to active, and the first outward signs of her recovery coincided, symbolically, with the beginning of the new year.

∾ EIGHTEEN ∾

New Year's Eve is gala in St. Moritz. There are elegant parties in private chalets, and in the glittering hotels, the Palace and Suvretta House, revelers drink champagne and dance far into the night until it is time, early on the morning of the first day of the new year, for a breakfast of caviar and scrambled eggs at Chesa Veglia.

The Raimonts were a family without tradition, except for one: Every year Alexander took a tower suite at the Palace and hosted a combination New Year's party and ski holiday. The family and key Raimont personnel were invited. This year, 1976, the year of Sergei's death, Alexander did not know whether or not to celebrate the holiday in his customary manner.

"What do you think, Alix?" he had asked, long distance, Milan to London in mid-October, when reservations would have to be made. "I wonder if it's too soon after Sergei. . . ." He let the sentence go unfinished.

"I'd like it, too," Alix said. Her father asking her opinion and advice had been, until Sergei's death, unheard of. "Sergei always enjoyed it, and it's the one time all year everyone's together."

"Do you think it's appropriate?" her father asked. "It's not too soon. . . ."

"No, it's not too soon," Alix said with more certainty than she felt. The fact was that the thought of having to live through the holidays without the one Raimont tradition would have been devastating to Alix; the harsh punctuations of death caused her to cling to any shreds of continuity. "I want you to, and I'm sure everyone will understand." Alix thought of the cliché "Life goes on." She realized how true it was.

"Then I'll make the reservations," Alexander said.

"I'm glad," said Alix. "I would have been very unhappy if you hadn't."

"Really?" Her father sounded surprised. For the first

218

time ever it occurred to Alix that she might be as much of
an enigma to her father as he was to her.

"Yes," she said, and this time she felt the certainty with
which she spoke.

"Then I'm glad I asked," said her father. "I want you to
be happy."

The conversation gave Alix courage for the talk she
wanted to have with her father. Since her conversation with
Grandmère, she had had lunch with Cartwright, and she
had decided what she wanted to do. The next step, as
Grandmère had advised, was to tell her father. St. Moritz
would give her the perfect opportunity.

Alexander picked up Yale and Alix at Heathrow in his
Lear for the flight to Zurich, where one of the omnipresent
Raimont limousines drove them the rest of the way to St.
Moritz. Jai Jai, six months pregnant, flew in from Paris;
Tatiana, happy to see Alix looking so much better, from
Southampton, and Liliane, nervously wondering whether
there would be more talk of divorce—Alexander had never
referred to the subject again since their brief conversation
in St.-Jean-Cap-Ferrat—drove in from Lausanne.

Alix was annoyed that her father had invited Jai Jai.

"It's bad enough that he invited her," Alix said to Yale
before they left London, "but you'd think she'd have the
discretion not to accept."

"What do you want her to do, Alix, stop living?" Yale
had answered. "I think you're jealous of Jai Jai," said Yale.
"Because she's beautiful—" He stopped in mid-sentence.

"And I'm not?" asked Alix.

"I didn't say that."

"But you were going to."

Yale didn't answer, and Alix knew that she was right.
She resented Yale's defense of Jai Jai, and Alix decided, for
the first time in her life, to compete. She could never be as
dazzlingly beautiful as Jai Jai, but she had weapons of her
own. At a fee of five thousand dollars plus first-class travel
expenses Alix had a makeup artist flown in from Hollywood for one day. He restyled Alix's hair and made up her
face two different ways: one for day, one for evening.
Then, as he stood by, Alix removed the makeup and, with
his commentaries and corrections, reapplied it until she

was able to achieve the same subtle un-made-up effect he had created. Alix was so pleased that, on top of his fee, she gave him a lavish tip. She then called Corinne de Sancheval and asked if she had three days free to go shopping with her. Corinne was periodically on the best-dressed list, and Alix admired her taste and Parisian chic. With Corinne's guidance, Alix bought several dinner dresses from Saint Laurent and a spectacular dress for New Year's Eve from Lagerfeld and casual clothes from the sensational new boutiques in the Place Victoire and in and around Les Halles. Underwear, Corinne counseled, should be ordered from Sabia Rosa in Paris, Fernando Sanchez at Bendel's in New York and Janet Reger in Beauchamp Place. When Alix left for St. Moritz, she left with six pieces of luggage, and even Yale, although he said nothing, was visibly impressed.

During the day Alix skied alone with an instructor, taking the T-bar from Corviglia to Tres Flores and making the downhill runs in her graceful, aggressive style. She skied the way she drove, and it showed a part of her personality not usually apparent. Yale did not ski with her; he did not know how to ski and had never wanted to learn. The first winter they'd been married and gone to St. Moritz, Alix had been amazed that he didn't ski.

"I thought all Americans were athletic," she had said in surprise.

"Not this one," said Yale. "My father spent his life sweating on a tennis court. When I was very young, I promised myself that the most vigorous exercise I ever got would be opening a bottle of champagne."

Alix had laughed. It was typical of Yale, typical of the unusual and unconventional attitudes he had about almost everything. Early in their marriage and for a long time after, his unconventionality was refreshing, and she loved that part of him. As he became more and more successful in his business, she realized that his original attitudes were the key to his success; he truly had brought brand-new ways of doing things into the stodgy, conventionbound world of the City. She still admired his originality, although now she realized that often it had the effect of excluding her.

While Yale spent his time in front of a fire, Alix skied,

and by New Year's Eve she had a healthy pink-beige winter tan. For the gala, she wore her hair, usually neatly pulled back, in a loosely waving, soft style, its volume forming a frame for the face the Hollywood expert had designed for her. He had given her a typed set of illustrated instructions, and Alix had brought them along with her to give to the St. Moritz hairdresser. Her dress, cut seductively on the bias, was of hammered silk the color of heavy cream, and for jewelry, Alix wore the ruby and diamond earrings Yale had given her for her thirtieth birthday.

When she had finished dressing, she studied herself in the mirror, something she rarely did. She looked different to herself. The wounded look in her eyes was beginning to go, and an unmistakable intelligence showed. Her skin no longer had the fresh glow of a girl's but the matte finish of a woman's. To herself, Alix looked older, but older in a way that conveyed experience and sophistication. In the Concorde and through the autumn in London, she had been crushed by what she wasn't; now, with the passage of time, she was beginning to imagine what she could be. She thought she had never looked better in her life, and as she shut the door behind her, she realized for the first time in her life she was looking forward to being seen. To someone who had always been shy and self-effacing, it was a thrilling moment.

Corinne de Sancheval in coral crepe de chine with diamonds, Liliane in white velvet with sapphires, Tatiana in dove-gray watered silk with black pearls, Jai Jai in lime jersey with her emeralds—the women at Alexander's table were dazzling, but it was Alix, with a brand-new confidence and ruby earrings brushing her shoulders, who attracted all the attention.

"She'll be worth at least a billion dollars," said a British marchioness without envy, "and tonight she looks like she's worth every single dollar of it."

Alix danced with everyone—her husband, her father, Raoul de Sancheval, Cartwright Dunne and all the top Raimont people. The party was ebullient and happy. Champagne cooled in silver buckets; roses and anemones in brilliant colors decorated the white-clothed tables. Women in

Paris dresses adorned with kings' ransoms in jewels wore tinselly paper hats, and men who controlled vast empires blew on child's noisemakers. For this evening the world was innocent, and Alix, enjoying herself, accepted Raoul's second invitation to dance. She followed him to the dance floor crowded with dancers, the rich and the glamorous reflecting back to each other their most glittering images.

"Alix!"

"Britta!" said Alix. She hadn't seen Britta since her break up with Sergei. Britta was as Scandinavian, as blond, as wholesome-looking as ever, and Alix, who had always liked her, was happy to see her again. Britta was with Pierre-Gilles, and when the introductions had been made, Britta spoke quietly to Alix.

"I'm so sorry about Sergei. I wanted to call. To write. To express my condolences. But I didn't know what to say. I was afraid, too, that you might think me pushy," Britta said, her sorrow and her confusion apparent.

"I understand," said Alix, aware of the aura of scandal that surrounded Sergei's death. Britta had certainly heard the gossip. "It's been very difficult . . . for all of us."

"I'm so sorry. It must be terrible," said Britta. Out of the corner of her eye, she saw Yale and Jai Jai dancing, obviously absorbed in each other. She wondered about Alix's marriage. "P.-G. and I have a chalet nearby," Britta said. "Perhaps you could come for a drink tomorrow at five?"

As Alix accepted the invitation, a man joined them.

"Hansjürg von Miesbach," Pierre-Gilles said, making the introduction. "Alix Raimont."

"Hansjürg and Pierre-Gilles were at Oxford together," Britta explained.

"Hansjürg was our leading literary light," said Pierre-Gilles.

Hansjürg, winter-suntanned, was tall and blond. His eyes, surprisingly brown in his otherwise-blond coloring, turned down at the corners and hinted of an intriguing story. His smile was warm, and so was his hand. Alix, in high-heeled sandals, was almost but not quite as tall as he was. Alix's first reaction to him was that he was the complete opposite of Yale. Hansjürg seemed open, relaxed, sure of who he was and where he belonged, without the high-voltage drive and the aura of mysterious secrets that made Yale exciting and also dangerous.

"And Pierre-Gilles was our idealist," Hansjürg said, not taking his eyes off Alix. Hansjürg, now president of the publishing company founded by his great-great-great-grandfather, had published the German translation of *Economie Politique.* "Now he's become an idealistic businessman, an excellent, if tricky, combination."

"Hansjürg is too modest," said Britta. "He, too, is an idealist. A twentieth-century Renaissance man."

Hansjürg blushed at Britta's compliment. It was an attractive blush, and Alix realized that she had never known a man capable of blushing. It endeared him to her.

"It's so rare to meet an idealist," said Alix. She was frequently embarrassed by her own idealism, a heritage from her mother, who had instilled in Alix the responsibilities entailed by money.

"Would you like to dance?" Hansjürg asked Alix as the music began again. Alix glanced at Raoul, who excused himself, saying that it was time for more champagne anyway.

"I saw you when you first came into the room," Hansjürg said, taking Alix into his arms. "I immediately asked if anyone knew who you were. Fortunately for me, Britta did."

It was Alix's turn to blush. She followed Hansjürg's lead. He was an accomplished, well-taught, but basically unmusical dancer. He was attracted to her, and unlike the men Alix had known who made a point of hiding their feelings, he made no attempt to conceal them. Alix, too, was attracted to him, but she was disturbed by the feeling, distrusting its immediacy. Nevertheless, his unconcealed admiration made her very pleasantly aware of herself and the moment. She enjoyed the feeling of her clothing against her body, the weighty sensation of the heavy earrings, the scent of her own perfume, with the increase in the warmth of her body at the emotions she felt, suddenly more noticeable, a mélange of ilang-ilang and rose and jasmine. They danced in silence, Hansjürg at ease with his feelings, Alix uncomfortable with hers, yet unwilling to relinquish them. Suddenly, before either of them had spoken again, the volley of sounds from noisemakers increased, and the band played the opening bars of "Auld Lang Syne." It was the stroke of midnight. Alix looked around frantically, wanting to find Yale. She could see him nowhere.

For the first time since their marriage Alix and her husband did not share the first kiss of the New Year. She turned to Hansjürg, and for days later both Alix and Hansjürg would try to remember the sequence of emotion and movement that led to the kiss, but neither could. Suddenly, with a natural movement, on the dance floor, in public, in each other's arms, they gave themselves up to the traditional first-of-the-year kiss, permitting it to fluctuate undirected by either of them between tenderness and the promise of future passion.

Hansjürg von Miesbach was, at thirty-nine, because of a tragedy that had occurred when he was too young to understand it and too young even to remember it, the head of one of Germany's most prestigious and profitable publishing houses. Hansjürg's father, the Baron Friedrich von Miesbach, had died for his political convictions under circumstances never fully clarified. Baron Friedrich, violently opposed to Hitler, had secretly published and distributed anti-Nazi writings throughout the Second World War at the risk of his own life and at the risk of the business that had been in the family since 1770, when it had published the early German Romantics, Schiller and Goethe and Schlegel, as well as translations of the Europeans Blake and Coleridge, Musset and George Sand and the Americans Hawthorne and Melville. Baron Freidrich survived the war almost to its conclusion, openly publishing noncontroversial material approved by Goebbels' propaganda ministry while secretly disseminating anti-Nazi material. As the Allies were poised in Great Britain planning the invasion of the European continent, Freidrich was betrayed. The identity of his betrayer was never discovered, and neither were the exact circumstances of Friedrich's death. According to one version, he was sent to Bergen-Belsen and gassed; according to another, summarily shot in the basement of Gestapo headquarters in Munich.

Hansjürg was two years old when his father died, the only son and coheir, with his sister, of his father's properties. Hansjürg, a boy without a father, grew up in a family of women, felt comfortable with women, an alien in the world of men. His mother, irrationally guilty over her husband's death, overprotected Hansjürg, coddling and catering to him until, when he was eight, Hansjürg's sister, Heidi, warned her mother of the possible adverse consequences of her indulgence. Her mother, a sensible woman, listened to her daughter's warnings and went to the boy's uncle, a chemical engineer, and her pastor, a worldly Lutheran, for advice. The two men agreed with Heidi, and, as a result of the consultation, Hansjürg was sent to a boys' school in Switzerland. It was a decision that Hansjürg always said saved his life, although at the time he was frightened and, for the first few weeks, cried himself to sleep every night. Separations, he would say, were traumatic to him, more so than for other people. He traced his abhorrence of separation to the unremembered but psychologically devastating loss of his father.

As a very young man Hansjürg worked summers in the family firm, a company brought almost to bankruptcy by the economic collapse of Germany at the end of World War II, as a mail boy, as a clerk in the bookkeeping department, as a typist in the production department. By the time he graduated from Oxford West Germany was well into the postwar miracle, and under Hansjürg's leadership, the position of the firm as one of Europe's greatest publishers was first consolidated and then expanded. As Hansjürg's business life blossomed, his personal life atrophied. Just as his sister had intervened in his behalf when he was a boy, she helped him see, when he was a man, that a life overly weighted in one direction at the expense of another would, ultimately, be unhappy. In his thirty-first year, for the fall and winter and early spring, Hansjürg consulted a psychoanalyst four times a week. His own suspicion that his father's premature death had deprived him of a capacity for intimacy was confirmed. His terror of intimacy was, at root, the consequence of a childhood terror that to love would be to be deserted.

Later that spring Hansjürg became engaged. Annaliese

Schaeffer was an intellectual, editor of an avant-garde journal which commented on the theater, ballet, music, poetry and literature. Dark-haired, intense, Annaliese was also a talented hostess, in whose living room the young and artistic-minded gathered for white wine and conversation. Hansjürg and Annaliese shared intellectual interests, as well as an idealistic attitude toward their future life together—they would dedicate themselves to the artistic and cultural life of their country. Hansjürg would contribute financial resources, and Annaliese her knowledge and personal contacts. Their wedding was scheduled to take place in the garden of Annaliese's parents' country house in the rolling hills several dozen kilometers outside Munich in late September, while it would still be warm and after their friends and relatives had returned from August vacation.

That summer Annaliese and Hansjürg went to Corfu for a holiday. There one night at a taverna they met Jāo Rondonio, a member of the Brazilian soccer team—a soft-spoken, gifted athlete. With Hansjürg looking on, Annaliese and Jāo proceeded to fall madly in love. Annaliese and Jāo, guilty, tried to deny to themselves and to each other what was happening. Jāo, unhappy at coming between Annaliese and Hansjürg, left Corfu. A month later, after trying to repair their engagement and failing, Annaliese, in tears, admitted that she wanted to be with Jāo. Hansjürg played the role of the gentleman and, suppressing his own tears, sent his fiancée off to join her lover.

The reality of a desertion in adult life awakened the most painful of Hansjürg's childish fears, and he withdrew utterly from personal attachments, devoting himself more than ever to his business, burying his loneliness in an avalanche of activity. When he saw Alix Raimont, he felt emotions he had thought forever dead in him.

Much later at Chesa Veglia, Hansjürg told Alix what had attracted him to her the moment she'd entered the party.

"You were with a group of people, but you seemed alone," said Hansjürg. "There was an air of isolation about you. You reminded me of myself."

"Are you lonely?" asked Alix, a little amazed at the quick rapport they had developed.

"Always," said Hansjürg. "And I think you are, too."

His words caused tears to sting at the back of Alix's eyes. He was, of course, right, and Alix felt uncomfortably exposed. Across the table, Yale was holding a mirror for Jai Jai as she patted on lip gloss. Her father had said goodnight just before one o'clock. He was leaving early the next morning for the walled town of Sidi-Bou-Said in Tunisia, where a group of oil rich Mideasterners wanted to build a luxury resort complex. Except for Hansjürg, Alix was alone again, feeling her loneliness, as she always did, with especial sharpness on holidays. She remembered suddenly the Christmas years before when she'd gone from her mother's Delaware house to meet her father, who at the time was still married to Andrea and was spending the holidays in Venice. Alix remembered the stranger who'd wanted to be a writer and who'd held her in his arms as a big, empty Air France plane had crossed the Atlantic. The memory, the tenderness and sadness of it, disturbed her, and as soon as she politely could, Alix excused herself.

The next day when Hansjürg telephoned her, the Palace Hotel reception informed him that Alix Raimont had checked out.

∾ NINETEEN ∽

On the third of January, 1977, Alix went to work in the London Raimont offices, three floors of a prewar building on New Bond Street. Under a plan which she and Cartwright had agreed on, and which, when she had presented it to her father in St. Moritz, he had agreed to, she would work in each department—reservations, purchasing, housekeeping, food and beverage services, acquisitions, finance and accounting—to reacquaint herself with day-to-day hotel operations.

Alix was surprised at how much she remembered from Harvard, at how much she had learned about the hotel business during the summers she had worked and how much she had absorbed by osmosis, simply by being her father's daughter, and while she enjoyed it, she worried about her father.

In the months since Sergei's death Alexander had begun to age. Each time Alix saw him, she was shocked at how lined his face had suddenly become, at how he seemed to have shrunk. He seemed shorter and thinner, as if there were literally less of him. Always decisive and driven, he now seemed indecisive and indifferent. He had placed a losing bid to erect one hotel in a four-hotel complex sponsored by the Yugoslav government to be built near Dubrovnik and didn't seem to care that he lost; he was hesitating about Raimont involvement in the resort being planned in Sidi-Bou-Said, unable, uncharacteristically, to make up his mind.

He began to worry about money, to fear that he would not have enough. Alix had the chilling thought that to him, his fear of running out of money really was the same as a fear of running out of life. He once asked a startled Raimont executive where he bought his shirts, how much they cost and if he was satisfied with them. On another occasion he asked a taxi driver how much he earned a week and then inquired if he was able to support his family on that sum. He wanted to know how much a bus cost in London, what it cost to have pajamas laundered in Chicago and the price of a Kodak camera he saw an American tourist use in Hawaii. He began to make certain economies, rich men's economies: When one of his fleet of planes wasn't being used, he leased it out instead of letting it remain in a hangar; he replaced the gaily painted ceramic ashtrays in his European hotels, a favorite tourist "souvenir," with inexpensive glass rectangles; and while in the United States he gave up the Evian water he had always ordered by the case.

Alix worried about her father, and she worried about her husband.

Yale paid no attention to his business, and he paid no attention to her. Alix didn't know what the trouble was, and when she asked if it were she, he said that it had nothing to do with her. When she asked if it were problems with WCD—she had begun to hear rumors in the London financial community—he said that it had nothing to do with WCD. When she asked him to tell her what was bothering him, he said, "Nothing," and shut Alix out.

Yale was unable to admit what was troubling him to Alix because he was unable to admit it to himself.

It had begun the night of the day Jai Jai and Sergei had eloped to Gibraltar. Yale had gone to Oliver Holborn's because, he told himself at the time, it was fashionable and he was curious. He had, after all, been curious about different things, fashionable at different times and in different places. In the sixties marijuana, in the seventies cocaine and, when he was much younger, cigarettes and then alcohol. He had tried them all, found them far less exciting than their reputations had led him to believe. He thought that an experience with one of the boys he met at Oliver's would be different, that bisexuality would be the ultimate experience, the ultimate thrill. In the beginning Yale was right. He would go to Oliver's, pick up a boy, tell him what he wanted, they would leave together. Afterward Yale would think about the next time, the next experience.

Gradually Yale began to resent his experiences at Oliver's because after the first few times they weren't as wicked, as thrilling as he had hoped, and Yale began to rage inwardly at the disappointment. The rage began to spread, echoing all the rage he had ever felt. Rage at his parents for not being rich, rage at Phillip Noyes for not leaving him more money, rage at Alix for being richer than he would ever be no matter how much he earned. Yale knew that his rage was unacceptable, knew that it was irrational. His love/hate relationship with the rich had turned to hate. No one must know; he could tell no one.

Yale was afraid of himself, afraid of the rage burning inwardly, invisibly, afraid of what he might do. He turned to Jai Jai because she, too, moved among the rich, had been used by the rich, had used them and had, by shooting Sergei, *gotten even* with them. Something that he, no matter what he did, had never been able to do. He began his liaison with Jai Jai because when he was with her, when he made love to her, marking both their bodies with her emeralds, he felt, finally, *superior* to them. The rich could buy anything; he, Yale, could do anything.

Yale felt an incendiary excitement when he began his liaison with Jai Jai. It was sexual excitement, constant, unrelenting; it was like being a very young man again, but even more so, it was an emotional excitement, all-consuming, addictive, thrilling. Everything else had been a disappointment, one way or another, but Jai Jai, what he felt with Jai Jai, Alexander's mistress, Sergei's wife, Sergei's killer, never was. Jai Jai never disappointed.

Yale's liaison began in Paris in the spring of 1977; his marriage ended in London in the same summer. The ending happened so fast, in such a tornado of passion, that Yale, who usually calculated first and acted later, made commitments he hadn't considered without contemplating the consequences. He wanted to marry Jai Jai; Jai Jai wanted to marry him.

"It's pointless to go on . . ." he told Alix on one of the few nights he'd spent in London since he'd begun the liaison. "I want a divorce." They were in the second-floor library, navy-blue, lacquer, terra-cotta and cream printed fabrics, a tranquil, intimate room, too small to contain Yale's explosive emotions. He wished he could offer Alix something, something to make her feel better, but what? She was the one who had; he was the one who wanted. It was the story of his life. "I'd do anything you want me to," he said. "But I want her."

"Jai Jai?"

"Yes," said Yale.

"Why?" asked Alix. "Why Jai Jai?" She'd sensed it was Jai Jai even before Corinne told her in so many words. She'd known ever since Southampton; she'd known with a part of her that didn't need facts, proof, gossip, rumor or the well-intentioned confidences of friends. What she wanted to know was not who, but why? What was there about Jai Jai that had such an irresistible effect? It couldn't be simply beauty; there were, after all, other women as beautiful as Jai Jai but none capable of producing the haunting impact Jai Jai seemed to exert. He father, her brother, now her husband. . . . "Why Jai Jai? What is there about her? What magic?"

"Jai Jai makes me feel rich," Yale said.

"Rich?" Alix was startled. "And *I* don't?"

Yale shook his head. "Feeling rich has nothing to do with money."

"What *does* it have to do with?" The irony of Yale's wanting a divorce because he had met someone who made him feel rich was not lost on Alix. She was the richest woman in the world, and she was about to lose her husband because he was in love with someone who made him feel rich.

"Feeling rich," Yale explained, "means I can do anything I want."

"Anything?" asked Alix. She thought of Daisy in *Gatsby* walking away from a fatal accident; she thought of Jai Jai in Mazatlán walking away from another fatal accident. It occurred to Alix that Yale might be walking into one. "*Anything?*"

"Anything," repeated Yale, "and everything." Then he said it again. "I want a divorce."

"Never," said Alix. She had promised herself she would never go through the repetitive sequence of marriage-divorce-remarriage that had so marked her early life and the lives of almost everyone she knew. A cycle that substituted motion for progress, that robbed emotion of its values, that insulted men and women and their uniqueness. She would never agree to a divorce. She would wait—Yale would tire of Jai Jai. Their marriage had not been a perfect marriage, but it was a good marriage—Yale had seen what there was in her when she had been plain and awkward and insecure. She had begun to change, and he had helped. Alix was not going to throw away a marriage for an affair.

The same week that Yale asked for a divorce, he made another request of Alix: He asked if he could buy the Belgravia house. At first Alix refused. Then, when she found out that he and Jai Jai were going to live together openly in St. Tropez in August, she agreed. To Yale's surprise, the contract specified that payment be made in dollars rather than pounds. Dollars were strong and getting stronger; pounds were weak and getting weaker.

"You have a smart lawyer," Yale said admiringly, even though it was going to make the house, already expensive, even more expensive.

"Yes," said Alix, choosing to let Yale think whatever he pleased. She saw no particular reason to tell him that it was she who had insisted on the dollar payment. It was the kind of thing she was learning under her father's and Cart-wright's guidance.

Alix moved into one of the penthouse suites of the London/Raimont, conscious of how her life was taking on a new shape. Yale, to whom the Belgravia house was more than just a home—it was, to him, the ultimate status symbol—wanted to make it into the most spectacular house, just as he and Jai Jai would be the most spectacular couple.

He hired Cole Whitelaw to transform it into a show-place. When Cole asked for a budget, Yale said, "There is none. Spend whatever you need."

It was a designer's dream; Cole didn't know it would turn into a nightmare.

In August, when Yale and Jai Jai went to St. Tropez, Alix's separation became known.

"You have no grounds anymore on which to refuse to see me," Hansjürg said. He called her throughout the winter and spring, and except in early September for two dinners in London when Hansjürg was there on business, Alix had been reluctant to see him. She was still married, and no matter how Yale behaved, Alix took it seriously; it was, of course, precisely what attracted Hansjürg to her.

"No, I haven't," said Alix, flattered at his persistence.

"I have a house outside Munich," he said. "Will you be my guest for the weekend?"

"Yes. I would be delighted," said Alix and they made a date for the last weekend in October—the first time they'd both be free. She hung up and rang for her secretary to begin the morning's dictation.

In the months since she'd begun working, Alix had become more and more confident, and gradually she made her stamp felt. She continued her father's long-standing policy of refusing to book tours in Raimont deluxe class hotels, although she encouraged the sales department to pursue group charters and off-season reduced-rate tours at the first-class hotels even more aggressively than in the past. With her father's and Cartwright's go-ahead, she had ordered estimates to be gathered for a top-to-bottom renovation of the Raimont/Brussels, which was feeling the competitive presence of the spectacular new five-hundred-room Sheraton, and without anyone's authority other than her own she had summarily fired the head concierge of the Raimont/Rome.

The concierge can be the tourist's best friend. He is, except for the elegant reception staff and the bar and restaurant staffs, the overseer of the entire street floor staff: key men, doormen, mail sorters, bellboys, elevator operators. He makes restaurant reservations, gets ballet, opera and theater tickets, reconfirms air tickets, reserves newspapers and magazines, pays for parcels and collect cables, sees that errands are run, packages received and messages delivered. Wearing the badge of his profession, the crossed *clefs d'or* on his lapel, the concierge knows everything and everyone in the city in which he works, regards "his" hotel as his domain, knows everything that goes on under its roof, is a gold mine of information and a fortress of discretion. He is a very Important Personage, and hoteliers are well aware of his value. A good concierge is worth his weight in gold, and he knows it.

Silvano, the concierge of the Raimont/Rome, had worked behind his imposing desk just to the left of the polished brass and glass revolving door for a dozen years. He had been hired away from the Excelsior at a great expense much as a valuable athlete is courted, given a bonus and won. Silvano, in his elegant gold-braided dove-gray uniform, pinkly barbered and impeccably manicured, the master of six languages, ran his domain like a private fiefdom.

One midnight in May, after having dined with some officials of CIT, the Compagnia Italiana Turismo, Alix returned to the Raimont/Rome and got on the elevator with two American couples.

"I'm so tired, I feel ill," said one of the women, middle-aged, attractive. She looked gray and exhausted.

"It will take me two days to recover," said the other woman, who resembled her and was, in fact, her sister. "I'm sorry we went."

"It was a big mistake," said her husband. "And it was my fault. I was the one who wanted to see Sorrento, and it was my idea to go."

Alix had noticed the tour bus outside the hotel when she had returned from dinner, but until she heard the word "Sorrento" she had paid it no attention. "Did you take the tour to Sorrento?" Alix asked the man who had spoken last.

"Sorrento, Vesuvius, Naples," he said, "and if you're thinking of going, I'd advise against it. It's too much for one day. You spend most of your time in the bus, and you're so tired you don't even remember what you've seen."

"The concierge says it's the fastest way to see some of southern Italy," his wife said, wanting to modify his negative tone.

The elevator came to a stop, and as the two American couples left, Alix wished them a goodnight. The Rome–Naples–Sorrento–Rome one-day excursion was a scandal. Alix knew that Temple Fielding devoted an entire paragraph warning against it in the most vehement terms. The trip usually left Rome at 7 A.M. and returned at midnight, and it was general knowledge that the tour operators paid commissions of fifty percent to the concierges who filled their buses. Supposedly, none of the personnel in first-class houses was involved, but Alix investigated. She discovered that not only was Silvano hard-selling the Naples–Sorrento excursion but that he was taking a hundred percent commission on theater tickets he bought from friends in box offices at discount prices and that he had innumerable "deals" with taxi drivers in which various "rain," "evening" and "rush hour" supplements were added to the meter fare and split between the drivers and Silvano.

As a businesswoman responsible for company earnings and as her father's daughter Alix understood the profit motive; as a hotelier who wanted satisfied guests to return and spread the word and as her mother's daughter she was appalled by greed. When she confronted Silvano, his defense was: "Everyone does it."

"Everyone in Raimont hotels does *not* do it," said Alix. "In fact, no one in Raimont hotels does. My father doesn't permit it, and neither do I," she added, and fired him on the spot.

The incident earned Alix respect and gave her an idea:

She began a monthly newsletter that was left in every room
with the room service menus and laundry, pressing and dry
cleaning lists. The newsletter suggested tours, diversions,
attractions and entertainments. With each, a price the tourist should expect fairly to pay was noted. It offered the
concierge's services to make arrangements at a flat fifteen
percent surcharge. In addition, it explained for American
tourists European tipping customs and suggested appropriate amounts. Although there was some grumbling from behind various concierge desks in the Raimont/Europe chain,
the feedback from guests was uniformly good, and as it
turned out, guests usually preferred to let the concierges
handle all the details, considering the 15 percent surcharge
well worth it. Eventually other chains adopted the idea,
and Alix was rewarded by the sincerest compliment of
them all: imitation.

∾ TWENTY ∾

Hansjürg von Miesbach's house was a castle. Schloss
Zauberwald, located seventy kilometers outside Munich,
was a turreted, stone edifice that Hansjürg explained had
been built in the fifteenth century, a period of enormous
commercial prosperity, as a hunting lodge by one of the
rich and worldly members of the Fugger banking family.
Set on a vast lawn in the midst of dark-green pine and
silver birch forest, the gray-stone building with its iron
gates seemed a fairy-tale castle when Alix first saw it early
on Friday evening as a gentle autumn mist blurred and
gentled its romantic façade. Lights burned behind the
many deep-set shuttered windows, and in the great hall a
fire crackled, the scent of burning wood fresh and wonderful.

The grandeur of the outside was offset by the coziness of
the interiors, with paneled rooms, comfortable upholstered
oversized furniture, wood armoires and painted wood

chests decorated with traditional Bavarian designs; the rush-seated chairs, also locally made, were naive and charming in their rough-hewn design and execution.

After a bath in a mahogany-sided tub triple the size of any Alix had ever seen and a nap, she came down to dinner. She waited not in the vast dining hall but in a library covered floor to ceiling with books published by generations of von Miesbachs. Stained-glass windows prevented the sun's rays from injuring the bindings of the valuable books, and long ladders rolled on rails to allow access to the volumes on upper shelves. An enormous twig basket of magazines in four languages was set on the needlepoint rug in front of the fireplaces. Alix had never, outside a public library, seen so much printed material.

"You don't read it *all*, do you?" she asked.

"Most of it, actually," said Hansjürg, the "actually" a clue to his years of English schooling. "Yes, I do. It's my business, but it's my pleasure as well."

"I wish I had the time to read. It was my favorite pastime when I was a girl," said Alix. She was not exaggerating the demands on her time. She was now working fourteen-hour days at Raimont, and twice a month she flew to Baltimore to carry on the charitable work started by her mother. Her father had been angry at first. Furious when he called her London office from Caracas and was told that she was in Baltimore, he had called Baltimore, and when Alix answered the telephone, he exploded: "Why aren't you in the office? Who gave you permission to leave London?"

"Nobody gave me permission," Alix had said. "I don't need anybody's permission." She was shocked at her own words. Never had she talked back to her father. Apparently her father was as shocked by her words as she was, for there was a long silence from Caracas. She waited for the outburst of temper she had become used to. Since Sergei's death her father seemed both to love her more and to resent her more. He showed his resentment by explosions of temper, always, so far, over business matters. Sometimes she didn't do things as fast as he thought they ought to be done; often he asked her to do three things at once and was furious, ten minutes later, when she hadn't done them all; once he blew up when she didn't know the terms of the fire insurance coverage for the Atlanta/Raimont when a touring rock group had set fire to a room; another time he hung up on her—Toronto to London—when he asked for the previous week's occupancy rates in the Madrid/Raimont and she asked him to hang on while her secretary brought in the figures.

Yet, when she made real mistakes—once she had OK'd a linen order for three Italian Raimonts without having the prices of competing suppliers checked, a seventeen-thousand-dollar error; another time she had failed to return a call from an agent in Bordeaux soon enough and a competitor had bought a vineyard's entire production, a coup that could be advertised and promoted and an error that cost Raimont Hotels prestige and would affect the depth of its restaurant cellars ten years hence when the wine would be ready to drink—her father was reasonable. "As long as you learn from your mistakes," he said, "I won't consider them unforgivable."

"What are you doing in Baltimore?" her father asked, surprising Alix, who was still braced for his temper.

"We're raising money for a new burn unit," said Alix. "Baltimore has none. Burn victims have to be sent to New York Hospital or Bethesda. Sometimes we lose them in the time it takes to move them." Alix went on to tell him about three men who had suffered third-degree burns in an explosion of a boiler in a primary school. One had died on the way to Bethesda; the others, suspended in saline baths, faced long months of therapy and skin grafts, and the outlook for their survival even then was still questionable. "The main initial problem burn victims face is infection since the protective covering of the skin is lost through burns. We need highly sterile situations immediately if there's to be any hope for them."

"Where did you learn all that?" Her father was impressed.

"I've been working with the board since Mother died," said Alix.

"It means a lot to you, doesn't it?" he asked. "To continue your mother's work?"

"Yes," said Alix. "It also means a lot to me to work with Raimont. But I don't like to be abused for it."

Her father did not respond to Alix's comment. Instead, he said he was calling because he had just had lunch with an Argentinian investment banker. A lot of Argentinian money was going into the United States, and a group of Argentinian investors was interested in a furniture factory in High Point, North Carolina, and the banker had asked if Raimont, who purchased large quantities of furniture, might be interested in buying. "What do you think, Alix?" her father asked. As always, when he asked a business question, he gave no indication of his own thoughts; he did not want to influence her.

"We're hoteliers. We don't know anything about the furniture business," said Alix. "Having a source, though, to make furniture to our design and for the best price is attractive." They continued to discuss the pros and cons of the idea, and the conversation, which took place a week before Alix went to Munich, was completed with no reference to Alexander's initial anger. Alix thought of the conversation as a new development in her complex relationship with her father.

"I always promise myself I'm going to read on flight," Alix told Hansjürg, "and I even pack a book with me. But I always seem to have a briefcase full of things stamped immediate."

"Are you complaining?" asked Hansjürg.

"No. In fact, come to think of it, I'm really bragging," said Alix. "I like it."

"You seem different from when I first met you in St. Moritz," said Hansjürg, realizing that it had been almost a year before. They were eating a delicate meal of veal with cream and wild mushrooms Hansjürg said were gathered in the nearby forests, along with a local white wine so light, so fresh it had the quality the French call *pétillant*. "Less lonely, I think," he said.

"I am different," said Alix. "I feel sadder"—she felt it unnecessary to refer to her mother's death, to the long separation from Yale—"sadder but no longer isolated. I feel needed. I've never before in my life felt needed."

"I understand," said Hansjürg. Feeling needed had happened to him, too, when he had taken over his family's business. He realized something similar must be happening to Alix. "When I met you, you were merely beautiful; now you have another quality that goes beyond beauty."

He paused to think of the word—confidence, he wondered, or perhaps a new softness, womanliness. While he was thinking precisely how to describe it, Alix thanked him for his compliment with a smile, and looking at her over the candles, he smiled in return and said, "Now you look just merely beautiful again."

If it was flattery, it pleased Alix enormously.

Hansjürg had always asked Britta and P.-G. about Alix and had heard disturbing rumors about her in the past year, but the way she looked and behaved contradicted what he'd heard, and uncertain, he did not mention anything to Alix.

After dinner they went into the small village with its wooden neat-as-a-pin storybook houses and its steepled church which managed simultaneously to project Gothic seriousness and Baroque exuberance. Over schnapps in a cozy bar, Hansjürg joined in the spirited discussion of the hunting season—hare seemed unusually scarce, while woodcock and thrush were plentiful—outlandish tales of the just-past *Oktoberfest* and a serious conversation about the wave of West German political terrorism that bordered on the epidemic. By the end of the evening plans had been made for a wild mushroom hunt the next morning in response to Alix's interest. They returned to Schloss Zauberwald and their separate rooms just past midnight. As he said goodnight, Hansjürg told Alix again that she looked wonderful. "More than just beautiful" were his words, and his tone seemed to say that he was surprised. Fleetingly Alix wondered how he had expected her to look.

The next day was enchanted. They rowed across a lake so still, so perfectly calm that it was like floating on a mirror. Later in the winter, Hansjürg told Alix, the lake would freeze and would be the scene all winter long of ice skating parties. Alix and Hansjürg and their companions from the evening before searched for mushrooms damp and sensuous in shape and scent, as rich as the earth in which they flourished. Alix in corduroy pants and sweaters and stout hiking shoes enjoyed the simplicity of the pleasures of Schloss Zauberwald, and it seemed an omen when, as they returned to the *Schloss*, a long procession of placid cattle led by their shepherds made their stately way down the high hills, their soft mooing carrying across the wooded valley. Alix couldn't quite believe her eyes. "There are garlands of flowers twisted through their horns," she said in amazement.

"They're wild flowers from higher up in the hills," said Hansjürg. "It's a custom here to twine them through the horns when the cattle come down for the winter. It's been done as long as anyone remembers."

"How magical," said Alix.

"Yes," said Hansjürg, seeing it anew through her eyes and finding pleasure in her pleasure.

That night Hansjürg gave a small dinner party. An architect and his novelist wife drove by from their nearby country retreat; the brewmaster of a famed Bavarian brewery and his wife, a boutique owner from Munich, and the priest from the Gothic/Baroque church in town formed the guest list, and Alix recalled how she had enjoyed the mix of people she had always welcomed to her New York apartment before she married Yale. It had been a long time since she had spent an evening with such a varied group since Yale preferred either business associates or jet-setters. Alix was stimulated and intrigued by the wide range of the conversation, and she told Hansjürg so when the guests had left and he walked her upstairs to her room.

"I knew I'd like you," he said in his intense way, "but I didn't know how much." They were outside the door to her room, and Hansjürg embraced her and kissed her, first gently, then passionately, a kiss that evoked in them both memories of the past New Year's Eve. Hansjürg took his mouth just far enough away from Alix's lips to be able to speak. "May I come in?" he asked, indicating the door.

"No," she said suddenly and without thinking. Alix pulled away from his embrace and went into her room, shutting the door behind her, leaving him hurt and confused. Alix didn't understand why, but she burst into tears, and when, finally, they had died, she wondered why she had said no when she meant yes.

A long time ago, so long it seemed to have been always,

Alix had promised herself that one thing she would never be was a poor little rich girl. No string of marriages and divorces, no long afternoons killed with backgammon and bridge, no eye tucks at thirty, followed by a full lift at forty, no sad and aimless middle age spent with a retinue of amusing homosexuals to advise her on clothes, makeup and decor. In the wreckage of her marriage, it was easy for her to respond to Hansjürg, and because it was so easy, she was suspicious of herself, of her feelings. Yale, she had heard, was no longer living with Jai Jai, and abruptly he had stopped demanding a divorce. Alix had allowed herself to think of a reconciliation, but Yale had totally rejected all her advances. She was confused and lonely, wanting to get involved with Hansjürg but afraid. Perhaps, she thought, that was why she had so abruptly cut him off the night before.

By three o'clock on Sunday Alix had not seen Hansjürg. She had breakfasted alone, read the Munich, London and Paris newspapers alone and lunched alone. Distracted, she remembered nothing she'd read; anxious, she'd barely eaten. She kept glancing up, looking around, looking for Hansjürg. She was ashamed at what she'd done, the way she'd done it; she was ashamed at her behavior, so inexplicable even to herself. She understood why he was avoiding her; in his place she certainly would have done the same. But she wished he'd appear; she wished he'd make things all right again between them. Whenever she and Yale had argued, he'd always been the one to patch things up, to send a little present, to apologize; all she'd had to do was wait. With Hansjürg she wanted things to be different from the way they'd been with Yale, and she realized that if she wanted things to be different, she would have to *be* different.

It took all the courage she had to ask the housekeeper where Hansjürg was, but she did it. And when she got to the carpenter's shed, it took even more courage to say what she had decided to say.

"I want to apologize for my behavior last night," she began. Just as it had to her father and brother, apology came hard to her. "I don't know why I acted the way I did. You must be completely mystified."

"I am," said Hansjürg. "You led me on, then slammed the door in my face." His tone was cold. He was hurt and angry. He had not allowed himself to feel anything since Annaliese. He had wanted Alix and shown it, and she had pushed him away. Additional bookshelves were being built for the second-floor hall, and freshly cut boards were stacked all over the floor, making it difficult to move. Alix wished she could reach out and touch Hansjürg, but piles of boards were a barrier between them. She was aware of the smells of construction: newly cut wood, turpentine and the heavy lubricating oil used on machinery. She reached out over the stack of wood, and if Hansjürg had moved only slightly, she would have been able to touch his sleeve. He didn't, and she felt a flash of resentment.

"Sometimes I don't understand myself," Alix continued her apology, "I do stupid things, destructive things. . . ."

"So I've heard," said Hansjürg.

"What do you mean?" Alix asked sharply. "What have you heard?"

Hansjürg hesitated. He wanted to lie. His eyes focused on the opposite walls, where, in assigned places outlined by stencils in yellow paint of their shapes, hung saws, pliers, screwdrivers, wrenches, hammers, coils of electric wiring, wood and metal planes. He looked everywhere except at her.

"Don't lie to me," said Alix, reading his mind. "Tell me what you heard."

"That you're unstable," said Hansjürg finally. "That you've spent time in a psychiatric hospital."

"That's not true!" said Alix. "How could it be true? I've been working since the beginning of the year." She paused and thought for a moment. "The way I behaved last night made you wonder . . . whether I'm in my right mind?"

Hansjürg, embarrassed, miserable, nodded. He had not told Alix the whole story: that she had supposedly tried to commit suicide on the anniversary of her brother's death; that she had been taken to a hospital to have her stomach pumped and then been transferred to the psychiatric ward. Hansjürg had not wanted to believe it. On the other hand, her brother and grandfather had taken their own lives, and there had been times in the year since he'd met Alix when ıer office had told him she was unavailable. Perhaps she'd been . . . "away." Hansjürg didn't want to believe what he'd heard, but the way she'd led him on, then, at the last moment, abruptly, irrationally shut him out seemed to be a kind of evidence.

"Where have you heard this?" asked Alix. She was furious; it was all such a blatant lie, and yet even Hansjürg was willing to at least consider that it might be true.

"I don't think I should say," said Hansjürg.

"How can I stop these . . . malicious . . . rumors if I don't know who's spreading them?"

Hansjürg thought over what she had said; she was, of course, right. "From Britta," he said finally. And then, wanting to protect Britta, he added, "Britta isn't gratuitously spreading this gossip," he said. "It's just that I always ask about you . . . I care about you, I think you sense how much . . . and, at first she didn't want to tell me but I pressed her. . . ."

"Please tell her it's not true, none of it," Alix began, and then she corrected herself. "No. I'll call her myself. I want to find out where she heard all those things." Then Alix asked Hansjürg a question: "Have you forgiven me for last night?"

"I *will* forgive you," he said. "But right now I'm confused and hurt and—"

"And angry," Alix again finished for him.

"And angry," he said. "And afraid. I'm afraid you'll just hurt me again."

"I'm tempted to make a lover's promise," said Alix, "and promise I'll never—"

"May I point out," said Hansjürg, interrupting her, "that we're not lovers?" Alix looked as if she'd been slapped.

Before she could say anything, Hansjürg looked at his watch. "Come, it's getting late," he said. "I'll drive you to the airport."

They said goodbye awkwardly without kissing, without touching. They were both conscious of a holding back, of a growing tension and uncertainty between them that were far more electric, far more compelling than a giving in to the enormous sexual excitement both felt.

She hadn't heard about Alix from *one* person, Britta said over the telephone from Neuilly-sous-Clermont to London. "Everyone" gossiped about Alix, Britta said, and she had heard different versions from different people.

"None of it is true," said Alix, pointing out that for almost a year she'd been at work every day. "None of it could be true."

Britta promised to stop the rumors whenever she heard them. Before they said goodbye, Alix and Britta promised to have lunch together the next time they were in the same city at the same time.

Alix hung up, wondering who was spreading such destructive gossip—gossip that threatened to poison her not-even-begun love affair. Alix had grown up knowing that there would always be those who automatically hated and envied her for being rich because they imagined that the rich never suffered, were never hurt, rejected, who thought that money bought invulnerability. There was nothing Alix could do about that; there was nothing, she was afraid, she could do to stop people from talking about her.

Upset, she forced herself to turn to the morning mail. On top with the return address of a Paris law firm was a registered certified envelope. Addressed to Alix Raimont, Co-executor with Alexander Raimont of the Estate of Serge Ramont, it informed Alix of the intention of Jai Jai Raimont, widow of Sergei, to press a claim for the widow's fifty per cent share of the residual estate.

Sergei's estate had been valued at a hundred and twenty-five million dollars. Jai Jai was talking about sixty-two million five hundred thousand dollars.

Alix Raimont had never had to fight for anything in her life. She had no instinct for it, no practice at it, and she wondered whether she'd have the courage to do it. She sat at her desk immobile. She felt defeated, and then, just for a second, a tiny spark of anger flared up in her, and then just as quickly as it had blazed, it disappeared.

∞ TWENTY-ONE ∞

"I must have luxury; necessity I can manage without." It was a very Cole-like statement, and Dante knew it was a warning signal. He wondered what was on Cole's mind. Cole lived beautifully in his Kensington house; he dressed in Savile Row clothes, beautifully brushed and pressed and never brand-new; he dined on simple foods accompanied by complex wines—and he owed everybody: tailors, florists, art and antique dealers, grocers, butchers, wine merchants. The days when it was considered the mark of a gentleman to owe tradespeople had long passed, and their demands for payment were no longer polite.

"What's the matter?" asked Dante. Humor was Cole's best defense. When something troubled him, he made a joke. "Money problems again?"

Cole nodded. "At my age it's no longer very amusing to be hard up all the time. My days of being able to enjoy bohemian poverty are over."

"Are you being extravagant?" Dante had been living in Paris, taking care of Cole's business interests there, while Cole had been in London running his business there.

"No more than usual," said Cole, sipping brandy from a crystal snifter, thin as glass thread. "I'm being evicted, for one thing," he said. "For another, not one of my suppliers will extend me any more credit." He took a ribbon-tied portfolio covered with hand-printed Florentine paper and handed it to Dante. It was filled with bills stamped overdue, letters from collection agencies, lawyers' letters and an eviction notice. The deadline was five days away. "The thing is," Cole said as Dante shuffled through the papers, "that I'm owed a lot of money."

"How much?" asked Dante.

"Two hundred ten thousand pounds," said Cole.

"How long overdue is it?" Dante asked, cursing himself for not insisting on running *all* of Cole's business affairs. At the time he hadn't wanted to appear to want to take over, and when Cole said he had a big job in London which he would bill through that office, Dante had not commented.

"Six months."

"My God," Dante said. "Why haven't you told me before this?"

"The client promised I'd get the money. I believed him. I didn't want to embarrass him," Cole said. Dante rolled his eyes. If Cole was one of the world's best designers, he was its worst businessman. "Besides, he's a friend. We know him socially."

"Yale?"

"Yale," said Cole. "I thought he was superrich. The papers said he was a financial genius, a wonder boy. I was sure he was good for the money."

"Not anymore," said Dante. "He's had a lot of financial problems." Cole listened as Dante spoke of loan losses, mismatched due dates, insider trading, questionably accelerated depreciation and artificially inflated P/E ratios. He didn't understand one word, but he understood the meaning.

"I guess I'll never get paid now," Cole said when Dante had finished. He was proud of the work he'd done on the Belgravia house. It was an extravagant neo-Egyptian fantasy, and now it looked as if he wouldn't get paid.

"Cole, let me?" Dante motioned to the portfolio and its bills and threats and deadlines and dunning letters.

"I'd never be in this mess if you'd been handling the London office in the first place," Cole said, his relief apparent. "I thought of it, but I was afraid to ask. I didn't want to make too many demands on you."

"I thought of it, too," said Dante. "And I was afraid to offer. I didn't want you to think I was being pushy."

They smiled at each other sadly. It was a poignant moment, and Cole summed it up when he said, "I wonder if everyone has the same fears we do or if we're really . . . different?"

"I think everyone has the same fears," said Dante, and then he looked at Cole and said, "After all, Cole, we're human."

The next day Dante flew to Zurich, where he withdrew two hundred and ten thousand pounds from the account

Alexander Raimont had established for him a year and a half before. Dante intended to pay Cole. Dante would collect from Yale. He would wait if he had to; Cole couldn't afford to wait.

When Dante returned to his small Montmartre flat, he was surprised to receive a call from Alexander Raimont.

"If you need money, why didn't you ask me?" Alexander said.

"I've already profited enough from the . . . tragedies of the Raimonts," he said. Apparently the Zurich bank had informed Alexander of the large withdrawal. Dante was impressed and uncomfortable; there was something terribly ominous about all the power that kind of money—Raimont money—carried with it.

"Why do you need so much money?" asked Alexander. "Perhaps I could help you out."

Dante had heard of Alexander's legendary generosity; now that he was on the receiving end, he was surprised at how flattered he was. Dante was reluctant to explain his relationship with Cole to Alexander, was reluctant to expose Yale's financial difficulties until Alexander, sensing his discomfort, told him that he already knew everything about it. Dante wondered for a split second whether Alexander, who had always hated Yale, had been behind his current difficulties but dismissed the thought.

"Cole completely gutted and redesigned the interiors of the Belgravia house," Dante said. "Yale owes Cole two hundred and ten thousand pounds for the job and has owed it for over six months now. I'm afraid Cole is never going to get paid."

"I think we can help Cole out," Alexander said when Dante had finished, "without your having to use your own funds. Will you agree to wait until tomorrow before you do anything? I'll call you back."

Dante agreed, unable to fight down the glow of pride he felt at having one of the world's richest men take a personal interest in his problems. Dante was quite surprised when, on the next day, Alix Raimont called. She was, she said, calling at the suggestion of her father. She invited Dante to London, to lunch in the Raimont dining room on the first Monday of February.

In a rust silk blouse and black bouclé Chanel suit, Alix looked both powerful and sexy. Dante had never seen her look so attractive, and for the first time he was startlingly aware of her resemblance to her father. She had his unusual, dramatic coloring, dark-blond hair that shaded off into healthily tanned skin with no line of visible demarcation between skin and hair. That oddity of coloring made the distinctive Raimont features stand out in bold relief: The eyes, large and oddly slanted down at the corners, were a clear, Tiffany blue; the nose, strong, straight, in perfect proportion to the size of the skull; the sensuous, wide mouth hinting of severity, and vulnerability, impossibly, at the same time. Alix was, Dante thought, a striking woman who would become more attractive, more commanding with maturity. Alix's voice, as she spoke to the steward, was soft, confident, assured; her manner, as she suggested poached turbot and a Sancerre, was that of a poised hostess.

"I would like to know what my husband is doing," said Alix straightforwardly. "He has suddenly stopped pressing me for a divorce. I thought you might know why."

"I'd prefer not to . . . get involved," Dante said, and paused. He was intimidated in the presence of Alix's self-confidence, and he did not want to be the one who told Alix the shocking details of Yale's life-on-the-fringes. "I really don't want to get in the middle of this."

"I don't understand," said Alix. "He was so anxious for a divorce. It's curious I haven't heard from him since January." Alix's self-assurance in what would have been an intolerable situation for any other woman—having to ask an almost stranger for intimate details of a spouse—impressed Dante incredibly. "I understand, for instance," Alix continued, "that Yale and Jai Jai are no longer . . . together."

Dante nodded. Perhaps, he thought, if he told Alix, they would be able to help Yale. Yale, he knew, was desperate and desperately unhappy. "Jai Jai left Yale in Cairo. I don't know the details, but she walked out on him. As far as I know, they haven't seen each other since."

"Do you know why?" Alix asked when the waiter had cleared the main course and served foamy lemon mousses

"Yale has gone beyond—" Dante was acutely embarrassed, not knowing how to phrase himself.

"Gone beyond what?" Alix was matter-of-fact.

"Well, Alix, as you must know, I'm one hundred percent homosexual," Dante finally said. "I believe Yale has gone far beyond that."

Alix stroked the silver handle of her large European-style dessert spoon thoughtfully. She remembered Yale's interest in offbeat sex, the party in SoHo so many years ago, the incident in San Lorenzo. What Dante was saying did not come as a total surprise. She assumed that Yale was now doing all the things she had refused to take part in. It was sad, Alix thought, and she told Dante so. It explained why he no longer wanted a divorce. If what Dante said was true, Yale did not desire Jai Jai, did not desire her, did not desire any woman.

After a moment's silence during which the espresso was served, Alix spoke again in her quiet voice with the intriguing accent that was neither American nor British.

"My father and I want to pay Cole Whitelaw for his work on the Belgravia house. We do not want you to have to assume, even temporarily, a debt of a member of our family." Before Dante could demur, Alix handed him a check made out to Cole; she had had it concealed under the Madeira place mat during the entire meal. "Don't refuse it," Alix continued. "We will not let you use your own money to pay my husband's debts. I'm sure," she added, "you can find a more productive use for it."

Dante nodded again. He had, in fact, been thinking of using the money in his Zurich account to capitalize the web of business he and Cole were planning. Dante accepted the check and, folding it, put it in his pocket.

"Thank you," he said. "You did not have to do this, but it will make a difference to Cole and me." Alix listened with interest as Dante described their plans.

When lunch was finished, Alix walked Dante to the elevator and waited with him until it arrived.

"Now that we've paid for Cole's work," Alix said with a trace of completely unexpected humor, "we'd like to see it. Perhaps you'll send photographs. . . ."

Dante agreed, and when the elevator arrived, Alix shook

his hand warmly and said goodbye. As Dante left the Rai- mont offices, he looked back up at the building at the inter- twined AR, the monogram identifying Raimont hotels throughout the world, on the canopy. He realized that not only did Alix look like her father and behave like him, but they even had the same initials. Alix Raimont was, Dante thought, not only the richest woman in the world but also the most interesting, the most intriguing, the most glamor- ous. He wondered how Yale could possibly have left her for Jai Jai.

As Dante left the building, Alix placed a call to her fa- ther in San Francisco. She told him that she had paid off Yale's debts, as they had agreed. She also told him that there was something she wanted to discuss with him in per- son. They agreed to lunch together in the bar of the Quo Vadis restaurant in New York City on the first Wednesday in February.

"I've heard of rich women who paid their husbands' bills," Cole said when Dante gave him Alix Raimont's check. "But I've never heard of one who paid the bills of a husband who left her for another woman. Why on earth is she doing it?" Cole wanted to know.

"Because Alix Raimont is a nice person," Dante an- swered. "She doesn't want anyone to be hurt."

Alexander Raimont was pleased when the first thing Alix told him at the Quo Vadis was that she had decided to divorce Yale.

"Good," said Alexander. "You'll be better off without him." He refrained from pointing out that he had cautioned her not to marry him years before. Alexander was a realist; he knew that I-told-you-so's accomplished nothing. He had given up trying to arrange a marriage between Alix and Paolo Barragan. He had met Hansjürg, had him investi- gated, and he approved. Hansjürg was not interested in her for her money; he had plenty of his own. But Alexander was curious.

"What made you decide to divorce Yale at this late date? Hansjürg?"

"It has nothing to do with Hansjürg," said Alix. "I decided to divorce Yale because there's no hope for us. Yale will never want me; he will never want any woman." Then she brought up the subject she had dreaded because her father's warning about Yale had turned out to be true. "A divorce is going to be expensive."

Alexander nodded. There had already been the payment to Cole; the mortgage on the Belgravia house and Yale's loans from WCD were still outstanding. "But a divorce will be cheaper than staying married to him. And besides, whatever it costs, it will be worth it. You'll be free."

Alix nodded. Yale had always told her that money existed to buy what you wanted. What she wanted now was freedom.

"You're lucky to be able to turn your back on him, to walk away from him," said Alexander, the envy in his voice obvious. Alix thought she knew what he was referring to.

"Jai Jai?"

"Jai Jai." Alexander nodded.

"You and Sergei and Yale," said Alix. "What is Jai Jai's secret? What is her power?" Alix knew it had to go far beyond mere physical beauty.

"Jai Jai makes me feel alive," Alexander said. For as long as he could remember, money had made him feel alive. When he met Jai Jai in Bequia, he was beginning to be sated with money, and it had begun to lose its magic for him. Jai Jai gave him the feeling that money always had but even more strongly, more intensely, and once he loved her, it renewed his passion for money, and he began to multiply the fortune he already had. Jai Jai made him feel immortal, and the birth of Jacqueline had confirmed the feeling.

"Yale once told me that Jai Jai made him feel rich; Sergei once told me that Jai Jai made him feel like a man," Alix said. She realized that Jai Jai's secret was that she, who demanded only to be admired and desired, could make a man's deepest wish, most secret fantasy come true. Jai Jai, obsessed with mirrors, was herself a mirror. She cast back the image each man most deeply craved. What none of them had realized was that there was a penalty.

Sergei has paid with his life. Yale has paid with the loss of his business, the ending of his marriage. Alix wondered out loud what price her father had paid.

"I've paid with my freedom," Alexander answered. For months the battle over Jai Jai's claim against Sergei's estate had been carried out in lawyers' offices in London, Paris, New York and Mexico City. The lawyers' fees for fighting Jai Jai's claim had already amounted to more than a quarter of a million dollars, and no end was in sight. Even if Jai Jai wanted to give up, Alexander knew perfectly well that her lawyers wouldn't let her. They were working on a contingency basis and weren't about to let go of a percentage of sixty-two million five hundred thousand dollars. The endless meetings drained Alexander, forcing him to think of Jai Jai, to be reminded of her, to be constantly confronted with the consequences of kisses on the mouth. He was a prisoner of his own passion.

"Buy your freedom back," said Alix, "the way I've bought mine from Yale."

Alexander nodded sadly. "But don't you see, I don't want my freedom. I still want her." Alexander thought of the weekend in Beaulieu, the days and nights since that he had spent with Jai Jai, compelled to see her, unable to resist, although for days he fought the need to pick up a telephone, to pass her apartment, to talk to her, to touch her, to feel her warmth, to receive the comfort from her that sustained him and shamed him. "I still love her."

"After everything?" Alix thought of Sergei . . . dead because of Jai Jai; of her own marriage . . . destroyed because of Jai Jai; of her father . . . exhausted, drawn, aged . . . because of Jai Jai. "After . . . everything?"

Her father nodded. "I still love her."

"Then tell me," said Alix, "if you still love her, why do you look so terribly unhappy?"

Alix's question, identical to the question Liliane had asked in Cap Ferrat the summer before, stopped Alexander short. It had the impact of a physical blow.

"Perhaps it's not what other people would call love," Alexander said. "Jai Jai is my obsession. My terrible obsession."

"You have used money your entire life to solve everything . . . why don't you use it to free yourself of your obsession?" said Alix. "Offer Jai Jai a settlement . . . get her out of your life except on your own terms . . . use your money to do it. . . ."

Alexander nodded, allowing himself to imagine how wonderful it would be to have Jai Jai in his power, to do his bidding. If he made a settlement, put strings on it, forced her to live on his terms. "Half of sixty-two million five hundred thousand is thirty-one million two hundred and fifty thousand," he said.

"She'll jump at twenty," said Alix.

In Paris on the Tuesday of Easter week, 1978, Yale and Jai Jai saw each other for only the second time since Christmas 1977 in Cairo. They had each been summoned to the offices of a lawyer on the Rue de Quatre Septembre across from the Bourse. They did not conceal their surprise at seeing each other, and the lawyer was aware that they did not exchange one unnecessary word during the introductions. It was certainly strange, considering what he had to tell them, but their personal life was none of his business. He had called them together to deliver the message he was being well paid to deliver.

"I have been instructed to tell you," the lawyer began, "that the Raimont family is prepared to settle with both of you. Mr. Warrant, your debts will be paid off entirely. Mrs. Raimont, a lump-sum cash payment will be made to settle your suit against your late husband's estate. There are, naturally, conditions attached to the offer."

A wave of relief went through the room, and Yale and Jai Jai looked at each other for the first time and smiled. The atmosphere in the room lightened, and the lawyer, who had been addressing them both, turned directly to Yale as he continued. "The board of Warrant, Charlton, Dover, upon the recommendation of the investigating auditors engaged by the London Bank, expects your resignation, effective immediately."

Yale swallowed. He felt as if the ground beneath his chair had suddenly opened up.

"Resignation, effective immediately . . ." the lawyer repeated, not sure if Yale had heard. "Do you consent?"

Yale wanted to refuse. Then he thought of the legal charges that were being prepared against him—he would be ruined in every financial market throughout the world—and of his debts—a half million dollars borrowed personally from WCD, the three-hundred-fifty-thousand mortgage on the Belgravia house, two hundred ten thousand to Cole Whitelaw.

"What happens if I agree?" asked Yale.

"If you agree, all charges will be dropped and your debts will be guaranteed by the Raimont family," said the lawyer. "You will leave this office unencumbered."

Yale nodded, relieved, resigned, resentful. He had no choice. When a billion dollars leans on you, he thought, you feel it.

"Mrs. Raimont," the lawyer said now that he had Yale's agreement, "the condition in your case involves your daughter, Jacqueline. . . ."

As the lawyer spoke, Jai Jai realized with tears she couldn't hold back the price she was being asked to pay: the Raimonts considered Jacqueline a Raimont baby, and they wanted to adopt her.

"You leave your daughter in the care of nurses and governesses," the lawyer said, "you are frequently away from your home weeks at a time and the Raimonts would like the child to be brought up under the care of an attentive, physically present guardian. In return, the Raimonts will make an offer in settlement of your claims against your late husband's estate. . . ."

Tears fell down Jai Jai's cheeks and she listened numbly. She had begun her action against Sergei's estate at Yale's behest. Unable to live on the hundred-thousand-dollar-a-year income Sergei had provided for her, Yale had urged her to press for more. "You'll get it," he had said. "You're his widow." When Jai Jai had expressed reluctance, Yale had merely said, "Jai Jai, they'll pay you off just to keep you quiet." And then, when Yale had left her, withdrawing his financial support, Jai Jai had found herself trapped by her own lawyers, who refused to let her drop the suit. It had been five months of hell. The large amounts of money frightened her, the endless meetings with phalanxes of lawyers and accountants at which she understood almost nothing, the constantly changing series of offers and counter-offers had exacted its toll in anxiety, sleeplessness, panic. When Jai Jai looked in the mirror, she no longer saw the most beautiful girl in the world.

"Mrs. Raimont, do you agree?" asked the lawyer, his voice penetrating Jai Jai's thoughts.

Jai Jai nodded, the tears preventing her from speaking. She had only half heard, but it didn't matter. She would agree to anything to get the torment over with.

"In settlement of your claim against your late husband's estate," the lawyer went on, "the Raimont family is prepared to offer a cash settlement of twenty million dollars. . . ."

The lawyer continued. Jai Jai and Yale looked at each other and smiled. They read each other's minds: twenty million dollars. For twenty million dollars they would do anything. . . .

PART SIX

THE RICH
AND THE
BEAUTIFUL

June 1978

∞ TWENTY-TWO ∞

The Hôtel du Cap is more than a hotel; it is a legend. A serene white and blue shuttered Second Empire building, it is set on a hill overlooking twenty-two acres of scented pine woods and rose gardens on the tip of Cap d'Antibes, and its elegant paths wind down toward the Mediterranean and the Eden Roc, the world's most elegant beach. The guest list is a who's who not of the year or of the decade but of the century. Scott Fitzgerald wrote about it; Chagall and Picasso strolled through its gardens; the Duke and Duchess of Windsor honeymooned in rooms number 33 and number 34, Marlene Dietrich and Gloria Guinness were among its great beauties and Aly Khan and Porfirio Rubirosa among its great playboys; Eisenhower and de Gaulle conferred here on matters of state; Nubar Gulbenkian and the shah of Iran, two of the world's richest men, entertained their guests there, and it was there on a heavenly day in June that Jai Jai Raimont and Yale Warrant were married.

Alexander Raimont, the bride's lover and former father-in-law, gave Jai Jai away, and Alix Raimont, the groom's ex-wife, was the first to wish the couple well after the vows had been exchanged. Jacqueline Raimont, who threw pale-yellow rose petals in her mother's path, was too little to understand what it meant when people said that her mommy was getting married or what it meant when they said that Alix was adopting her. She did know, when she looked at her mother, that she had the most beautiful mother in the world. And she knew, when she looked at Alix, that she loved Alix more than she loved anyone except maybe Alexander, who always made such a fuss over her and made her feel she was the luckiest little girl in the world.

Two hundred and fifty guests, among them the most sophisticated people in the world, swirled around the ground floor and the gardens and even spilled out onto the pebbled, curved drive where Rollses and Bentleys and mint-condition Duesenbergs seemed the only cars equal to the elegance of the setting. The guests had been flown in from around the world at Raimont expense, and although no one person knew the entire glamorous and scandalous story, there were many who knew parts of it.

Corinne de Sancheval had organized the wedding. Half a dozen engravers worked through the night; half a dozen penmen, two of them flown in from Washington, D.C., specialists in Spencerian script, labored at hand-addressing the envelopes. With the assistance of Raimont chefs and sommeliers, she had ordered the food, the wine and the champagne. She had personally selected a dress for Jacqueline and accompanied Jai Jai when she chose hers; she had ordered the flowers and supervised the decorations, arranged for the mayor of the Ville d'Antibes to perform the ceremony and selected the two string quartets that provided continuous music.

Corinne thought she understood perfectly why Alexander Raimont had allowed his mistress to marry. Raoul did not, and Corinne explained it to him.

"Many married men prefer to have a safely married mistress. It's much safer than an unmarried mistress who might make tiresome demands for marriage and might even reveal the affair to the man's wife. All in all," Corinne said, "it's much safer, much more civilized."

"I suppose so," said Raoul, who did not know that years before, Esau Yakov had approved of him before Corinne agreed to marry him. "But I'm old-fashioned. I still believe in love."

"So do I"—Corinne shrugged—"but I'm not a billionaire." And then she turned her attention to Mignonne Mireille, who was with her newest lover, an exceptionally handsome young man at least ten years Mignonne's junior.

For Gilberto Rodríguez, it was his first trip to Europe, and whatever he personally felt about the rich and the beautiful and the way they walked away from fatal accidents, he said nothing. Discretion had, after all, brought him rewards beyond his most extravagant dreams.

In the weeks following Sergei Raimont's death Gilberto's early retirement at full pension was arranged with the Mazatlán police force, and he was hired as head of all security for the Raimont/Mazatlán at a salary that would allow him to send each of his four children to college. Additionally a Mercedes automobile, coincidentally the same burgundy red as the one he had so often seen Sergei Raimont drive, was put at his disposal. He had, in the two and a half years since Sergei Raimont's death, got to know Alexander and Alix Raimont during their frequent trips to Mazatlán. Unlike his fellow Mexicans, who often looked down on his Indian blood, the Raimonts treated him without prejudice and with the respect he had so often had to struggle to obtain. When the wedding was over, Gilberto would not return to Mazatlán because he had a new job. When Alexander Raimont had announced the appointment of Alix to the vice-presidency of Raimont/Europe one week before the wedding, a new life insurance policy was negotiated reflecting Alix's value to the company. As part of the terms of the policy, the company required that Alix be attended at all times by a personal bodyguard.

She had not hesitated to select Gilberto Rodríguez for the job, and he had not had to think twice before accepting it. He had just come from a secret place in southern California where he had completed a six-week course in weaponry, karate, evasive driving techniques, explosives disarmament and other antiterrorist tactics. In a well-tailored dark suit he blended in perfectly with the other guests and unobtrusively hovered close to Alix, never taking his eyes off her.

Jai Jai Raimont did not seem to remember him, and Gilberto did not introduce himself; he did wonder, though, if her second husband knew how her first husband had died. . . .

For Cole Whitelaw and Dante Mascheroni, it was the third big celebration in as many weeks. Cole Whitelaw was becoming *the* celebrity interior decorator. His business had been organized by Dante along the lines of the great Paris dress designers and capitalized with one million dollars from Dante's Swiss account. The work he created for private clients was equivalent in luxury and extravagance to the couture originals, while his mass-produced fabrics, furniture and accessories paralleled the less expensive but just as sought-after boutique lines. While Cole devoted all his energy to creativity, Dante handled the business. Dante had turned Cole's design of Yale Warrant's Belgravia house into a triumph; photographs appeared on the covers of French, English, German, Italian and American decorating magazines—a "first" since ordinarily the competing publications insist on exclusives.

Cole had gutted the entire interior of the Belgravia house so that the first floor now rose to triplex level; he had had the interior wall demolished, the side walls reinforced to support the weight of the ceiling, and the sleeping, dining and living areas were now separated not by screens, curtains or sliding panels but by an entire palm forest lit from above during the daytime by a skylight and at night by floor spots that cast shadows of the leaves of the tropical trees. The furniture, custom-designed by Cole, had a strong, classic Egyptian influence. The effect was dramatic, exotic, spectacular, and as a result of the photographic attention it created, would-be clients besieged Cole from four corners of the world in search of something equally original for themselves.

In quick sequence Dante signed a contract with a large North Carolina mill for sheets designed by Cole, with a Milanese furniture manufacturer for an entire line of Egyptian-influenced furniture and with a Fifty-seventh Street fabric-and-wallpaper house for an exclusive line. Dante was currently working on a licensing arrangement for fragrances for the home—sachets, drawer liners, candles and potpourris in scents reminiscent of the souks—as well as negotiating with publishers for a Cole Whitelaw book.

"He's as queer as a three-dollar bill," said Cole, speaking of Yale. "I cannot for the life of me imagine why Yale is marrying her. He'll never touch her."

"He's marrying her," said Dante, "for twenty million dollars." Dante, one of the few people on earth who knew what really happened in Mazatlán, was not surprised by anything Jai Jai did. He was slightly afraid of her, slightly in awe of her; he was glad he had made a new life for himself. A new life that had nothing to do with her.

"Chacun à son goût." Cole shrugged, thinking that for all the outrageous things he'd done in his life, there were many things he wouldn't do for a million or even twenty million dollars. One of them was marrying without love. . . . Cole looked at the champagne in the tulip glass, considered forcing himself to drink it, then replaced the untouched glass on the butler's tray. Perhaps if he didn't drink it now, he'd be able to enjoy it a week from now in Tokyo.

The prince and princess de Lalande-Dessault had flown in from Stockholm, where they had been living now that Pierre-Gilles was running the Sundsvall steel mills. Britta thought Alix Raimont had never looked better and told her so, and she was surprised that Alexander, who had always been so frigid when she was having her affair with Sergei, was cordial and welcoming. Britta and Pierre-Gilles had a good time at the wedding, seeing friends they hadn't seen for a while, dancing, drinking champagne, eating exquisite food. Still, Yale had once been married to Alix, and Jai Jai had been Alexander's mistress; it was not an ordinary boy-meets-girl love story.

"I still don't understand," said P.-G. while he and Britta were dancing, "why Yale is marrying her. As far as I know, he blames her for his divorce, for having to resign from WCD. . . ."

"Jai Jai's worth twenty million dollars now," said Britta. "I guess that much money can change a lot of things."

"Charming," said Pierre-Gilles, "just charming."

"I doubt," said Britta, content in her husband's arms, "that they will live happily ever after."

In Washington, D.C., Preston and Delia Cunningham had with regrets declined the invitation. They were in the middle of defending the sister-in-law of the President of the United States, who had been accused of murdering her husband, the President's brother.

"I wish we could go." Delia, who had married Preston when they'd both been starving law students, sighed. Their wedding dinner had been fried egg sandwiches. "I've never been to a high-society wedding."

"How can you be so romantic?" asked Preston. "You know what Jai Jai is like. She was sleeping with her father-in-law during her first marriage, and I can guarantee you a second marriage isn't going to change anything."

"I could buy a beautiful dress and dance and drink champagne," continued Delia in her reverie. "I'd wear flowers in my hair and leave my glasses at home and have a professional makeup man do my face. . . ."

As she dreamed on, Preston wondered that his wife, who dealt daily with greed and murder and lies, could be at the same time such a romantic. It was, of course, why he had fallen in love with her twenty years before and why, to this day, he was just wild about her. When this trial was over, he decided, he would take Delia to Paris and make every one of her dreams come true: He would buy her clothes and makeup and flowers for her hair and dance with her in romantic nightclubs while champagne cooled in silver buckets. . . .

In London, in Belgravia, the Chinese couple Yale had hired were preparing the house for the return of the newlyweds, polishing, dusting, arranging flowers, stocking the liquor cabinet, the basement wine cellar and the large pantries, while in a grimy flat in South London a young man removed his brass-studded black leather gloves to open the telegram that was waiting for him. Yale Warrant wanted to see him Thursday . . . at midnight.

The young man smiled. The last time he'd seen Yale Warrant for fun and games, Yale Warrant had given him an emerald bead. The young man had thought it was glass, but just to be sure he had taken it to a jeweler. He'd been amazed to receive five thousand pounds for it. Perhaps Thursday at midnight there'd be another little green bead. This time he'd tell the jeweler he wanted seven thousand pounds or he'd take it somewhere else.

Alix was the first to wish Jai Jai and Yale happiness. With Jacqueline and Hansjürg, she was the first to leave. With Gilberto Rodríguez driving, they headed toward the Côte d'Azur airport. Their initial destination was Munich, where Hansjürg was giving a party for an exiled Russian poet whose verse he published. After that, to Sidi-Bou-Said, where Alix was joining her father to sign the contracts committing Raimont to the planned four-hotel complex with Robert Trent golf course, shopping mall, four swimming pools, two freshwater, two seawater, twelve Har-Tru tennis courts and a planned Olympic stadium which would bid on the 1984 games. As they drove toward Nice, the Mediterranean on their right, Alix, who had been very quiet, said, "I'm glad that part of my life is over."

Hansjürg knew she meant Yale, her marriage to him, and he understood. Although Alix had been very discreet in speaking of Yale and their marriage, between the gossip Hansjürg had heard and the few clues Alix had given him, he sensed it had been very painful for her. More than her marriage had died; her innocence, her illusions had died with it. "I'm surprised you went to the wedding," he said. "I'm surprised there *was* a wedding. I gather it's not exactly a marriage made in heaven."

"Some people will do anything for money," said Alix. Her tone was flat and final, and Hansjürg dropped the subject. She turned in her seat to check the car traveling behind them. The nurse followed with Jacqueline.

For reasons of safety, Alix and Jacqueline never traveled in the same automobile, but Alix turned back to make sure that the second car was still following. Alix was extremely protective of Jacqueline, showing a strong, maternal side to her character that came as a charming paradox to her sophistication and poise. Alix had once told Hansjürg how she felt. "I never felt I belonged anywhere," she had said, "I blamed it on place. There was never anywhere I thought of as home. But I was wrong. I realized later that we don't belong to places; we belong to people. I belong to my father; I belong to my mother. They are inside me. What they gave me *is* me. No one can ever take it away. I want to give Jacqueline that feeling. It's the most important thing I can do for her."

Hansjürg agreed. Alix had struggled with her conscience over Jacqueline. She felt it was wrong to separate her from her mother, but when Jai Jai, absorbed in her flamboyant affair with Yale, left Jacqueline first with one nurse, then with another, Alix finally agreed with her father. Jacqueline was a Raimont baby, and Alix was devoted to her.

Hansjürg thought Alix looked happier and more relaxed

the farther they left Cap d'Antibes behind, and for a while they drove in quiet intimacy. "I know it's a cliché to propose right after a wedding," he said as the car swung into the airport, "but will you marry me?"

Alix wanted to say yes, and this time she said what she meant.

The free-standing elevator in the center of the lobby of the Hôtel du Cap is glass, and it rises within a glass shaft. Jai Jai, who knew how to make an entrance, also knew how to make a departure. At the very height of the glittering reception she and Yale got into the elevator, and as it rose slowly, its beautiful couple on display like diamonds in a jeweler's window, the crowd gazed upward, following the ascent of the elevator with hundreds of envying eyes until the glass cage and its occupants disappeared from view.

Jai Jai and Yale had what everyone in the room wanted: They were young; they were rich; they were beautiful. Yale and Jai Jai had that day achieved their heart's desire: They were the people other people wanted to be.

Only one person knew the whole story; only one person had declined without cause the most sought-after invitation of the decade; only one person had refused to attend the wedding. In Paris, Roman Bartok reclined on his couch, a Charvet robe the texture of heavy cream sensuous and comforting against his naked skin, and while Jai Jai and Yale exchanged vows in Cap d'Antibes, he dictated the first line of his newest book to his loyal secretary: "Theirs was not a wedding made in heaven but a marriage conceived in hell. . . ."

✎ TWENTY-THREE ✎

Alexander Raimont, everyone at the wedding had remarked, must have found the fountain of youth. He had, everyone agreed, never looked better. He had never seemed happier. He had never been more charming, more magnetic. He was the host at the wedding, seeming to enjoy it more than anyone, smiling, excited, expansive. Among the last to leave, he was meeting his plane at Nice. It would take him to Sidi-Bou-Said, where, two days later, he would meet Alix, now vice-president of Raimont/Europe.

He walked down the front steps of the hotel and told his driver to take him to the private hangar at the Côte d'Azur airport. As the big car turned out the curved driveway, he began to think about the complex to be built at Sidi-Bou-Said. With ultimate costs projected at a hundred and seventy-five million dollars and an eventually projected annualized profit of seventeen percent, he would be able the next year to start a duplicate. Bodrum, on the Turquoise coast of Turkey, called in antiquity Halicarnassus, was one of the few ideal, still-unspoiled tourist areas in the world—there was a lovely harbor, ideal for yachts and cruise boats, ancient ruins, pine forests and white beaches, picturesque caravans of camels, exquisite seafood and inexpensive and delicious local wines, exotic native markets, a Crusader's castle guarding the harbor and across the narrow inlet, the Greek island of Kos, where Hippocrates taught at the Asclepion, could be seen. Alexander's approach to the Turkish government had been heard with enthusiasm.

Alexander looked forward to telling Alix about it. Since Sergei's death they had become more than father and daughter, more than business partners. At lunch in the Quo Vadis they had become allies; on Good Friday they had become accomplices.

267

"You're right," said Alexander at the Quo Vadis. Espresso had been served, but it cooled as father and daughter spoke. "She'd jump at twenty million dollars."

"Then you'll be free of her," Alix said.

"I don't know," said Alexander. For the first time in his life he doubted the power of money. "I'm afraid it will take more than money to make me stop wanting Jai Jai."

Alix's heart went out to her father. It was terrible to see a man made powerless, and she wanted to say something, to do something to end the enslavement that robbed him of his will, his drive, his very essence. Before she could think of what to say, her father spoke, changing the subject.

"My problem with Jai Jai isn't our only problem," he said. "Cartwright is reluctant to have you named vice-president of Raimont/Europe." For several months Alexander had wanted the announcement made. Alix had worked at Raimont for more than a year, and it had still not been officially announced that she was being groomed to succeed her father as chief operating officer in Europe.

"Why? Because I'm too young?" Alix was thirty-two. Not *that* young.

"He said that he's heard rumors that you're 'unstable,'" Alexander said. He paused, reluctant to go on but driven by his paternal curiosity to know about his child, by his paternal need to protect her. "And that you've tried to . . . take your own life." Tears suddenly appeared in his eyes. "Is that true? Did you? Alix did you try to"—with an enormous effort, he forced himself to pronounce the words again—"kill yourself?"

Alix shut her eyes for a long moment; when she opened them, Alexander thought that the tears in them answered his question affirmatively.

"But why?" Tears flowed down his face, and he did not care, did not notice that others in the dining room looked at him curiously. "Why, Alix? Why?"

"Because I thought it was my destiny. Because of Grandpère, because of Sergei. . . ."

"Because of Sergei?" Alexander was stunned. Then, very slowly and very deliberately, he asked Alix a question: "Alix, how do you think Sergei died?"

It was the question that had haunted Alix. Now dramatically, unexpectedly, it had been asked of her.

"Like Grandpère," Alix said, "he committed suicide."

The word seemed to leap into the air; Alix feared it would devour them.

"Where did you get the idea that Sergei took his own life?" Alexander asked. To Alix's surprise, he did not flinch, did not back away.

"From you . . ." Alix said. She recalled as she had a thousand times, her father's exact words: *Jai Jai and I were seeing each other . . . Sergei found out . . . Sergei had a gun. . . .* Alix stopped short. . . . Had her father said that Sergei shot himself? Or was that her thought? Her phrase? Alix looked at her father and asked the question she had thought she would never be able to utter: "How did my brother die?"

"Jai Jai," he answered. "Jai Jai shot him. I got her off."

Alix closed her eyes, and Alexander was afraid she would faint. The color drained from her face, it seemed to drain even from the roots of her hair and then, finally, she opened her eyes. As Alexander looked into them, identical in color and shape to his own, he felt as if he were looking into a mirror as he spoke.

"You're obsessed with Jai Jai because you feel responsible for Sergei's death," said Alix, excited with a sense of sudden revelation. She had the unmistakable feeling everything was about to fall into place. "Jai Jai knows it, and your guilt is the weapon Jai Jai uses to enslave you. Jai Jai will destroy you with your own guilt, just as Yale undermined me with my own insecurities and now is trying to destroy me with my own letters. We have a choice: We can remain in their power or we can get them in ours." Alix paused for a moment and then said to her father, "I think we have more weapons than we imagine, and I think I know how to find out what they are."

Alexander Raimont nodded. In a few succinct words Alix had named the roots of his obsession and, by naming them, had already begun to loosen their stranglehold over him. Alix's voice was angry and determined, a tone Alexander had never before heard in it, a tone which thrilled him. . . .

"Can you come to Paris with me later this week?" Alix asked, and knew the answer before she asked the question.

Roman Bartok's long-awaited book had not been published, and it was already his greatest success. Worldwide publishing rights, movie and book club and magazine rights had already earned him more than five million dollars. No one had read it yet, but everyone talked about it. Bootlegged Xerox copies of the manuscript sold in the black market for ten thousand dollars apiece. And Roman occasionally wished he had never written it.

The book was a thinly disguised portrait of Jai Jai Valerian. In it, Jai Jai was pictured as a legend in her own time, a romantic heroine whose glamour and fascination rivaled those of any woman in history. The book told of her affair with the richest man in the world, of the mysterious scandal-shrouded death of her first husband, who happened to be her lover's son, of her fabulous jewels, her emeralds in particular and of the erotic use to which she put them.

Roman's lawyers had cautioned him to be careful, and their warning turned out to be accurate. Word about the book had no sooner begun to circulate when Roman felt the repercussions. Three of his former intimate friends—the wife of a cousin of the queen of England and a married couple, he South African, she American, who owned uranium mines in South Africa and fifteen blocks of Park Avenue between Fiftieth and Seventy-first streets—had stopped speaking to him, stopped inviting him to their parties, stopped asking his advice and sharing their confidences.

The penalties Roman paid weren't only social. One evening at dusk in the Bois de Boulogne, a fabulously wealthy Texas oilman who thought Roman's book was about *him* stood by and watched while two hired thugs from the Paris underworld beat Roman badly enough to send him to the hospital for two weeks.

Alix Raimont had read the manuscript, obtained for her by Hansjürg, in early spring. Her father had been disguised as a Greek shipping owner, Sergei as his playboy son and herself as his shy, unattractive daughter. All of it troubled Alix; the part that angered her was the way Roman had glamorized Jai Jai and Yale's flamboyant love affair. Apparently Roman knew everything; Alix thought it reasonable that he would know why Yale was trying to destroy her reputation, her personal and professional lives. When Alix called from New York to ask Roman to meet her and her father for drinks at the Ritz, Roman was flattered and set the date for five P.M. on the afternoon of Good Friday. Drinking in public on a sacred holiday was the kind of outrageousness that not only appealed to Roman personally but also was, as he had learned, good business: It built his image as daring, scandalous, out-to-break-all-the-rules.

The Ritz bar was virtually deserted, and Roman, who was fascinated by the rich, looked forward to meeting Alexander Raimont. Although, because of his friendship with Jai Jai, he knew as much about him as if he had been his biographer, he had never met him in person. Roman, still on crutches from his beating, occupied two chairs in the bar: one for himself; one for his leg, still in a cast. His left arm, in a paisleyed sling, rested against his body, and Roman, who arrived first, watched as Alexander and Alix entered the bar.

Roman had a trick to help him invent the characters in his books: He always imagined how they looked naked. He knew that if he saw Alexander Raimont stark naked, he would still know that Alexander Raimont had money and power and control. It was in his pores, in the precise, graceful movements of his hands, in the economy and strength of his strides. He understood immediately Jai Jai's obsession with Alexander; there was a central mystery about him. Roman sensed that Alexander guarded his emotional privacy to the extent that he was almost impenetrable, and it was that challenge, the challenge of getting him to respond, that must have so fascinated and frustrated Jai Jai.

What surprised Roman was that Alix, whom Jai Jai had always described as plain and unattractive, was exactly as magnetic as her father; she moved with the same graceful strides, used her hands, the nails unlacquered but immaculately manicured, in the same precise way, had his eyes, his nose, his mouth, the same coloring of skin and hair. Alix was one of those creatures, thought Roman, who seemed destined from birth to move in only the rarest, most exquisite of ambiances. And above all, she seemed to share the same central emotional mystery as her father. Roman wondered, as the introductions were made, what secrets father and daughter shared.

Roman ordered a vodka, Alix, Perrier and Alexander, an Evian. When the drinks had been served, Alix turned to Roman.

"Yale is trying to destroy me," she said without preamble. "I thought perhaps you might know why."

"He's jealous of you," said Roman.

"Jealous?" Alix was surprised.

"You're everything he ever wanted to be," said Roman. "He's in awe of you."

"But he never said anything," said Alix. She remembered how Yale had told her she couldn't succeed at Raimont, how she couldn't carry on her mother's work.

"Of course not," said Roman, sipping the vodka, an iced Stolichnaya served in a small cut crystal glass. "If he admitted it to you, he'd lose his control over you."

Alix thought of all the times Yale had disparaged her, compared her unfavorably to other women. . . . The spark began to glow; she began to feel its warmth. Alix nodded, agreeing with Roman.

"If it's any comfort to you," Roman said, "you're not the only one he's trying to destroy." Clumsily, because of the paisley sling, Roman rolled up his shirt sleeve and showed a scar that ran from waist to elbow, deep, red, ugly. "Yale," Roman said.

"But why would Yale want to do that to you?" said Alix, shocked, knowing she was about to step into an unknown territory, a place that frightened her and yet drew her forward, the reason she had asked her father to go to Paris with her. "Why would Yale hate you that much? He's not even in your book."

"It's not me," said Roman. "It's Jai Jai. This"—he gestured at the scar—"is her Valentine's Day present."

Alix and Alexander looked at each other, a deep look, a look they both understood, a look that no one else could have interpreted.

"I thought," Alexander said, perfectly calmly, "that Yale and Jai Jai were lovers."

Roman shook his head. "Not anymore."

"What happened?" asked Alix. "Tell us what happened."

Roman Bartok's public talent was as a writer; his private

talent was as a gossip. It was a talent he loved to display. Roman, his vodka untouched, began his story.

"I was in Jai Jai's apartment on Valentine's Day evening," Roman said. "We had gone out to dinner and come back for a cognac when Yale called. He asked if he could come over. He had something for Jai Jai.

"Jai Jai was anxious to see him. She told me that her emeralds were still in Yale's safe-deposit box—she had removed them from the vault of the Morgan and put them into Yale's box when they were lovers. She and Yale went out frequently, and Jai Jai wore them often. Yale enjoyed going to the bank and signing out Jai Jai's necklace for her and bringing it to her. He told her that it gave him a thrill to walk through the streets of Paris with a quarter of a million dollars' worth of jewelry in his pockets. He'd bring the necklace to Jai Jai, and they had a lovers' ritual of making love while Jai Jai wore the necklace before they went out.

"When she walked out on him in Cairo, she forgot about the necklace in her anger. She had been pleading with him ever since to return it. She had some letters you'd written to Yale," said Roman, turning to Alix. "He had been asking for the letters, and Jai Jai thought he would bring the necklace and exchange it for the letters.

"Yale came into the apartment carrying a small tissue-wrapped parcel. I could see Jai Jai's relief. When Yale opened the wrappings, though, he pulled out a knife. A vicious, straight-bladed sporting model, and telling Jai Jai that everything was her fault—the breakup of his marriage, the demand for his resignation from WCD—he lunged at her. I threw myself between them, shoving Yale off-balance just enough to deflect the thrust."

Roman unconsciously rubbed the scar where it itched. He had fallen in love with Jai Jai because she made him feel the one thing he had always doubted: she made him feel he was an artist. Because of Jai Jai, his newest book was his best. His next, he knew, would be even greater. In his next, he had decided, he would tell everything he knew. He was tired of being discreet about the rich and the beautiful.

"Isn't Jai Jai afraid of him?" asked Alix. "What happens the next time if no one's there?"

"I asked Jai Jai the same thing myself," said Roman "I'm still chilled by her answer: 'I can take care of myself, she said. 'I got away with it once; I'll get away with i again.' "

Alexander Raimont seemed riveted at attention. Roman wondered what he was thinking.

"But why did Yale want my letters?" Alix asked in her intriguing accent. She was composed, attentive.

"He wanted to sell them," said Roman. "He had been asking me about various newspapers. . . ."

"And who has the letters now?"

"No one," said Roman. "After Yale's attack, Jai Ja burned them. She was determined that Yale would never get them."

"I see," said Alix. She thought that Yale had almost ruined her with gossip; with her own letters written in the depths of a suicidal depression, he would have had proof. "This is all very interesting," said Alix.

"Good gossip is like money," Roman said. "It's no good unless you spread it around."

Both Alix and her father smiled. Roman thought they smiled in appreciation of his bon mot and, wanting to leave on a positive note, excused himself, saying good evening.

As Roman left the Ritz bar, he stopped in the doorway to look back. They were already gone. The richest man in the world and the richest woman in the world had already disappeared. Roman's untouched vodka—he never drank when he worked, and he was about to begin a new book—Alexander's half-finished bottle of Evian and Alix's Perrier, now gone flat, were being removed by a waiter, who picked up the tip, looked at it and pocketed it with a look of pleasant surprise.

As Alix and her father crossed the splendid and ornate lobby of the Hôtel Ritz, the drama that was taking place was invisible to passersby just returning from the three-hour-long Good Friday services.

Alexander was consumed by thoughts of obsession and emeralds, money and revenge. The emeralds, the gift he had given in love and need and passion, were now being used on the altar of another man's desire. The force of the image broke down the floodgates of grief Alexander had held in, and the guilt he had suppressed over his son's death almost crushed him. Memories of the passionate enslavement to Jai Jai flayed him, and as always, when he feared annihilation by passion, Alexander thought of money, money that could save him, buy him anything he wanted: life, death, immortality.

And then he thought of twenty million dollars. He had planned to barricade it with snares and traps of legal procedure, to tie it up with skeins of red tape so that it would be years before Jai Jai ever saw a penny. But Roman had just told him—and shown him proof—that Yale wanted to kill Jai Jai. . . . If Yale succeeded, Alexander would never have to pay a dead woman. Roman had also said that Jai Jai wasn't afraid, that she had got away with it once, would get away with it again. . . . If she murdered Yale—in anger or in self-defense—this time, Alexander would do nothing to get her off. He would never have to pay a woman in prison, a woman stripped of her powers and her rights.

As thoughts of money and death crossed Alexander's mind, he realized he felt something he hadn't felt in a long time. He felt free. Free of his obsession, free of his enslavement, free, finally, of the addiction that had begun in Mexico, one night in a marble bedroom, with kisses on the mouth. He looked at Alix, walking next to him, their strides matched, and wondered how to put his feelings into words.

"I think," he began, "there ought to be conditions placed on the twenty-million-dollar settlement. First of all, Jacqueline. . . ."

As Alix listened to her father, she thought of what she had learned in the past two days: that Jai Jai had killed Sergei and that she had no compunctions about killing again, and that Yale, who had once said that feeling rich meant he could do anything, now included taking Jai Jai's life in his definition of anything.

As her father had thought of emeralds, Alix thought of rage. Rage at Jai Jai for killing her brother and binding her father to her in an unholy guilty secret, a secret that had led Alix to think that Sergei had taken his own life and that she shared the same fatal inheritance. Rage at Yale: rage at Yale for leaving her, for telling her lies, for telling her that she didn't make him feel rich, that she wasn't beautiful enough, bold enough, dazzling enough; rage at Yale for be-littling and diminishing her in word and deed, for telling her she could never be of value to Raimont, could never continue her mother's legacy; rage that she had been faithful when he had been faithless; rage that he had returned her loyalty with betrayal; rage at him for trying to destroy her the way he had destroyed himself and now wanted to destroy Jai Jai.

"And the second condition," her father continued, "will be a marriage. . . ."

"If two people ever deserved each other," Alix said, "it's Jai Jai and Yale." She realized as she spoke that she did not care if Yale murdered Jai Jai or if Jai Jai murdered Yale or if they murdered each other or if they lived for-ever, condemned to each other. . . . It just didn't matter to her anymore.

As Alix and Alexander left the Ritz lobby and stepped into the Place Vendôme, planning the details of a wedding that was a murder, Alexander suddenly stopped and, turn-ing, looked back.

"The Ritz has always been one of my favorite hotels," he said.

"Don't tell me." Alix laughed. "You'd like to buy it."

"Why not?" asked Alexander. "I've never been able to resist beautiful things."

And as he spoke, he thought with a slight sense of irony of Jai Jai, another beautiful thing—it seemed she was someone he had once known, a very long time ago.

"Why not, indeed!" said Alix. "It would be a thrill to own the Ritz." As they spoke of opening negotiations for the Ritz, Alix realized that for the first time in her life, she felt rich.

EPILOGUE

August 1978

The twelfth of August is the first day of grouse shooting in Scotland. On the fourteenth of August, word of Yale Warrant's death in a tragic shooting accident involving his wife, the former Jai Jai Valerian, was carried in newspapers on both sides of the Atlantic. Alexander Raimont, in Chicago, telephoned Jai Jai, who was staying with Lord Lothian, the host of the shoot, on his forty-thousand-acre estate bordering the river Dee. Alexander's indifference toward Jai Jai, his sense of freedom from her evaporated as they spoke, and Alexander offered her any help she might need. They both knew he was referring to the kind of help he had been able to provide in Mazatlán. Jai Jai thanked Alexander for his offer but said there was nothing at all he could do; everything had been taken care of. Lord Lothian had been protective, concerned, efficient, indispensable. For the time being, she planned to stay with him.

Alexander Raimont wondered what kind of a man Lord Lothian was; he had, of course, heard of him. He was in his early forties and had inherited a vast fortune founded in the nineteenth century on the rich coal and iron deposits between Ayreshire and Fife and expanded by each generation until the present Lord Lothian controlled vast, worldwide mining, manufacturing and banking interests.

Alexander made a final offer of assistance, knowing as he made it, that Jai Jai did not need him. She had found a new lover. As Alexander said goodbye and hung up the telephone, he found that he had already begun once again to want her.

For a moment he indulged himself in speculation. He wondered if he would ever be free of Jai Jai; he wondered if he would ever *want* to be free of her. He then instructed his pilot that their next destination would be Edinburgh and ordered him to obtain the necessary clearances and to file a flight plan.

ABOUT THE AUTHOR

RUTH HARRIS grew up on Long Island's North Shore and graduated from Sarah Lawrence College. An editor and freelance writer before turning full-time to fiction, she is an avid traveler who, between trips, divides her time between a Manhattan apartment and the eighteenth-century house in which she grew up. She is married to Michael Harris, also a writer, and is currently at work on her third novel, *The Last Romantics*, which will be published in hardcover in the spring of 1980. Her first was *Decades*. Of her talents as a novelist, columnist Liz Smith says, "The novels of Ruth Harris are just the *sine qua non* in getting away from one's own drab existence. . . . Harris can tell you about the most glamorous woman in the world . . . and the one man rich enough to afford her. . . . What's more she can tell you with more style and verve than many others who have won fame and fortune writing in the same vein. Harris has an eye for detail that is truly incredible. . . ."

RELAX!
SIT DOWN
and Catch Up On Your Reading!